The Gathering
Book One of The Dark Road

Jonathan Graef

Copyright © 2016 Jonathan Graef

All rights reserved.

ISBN: 1523962615
ISBN-13: 978-1523962617

DEDICATION

This entire series is dedicated to my wife and children for suffering my long hours, frustration and endless bantering. Patience of saints and unending warmth- no one could ask for a more loving family.

Prologue

A brief, known history of the world...

No one really knew what had turned the once reverent and dignified country of Ilmaria to its dark path of malevolence. Some had speculated the surreptitiously gradual corruption was caused by the unscrupulousness from its immense affluence and supremacy and that the hierarchy fell to its own avarice. Others contested to some more tangible force crept down from the mountains and into the hearts of the populace. Yet others spoke of dark delving and vile rites committed behind closed doors that eventually gripped the masses. For whatever reason however, it happened.

Those who did not turn sinister fled, fearing for their lives and secretly gathered in the south lands. Beyond the difficult mountains stood an ancient ruin of a holy place, the Shammash Cathedral. The Cathedral was erected to worship Shammash, the God of Light and Life. It was there that the stanch revolutionaries would exchange secret information, lend much needed aid to one another and stand their ground. However, the creeping fear of eminent danger, steadily worsened by wild uninformed rumors, became thicker and quietly stifled people's ability to unaffectedly breathe let alone slumber well even on bright moonlit nights.

Whoever was able bodied or determined enough fled the Cathedral and hid in Sanctuary, an undersized town constructed on the western edge of the tall jagged peaks just through the rugged pass. Sanctuary was so named by the bold people who escaped there. It was to be a safe area where they could go for refuge, hear news and ultimately to hide. Their effort for maintaining secrecy did not last long, though. That defenseless community was the first to be struck. The dark hammer of Ilmaria fell quickly and without pity. Fiends were loosed to hold ranks in elements of the force that came to be referred to as the Black Tide, for it washed away everything in its path. The powerless Sanctuary swiftly became a smoldering field of slaughter.

The hushed rumors of the Ilmarian Royal Family being furtive practitioners of the black arts may have been true, for an army of evil creatures raged across the lands like a swift storm. Undead, hideous monsters, devils and other horrific things beyond identity waded over the entire continent leaving less than the dead in the wake of their destruction. It was then that the words such as vampire and phantom became known. Other names became notorious as well-hideous and unholy names: wraith, werewolves, the dreaded shades, screamers and ghouls also became infamous.

In those dark days and even in the much brighter days before, there lived a Messenger of the Gods, a Chosen One. Her name was Gajana and she was worshiped as a goddess. Her nameless origins have remained as confusingly mysterious as her immense power and vast magical knowledge has remained unequaled. Few solid facts are known about her but fanciful conjectures are abundant. A singular set of writings, the Sacred Scrolls of Migru, are the official and accepted source of information concerning the happenings of that time. Any book, scroll, tome or other text is weighed against the Scrolls for validity. Within the Sacred Scrolls, reputedly, Anu, the chief god of the pantheon, had chosen her himself, had personally taught her the ways of the cosmos and tutored her in the very essence of magic. Gajana was then charged with telling the ignorant world of the ways of Heaven and to help men and elves work together without discord.

It was she who swiftly took the lead against Ilmaria and all its ungodliness. She sought the two great warrior clans and met with them in secrecy to unite and collectively destroy the evil. The Montigans, the larger of the two, had the greater history of heroes and men of renown. The other family, the Drathmoore's, was not as influential, had less authority and was smaller. However, they were the strength of the battlefield. The Drathmoore cavalry knights were unmatched. By the direction of Gajana the two clans sealed their alliance with a marriage and went into combat.

The clans met the already blood soaked battlefield on the eve of the first crescent moon. As the scant light was swallowed by black clouds, the Darkness and the last hope of the world clashed. For three months, the crusade raged on. Slowly, the Darkness began to envelop them. Even with Gajana ardently fighting side by side with them, the army shrank smaller and smaller as the casualties mounted. Until…

Forged at the birth of the world, Mardakkar, the first holy sword ever constructed, sat in a faraway desolate land surrounded by evil. So it is rumored the sword was fashioned in Heaven by the gods themselves. The Montigans secretly sent an expedition to recover the legendary blade. It was locked away in the crypts of Cutha, the City of the Dead and was guarded by Iak Sakkak and his hoards. Sakkak, one of the generals of Ereshkegal, the Great Dragon, the source of all evil, was a foe not to be fought by sword.

In a great heroic feat, they reclaimed the sword from the depths of Cutha and brought the blade into thunderous reality before the malevolence of Ilmaria. Gajana, weapon in hand, rode head first into battle and on the third crescent moon, three months to the day, the Darkness fell. In a swift stroke of military *genius led by Gajana, the Black Tide was shockingly overwhelmed. The few remaining fled across the lands to hide. All was great and done, until the storm came...*

The blackest clouds ever to cast shadows on the earth, crept across the sky glaring with unseen eyes over all the land. Lightning crashed the earth and thunder roared so furiously that many thought the world was ending. Some people were driven mad. Some people committed suicide. The wise men knew something else was amiss. The Montigans and the Drathmoores having been almost eliminated in the war, reluctantly ventured forth to discover the source of the new evil.

After four day's ride, the crux was discovered. Halfway between the Darkwoods and Blackmoore Tower, a circle of vile priests gathered and had begun their work. With the aid of the demon lord Tzathaogguah, the most hideous and destructive creature was summoned. The Alal. With claw and teeth and speed of lightning, it devoured everything it could see. Most horrid was Alal for it proved unstoppable by all champions of the land. It towered over trees, moved three times the speed of a horse and was impervious to even the most powerful magic used against it. The terror seemed unremitting, the sorrow appeared unending. No human, elf, or peaceful woodland animal was safe. It ate and killed without rest or pause. The most powerful wizards in the land tried in vain to rid the world of it. Priests failed. Warriors failed. All died in horrible ends. Its hunger was as ravenous as it was endless. Worst of all it seemed unstoppable.

A group of wizards, led by Gajana, the last of Paragon, gathered in secret to make an end to this monster. For weeks the work went on, unaware of what had unfolded. Before the Black Tide, they numbered close to three hundred. Now, the Montigans and the Drathmoores were reduced to nine knights in total. The great sword Mardakkar was lost while battling Alal. The hope of the land waned low. The single gargantuan horror had ravaged over a quarter of the continent and showed no sign of slowing or stopping. At last though, the wizards' work was done.

In a furious battle, the new device proved its worth. Soulbreaker, a powerful sword, was brought to the field. Evil was created to combat evil. The blade was hammered from an ore found only in the darkest depths of Hell itself. Its vile force was comprehended as it drew the life from its victim to further fuel its own power. Bit by bit the horrific Alal was cut to oblivion. After three days of conflict, the violence became silence and the land finally grew still. The dark wizards were mortified. They stood and watched the promise of the Ancient Ones, the dark gods, fall to the ground. They were attacked and their numbers cut down to five as the last Montigans and Drathmoores pursued them into the mountains. The dark wizards vanished and went into hiding. What remained of the fled dark army that went into hiding was systematically hunted and crushed by Gajana and an elite group of soldiers chosen and trained by her.

Rumor had it they formed a coven called the "Talismachiem." They were the "Demons who would lie in waiting" whose sole purpose became to expand in total secrecy and surface when their time was right and take vengeance on the Montigans and the Drathmoores and on all existence. That was almost five hundred years ago, no threat ever came and whisper of them ever was heard.

In those days also, the time of Gajana had come to a close. She departed the world through the Gate of Death, leaving behind many legacies for the world to follow. It was her that invented the calendar that the world used. It was her that wrote many of the texts used to govern the lands and from her came much of the technology used in the world to this day.

Peace filled the very air and breath of the countryside. The few surviving inhabitants of the earth thus began to rebuild and create new civilizations. Without that evil force, the mysterious Soulbreaker was of no use and so the gods saw to its disappearance. A promise was made back then that Ilmaria's corruption would never happen again. The Montigans and Drathmoores had then razed the Temple of the Dragon to the ground and went about founding a new kingdom. Paragon, it was named and was to be the model for all other countries on the earth. Magic was henceforth outlawed there and its practice could be punishable by death. The horrors that threatened to vanquish the world soon became mere shadows of the past. History quickly turned into tale that quickly turned into fable as the years progressed without the weight of apprehension.

To this day, "The Promise" has been diligently kept by both the Montigan and Drathmoore families and Paragon remains the most powerful nation in the entire world.

Near the Hill of Standing Stones

Just after midnight, three years ago

The frozen branches of scattered trees tore at her exposed skin as she ran for her life. She didn't know what direction she was running in and she didn't care. The girl only knew it was after her and she had to get as far away as her legs could carry her. Terror had enveloped her so tightly that she could barely feel her feet passing through the thick snow or hitting the cold ground as she bolted. Tears froze on her face but she did not notice that either, she could barely see where she was going the dark woods.

Suddenly her face was in the snow. Too many moments passed as she lifted her head, trying to understand what happened. When she finally realized she had tripped and fallen, the girl scampered wildly to get herself running again. *No, no, no, no*, she screamed to herself. *Must get away. Must...*

The unearthly howl from somewhere behind and above her froze her for a moment. She couldn't help but stop and listen as its echo reverberated through the silent trees. Even the forest seemed to feel fear. Scrambling to a nearby tree, she moved around it and hid as her panting breath pulsed out jets of condensation. Her head and back pressed against the frozen bark and her heart pounded in her ears. She tried to listen. She tried not to cry. Everything was quiet, silent as an old tomb, and only the faint whistling of a distant wind could be heard. Thoughts raced: How had she gotten here? What had she done to get herself in this predicament? She slowly peered around the trunk, squinting into the dark of night. Nothing moved. Did she even hear that noise? Was it real? The tree she sat against seemed a good a place as any to rest as she thought about how she had ended up there.

Hours earlier, the girl had decided she had quite enough of following her master through thigh deep snow in the freezing cold of night. Large flakes had been lazily falling for two days straight and no one had seen sunlight for over a month. Even during what should have been midday, the dimness resembled bleak twilight. Those were strange times indeed; and no one remembered hearing or even seeing any birds. Evil had come to the countryside. The girl drew her layers around herself tighter to fend off the cold. Even though she was only a girl at thirteen, she was not stupid. She knew. She knew that chill was not just the weather, it was Death drawing closer. The girl had followed her master enough to know what it felt like, and wished she never had been sold to him.

Her name was Alizee, and coming from a poorer family was not quite bad enough; she also had a younger brother. Since the family could not afford schooling for both of them, she was pulled from her teachers at the age of ten and sent to work to earn money for his education, like any good little girl should have done. At the time, she did not resent it because that was how everyone's life went. But when her meager wages were not enough the family suffered, and so did she by the hand of her father and distain of her mother.

On a dark night the previous summer, a stranger had called. He was richly dressed, spoke with an educated foreign accent and carried more gold than the family would see in ten of their lifetimes. It was a small pouch that only held thirty or so coins, but it was enough. Alizee was sold to him and her parents barely waved farewell before counting their new fortune. With tears streaming down her cheeks, she was dragged away by her arm while she stared at her house shrinking in the distance. Her heart broke as the lights of the place she called home dwindled.

Since that time, she was a pack mule for her owner. The stern tyrant, Atto Liguell Kiesinger, seemed to never let her have a moment's rest. When she was not carrying things she was cleaning or cooking. When she cleaned the wrong things or even touched them, it would take days for the wounds to heal enough for her move around. She had become a quick pupil to pain but her curiosity had kept her eyes and ears open even when her fingers were kept at bay. She watched him change over that time. Slowly, he did not groom himself as much and did not dress as sharply. Also, he seemed to talk aloud to himself or to no one. Alizee did not fully understand what she was watching but she knew that he was somehow crumbling, slowly going insane.

Atto, Liguell or Kiesinger, as he was called by different people, was a dark and vile man and everyone who spoke with him seemed to treat him with great respect. Later, she figured out that it was fear, and she came to learn why. Kiesinger was Craftuser, one who practiced the arts of magic. It was not the street kind of magic that people performed for a few measly coins, it was real magic, scary magic. It was the kind that made the dead speak. It was the kind that made shadows move as the room became cold. It was the kind that drew...*things*, terrible things from somewhere else. Her life was a nightmare.

She shook her head as she sobbed against the tree in the falling snow. She wished she were somewhere else. She wished none of that had ever happened. Her eyes screwed shut as she sobbed harder. She wished she was dead.

Suddenly there was something touching her cheek! Alizee opened her eyes wide and tried to scramble backwards but she was already against the tree. There was nowhere for her to go.

"Shhh, little one," the voice said to her. "I will not harm you."

It was a woman! Turning her head quickly, Alizee looked at her. The woman had an ornate gold tiara holding her long flowing black hair and very deep dark eyes set into her sharp featured face. She wore a flowing dress of dark blue silk that was trimmed in gold threads and had a stout looking staff leaning across her knees as she squatted to talk to the young girl. Her skin was smooth and very pale. She was beautiful. Alizee instantly stopped squirming and blinked at her.

"Who are you?" she asked the mysterious woman who smiled with her dark red lips in response. Lifting her slender hand, the woman gently reached out to Alizee and brushed the tousled hair from the girl's face. The woman's long fingers were dead cold.

"I am Shazandra Melleriene Lanariel," she said with a warm smile that never reached her eyes. "But you can call me Zandra. I know my full name is a mouthful."

Alizee seemed to have forgotten all about Liguell, the unearthly monster that was chasing her, the altar in the middle of the stones, all the blood...

"Aren't you cold?" asked Alizee, noticing that the only clothing the woman had was her silk dress. Even with its layers, there was no possible way it could keep anyone warm enough. Alizee knew that from the cold touch of her fingers.

"No, my dear," Zandra spoke while still smiling. "The cold does not trouble me in the least." She took Alizee's gloved hands in her own and stood. Her staff rested in the bend of her elbow as Alizee rose as well. The woman was tall and towered over the short shivering girl. "Now then," she said as she bent down and caressed the girl's cheek. "Let's get you to someplace different, shall we?"

The two had walked, side by side without speaking for a few minutes. Alizee kept glancing around the forest looking for her master, half expecting the sinister man to jump out at any time and scare her to death. She felt strangely safe with the tall thin woman striding graciously beside her. She looked at the woman's solid staff and noticed the glimmering gold and silver that was set into the dark lacquered wood.

"It is made from acacia," the woman told her. "It is a very special tree that has many special properties."

Alizee did not think to ask how the woman knew what she was thinking without her even looking. Instead she tried to look at the intricately carved surface that was covered with what looked to be lines and glyphs. Her attention was broken when the woman abruptly stopped walking. Alizee glanced to the woman then looked around to see where they were. Her heart leapt into her throat. She was right back where she ran from, atop the Hill of Stones!

"Atto Kiesinger," the woman sharply addressed, her voice sounding like a cold wind blowing over old dry bones. "Have you been distracted these past few moons?"

Liguell turned sharply, startled from hearing the woman's voice. His blood seemed to drain from his face as his eyes became wide. She noticed he looked around furtively before fully facing her and then bowed dramatically.

"Mistress Shazandra," he greeted. "I had not anticipated your arrival."

Alizee was trembling but not just from the cold.

"I did not think you would," the woman snapped. "However, what did you expect? I gave you a task to complete and then I hear nothing from you in months." Her dark eyes became impossibly darker. "What have you been doing with your time instead of what I told you to do?"

"I... I have... not been very occupied with..."

"I found one of your strays," Shazandra interrupted, causing Alizee to look up at her with terrified eyes. The last thing she wanted was to be given back to Liguell.

"Oh... I see," he replied absently. His attention was clearly elsewhere as if he was expecting something. Shazandra looked past him at the stones of the hill and a grim look came on her face. "May I have her returned?"

Alizee was about to panic.

"No," the woman answered dispassionately. "Not until you tell me what you are doing here."

Suddenly, they could faintly hear a subtle yet disturbing sound of an echoed whisper. It sounded harsh and hateful and pushed into their minds. Alizee realized what the unnatural chill in the air was that she had felt earlier...it was whatever made that voice, and it was there at the hill.

I want out...

I hate her!

Get me out...

"Someone does not like you being here, *Mistress*," he said with a snide tone that resembled oozing slime.

Before she could respond, they all heard the buffeting of large wings. The forest below them seemed to tremble in fear as the monstrosity came down from the night sky. It howled. That was the sound Alizee heard before. She did not know where to run or how to hide. Her knees became weak and she dropped where she stood into the snow. Time seemed to almost stop. The large flakes of snow that still fell lazily from the black above seemed to nearly hang motionlessly in the air as she watched. She became acutely unaware of the forest around them, the ground, the cold of the air, and even the whistling winds. She watched the white flakes in the air suddenly move toward her. From the black behind Liguell, emerged a gargantuan horror that seemed to slam against the hillside. The ground shook from the impact and a wall of snow was cast into the air. Before the snow settled, it roared with the stench of burning sulfur and the decay of a thousand graves. It stepped forward and the ground shook again. She could see the tips of its wings stretching outward almost around the hill! Before she could make out its head, Alizee fainted in the snow.

"Ozadogguah," the woman said flatly. "I might have known…"

"Yes!" Liguell melodramatically shouted in triumph. "It's a spawn servitor of Tzathaogguah, the Demon Lord of…"

"I know what it is," she interrupted. "Did you forget who taught you?"

"Never, Mistress. I would never forget…that," he spoke sarcastically with a perverted smile.

"But you did," Shazandra said as she began walking around the edge of the hilltop. "You completely forgot. Or were you just being petty and spiteful by not reporting to me?"

He watched as she calmly walked but was completely oblivious as to why. Behind him, the hellish creature sporadically quivered in waves, making the ground tremble.

"I… I don't… serve you any longer, Mistress." That seemed difficult for him to say.

"I can see that," Shazandra said as she looked at the huge creature behind him. She was almost where she wanted to be but did not think of it. Shazandra knew better. "But the question is: who is your new master?"

"Ha!" Liguell barked. "That's an astoundingly simplistic answer!" He was almost laughing but it carried a maniacal tone of desperation. "I have found my true master… an *authentic* immortal… a goddess."

"So," she replied as calmly as ever while still strolling. "Does this *goddess* have a name?" Shazandra was taunting him. He always had a problem with his temper and whoever this goddess was did not help him get any better. They both worshiped the Ancient Ones, the dark gods, and there would be no reason for his dissention. So, who was this goddess?

"Oh," he said while canting his head. "I think you know who it is… and she definitely remembers you."

Shazandra stopped cold. Three mere steps from the place she wanted to get to and she had halted in her tracks. *Impossible. She, she…*

"She wants out," Liguell chillingly finished the sentence in her mind. The monster quivered again with a violent tremor. "And she wants vengeance."

They cannot get her out, Shazandra thought. *The keys…*

"There are already servants digging for the keys, Mistress," he spoke as if he could hear what she was thinking. Was that possible? "And if that does not work…there is more than one way to open the Vault. Remember?" His head threw back with a hideously mocking cackle.

The Messengers of the Black Mage! The Three Servants of Nammtar, the Ancient One, the Dark God of Secrets, could maybe… For the first time in over four hundred years, Shazandra felt fear. He had given up her humanity, and her very soul, as a trade for becoming immortal. Her worst nightmares were coming back to haunt her. She looked at Liguell with her black orbs and tightened her grip on the staff.

"Excellent," he sneered. "A fight… this Ozadogguah has not had a tussle since the time of Gajana, right here on this very spot if I recall."

"I have no quarrel with it, Atto. This matter is between you and me." She took another step.

"I'm afraid not," he chuckled as he shook his head. "It has been given to me, on loan so to speak."

"Those are never given on loan. You dung licking moron!" She took another step and there was just one more. Maybe she could stall this long enough. "You are being used. After which, they will discard you like burned rubbish."

"I don't believe so," he said with his twisted smile still smeared across his face.

"Then you are a complete idiot," Shazandra replied. "…A special manner of stupid."

She took her last needed step, placing her in perfect line with the tall stones of the hilltop. She knew that she was unequipped and ill prepared to battle an Ozadogguah on such unholy ground. But she knew that she could get away and warn the others.

Her staff was thrust through the snow and a blinding light suddenly burst from the shaft. Liguell shielded his eyes, screaming in pain. The creature howled and retreated back down the hill, trying to shield itself from the searing light. Shazandra could no longer be seen through its brilliance.

When it faded, she was gone.

Sometime later, Alizee became conscious in a damp stone room. She had no clue where she was or how she got there.

Looking around, at her strange surroundings, Alizee became aware that it felt disturbingly similar to what Liguell had to study the Crafts.

"Tell me everything you know," her enraged master's voice came from behind her. "Now!"

Alizee slowly turned in the chilled gloom of the stone room to see a figure slowly lumbering toward her. It was mostly skeletal with grey rotting flesh clinging to its bones and was draped in equally rotting black tattered robes. Where eyes should have been, there were two deep points of burning red light. The young girl opened her mouth with a blood curdling scream.

"Tell me!" shouted the figure with an earsplitting volume that shook the stone walls and caused dust to fall from the ceiling.

Without thinking, and still in shock, the trembling Alizee managed to whimper, "Where is Zandra?"

"Don't speak that name again, brainless twit!" He hobbled ever closer to the young girl who seemed to be shrinking away. "Stop wasting time! Tell me now! What do you know of her? What do you know of Shazandra?"

Regressing, Alizee continued, "I don't know…She was nice to me! That was all!" Her voice struggled through terrified sobs.

"That makes you a gullible and naive idiot. She is nice to no one!" Liguell Kiesinger rebuked. As he neared, Alizee could feel the air around her become cold and felt the unseen fingers of vile energy insidiously weaving themselves into everything close to the skeletal creature.

"No!" the young girl wailed. "Please, no!" She began to shake uncontrollably and a puddle of urine formed under her. "Why do you hate me so much?"

His boney hand reached out and grasped her face like a frigid vice. Shaking her head, the corpse-like Kiesinger mockingly replied, "You imbecile, I don't hate you. I just don't care anything about you."

Less than one week later, a near mindless dried cadaver carried old books into Liguell's study. Not being very dexterous to begin with, or very bright, she now served as nothing more than a common laborer. Her fate was not much different than before, but in this state, Kiesinger felt better not having to feed and water her. She, or now it, stumbled while carrying her bundle, dropping the ancient tomes onto the stone floor and breaking their bindings. The ancient pages slid across the stones. In a flash of anger with eyes burning like orange flames, the skeletal Kiesinger spoke a single word, and poor Alizee's remains abruptly scattered across the stones in a cloud of fine dust...

Somewhere in the wild

Just after nightfall, Present Day

She poked aimlessly at the crackling fire. Her curvy brown tresses waved gently in the subtle wafts heat while its incandescent light was reflected in her sad hazel eyes. The yellow flames and orange embers provided no comforting warmth. The occasional hiss and pop from the fire seemed to invite a fragile dialogue that she had no interest in engaging. It was tepid that evening but her chill came from inside and everything to her was beginning to seem futile. The arduous four-month trek on foot, her plea for rescue, even the aid that was sent with her, seemed to be useless; insultingly useless. And so nothing provided comfort.

Earlier she distractedly picked at her unappealing food. She knew she needed to eat in order to maintain her strength and to get proper sleep as well. Even those seemed pointless. Why bother? She felt weary but not from physical exertion. She felt dejected. Glancing up from the dancing glow before her she looked at them and felt a sickening disgust. They were sent to help, or so she was told. But she knew better. These two were sent to pacify her perceived insanity. How could she be possibly telling the truth? No one had ever seen the absurd horrors she spoke of. After all, such things did not actually exist. Kneeling by the luminous fire that was far from the capital city, she could imagine and almost hear the disdainful conversations that took place behind closed doors. She must be crazy. A back woods illiterate with an over active imagination speaking of the sheer impossible as if it were unadulterated truth, weaving fanciful tales of twisted mythology and questionable superstition that she could never prove. She was just another unfortunate peasant without any recognized education or realistic mindfulness.

She was however, something rather different and

predominately unseen by most city dwellers. Ruelina was an elf and a ranger, one who was "tuned" to the forest and nature. Most people considered rangers to be "rooted" to the trees and loners. Neither of which was very accurate. More to the fact, the hills and forests could be filled with fierce and cunning creatures and rangers were the forest's guardians. Rangers formed a bond with the land and became its defender and sometimes protected those who ignorantly wandered through the wild. Those who did understand a ranger's function in nature sometimes referred to them as "Guardians" or "Keepers." Being so in touch with nature, they were also extremely skilled at survival, hunting, tracking, herbal medicines, hiding and stealth as well as most anything that did not involve city living. Many were also craftsmen and sometimes skilled musicians. The role suited her well.

As Ruelina coldly starred at them her head shook in disbelief. They were her great hope? That is what she walked almost three long months for? Now she tended to their survival. How ridiculous. Did she not explain where she was from? Did she not describe the deaths and fear? Did they not understand how far outside their accustomed civilization they would be traveling? Why send only two and why send those who were neither equipped nor experienced for the wild? She almost felt pity for them. They had no idea what they were literally walking into. They brought inadequate weapons, were ill informed, had no reinforcements and were sent leagues away from civilization. What were they thinking?!

Morons, arrogant unthinking morons, she felt. Her discouraged gaze cast back down to the fire. Again she poked at it so the air would keep flowing and it not extinguish. She knelt by the fire with her back to the road that lay not far to the south and faced northward into the darkened woods. Slowly she shifted uncomfortably in her kneeling position, feeling her feet losing circulation. How long had she been in that awkward position, hours? She had been that way at least since sundown, just after she cooked, and that was after she hunted and dressed the small deer. No wonder her muscles were cramping. It was also just after admitting to herself, again, that unless she did most of the practical work those two would starve on their own. They weren't just *no* help; they were useless. She could feel the two men had been looking down at her for being a woman. If either of them had been paying attention they would have seen her rippling muscles as she dragged the deer to their camp. She had more the frame of a fighter than a helpless woodland woman.

Who were they anyway? A priest and a plainly dressed "investigator" of some kind? Investigator? Ha! He did not even believe her, how could he "investigate" anything? This was her great accomplishment? Walking for weeks only to bring back…*them*? They had contemptuously laughed at her in the city and they would disdainfully laugh at her when she returned home. *Even the gods, if they really exist, must be laughing,* she thought to herself. The utter humiliation was one thing, but the overall futility of that whole venture was becoming unbearable and was over shadowing her sense of disgrace. How many more had died since she left for help? Would there be anyone left? Anything?

Probably not, or very little if anything or anyone. Her modest home sat in the heart of silent woods with nothing around but miles of trees. Isolated from any existent civilization, her tiny community was very self-reliant and that is exactly the way they liked it. There was no need for the clutter and noise of city life. With cities came crime, corruption and the destruction of Nature. The land is wounded by mining for materials one does not need to survive, forests were cut without cause and animals are killed for sport or driven from their homes by vicious hunters. People did not need to do such things. Large clearings of land for picturesque gardens were destructive. Killing woodland creatures for stylish clothing or trophies was destructive and disrespectful. Digging into the ground for gold or silver was also superfluous and something close to raping the land. All one needed was just enough food and shelter to survive, anything more than that appallingly distracted and corrupted one's natural state. Life was not meant to be spent trying to acquire more objects, wealth or land that would outlast anyone anyway. Such was the way of cities and their "civilized" ways. Love and virtuous living by the ways of the gods was all what one really needed and anything else was a poisonous distraction.

Her village had existed that way for a few generations. Living alone, away from the corruption of city life and supporting themselves with only what was absolutely needed from the land had worked very well for them. They had reached an almost perfect equilibrium with the forest. Peace reigned...until *they* came.

What would remain? Anyone who was even remotely capable of defending their homes had already been killed or altogether vanished. It was no wonder, though. How can one fight an opponent that they cannot kill and are outnumbered by? Brazen, the enemy had become. Legend spoke of them moving only at night. Now they attack in daylight. But that was months ago. What would be left of her home?

Another log was placed on the fire and her lips pursed as she fought to not bite her own tongue. Perhaps she should have. Maybe throw something. She felt like screaming. Looking down at her slender yet calloused hands she noticed she was beginning to shake. It was far from the first time. The problem was she felt as if she was losing control day by day. Every exasperating hour she spent with those two grated on her nerves. At least those two finally quit trying to engage her in a mindless conversation. Their petty questions ended weeks ago when they lastly admitted to each other that she was just not talkative. In an attempt to be pleasant, they had inquired her about her home, her family, her friends, her life philosophy and beliefs. Nevertheless, they were answered only by single words or none at all. It was perhaps not the best way for all of them to start out. What was she to do, though? Was she to treat them with great respect? Speak to them about things they really did not care about? Smile to them when she felt like scowling? Laughing with them when she felt like destroying something and crying?

There was also her fear, a deep welling of sheer apprehension when she considered her return. No one was able stop the horror that came to the woods around her home before. She was returning without any real aid; how would the terror be stopped? What would be done? Who would do it? There were too many questions and too few answers. Again, she began to tremble. *Breathe slow,* she told herself. *Just breathe…*

She began to remember the stench of old death and the horrid sound of labored air rasping through fangs in and out of rotting lungs that had not needed to breathe in many long dark years. Ruelina remembered the burning malevolent eyes that peered through the darkness carrying a leer of hatred and worse yet, a ravenous hunger that could be felt in the cold pit of her stomach. Leathery grey skin slowly rotting was pulled taut over muscle and sinew that somehow retained or gained lethal strength. They had claws, more like talons, long and black on both hands and feet. Never did they walk upright. They scuttled swiftly using all four limbs, hissing and snarling as they would give chase. She imagined how they would rip the flesh from the dead and crack the bones in their jaws as they fed. She remembered her sword cutting deep through the shoulder of one and into its chest while it continued its assault, seemingly unable to feel pain.

Finally, with a focused exhale, she abruptly stood and brushed some of the pale dirt off of the worn leather skirt she dressed in. Realizing that was also useless since they had spent weeks in the dirt already, she frowned even more. Tightening her soiled belt and glancing up to the stars in the night sky still trying to shake off her chill, she began to walk off with a purposeful stride. She was determined to just walk into the black of night a moment or two, needing to just get away for a while lest she scream. Her stride was not even broken upon hearing a voice; rather, it spurred her on in the already lost hope of getting away without being noticed. The voice was from one of *them.*

"Wha- wait," he stammered. "Where are you going?"

Kaeleb was his name… maybe. She did not really care anymore.

Glancing back through narrowing eyes and clenching her jaw she felt like shouting, *Away from you!* Instead she curtly hissed, "I'll be back."

At that, she vehemently continued without the slightest hint of any invitation to further speak of it. The two men looked at each other dumbfounded as to why she abruptly stomped off.

"I hope she is coming back," one of them said.

By the Heavens, she thought. *I hate humans,* and continued into the darkness…

Somewhere in the wild...

That Same Night

He took a few moments to study the stars in the night sky. The fire behind him cast a soft glow as their guide, Ruelina, tended to its maintenance. The wind, as it had most night nights over the past few weeks, tugged at his grey cloak and gently caused his brown hair to sway. But a least it was not raining that night. Not that he minded rain but it did make the next day of travel a bit uncomfortable in wet cloths. Since he was not accustomed to travel outside of Paragon City, much less that far out into the wild, the normal habits of traversing the forest without normal comforts of the daily life he was used to. In two days they would reach Silverwood and maybe he would have a decent bed to sleep in instead of the hard lumpy ground he now found himself trying to rest on.

Ghouls, he chuckled to himself. *Ignorant peasants*. Everyone in the civilized world knew there no such thing. The old fanciful stories of uneducated masses must still be "haunting" the remote countryside. Again, he chuckled to himself at his own cleverness for making a pun.

Smythe Gibvoy was very intelligent, one of the most intellectually gifted in the entire country of Paragon. He had been educated in the best colleges, fluent in nine languages, schooled in mathematics, alchemy, geography, astronomy and other more obscure subjects. He was only assigned to the most difficult or the most challenging and always those that required the utmost...discretion. To send him to Silverwood, he had surmised a few weeks ago, would mean that someone in Paragon City is taking a very keen interest in the events that were afoot there. Something obscure must have been happening there and that something needed his very subtle exploration. He reflected thoroughly on this day after day since they left the City a few weeks ago, making certain he did not carelessly overlook any detail in his mind.

After The War, it had taken over four hundred years for the forest and wildlife to come back after all of the land, hundreds of miles worth, was completely laid barren and desolate. In the time just after The War, no one could even see grass for many, many miles. As far as one could look there was just dirt and rock and the unmistakable stenches of brimstone and blood. However, after all that time, hard work and much cooperation from everyone in the world that would help, the lands were finally green and teeming with life again.

So that must be it, Smythe thought to himself. *Someone wants to harvest the silver for their own profits at the expense of helpless Paragon citizens.* Now the question was who? Who would do that? He had thought at length. *I must enlist aid from Boregar to solve this.*

But that was another problem. The elven girl, Ruelina, said they went to Boregar for aid and received none. Does that imply that someone in Boregar was involved? Either way he was there to look into the matter and it would not be a simple one at that. Nothing was ever simple or easy if he were sent.

What puzzled him even more was the strange fact that a priest was sent with them. *Why send a priest to look into this? Why would the Church be interested in this?* Specifically, why was the church of Enki becoming involved? Enki was, in fact, the god of war. How puzzling indeed. He understood, at some length, why he himself was being sent. That seemed easy to grasp. But a priest? Yes, it was also true that Enki was the patron god of Paragon. Why not? Paragon society was based on the warrior class. Who better to be an advocate than a priest of the realm? However, anyone from the military could have been sent. Especially if they had truly believed the threat was real it would stand to reason that a group of soldiers would have been dispatched rather than a single priest. So again, why was the church getting involved? Puzzling. Even more perplexing was that they had sent Kaeleb Miryd. Not that he was particularly gifted, so to say, but he was famous. Kaeleb, he had heard rumors, was supposed to be a *genuine* priest. He was not just another man with a title and a sword.

Purportedly, and yet quite unproven to Smythe's standards, he had been "touched" by Enki and could do…things, things that other people, even other priests, could not do. The man was either a bona fide saint or a clever deceiver. After months of travel, Smythe had not yet determined which one. It seemed the opportunity to put the good brother to the test had not presented itself.

As he continued to stare intently at the sky carefully watching the subtle movement of the Heavens, as he usually does on every clear night, the other man in that little group of three approached him from his flank. Brother Kaeleb was dressed in the traveling blue and light grey that every devout member of that clergy wore when traveling. It would look disturbingly strange to anyone outside of Paragon to see a priest wearing chain mail armor and bearing a long sword at his side. But it was Paragon and such things were expected, especially for priests of Enki because those blades were not just a decoration. Every priest of Enki was well trained in their use. Theirs was a cast society where the military held the highest position in the land. Other clergy, not of the war god Enki, came next in line of social status, followed by merchants, skilled artisans and laborers. Even below thieves however, were mercenaries. No one could be lower than one who sold their sword without honor.

Kaeleb inhaled and exhaled deeply when he reached Smythe's side. Not looking up the sky, since he already did that days before and knew what Smythe was doing, he began to converse.

"I do not feel our guide is very pleasant."

"Hmm," replied Smythe. "I would guess not since her whole village is in danger of being destroyed." He spoke flatly, continuing a game he began the first day they met.

"I realize that." Kaeleb was getting a little of tired of whatever Smythe was doing with his manner of talking. He could feel Smythe was up to something but could not tell what. "I was speaking of her thoughts toward us."

"Yes, I agree." He still spoke without looking at Kaeleb. "Perhaps she was hoping for something much more than just the two of us."

"If her ghoul story is true, which I am not inclined to believe just yet, then the two of us may not do much good."

"Precisely," Smythe still spoke impassively. "However you do must admit something…" Still playing the game, he wanted to see how imperceptive the priest was. Kaeleb was, after all, predisposed to a narrow and fundamentalist view of the world being a priest and all.

"Yes," Kaeleb spoke in the same flat tone as he turned to walk back to the comforting campfire. "Something motivated her to walk for four months on a hope that she would find aid for her home."

Smythe took his eyes from the stars to watch Kaeleb slowly return to the campfire where Ruelina crouched. That was surprising. He did not expect the priest to think that way. Perhaps the man would be of some use after all. With that he returned to the camp.

When he reached Kaeleb who was already sitting on the ground, Smythe sat down within talking distance. Not so close as to appear friendly but not so far as to appear obstinate any longer either. He reached over the fire and removed a stick of deer meat that Ruelina had prepared earlier. It was a bit dry from being on the fire for so long, but that did not matter so much to him. Smythe quickly learned on the trip that hunger won over taste.

Suddenly Ruelina stood and brushed herself off. The two men looked to one another then back to Ruelina as she turned to walk away. Kaeleb became more concerned for her feelings than he had before.

"Wha- wait…where are you going?" the priest stammered with sincere concern and was about to stand to go after her and see if he could get her to talk about what was bothering her. Sharply, she spoke over her shoulder without slowing her stride.

"I'll be back," she hissed. Her harsh tone invited no more conversation.

Kaeleb looked to Smythe and said, "I do hope she is coming

back."

"She can care for herself," Smythe quietly replied, making certain that she could not hear while watching the back of her head vanish into the darkness.

"I am not concerned for her use of a sword nor that we may not be able find Silverwood without her." He was irritated with the cold obliviousness of Smythe's demeanor and poked a little harder at their campfire. "I am concerned for *her*. She is very troubled and I am here to help. If that means I can settle her spirit so she can get some rest, then so be it. She is about to fall over from exhaustion and, if you didn't notice, she eats and sleeps less and less the closer we get to her home." Kaeleb looked away from Smythe, casting his concerned focus onto the fire to take over where Ruelina left off.

Oh, I noticed, Smythe thought to himself. I noticed more than you know…

Paragon City

Two months before the present day

Above the loud reverberating thump of hardened leather boot heels sprinting along the grey cobblestone walkway that was crowded with people, amazingly, a voice billowed.
"Tobin!"
A young nobleman donning a fine tabard over his gleaming chainmail quickly turned and warmly smiled, recognizing the voice of his life-long friend. They had grown up together from happy children running through the local fields and slaying furious dragons with wooden swords. Since both of their families had close ties with one another it seemed only right for them to encourage the children's friendship. Eventually they attended war academy years later as classmates and even stood shoulder to shoulder on a battlefield. Their victories that day at the Battle of Southmar Planes made them heroes here at home and were consequently knighted for having maintained the integrity and security of the kingdom of Paragon. Sir Emerik Montigan and Sir Tobin Drathmoore were both knighted side by side before the age of twenty two.
Tobin raised his brown leather gloved hand and waved to his running friend, waiting for the distance between them to shrink. When he slowed to a stride, Tobin bowed and in a deep voice bellowed out, *"Prince* Emerik!" He liked melodramatically emphasizing the word "prince" while in public. It was quickly returned with a disapproving glance from Emerik. He never favored his friend calling him by his title. It was acceptable for everyone else, just not Tobin. Friends should not be caught up in titles and such things when speaking to one another. Emerik always felt that when one did so, they spoke to the position and not the person and that was undesirable among friends. Both were well known members of the two families that founded and governed the vast country. But in his heart Emerik did not even recognize that the Montigan family were royalty and occupied a higher station than the Drathmoore's and definitely did not hold his dear friend to such things.
"Where are you off to?" Emerik asked while slowing to a walk beside him. The two were warriors with the aura to match.

Without looking, people would move from their paths. Both had penetrating stares that would cut through stone and muscles of hardened steel.

"I was about to check on Perry. I have him practicing with a halberd this morning and wanted to see how he was coming along."

"Ah," Emerik replied. "How's his training progressing, anyway?"

"He's an excellent squire," Tobin noted while looking to the congested road ahead as if fully considering what he just said. Watching all the defenseless people go about their daily lives while he was there to help protect them from any enemy that would ever present itself. With a nod he added, "He'll be a fine knight. How about yours? Is Dyrrany faring well?"

"Yes!" He sounded surprised, not expecting the question to come. Emerik had something on his mind and the seemingly casual meeting with his friend was actually quite purposeful.

Tobin glanced over to him with his wrinkling forehead as he wondered what Emerik was up to. They have spent most of their lives together, after all, and one cannot spend that time with another and not get to know them.

"What are you planning?" he spoke with an exaggerated exhale.

"You have that look again, my friend," Emerik noted. There was no look but he wanted to carry the conversation for the sake of building up his friend for a surprise.

"What look is that? The one where I asked if you have something you're planning?" A smirk crept across Tobin's lips.

"You look as if you long for something."

"Really?" Tobin asked while tilting his head and pondered where Emerik was going with all that. "What would that be?"

"You miss war," replied Emerik with certainty. That statement, however true, caught Tobin by surprise. His eyes widened with a lift from his brow as his gaze cast to the worn grey stone they walked along. Oh, how true that was. It had been what, almost three years? Images of Southmar Plane flashed in his mind. Yes, he had to agree, he did miss the battlefield and no amount of sparring practice would serve as adequate substitution. He had even fought six at once and yet, still did not feel the exhilaration that he did when in real bloody combat. Emerik looked at his friend and watched his mind wander. It wandered exactly where the prince intended it to go.

"Want to go back?" Emerik asked finally. Tobin blinked as if jolted from his musing by a slap on the nose.

"Where, back to Southmar?" He was confused. The potential war was over with that single battle. Why return to an empty field?

"No, man!" hollered Emerik. He leaned in and spoke slowly and forcefully as if driving the point with a maul. "Into battle," he said smiling with a twisted gleam in his eye. Tobin's eyes widened as he began to grow excited. He could not help the beam from creeping across his face.

"A war?" he finally asked. Tobin knew nothing of any war brewing but the very idea lit a candle deep inside him. Tobin's comment was however, a bit louder than Emerik wanted. In a hushed voice he explained.

"No, no, no. Not a war, but a battle none the less and I have been working on our involvement for weeks now."

"That is what you have been up to!" Tobin exclaimed. He wondered what secret little thing his friend had been whittling for the past month. "So, who is our enemy? Where are they? What are their numbers and how are they armed?" He was unable to conceal his excitement at even the remote chance of being in mêlée again.

"Shall I tell you now?" Emerik asked with an obvious smirk.

"Yes!" Tobin said a bit louder than even he wanted. It had to be something to keep secret if his twenty year friend had remained quiet about it. He looked around to see if anyone on the busy street was paying them any attention. Satisfied at the apparent lack of attention, he leaned toward Emerik as they walked. "Yes," he repeated. "Tell me!"

"We fight ghouls," Emerik announced. He kept walking a few steps before realizing Tobin had abruptly halted and stared at him as if Emerik had told him the entire sky itself just turned green while growing a second head. Tobin obviously fought for some constructive thing to say, struggling against something ill-mannered that was about to burst from his throat. His face twisted and his hands gestured as one thought after another was rejected from speech. Finally, he uttered the only thing that made any sense to say at that time.

"What, your Highness?"

Emerik scowled underscoring his dislike of his friend's formality. "Ghouls," he firmly stated. Taking the few steps toward his friend he repeated a bit slower, "We fight ghouls."

Tobin shook his head in disbelief and settled his eyes on Emerik's. He took his friend by the arm and moved to the closest wall of a building on the street. Emerik allowed himself to be led, knowing it was hard for Tobin to accept. When they reached the random point he hastily picked out, Tobin took a deep breath and curled his lips. He's gone mad.

"Emerik," Tobin spoke while placing a comforting hand on his shoulder. "There is no such creature as a ghoul." He was hoping to re-educate his friend who obviously forgot that small detail.

"I know," he said with a smile however, somewhere inside he could not help but feel that perhaps they did. His unrevealed experience taught him that. Tobin, though, truly looked at his friend with earnest concern for his mind.

"Then what are you talking about?" the knight asked.

"Ghouls are attacking a small elven village about a thousand leagues from here."

"Ghouls…Ghouls are attacking?" Tobin remained confused.

"Yes, I heard it myself a few weeks ago inside the Gold Court."

"You heard this?" Tobin asked, still in disbelief.

Emerik gave a single nod and retained his smirk.

"With your own ears?"

Another nod from Emerik.

"Who spoke of it?"

"A simple peasant, an elf girl from there." He glanced at Tobin but neglected to tell him that it was he who helped her gain admission to the Court. Without him the girl would have been laughed out of the gates. "She walked a thousand leagues to pray for our aid."

"Ghouls," Tobin said again, still in disbelief.

"That is what she said," Emerik announced. "And I am inclined to believe the danger is real."

"So…now you believe in ghouls?" They both began to continue walking down the busy cobblestone street. Neither wanted to draw undue attention to themselves, but Tobin began to wonder if Emerik had been hit in the head too many times.

"No, my friend, I don't. On that I am still unconvinced." Emerik's eyes cast away from Tobin as he pretended to scan the crowd for an eavesdropper. Not only had he just lied to his lifelong friend, he was also losing Tobin who starred at him hoping to receive some sort of statement that could be accepted as evidence that he had not gone mad. "However, I do believe that the people of the village are being killed off and the place is in danger. Also, so do others. They are inclined to believe that as well."

"Why?"

"Because," Emerik replied. "We are speaking about the elven hamlet of Silverwood."

"Silverwood?" The hamlet was famous for a superstitious rumor that silver grew into the trees.

"Yes. The Royal Ministry has assigned an investigator to determine the validity of what the elf girl spoke. They departed for Silverwood about three weeks ago on foot. But we should catch up with them by horse without difficulty. Also, I did some asking. It seems that the rumors are true…silver does grow into the trees."

"Whoah!" Tobin exclaimed. "That's incredible."

"Yes."

"How is that possible?"

"I do not know. Perhaps another mystery of the gods?" Emerik shrugged. "Or maybe some vile magic is afoot. No one can say right now without going there to see."

"Magic?" Tobin spoke darkly. "That can still be punishable by death if I am not mistaken."

"No, no mistake, you are quite correct." Again, he was hiding something and luckily Tobin was still none the wiser.

"So I had hoped," Tobin added with serious tone. "I would not have liked for that law to have been changed after all these years. Over four hundred years, actually."

"Four hundred eighty seven," Emerik nodded in agreement.

"With good reason," he preached. "Such things are the work of evil." He looked to his friend who merely strode beside him in silence. "Well," he spoke. "I should not be telling you of this, you should be tutoring me!"

"Yes, well…" Emerik said dismissively.

"You are still a Paladin, are you not?" he rhetorically asked.

"Yes," Emerik answered, knowing Tobin understood that

already. "Only my cousin Kyron and I study The Path. No one else in my family felt the Call." Tales of old spun yarns of devout warriors who received a pull toward a faraway place where they would be isolated and wracked with mental, emotional and physical anguish in the name of their god. When they returned, they proved the possession of certain abilities not held by normal men. But such things were thought lost since the days of the gods had passed and the heavens fell into silence.

Suddenly the prince remembered Tobin and himself jesting a few years ago about him ever becoming a paladin, a holy warrior in the service of an Elder God, and how no one ever received the Call anymore. Enki, once called Adad, was the primary deity in Paragon since He was the god of war in a society of warriors but "Paladin" became more an honorific title than an actual proving of the Call. Emerik's and Kyron's Calling had changed all that. No one had seen that in over four hundred years and no one could understand why those two, of everyone in the world, had gone and returned as Paladins. In ancient times, when the world was polluted with scheming Craftusers, unholy priests, bloodthirsty monsters and infernal fiends, the paladin was the last inextinguishable hope. Their staunch devotion to holiness, an undying will for social stability and a power to defeat evil that bordered on the supernatural were the three primary weapons against villainy in all its forms. Few possessed the devotion to walk their narrow path, fewer received the Calling to become one and even fewer yet remained paladins. That life was fragile and easily broken. But for those who held fast, they were rewarded with unnatural power to safeguard, heal and vanquish.

The paladin-prince and knight both walked briefly in silence, each deep within their own thoughts. Emerik's thoughts, being darker than Tobin's, arrested his mind. The memory of his private horror still haunted him. Tobin finally spoke.

"So...why Silverwood? Why is it so special?"

"I do not know," shrugged the paladin-prince. "It is a tiny little village. I guess thorp would be a better name."

"A what? A thorp?" questioned Tobin. "What's a thorp?"

"Yes, a thorp is what you call something smaller than a village, like a very small hamlet."

"Why not just say 'very small hamlet' then?" Tobin was a man of simplicity and did not like anything to be complicated.

Emerik Chuckled, "Because 'thorp' is shorter."

"But no one understands that word," Tobin argued.

"Looks like you just learned a new word then," said Emerik with a broad smile.

Tobin pondered.

"Thorp," he said again as if teaching himself not to forget.

Both smiled then Tobin fell briefly into an awkward silence.

"Do you hear what they are calling you?" Tobin asked.

"Who is 'they'?"

"Well, 'they' are the nobles of Paragon."

"No, I have not heard. What are they calling me?" He had a slight look of concern on his face.

"Well, because you seem…different from everyone else they made a name for you."

"Different how?" Emerik asked. "What name?"

"Your interest and compassion in commoners and your display of affection or respect for peasants had earned you the name 'People's Prince' among the nobles," explained Tobin with a smirk.

"You are joking," he balked.

"No, I am afraid not," Tobin calmly replied but retained the half grin.

"They actually wasted their time with that?" Emerik paused. "And 'People's Prince' is the best they can think of?"

Both looked to each other and laughed. After their amusement quieted, they kept walking and then Tobin began again. "So where do ghouls fit into this? We were actually speaking of ghouls, right?"

"That is correct," Emerik answered in confidence. "Unholy aberrations that feed on corpses, they are the walking dead." He folded his arms. That was much more than he0020wanted to say. "Well, according to the books on mythology from our library," he quickly added, not wishing to sound like an authority on that forbidden subject.

"You have been reading…" Tobin's point trailed off. He noticed. There was no avoiding it now.

"A little, yes," admitted the paladin.

"But, Emerik, that's myth. Ghouls don't exist."

"Most probably so and yet perhaps not. But think of this, my friend…if not, then a group of mere men are attacking and trying to force the elves out of Silverwood, no doubt to harvest the silver from the trees. This is something the elves there have been struggling with since the trees grew back after the Great War. However, if they do exist then it falls to the responsibility of the kingdom to protect its citizens from such evil. Either way, we save a village and must do battle to accomplish this." He slapped Tobin on the arm. Hopefully he still kept his secret. Not that he was malicious in his deception; he currently did not know how to sort out his experiences yet. Night time was the hardest. Slowly, Emerik watched an eager gleam appear in Tobin's eyes.

"So it is off to battle then! How many are we bringing with us?" he spoke happily.

"Just us and our squires. That is all we need. From what the elf spoke their numbers are less than eight." He looked squarely at Tobin before challenging, "We can handle eight peasants, correct?" Tobin thought on that only for a moment because there was no way he was going to shrink from any taunting, especially when the enemy was mere peasants. Either way, they would be heroes. Especially if what he felt in his gut was correct.

"Is not Silverwood a far travel for us to defeat a measly eight?"

"Non-sense," Emerik smiled. "Boregar City, Paragon's Shining Star, is where my cousin governs and is not but a day's leisurely travel from there. It would be a nice visit and see something away from here for a time. Want to go on holiday after we tend to this?" It took Tobin very little time to process the whole plan.

"Well," he enthusiastically spoke while beaming and clapped his hands in a singularly loud slap. "When do we leave!?"

Emerik merely smiled. Again that haunting thought came to him. As they walked off to prepare for their journey, Emerik could not stop thinking....*Am I doing what's right?*

Paragon City

Four Months before the present day

Smythe began to climb the long flight of decoratively carved stone stairs. Silently, he chuckled to himself again just as he did each time he came there. Magic was forbidden in the land of Paragon…if only they knew. He stopped on a landing in front of two very large and intricately carved ancient looking doors. Their surface was antique, the wood petrified over countless centuries. Many shapes of writhing bodies, both of men and women some of which were far from humanoid, twisted, danced, climbed or crawled over the doors that had no handles or visible hinges. Smythe placed his fingers into the gnarled folds between the carvings and closed his eyes.

"Anat biti sa eribusu," he spoke.

A lifelike moan bellowed from the rigid seams but the doors did not budge.

"Bastard changed the passwords again," he cursed. Smythe irreverently banged on the aged doors with his fists and shouted with impunity. "Scarecrow! Come on, do I have to burn these down again?!" He did not care if it was a secret entrance nor did he cast a concern that someone may have heard him shouting and pounding. He was an operative, true enough, however, when he became impatient because of stupidity his concern for surreptitiousness quickly vanished.

The doors unlatched and groaned as they opened. There was no one that pulled at the giant wood but they parted none the less. Smythe scanned the office, as a habit, to notice anything strange, unusual or out of place. He was working and he was trained to be observant. It was not that he distrusted the superiors in his organization; after so many years he simply did these things without conscious thought.

Most everything was in the same place as it had been when he left almost five months ago. There were exactly one hundred and sixty-six books in that office. Smythe, having been bored one day while waiting for his superior, took the time to count and memorize the title, shape, color and position of every single book. Upon each return, he would scan all of them and note where the new books were and their respective details. That day, there were no new additions however some were in the wrong place. He noted that and looked to his administrator.

Smythe's eyes instantly fell onto a meticulously crafted and very large orrery. Normally, these were an astrological sculpture that generally displayed the solar system in relative motion and did so in great detail. No particulars were omitted when the only twelve in the world were created, including the paths of the planets were even elliptical not circular and their orbits were tracked through three axes and not just two. It was an invention of the late Lady Gajana and only a handful of people in existence knew that the Earth was not the center of the universe, let alone how many planets there were in the solar system or how they moved. Exactly how Gajana knew of these things no one could tell and credited it to her goddess-like position.

That particularly large orrery was quite different than all of the others as well and, of these, there were only two left of the original three: that one and another that rested in Rokal at the University of Thaumaturgy in Ilranik City. Likewise, both of those were constructed by Gajana over five hundred years ago. Both forms of orrery are actually copies from much larger ones she had constructed many years before. During the Great War, the originals were destroyed and only those few now remained.

The orrery was different in that the planets on it were ancient relics in the forms of figures or depictions with symbols and had a white globe at the center. It was an orrery for tracking the forces and planes of the Cosmos and it was not moving.

A large pair of hands was open with elongated knobby fingers spread and his head was tilted back as he spoke the mantra. He was tall- being well over six feet, yet gaunt. His dark hair and shadowed eyes stood in disturbing contrast to his ashen skin. Scarecrow, as he was called, looked almost like a skeleton that could smile and wore gloomy clothes that hung loosely on his body much the same as they would hang on a hook on the wall. That seemed fitting since the specialized school of magic he recently had chosen was necromancy; the magic of the dead. Since the only way to get to the spirit world was to die, a necromancer may look a bit corpse-like before their end, having accelerated the entire dying process through their arcane study. Smythe had guessed his name "Scarecrow" came from his emaciated appearance. The sight was rather disturbing and the name rather appropriate.

Their "organization" was more like a clandestine police or secret society. They existed in every country, in every culture and in every level of society. The Brotherhood, or "The Order" as they called themselves, monitored the development and use of magic technology in every corner of the world yet utilized magic to accomplish that goal. It was a response from the problems before the Great War, from the fall of Old Ilmaria, and in fact was still called "The Promise." Secret whispers within the secret group held the rumor that they had been given their charge from Gajana herself. Perhaps that is why their hidden headquarters rested within the city of Paragon itself. Or maybe that was a device created by the Montigans and Drathmoores. Either way, the Brotherhood's master, who simply went by the name Bale, reportedly only answered to King Malazar of Paragon.

Using illegal magic to curtail illegal magic, the idea drew a smirk across Smythe's lips from time to time. What wiped that smirk away were the other deeds he knew were done, and even those he had to do himself, in order to control magic in the world. Sometimes those memories kept him up at night. Sometimes he wept in silence. Most people would never accept what had been done, the vast numbers of people killed, tortured or made to simply vanish…and worse. He knew the Brotherhood had destroyed entire cultures, deceived and subverted governments, subjugated thrones and worse, just to maintain control. But who was controlling them?

Smythe stepped in through the doors which autonomously closed behind him while he felt he wanted to be elsewhere. He did not mind working for the organization but he would rather have a much less unsettling superior. As Smythe had seen much in the world that most people do not, Scarecrow, or what remained of him, gave him disquieting shivers. Smythe had decided a few years ago that even shaking his cold hand was to be completely avoided. Being there made Smythe more than a little edgy and uncomfortable.

"…Imdikula salalu musha u ura qu u imtana alu u pi ia…" chanted Scarecrow.

"Deciding which color to paint this place again?" Smythe asked with thick sarcasm. Damn, he did not want to start that way. His desire to leave as quickly as possible would become evident soon enough and there was no need for being that crass that early in their meeting.

"Those doors are older than the last ones you burnt down," he informed Smythe while ignoring the question. His voice was disturbingly lower than it should have been for someone so skeletal.

"That last time was an emergency, remember?"

"So, this is an emergency?" Scarecrow asked still without looking at him.

"No," Smythe explained. "For changing the passwords and not letting me know…I would have done that for spite."

Scarecrow did not think Smythe was funny.

"You're back early," Scarecrow mentioned without taking his eyes from the orrery.

"I grew tired of spending your money." He stepped to the desk to casually glance at what Scarecrow was currently working on. His brow creased. *What the…*

"But I am sure you spent enough." He turned to Smythe who avoided looking him the eyes. Smythe did not want to see those midnight black orbs any more than he had to.

"Well, I do have a certain standard of living."

"Tell me you found it," he spoke as he crossed the room toward Smythe.

"I found the vault."

"That's not what I asked," Scarecrow said uncaringly.

"I cannot help it if Sydathrian monks with vows of poverty don't take bribes," he said with a shrug and hoped it could afford him some time to subtly peek at the papers and books on the desk. What he saw was most curious. Scarecrow, however, strode toward him in a most menacing manner. When Smythe perceived that, he calmly pulled from his pocket a small ebony and gold relic. It stopped Scarecrow cold.

"Even you can be fooled." Smythe's small games with Scarecrow helped him lessen the tension he felt each time they saw one another. It was not Scarecrow who was ill at ease and Smythe doubted the man was capable of any emotion aside from anger.

A reluctant grin cracked Scarecrow's stern features as he gazed at the icon. He took the artifact in his bony fingers and stared breathlessly at a gaunt figure bracing itself against a cosmic wind.

Smythe was careful not to let Scarecrow touch him as the figurine was grasped.

"Six-hundred-year old depiction of a sephiroth in the fourth realm..."

"Right...So, my task is completed, yes?" Smythe had quite enough of that room and that man already and it had barely been two minutes. He put out his hand and opened it, expecting to be given something in return.

Scarecrow ignored his outstretched palm, turned and walked back to the orrery to slide the relic precisely onto one of the many rods jutting from it.

"It should counter the Shadow plane..." he announced absently.

Shadow plane? Why would he be so interested in that?

"That damn thing is never going to balance." Smythe had watched it before and just wanted to leave. Scarecrow could play with his ancient toy without him or Smythe could come back when the room was less crowded.

Scarecrow let go and the complex machine actually started to move and turn. Smythe was somewhat intrigued as it clicked and pinged until the newest relic collided with another and the orrery jammed to a halt. Scarecrow deflated and stared at Smythe suspiciously who was still pondering the question of why Scarecrow was so interested in the Shadow Plane and why he was using that figure.

"Must I remind you of what delivering fake relics will do to your health?"

Smythe was snapped back into the room and out of his own head with that threat.

"It's authentic, Scarecrow, you just have the wrong piece. By the gods..."

The two had a staring contest. Smythe's rigid face was only broken by a cough and Scarecrow sighed then looked away.

"What? You never cough?"

Scarecrow reached into his desk and handed over a small sack of coins.

"There had better not be any copper in here this time," Smythe said as he took the sack. Scarecrow was not the only one who could give a threat in the room. He turned to the desk and opened the sack to count the coins. They were gold, sure enough, but that was not what he was truly interested in. Smythe wanted to see more of what Scarecrow was studying. Strangely enough, he usually did not care but that time something in his intuitive self was driving him to look and to understand.

"So, why did you make your trip short?"

Smythe stopped acting like he was counting the coins and actually thought about it. Or that is what Scarecrow believed. In reality, he was taking all that information from the desk he had gleaned in those few short seconds and weighed it against what books were out of place or recently used on the shelves. There were noted points which were devoid of dust and the misplaced books, especially for a devoted wizard, suggested haste. There was something he was keeping from Smythe.

"I don't know... Just a feeling. Something I saw in the sky, actually." Smythe laid some bait to see if Scarecrow would nibble and he did.

"Really? In the sky? What did you see?" His tone became one of concentrated interest.

"I am not really sure…it looked to me like a new star in the sky."

"You did? Where?" Scarecrow asked with complete sincerity yet with a tone suggesting he was thinking of something else at the same time. Smythe knew the game and decided to end it as quickly as possible and get to his own library. He knew Scarecrow was already aware of the game as well and he also knew he needed to get out of that office before the situation became dangerously unhealthy: for the rest of the population sniping at your superior could get you fired, sniping at Scarecrow could make that turn of phrase quite literal.

"It is just beside the northern part of the Large Dog constellation. I noticed it just before sunrise a few days ago." That was a lie. Smythe noticed it a few months ago while he was still on his way to Sydathria through the desert country of Pnath. Thankfully, Scarecrow was just as eager to get Smythe out as Smythe was to leave and did not perceive that he had just been lied to.

With their mutual farce of politeness and brief farewells, Smythe managed to not rush out of the door but to casually walk as he passed through the ancient portal. He unhurriedly walked down the great stone stairs to the bottom. When he reached the door to the outside he stepped through and into the tavern that served as a front for that location of the organization.

There were many such places scattered across the kingdom of Paragon, including in the capital city, as well as throughout the rest of the continent. They watched the world and controlled its technology with magic. It was they who ensured that spells and devices of only a certain level of power were accessible. They scrutinize and monitored everyone and everything to see that no one became too powerful. But as he exited the tavern and made as much haste as possible without drawing any attention to himself, Smythe had to wonder just then... *We supervise the world in secret, but who is supervising us?*

Later, Smythe was pouring through his own books and tomes to grasp and understanding of what he just observed. It was far too unusual to be casually discarded. Scarecrow knew something and he was not telling Smythe what it was. However, that was not the issue since that happened on a nearly constant basis. The difference was how Scarecrow behaved that time. He had sent Smythe to the far side of the continent to retrieve a small obscure item held in a monastery by a group of monks and then return with it only to learn that it was to be used in a cosmic orrery and paid more than any other assignment ever did. Step by step, Smythe reviewed the events.

First, he was sent to Sydathria. He did not know how to speak Sydathrian and, since his skin did not have a yellowish tint and his eyes were not shaped the same, he could not even look like one and blend in. *Why send me there? Was Scarecrow that confident of my ability or was there another reason?*

Second, the item in question was an ancient icon with a seemingly unknown origin, unknown at the time but not a mystery any longer. It was for an orrery that tracks the Cosmos. That having been said, why did Scarecrow want that particular icon out of the hundreds that are said to exist? Also, how did he know that one was all the way in Sydathria in that monastery?

Third, why was balancing the Shadow Plane important for the orrery to move? What was happening there that was causing problems or would soon be happening?

Forth, the icon Smythe retrieved was a sephiroth, an emanation or sphere of the divine energies that shape and move the Cosmos. The particular one he retrieved was of the Fourth Realm that was the aspect of "Mercy" and was one of ten that walked along twenty two paths and through five veils. Strange how Scarecrow would think to balance the Plane of Shadow with Mercy, since that Plane sat roughly what could be described as "between" the ethereal and the netherworld. That is obviously why it had been given the name Shadow. What was not so obvious was Mercy. Using the celestial aspect of mercy could only imply that that something godly yet cruel was happening there. Scarecrow must have been on the correct path since the orrery began to move however, the Plane of Shadow collided with another and the Cosmos halted.

What was the iconic representation it smashed against? Smythe struggled to remember but could not. He wanted to leave so badly that he had overlooked that small yet seemingly important detail. He would have to go back for that.

The books that Scarecrow had been pondering over on his desk were old maps and navigational charts depicting the eastern regions of the continent and out into the ocean. The papers were old and well used so obviously they were…creatively acquired like all other documents and items the organization possessed. The misplaced books were all concerning the same subjects: astrology and astronomy. *So…why was Scarecrow, a necromancer, so interested in astrology, maps of the earth, charts of the skies and balancing a cosmic orrery with Mercy in the Shadow Plane?* Something was very wrong.

Just then, there was a single rap at the back door of his house directly before a folded paper was slid under its crack. Smythe waited his obligatory count to sixty and then calmly walked to the rear entrance of his home through his kitchen. His abode was not very large; however, he did hot have to pay anything for it. That was one of the benefits of the organization, a free place to live.

Reaching the door, he noticed the paper on the stone floor. Bending down he retrieved it and never opened the door. It was quite customary and he had learned the routine long ago. When needed, the organization would send a messenger to the agent's home with a folded paper. The messenger did not know to whom he was delivering it nor did he know what the message was or what it meant. Each message was individual for each agent so that even if another agent acquired the message they would not understand what it meant. He opened the paper. To anyone else it would have looked like a doodled mass of curves and lines. But it was not so. Smythe learned it when he was brought into the Brotherhood. In their secret language called Awatium, "Bridge" was the only word.

So soon? He thought to himself. I only just returned. He draped his cloak over his body to drive off the chill of the night and promptly exited his home and made his way to the bridge.

There were over one hundred different bridges of wood or stone in the capital city but Smythe knew which one he needed to go to. There was a grand park in the northern district that held most of the affluent homes and business of the population here. In one area, there were two stone bridges that spanned a network of beautiful yet twisting walkways that wound their way through the surrounding lawns and gardens. His destination was the under path of the western bridge. When he arrived there was already someone there, leaning against the stone support of the span. Silhouetted by the streetlamps and moonlight, Smythe watched as the figure took a loud swig from a jug and then attempt to sing into the night.

Smythe approached with a frown. The figure dressed in dirty tattered clothing and reeked of stale wine. Smythe strode casually along the path in an attempt to pass the drunkard. But it did not work.

"Spare a coin could you?" his voice slurred. "I'm good for it."

Again, Smythe frowned. He reached into his pocked while glancing around to see if anyone else was watching then handed it to the man.

"Oh! Silver! You are most generous, milord!" he breathed heavily on Smythe who backed away.

"You smell."

The drunkard looked to him and began to complain.

"Hey...you'd small too if you had some a dis." The drunk tried to hand Smythe his jug but he passed it away.

"Will you quit that, already?"

Looking down the drunk watched as some of his wine sloshed out from the jug and made a small splash on the cobblestone.

"What cha doin'? Dis not cheap ya know!" He fell into Smythe and clutched his cloak. Smythe grasped him to keep the man from falling and while they held onto one another, the drunk spoke in his ear.

"I have a message for you." His voice was suddenly low, clear and controlled. "I am not really a beggar."

"I know that," Smythe answered impatiently in a harsh whisper. "Did they just hire you? Are you new at this? Stop all this nonsense!"

The drunk stood and straightened out Smythe's clothing. Smythe, meanwhile, could not abide stupidity and slapped the man's hands away from his cloak.

"Stop that!"

The man looked around for a second appearing quite sheepish. Smythe grasped him by his jacket and drug him over to the wall and pushed him against it a little harder than he meant to.

"What is the message?" Smythe whispered through clenched teeth.

"You don't have to get so angry. I was just acting as if..."

The look in Smythe's eye let him know it was useless to explain.

"Fine, tomorrow you leave for Silverwood."

Smythe blinked.

"Where is Silverwood?"

"It lies to the far north and east of the country, close to the border with Ib. Nearest settlement is the city of Boregar, a trade port for goods exchanged between the countries of Ib, Rokal and Paragon." He spoke plainly yet quickly in a very business-like tone that greatly contrasted his earlier performance.

"What is the task?" Smythe sounded impartial yet without a hit of patience. He did relax his grip a bit, though.

"Investigate any activity concerning ghouls and report the matter to Bale, himself."

That name made his heart skip a beat. Bale was the master of the whole organization. That could not be.

"Bale?" Smythe swallowed, audibly hard, after saying that name.

The man nodded.

"Grandmaster Bale wants me to report my findings directly to him?"

"That is correct. This has the highest priority," he spoke with a grave tone while looking Smythe in the eyes. "The Order wants proof, by the way."

"Proof of what?"

"Proof of the existence of ghouls. Tangible and verifiable proof," he acutely answered.

"How am I supposed to get that? Ghouls, they don't exit."

"That is your matter. I am only relaying your assignment."

"I do not know anything about them either, except…they are not supposed to exist."

"That," the man said, "is also your matter."

Smythe knew then he was not going to get anywhere talking to him. *This is gohram crazy.* "Anything else?"

"As a matter of fact, yes there is." He explained, "Tomorrow you will report to the Golden Hall to meet the Brother Kaeleb Azhwan Miryd of the Temple of Enki and you will be guided by Ruelina, a townswoman of Silverwood. She will fill you in on the background details."

Smythe reeled, "Other agents are going with me?"

"No," he answered. "You are the only member of the Order in that group. Kaeleb is a priest and Ruelina is an elf from that town who also happens to be a ranger."

You have got to be joking, Smythe thought to himself before asking, "An outsider is going to fill me on the details? Since when have we begun doing that?"

"Since time is short and intelligence from there is sketchy at best." The man pushed his way past Smythe who could only stand there and stare. He stopped though, and turned back around to operative. "Remember," the messenger reminded him, sounding more like a warning. "Tangible and verifiable proof."

"Yes, of ghouls." Smythe spoke to reinforce to the man he understood.

Without so much of a nod, the man turned and walked off, casting the jug away into the brush without care.

Ghouls, Smythe thought. *First an unbalanced Shadow Plane and now I am going to hunt a peasant myth I am completely uneducated about, out in the middle of nowhere, with a priest and an illiterate peasant and I will have no assistance if I need it…Bloody Hell.* With a sigh and a frown, Smythe trudged back to his home as the night became a bit colder.

Paragon City

Two weeks before the present day

He moved with the same amount of sound a shadow would make passing over the floor. The stone bricks of the corridor gave no one any hint he was there. Wearing black fabric, creeping with an unnaturally silent fluidity and grace along with his stealthy progress down the corridor, he would have given the impression of being living darkness, but no one could see him.

His disturbingly cold gaze scanned the corridor ahead as he listened behind and perceived that no one was anywhere close he needed to be concerned about. He heard two Paragon guardsmen in the next room chatting idly about the news of the day and of inaccurate rumors of luxury and life of ease in some far away kingdom neither would ever visit. He had no reaction. He cared little about the concerns of most people, especially when he was here with great purpose. This night, again, he was an envoy; his message was death.

The guardsmen's voices were muffled through the stone wall and heavy wooden door. In a single glance, he regarded the closed door with its wrought iron reinforcements and heavy lock. He suspected as much. It was a government building and everything within its walls was funded by the Paragon throne. Every table, spoon and guardsman was owned by the regime. Even the recipient of his message was government. But that did not concern him either. Everyone had to die some day and it just happened to be that person's time. Someone would miss them when they were gone. Some would mourn their passing. The government would look for their killer. However, none of these things concerned him either. He had a task to accomplish and nothing would keep him from completing it. Nothing could keep them alive.

The basic responses to killing are distinct, although they vary in duration. At first there are feelings of concern: Will I be able to kill the enemy or will I "freeze up" and "let my comrades down" at the moment of truth. Remorse usually comes after killing for most as a collage of pain and horror. "...I felt disgusted...I dropped my weapon and cried...there was so much blood...I vomited...I felt regret and shame... These emotions come from a sense of identification or empathy for the humanity of their victim.

This particular killer, however, had none of these feelings and he had denied his own attachments to humanity to such an extent that he felt very little empathy. Empty, hollow and cold, he had become one who had more compassion for an animal than a human child. Having killed so many and buried his emotions for so long he would save a cat before he would consider rescuing a baby. This man was not without the realization that he had become a monster inside, though, any questions of morality concerning his actions had passed away long ago. Good, evil, salvation, redemption, penance and absolution were words that had no meaning for him. Maybe they applied to others but if there were gods in the Heavens, he accepted his soul was damned long ago and there was nothing to do about that now. Paradoxically, however, he believed in what he did. He was devout in his belief in fate and destiny to such an extent that those who died by his hand were meant to die in that manner and if one were to pass through the gate in another way then that is as it should be. He was not making the world a better place by killing those who would never be arrested or sentenced for their evils and wrongs; he was providing a passage to death which held less suffering than many other forms. Never in his years had he ever killed a good and decent person, whether they were men or women. Not one was innocent or remorseful of evils they had done but would beg shamelessly for their lives with teary eyes and insincerely apologetic tongues. But then again, he was not their judge or jury. He was not given to evaluating or offering salvation. He was only their private, their silent, executioner.

When he reached the end of the corridor he found the staircase he was looking for. The map of the mansion was memorized over a week ago, along with placements and routines of every guard and servant in the place at any time of the day. He was a professional and within the Brotherhood, for those select few that even knew of him, he was the best in the world.

He paused momentarily to listen for anyone approaching from the upper floor. Satisfied no one was there, he swiftly and silently glided up the spiral stone stairs like a phantom. Upon reaching the top he paused, perplexed and concerned, at what he saw. The torches here were not lit.

He quickly glanced around the room seeing only the two windows and the single corridor opposite the stairs. It was everything he expected to see, expect the torches. Seeing nothing else unusual, even on the raised ceiling, he began to glide along the wall's surface to the arch of the hallway. He smoothly crouched under the stone frame of the window while he made his way. Reaching the archway he quickly peered down the hall. Only two doors, exactly like the map, one at the end of the corridor and one to the right just a few feet away. He was interested in the closer one. There was light coming from under that door but none from the other at the end of the hall.

With his back to the wall he began to cautiously move toward the door. The lock was a simple one and would easily be rendered ineffective with the acid he carried. Then, quickly and efficiently, one simple yet precise stab with his long thin dagger coated in poison would be the climax of the night's actions. If the strike itself was not lethal the poison it carried would be. Either way was death.

He froze in mid step.

He felt the light touch of something on his thigh then nothing. Damn! He should have known better. He cursed himself before quickly moving backward out of the archway and into the previous room with his senses more alert.

All too late he had felt the thread that warded the archway. With the thread broken his element of surprise was lost. Now he would have to fight to reach his target, if they were where they were supposed to be. The sound of approaching footsteps brought is mind into focus. None of that mattered now: he still had his task to complete.

Heavy boots with the unmistakable clank of armor became louder as a man came to the closed door. *They knew someone was coming! Someone told them? How else would they know?*

He only heard one person approaching him from the room. That made no sense. He quickly looked at the archway. It was high, rising in a curve at least twelve feet at its apex. He had a plan. The assassin waited for the door to open before he sprinted silently toward the far wall of the tight corridor. His eyes narrowed in determination as the door latch clicked before the heavy door groaned open and light poured into the corridor from inside the room. He was already running.

Placing his foot onto the far wall while in mid stride, he ran up the wall and stepped onto the ceiling of the hallway. By the time the guard reached to draw his sword, a vice like grip clutched his jaw and helmet. The assassin used his unnatural momentum and spun while he was inverted. The guard gasped in surprise as a blur of black shadow moved past his head. *Was someone running on the ceiling?* A chill gripped him when he saw the dim outline of a face with frightfully piercing eyes on that swift moving shadow. It was only a brief moment of lucidity before the sharp pain of his broken neck reached his mind. Then all was dark.

The assassin gracefully landed inaudibly on his feet inside the doorway. He used his motion to drag the lifeless body into the room. Since there was no point in maintaining stealth any longer and he dropped the lifeless body onto the stone floor. The sudden thud and ring of metal armor reverberated in the stone room and disturbed the silence like a sudden alarm. Drawing two short swords from his back while at the same time smoothly closing the door with his foot, he swiftly scanned the room for his opponents. But he found none!

Alone at a small reading table was a well-dressed woman sitting with her hands folded nervously in her lap. She kept her eyes on the floor. Dressed in a fine brown and tan gown trimmed in gold she looked more that she might be going to a dinner party. Her long blonde hair was elegantly wound with pins of gold and silver. A lantern on the table gently lit her delicate features and accented the lines of fear that she fought feebly to keep from showing on her face. Still, she did not move.

He slowly lowered his swords but became no less ready for any impending attack. Again, he looked around the room but perceived no attackers. It, as he knew, were private chambers. The bed was richly covered in fine silk linen and expertly carved of mahogany. Stained glass doors artfully depicting the symbols of beauty of refinement remained closed. The reading table she sat at had two chairs with cushions and the table itself was set with marble and pearl. He was bewildered. He looked at the woman as she sat immobile yet trembling.

Her heart pounded in her ears and her throat was dry. Her own tongue felt three sizes too big in her mouth. Trying to swallow the lump in her throat her lips trembled as she momentarily felt herself losing composure that she struggled so desperately to maintain. Dignity was her last asset she held since she knew her life was moments away from being taken from her. Maintaining her self-control was essential for what task she had chosen to complete that night. Like him, she would not be thwarted from her goal. Both would get what they wanted if she could only stay his hand for a time and hope he was receptive enough to listen.

The first attempt to speak ended in failure as the words stuck on the lump in her throat. Her eyes teared. She swallowed hard and cleared her throat. Just a few moments. Please, just listen to me, she thought to herself.

"Um," she finally uttered. "Could you sit?"

"Why?" he answered flatly, expecting an ambush. Was there a poison needle in the seat or some other trap? Was there someone here he missed?

"Please," she spoke with a shaky voice. "I know why you're here. But, I just want you to listen to what I have to say."

"You'll not talk me into sparing your life. You are wasting my time." He took a few slow steps closer still looking for some waylay or trick. People usually begged for their lives. It was very predictable and not belittling in the least from his perspective. Those not ready to die would naturally cling to life since they would not accept the inevitable.

"I've no intention of doing any such thing. I just want you to listen." Finally she raised her eyes to meet his. She was shocked at what she saw. It was his eyes. They were singularly the most beautiful and simultaneously the saddest eyes she had ever seen. For a moment she was lost in them. She could not tell if they were brown or green but his eyes were gorgeous. Under different circumstances she would have entertained the un-ladylike and perhaps improper act of just starring into them for hours.

"Why?" he said flatly as he took another step forward. Just one more and he would be about sixteen feet away, just enough distance for his skill to close and cut her down before she could flinch.

"Because," she said with all the determination she could muster. "We work for the same people."

That stunned him. *Was I here to kill her? How would she know who I work for? She must be bluffing.*

"I'm not here for you, Lady. I am here for Merrin. Where can find him?"

"I am Merrin. You're here for me." *They did not tell him who I was? Why?*

His brow creased. *She was Merrin? Why did they not tell me Merrin was a woman?*

"How do I know you're telling the truth? You could be distracting me while he gets away or the guards come to kill me."

"My guards are no match for you. Even if twenty came into this room you'd kill all of us and be gone hours 'fore the sun rose and I doubt you'd ever be injured." She spoke with confidence and fear. Yes, she was still afraid of death. Merrin swallowed again. "I can ease your doubt with a single question."

"Truly?" He was wasting time. "And what question would that be?" He took the last step he needed and tightened the grip on his swords. If he did not feel at ease after he allowed her to speak she would be dead before she fell to the floor.

She took a deep breath knowing if he did not care she would die and no one would know why she was being killed. Since they did not let him know she was a woman there must be other things he was not aware of. Regardless, she had to try. Mustering her strength she looked him dead in the eyes and spoke.

"Where can I find a good cloak?"

He stopped. That was the right question to ask. Only one way she could know that. She had to be part of the Brotherhood also. It was the first half of the secret phrase used by members to identify themselves to each other. What was happening here? He studied her for a while without moving or saying a word. The silence was thick and tense. Finally, he cocked his head to the side.

"What do you want?"

"I want you to listen to what I have to say then kill me as you came to do." She felt relief. If she got him that far then she got what she wanted. They both would.

"Fine," he said still speaking impassively. "I will listen then you must die."

"Yes," she answered. "That is all I want."

He walked slowly over to the empty chair and carefully sat down. He visibly saw some of the tension leave her body and felt the sincerity from her eyes. He did not however, lessen his awareness. If anything were to happen that he did not like she would still be the first one to breathe her last.

"Um," she asked as he sat, "may I know your name?"

He was perplexed as to why she cared.

"I am called Windwhisperer," he answered. Becoming personal with someone he was about to kill was not his way.

"Sorry, I was not asking for your professional name. I want to talk to you not your duties." Speaking to the man and not the assassin would help her.

He stared at her for a while before finally answering.

"Thelial...My name is Thelial." He thought it would not harm. No matter what happened, she was going to die anyway so it could not hurt.

"Thank you, Thelial." She managed to actually smile a sincere smile despite her apprehension.

"For what?"

"For giving me your name and for listening. I want you to know why I am being killed, Thelial. It is why they sent you. It is very important."

"It usually is important. But why do you think I am here and not someone else?"

"You are here because I learned something I was not supposed to. You are here, and not someone else, because you are probably the most reliable...Our people really want me dead."

After she finished telling him what she needed to she thanked him again for listening but he did not reply. He frowned darkly. Thelial only asked if she was ready. With tears streaming she nodded and closed her eyes. She told him that she regretted not being a better wife and mother and that she could have shown her family more devotion and outward affectionate love. She then asked him to make it quick. He did. That was the first time anyone asked to die when he came to kill them. No one had ever died with dignity like she did.

He departed like the shadow that had arrived. Still, no one else even knew he was there. Perhaps sometime in the morning someone would discover her lying peacefully in her bed still dressed for a dinner party that she would never see. From the street he looked up to her window and gritted his teeth. She was the first he killed that did not deserve to die. Merrin was not evil. She was not a bad person. She did not break the law. Merrin's crime was accidentally learning something someone else did not want her to know. They felt threatened by her and sentenced her to die for it. She died to ease someone else's fear. Now, he knew what she knew. Merrin told him what had gotten her killed. However, he was not returning to report that to his superiors. He had to go somewhere else.

Right then, he needed a certain friend. She was many leagues away and he had to hurry to get there as soon as possible, especially since he had to confirm Merrin's tale. To do that himself and to get to his friend were in nearly opposite directions. Both locations were at least four months away from Paragon City if one walked fast and hard. That would make a normal man's travel more than eight months from one point then back to the other: he did not have that much time. The agent preferred to travel by night using the cloak of darkness and shadow to make his movements all that much easier. He decided to begin right then. He would head to the southwestern mountain range in Lomar Province just to the west of Southmar Planes, verify what he needed to and then make for the tiny village in the forest.

He had not seen that secluded forest hamlet for many years. The shimmering of the trees always helped him feel better somehow, especially when it rained there because it sounded like magical chimes when the drops struck the silver in the leaves. The land there was alive and it was where he secretly went to balance himself. Too bad he was not going there for a holiday. He would need one after seeing the ruins in the mountains. At last, after frowning again, he slipped into the shadows the same way he had done over a thousand times before.

But just then, Thelial knew after that night nothing would ever be the same…

Temple of Black Ash

Three years before the present day

The murk of the shadows was as thick as the cold they embraced. There was no light in the deep of the mountain temple and they did not want there to be any. Three shapes shambled easily through the darkness, needing no light to navigate their way. They resembled skeletons, dressed in tattered rich robes and dressing and adorned with rune carved jewelry and wearing crowns of ancient designs. Pinpoints of red flame had replaced their eyes many hundred years ago and their flesh rotted unnaturally slow on their bones. When they reached one of the farthest chambers, they could see their comrade sitting in a massive ornate throne, just as she, or it, always did.

"Why have we been petitioned to convene?" One of the lumbering skeletons asked.

"She said not," the one seated in the throne offered. Its voice was clearly female but chillingly inhuman, sounding like a cold desert wind blowing over old dried bones. "Save to be adamant about the urgency."

Collectively, they felt space and time twist in the room. The fabric of reality stretched as they all casually turned at once to view the singularity. Abruptly, the fifth member of their group stepped forward.

"Ah," one spoke with a voice similar to acid eating away wood. "The Night Queen graces us with her presence." He, it, bowed with a hint of melodrama.

"Why do you insist on childishly creating new titles for me each time we meet?" the new comer asked as she stepped forward more gracefully than any of the others. "You can call me by name, Shazandra."

He did not answer but turned and shuffled away toward the throne instead.

"Come," one of the other's spoke. "Tell us what this is all about." Another he, or it, motioned for her to come toward the throne.

"Of course," she said softly, as softly as a skeletal

abomination could. "Also, as an aside, I would like to know how our plans are progressing. But first, an explanation as to why I called everyone here."

When they gathered, Shazandra wasted no time in getting to the point. In the moment before she began her explanation, she glanced at her fellow creatures and noticed how repugnant and miserable the notion of all of them was: people who willingly traded their souls for immortality to exist in a slowly decaying shell. She sighed to herself, not having the need to draw air through lungs that broke a few hundred years before.

"We have a problem," she flatly stated. "I am sorry for bringing us all together to deliver ill news but it is the truth none the less."

"What be this problem?" the one called Yathagra asked.

"Someone is on the verge of unearthing and opening the Vault."

"Rubbish," the one who first greeted her spoke, sounding impossibly more acidic. "We have concealed that place from all eyes and all knowledge. We have even taken steps to remove any and all nearby occupation. Who could possibly know of it?"

"Please, Bale, do not be insulting. What I say is not rubbish or bunkum in any regard. I know because I have seen it with my own eyes," Shazandra insisted. Every time she spoke Bale started an argument. Perhaps his deteriorated brain managed to forget that he was the reason they were all in this predicament in the first place.

"You don't have any eyes," he quipped, speaking of the empty sockets in her skull left when her eyes rotted away years ago.

"Stop wasting our time, Bale, and let her speak." The one called Azalan scolded Bale with a snake's hiss. "I traveled from another plane to get here and I cannot abide useless wrangling."

Bale shot him an enigmatic glance but said nothing further.

Seeing she had an open floor, Zandra continued.

"There is one who follows what he names a goddess in the same vicinity as the Vault, rather directly above it." She paused to look at everyone. "He spoke of this goddess knowing who I was, wanting out, wanting vengeance, the Keys and..." she hesitated. "He mentioned the *other* way of opening the Vault."

If corpses could curl a brow, they would have.

"He was also, as he believed, granted an Ozadogguah and

seemed to regard it as a pet. I know this to be true because I saw it myself and he was more than eager to have us fight." Zandra looked to the others for their reactions. Most stared at her expressionless. Except Bale, who seemed to omit replying to Zandra and looked to Bethny, the one seated on the Throne.

"What do you see?" he curtly asked.

Slowly the skeletal form looked to him with a cold dead stare. Red points of light glowing from inside empty eye sockets of their fleshless skulls made any appearance of anger, sadness, fear or frustration were impossible to discern. Bethny seemed to look at all of them at once and at each of them as individuals all at the same time. The disturbing stare continued for a bit longer than comfortable.

"I see a winged darkness," the skeleton answered. "I see her calling to anyone who would answer. I see…" her voice trailed off.

After a few moments, Bale pushed, "See what? Go on! Continue!"

"I see that Tsaogguhua has risen." She added, "The Black Serpent is freed."

"That would explain the Ozadogguah," Bale snapped. "One is never without the others." Those were the spawns of Tsaogguhua, the Ozadogguah, and were quite small in comparison. Zandra remembered it barely fit on the Hill and knew its master was over a mile long.

An unreadable silence fell upon the coven as they looked to each other and yet did not. The frigid stillness passed for a time before a cracking dry voice slithered through the air.

"Well then," Alazan announced. "It is time for another war. Man against man; a most violent conflict with no victors. Perhaps another world war? Soak the earth in blood and let the seas turn red. Blot the sun with smoke and soot while the planet burns to cinders." It stood with the discordant creaking of bones and slowly turned to leave. "I will make my final preparations for the Device while you all tend to the devastation…The end of all will be coming soon. One way or another, it is best not to defer the arrival."

"We have been behind every plague, famine, disaster and war for the past five hundred years. We almost accomplished the annihilation of both races of men and elf before," Yathagra reminded them of the obvious as he stood to depart as well. "Given the magnitude of this most recent revelation and sign, perhaps we could actually be successful. We need not fear Gajana's interference this time."

"The Dark Powers are returning," Bethny stated. "We should hasten to prepare and greet them."

As the coven went their separate ways Bethny, trapped on a throne that was not hers, watched them disappear in disturbing silence. Watch. Listen. Learn. That was all it did. It saw into Zandra's head and knew what she thought. Bethny saw everyone else's thoughts as well and could read them as easily as she could one of her numerous books in the far study. Without lifting a bony finger or turning one single page, she could read any line of text even if the volume remained closed. Bethny just never told them she could see their thoughts just as easily, as well as nearly all things past, present and future. Bethny saw what was to come in pristine detail.

I did not choose my path, this way, it thought. *But if I must follow it, then I shall damn every last one of you to it as well.*

Just outside Silverwood

Early Afternoon, the Present Day

The tall majestic trees stood proudly keeping watch over the land for more than the past four hundred years. Their substantial bark and roots were sturdy from being diligently tended to by the local Elves. The warm summer sunlight peeked through the canopy of leaves to never leave the lush foliage very shadowed. As large as the aged trunks were, the rich forest pillars were scattered and the small group could easily see quite a far distance. The reverberating sounds of active life were a peaceful reminder of the exquisite beauty of the earth away from the city.

Ruelina was remaining abjectly silent. She knew all this pristine beauty would end. She knew all the astonishing sounds and rousing smells and picturesque colors would be gone from their sight within a few miles. All of it would be replaced by a landscape of death and decay. Glorious towering trees would be grotesquely substituted by hulking masses of metal. Silverwood's trees had died away and only tarnishing silver skeletons had remained. The chirping of birds and the prancing of deer would be replaced by the cold shrills of wind whistling through metal shards and when not, would echo the despairing silence of a graveyard. Her home was becoming a necropolis. It was becoming something ghouls would gather toward anyway. Death and undeath. Why not?

She sighed dejectedly. Looking at the lazy crest of the next rise she realized they were closer than she had remembered. The deathly silence would be deafening within the hour. It had been some time since they stepped from the well-traveled main road and trekked along that path. Ruelina called it a road but neither Smythe nor Kaeleb were quite convinced that anyone could easily get a wagon down here; which was a deciding factor for what constituted a road. If not then call it a path. But okay, they will call it a road also.

After a bit farther, but long after Ruelina had noticed, Kaeleb began looking around the vast woodland a bit differently. Ruelina wanted to see which of them, if at all, would notice that everything was still green but there was no sound. It was completely silent; no animals and no insects.

Ruelina felt Kaeleb lightly tap her on the shoulder and turned to see his questioning look. Her communicative gaze answered his question without a word passing between them. She had conveyed to him that the feeling of unease would become much worse very soon.

Kaeleb slowly nodded in a gloomy understanding and cast his troubled glance down to the packed ground of the path. They both glanced to Smythe and realized their companion felt nothing yet. Kaeleb continued to look at the dry soil. This was not good, they realized.

The longer they walked the more he comprehended that the trip was not going to be pleasant. Something quite sinister was at work there. They had not gotten to Silverwood and he was already beginning to feel something was very wrong. The oblivious nature of the "investigator" beside him hid not help ease his feelings. Instead, it made them worse. Kaeleb had learned long ago that sometimes evil is not always so apparent and was usually surreptitious.

Or perhaps that was his gift. Maybe Enki had given him a capacity to discern harmful intent when he did not give it to others. At the strangest times that facility came in very good service. Problem was that Kaeleb had no control over it. He only seemed to feel what Enki chose for him to.

Ruelina kept looking more ahead than at the ground or sky as she had before. It mattered more that something would come after them from the forest and that it would be something unnatural rather than any forest animal. The only reassuring thing was that she did not smell the stench of death…yet.

Something was not right. She heard sounds of a tussle from further down the road. Quickly yet quite cautiously Ruelina moved to the right side of the road, along the line of foliage and up over the lazy rise. Kaeleb and Smythe saw her doing that and hastily followed.

"What is wrong?" Smythe asked in more confusion then earnest care.

"Someone's in trouble," she promptly answered over her shoulder and continued to the crest of the road.

When they stopped the two from the city saw nothing but a continuing empty road extending narrowly before them, curving gently to the right and vanishing in the thick underbrush.

"Who?" asked Smythe. He was beginning to wonder if this little elf was not a bit insane somehow.

"Shhh!" she spat in a whispered voice. "Keep quiet." She peered down the vacant road listening intently. It was evident that her hearing was much more acute than her human companions. It was disappointing, hearing what they could not. How could she convince them if there was really something happening? Maybe she would have to wait until the danger came and slapped them in the face.

"I see nothing," said Smythe quietly.

"That doesn't change the fact that someone else's out here with us," she retorted.

Then, she heard it again. Yes, it was a struggle. It was a muffled woman's cry of fear and pain with movement of others that were in her area. The others were heavier and thicker sounding. Men? She could not tell yet.

"A woman. She's in trouble," is all Ruelina reported then began moving along the roadside as quietly as she could.

Kaeleb followed trying to move silently however, his skills in stealth were horrible. He noticed where and how Smythe was moving. Smythe had been concealing his abilities, repositioning to the other side of the road into the underbrush where he would have an advantage from a flanking. When had Smythe learned about stealth and laying an ambush? It was not part of any investigator training that Kaeleb ever heard of. *After all this is over*, he noted to himself, *I will ask Smythe about that.*

When Ruelina stopped and crouched Kaeleb did also. He looked at the intensity Ruelina displayed as she lowered herself and silently readied her bow, a natural hunter in motion. Suddenly, she seemed more like a predator than the cute little saddened elf that was guiding them.

Ruelina's focus was on the road ahead. She knew they were close enough to Silverwood that it may be someone she knew. There were no other settlements out that far. So if it was not someone from her home then it was a trespasser causing problems. Either way, she was not about to be very forgiving. Ruelina knocked an arrow and quietly drew back her bow aiming down the road. Then, she waited.

Minutes later, the small group came into view. Kaeleb drew his sword as quietly as he could while watching the small band appear down the road.

There was a rather tall man, a human, striding ahead purposefully. He wore thick cotton shirt and pants with soft leather boots. A short sword was strapped to his side. His dark blond hair was unkempt and outlined the disgusted look on his face like a tattered hood. Then the others followed behind him. Two similarly dressed human men were dragging between them a young and very frightened elf woman.

Ruelina quickly recognized her. Clarissa! She was from Silverwood! Her and her husband owned a shop where they sold lamps, plates, eating and cooking utensils, everything the average home ever needed, they seemed to have.

"Let go!" she screamed, still struggling against her abductors. "Where are you taking me?"

The apparent leader abruptly stopped and turned on his heel. His hand quickly reached out and grasped her by the throat pushing her head back and squeezing her neck. She tried to gasp but the strong grip cut her air short and her face began to redden.

"I said shut up," the man hissed. "One more peep and I'll bleed you." He roughly tore his hand from her neck and her head slumped forward. She inhaled sharply searching for air before beginning to cough. He turned back and resumed striding up the road. Clarissa sniveled and become obviously weak as her feet dragged but her captors yanked her effortlessly up the road.

"I just want to know why, why you're doing this to me," she sobbed.

The leader spun again back to face her as he drew out his sword. Malice flashed in his eyes as he lifted the sword to bring it down on her head. She closed her eyes and turned away not wanting to watch the blade sink into her skull.

"Who are you? What's your business?"

The voice was angered, commanding and shockingly female. The men looked into the trees in all directions for speaker. The leader turned away from the woman and lowered his sword.

"Looks like we've got guests, boys!" he said.

"It's you who are guests here and you're very unwelcome," Ruelina answered. "Let'r go, now!"

The leader merely laughed, followed in his guffaw by the other two who still clutched Clarissa tightly by the arms.

"I am afraid we're not going to do that, girl," he said finally, still not knowing where she was.

"Wrong choice," Ruelina said gravely.

The leader heard the "thunk" of a bowstring. Too late to move he saw the blur of the arrow as it flew past his head. His first thought was that she had missed. But he quickly realized he was wrong as the searing pain reached his brain. The arrow ricocheted off his skull just above his left ear. Blood began to seep down his neck as his hand reached up to cover his wound. He yelled in pain and anger. Turning his rage to the closest victim, he swiftly spun and stabbed the captive woman in the stomach with his sword.

As the other two released Clarissa, Ruelina had already begun aiming another arrow at the leader. The other two began rushing toward them. Kaeleb stepped out from his hiding place with his sword drawn. As he reached the road he looked at the two as they quickly approached. Something was very wrong, Enki was telling him. They were not normal...

Thunk. Another arrow shot from Ruelina's bow. This time it passed above his left shoulder flying harmlessly into the forest. He smirked. After releasing his sword, the impaled woman slowly slumped to the ground. Turning back to the archer, he fell forward onto his hands and knees. When he looked up, his face had changed. His teeth were fangs and his skin was pulling tight against his bones as he began to change. A growl came from deep inside him, sounding less human every second.

That was really not good. Kaeleb felt something was very evil from them, unnatural. However, he seemed much better schooled and had much more fighting experience. As they clumsily lunged to attack he easily stepped to the side of the two and struck one with his long blade. Kaeleb felt the solid blow against something very hard. Armor! They were wearing armor under their cloths?

Kaeleb glanced to where he had struck to see what protection they were wearing. As they wheeled around his blood ran cold and fear welled up inside of him. Through the slash in the one's shirt he could just see flesh. They were not wearing armor. How could his sword not cut flesh? As panic began to rise within him he felt his heart pounding in his ears.

Ruelina readied another arrow and aimed as best as she could despite her welling sense of terror. Before her eyes she witnessed a man changing into a beast. His skin changed, his bones cracked, hands became claws, teeth became fangs and his arrogant laughter became a ravenous inhuman snarl. He was less human and more a dog-shaped lizard. Was that thing ever human or was that it's real form and it was just pretending to be human looking? With trembling hands, she released the arrow aimed for his chest.

His words began to come from his lips before Kaeleb ever realized he was shouting. It was happening again, as it seemed to have happened such times in his life before. It was also something which occurred, at times, without his control. Enki was with him always.

"Enki, zi dingir kia. Lu wabalu isakku mahasu ina rabishu!" Kaeleb felt the presence of Enki as energy flowed down over his body through is arm and into his sword. He felt his fear quickly melt away as the divine spirit imbued him from above. The men in front of him lunged for another attack, wielding claws and leering with fiendish eyes.

Smythe felt he must quickly to aid in their survival. With a sense of apprehension, yet feeling somewhat comforted by his hiding position, he did what he thought he would never have to do in the presence of others. He cast a spell.

When Ruelina watched her arrow strike the chest of the beast, after already being in motion to knock another arrow, she witnessed one of the most mind rendering events of her life. The arrow penetrated its chest and she watched as smoke began to pour from its wound! As she began to aim the next arrow amidst its reverberating howl of pain and anger, it started sprinting at her. Ruelina never felt such an unnatural hatred from anything, including the ghouls, as it crossed the distance with inhuman speed. In haste she released that arrow. It passed harmlessly by. Without time for thought, Ruelina dropped her bow and drew her sword fearfully readying herself in what little time she had for close combat with whatever that thing was.

As the two assailants lunged at Kaeleb, out from the corner of his eye, he saw what could be described as faint shimmers of energy moving like lightning. They struck the body of the closest beast and knocked it off balance, screaming in pain and surprise. Kaeleb, being no stranger to melee, took the opportunity and struck downward with his divinely enchanted sword. The steel cut deep into its back and it screamed again in anguish.

When the beast neared Ruelina it wasted no time to attack, swinging its claw at her head with smoke still pouring from the arrow that remained in its chest. Ruelina shouted in surprise and barely ducked as razors cut the branch above her scalp. Sounding like it came from a distance, Ruelina noticed bark from the tree passing through the air as if in slow motion. She was moving in slow motion as well. Panic gripped her and her mind struggled in desperation to process what was happening. That was the last thing she remembered.

From a distance, Kaeleb heard Ruelina scream in abject terror then recognized the sound of someone sprinting through the forest away from their position. Nothing he could do now. His strike came swiftly into the creature's skull. The steel passed easily through its bone spraying more blood onto the road. Kaeleb saw just in time that the other had already begun to lunge at him. All he could do was drop and raise his sword to offensively shield himself from the attack. In his surprise, the creature suddenly began to pass through the air slowly! Kaeleb blinked in disbelief. It was actually lunging against all natural perceptions of movement! How?

Smythe then emerged from his hiding place, sword ready and knowing that his spell to slow the creature had worked. Without a yell or any word at all, he started to sprint across the road to join Kaeleb in the fight. He had seen Ruelina flee in terror somewhere deeper into the woods. Damn her! They needed her sword!

When Kaeleb noticed he could move at his normal speed, and that it was no illusion, he took the initiative and thrust his sword deep into the beast's chest with every amount of strength he could muster. He felt the blade pass through its spine and watched it emerge from the creature's back. That was not in any altered speed of motion and the two fell to the ground with Kaeleb landing on top.

As the lead creature turned to Kaeleb and Smythe, after briefly watching Ruelina flee, it snarled in an inhuman glee realizing it now had the element of surprise…

Just outside Silverwood on the same road

Same Afternoon

The clopping sound from the leisurely pace of the horses faintly echoed throughout that beautiful forest. None of the four had ever seen such vivid colors before! Everything here was so very...alive. Sights, smells and even the feel of the air were all different here. It was a place the likes of which they had never experienced before. The vast fields and forest by Paragon were truly a sight to behold; however, that forest was something else altogether. It was, for lack of a better expression they decided, alive. It was very much alive. Not that their home was not, but this was something...different. They wanted to use the word "magical" to describe it though could not. Even the vaguest mention of anything arcane was severely frowned upon.

Paragon itself, the entire country, from its very foundation after the war, had held that all magic was a root of terrible evil and was thus banned from all practice. Any item that even thought to hold even the most minor enchantments was captured as contraband and the possessor punished. Most of the times, that penalty was capital so many were put to death after the war. Presently, it was rare such sentence was enforced as the knowledge and material to practice spellcrafts were no longer available to anyone. After being seized the items were destroyed so there was no way for anyone to follow down the old path of corruption that led to the ruination of Ilmaria. In Paragon, the Craft was dead and no one dared think of actually attempting its study. Even if they did, all the tomes containing the elementary principals were burned and the teachers put to death long ago. The world was safe from that threat now.

The gods did impart their influence, however, but that only through people and since there were no miracle workers moving mountains or turning rivers into blood, the idea of divine presence had begun to fade into the writings of fable and myth. The superstitious and those who were somewhat touched in the head would always speak and preach of the gods' presence or hearing the voices of the gods. But such people were also ignored or, if they became a danger to others in the community, put in prison. Few now actually believed that the dark powers, commonly whispered as Ancient Ones, or the divine consciousnesses in heaven, the Elder Gods, were even in existence now. Maybe they were just tales and fables from an age that had long past.

Those who did not hold to that growing belief still held that the gods would not always be noisy and could chose to remain quiet. Direct involvement was rare, if at all and since they did not wish to say the gods did not really exist out of fear of being wrong, they preached the other instead.

As the small group rode casually down the narrow road, noting its nonuse, Emerik and Tobin both heard the unmistakable sound of a woman screaming. The voice came from ahead of them somewhere farther along their path. They both looked to each other.

"Was that what I think it was?" Tobin asked, somewhere deep inside, hoping that it was sounds of a struggle. Tobin, if for nothing else, was bored and felt out of place if not engaged in some combat of one for m or another.

"Let's go see," Emerik said at once.

With a shout to spur on their mounts they galloped toward the woman, whoever it may have been. Their two squires did not hear their brief conversation but only noticed their teachers suddenly race forward. Buy natural order of their training Perry and Dyrrany were directly behind them.

When they came to the top crest of a rise in the road the four saw a struggle indeed. Two men, one obviously a priest of Enki were engaged in combat against three inhuman adversaries! Both starred in disbelief as no such creature was ever spoken of before.

"What the hell…" was the only fragment that Tobin could utter. How could this exist?

Emerik felt the presence of Enki empathically telling him the abominations must be destroyed. Wasting no more time he shouted over his shoulder, "Lance!"

Dyrrany quickly rode into action. Coming up to his right side, Dyrrany brought Emerik's lance up to him. Taking it with a firm grip Emerik readied himself in the saddle for his charge.

As Dyrrany approached Emerik, Tobin agreed with the hasty plan of action. He raised his right hand almost daring Perry not to understand that he swiftly required his lance as well. However, Perry was well trained and was already following Dyrrany's action.

When both had their lances and were ready, Emerik slapped his visor down on his helm and lowered his lance because of the short distance. Both urged their warhorses into a full gallop as quickly as they could, realizing they may not have the space to get enough speed. They hoped that the horses running down slope would make up for that.

Emerik steered his mount to the right to charge along the line of foliage. He saw one fiend slowly creeping on the priest who seemed unaware of its impending attack. Tobin, however, stayed in the middle of the road. Nothing was going to pass him uninjured.

As the leader crept up to the priest's flank, he slowed to a stop; the perfect distance to launch a perfect surprise attack. Its clawed hands fanned out, imagining the sharp points ripping through the human's armor and flesh. Lowering itself to a crouch it prepared to pounce. A panther would have been envious of its grace and power.

Kaeleb turned to his right to ready his posture for another beast's attack. He was totally oblivious that he had just given their leader his back. He was completely vulnerable. Smythe, upon seeing this, quickly sprinted forward to help Kaeleb. He knew the priest would not last much longer if he did not do something and quickly. The beast before Kaeleb quickly stepped to its left then lunged.

Just after that beast's attack, the leader lunged as well, having timed their attacks together. The priest would be torn to shreds as he screamed. Blood, the leader wanted to taste his blood. As it was fully in the air, with all nails of its claws ready to sink through the links of the priest's armor, it could just feel this human's death. The beast was close enough to see the cloth beneath the man's chain mail. Then suddenly it felt jarred and saw empty road. The beast felt as though it were floating. What was happening? Confusion gripped it as it quickly struggled to grasp what was happening. Tree after tree was racing by. It was flying sideways down the road!

"Argh!" Emerik exclaimed in frustration. It was the third time that happened! Again an opponent was stuck on the end of his lance. The point ran clean through the beast as it was in the air, piercing it just below its shoulder through its ribs and perforating the other side of its body.

The first beast stumbled as it tried to halt its attack. Did it just see something big pass by? Where was their leader? It looked to its right in time to notice the sharp point of Tobin's lance pierce its neck. As the lance penetrated deeper and widened, it felt its flesh rip and its bones snap. Blood sprayed as its neck tore on the left allowing it to slide off the lance and fall to the ground.

Smythe stopped abruptly as the unmistakable shape of a man on horse had sped by with a blur on the other side of Kaeleb. Then another passed by directly in front of him. The Investigator watched as the man on horseback rode through the spray of crimson as if he galloped through soft rain.

What was that? Kaeleb whirled around to see nothing behind him. Was that a horse? Then again at his rear the same sound and feeling. He felt the ground shake…heavy horses. War horses! Who is this? He quickly spun to look down the road and saw the backs of two mounted cavalries as they sped from their charge. One was dragging a fiend on his lance!

The paladin had to do something quickly or the weight would push his lance tip into the ground and throw him from the saddle. He steered slightly leftward and dropped his lance. Circling abruptly back the right Emerik drove his armored horse over the fiend, trampling it into the ground under the hooves of his mount.

The beast had felt the searing pain of something in its chest. It could not breathe. It could not scream. It could barely move. While in the air, it looked to its left and saw a large horse's head and just behind that a man. Man? Its lips drew back in a snarl of vile hatred. It wanted to taste this one's flesh as well. No human or elf would ever escape its fury. It would shred every last one of them if it could! Suddenly, it felt itself falling prior to its feet smacking the ground. The fiend felt off balance with a lance still piercing its body and before it could steady itself, horse's knees forcefully slammed into its chest. Its short but swift plummet to the dirt in the path was helped by falling hooves as the heavy mount trampled it into the road.

Tobin was able to slow his horse and turn for another pass. Readying his lance again he began to spur his mount onward but then stopped. He starred transfixed at the beast in the road that he had just run through with his lance and watched as thick wisps of smoke rose from its wound. Smoke? What strange feats were afoot here?

Kaeleb also looked and saw smoke rise from the fiend's gaping tear in its neck and shoulder. Its head barely attached at the spine and blood poured onto the dirt, all the while it writhed slower and slower. Smythe took the last few steps to reach Kaeleb and glanced at what the priest was looking at. Smoke? What the hells?

Emerik wheeled his horse around again and began another charge. The beast was prone yet trying to move with his lance still protruding from either side of its chest. At least two feet of lance point was jutting from its side while the rest with the handle was out its other flank. Being without his lance Emerik drew his sword. As he swiftly approached he saw smoke emitting from its wounds where the lance was penetrating as well from the arrows that still protruded from its chest. That was of no consequence to him at the moment since an unnatural beast was still animate and that abomination still required a sentence of death for its very existence. With a sure hand he raised his sword and leaned in his saddle to strike downward at the still prone fiend. With a blinding slash Emerik hit the beast solidly in its head and continued to ride onward. Glancing back, he noticed something that disturbed him. His sword did nothing! The fiend had no wound! How could his sword have no effect? Abruptly he pulled the reigns of his mount. His horse whinnied at its head being jerked backward and its front hooves came off the ground.

"Dyrrany!" Emerik spat. Without waiting for his squire to arrive he dismounted and readied his shield while advancing to the prone fiend. It still struggled, although more slowly and still fought for its breath which would not come with a lance through its chest.

When Tobin noticed his friend closing distance on the prone beast he quickly spurred his horse to the other with the gaping hole in its neck. When he reached it, without halting his mount, he drove his lance through the beast's chest and into the ground. He could hear from behind him the fiend's gurgled cry then silence. Glancing back, he saw his lance sticking up from the ground with that…thing impaled by it. It was no longer moving.

"Perry!" Tobin called out. "My horse!" With that, he dismounted to join his friend. If Emerik was to get into a struggle he was not about to sit in his saddle and watch. Perry quickly rode up and took charge of the reigns, leaning Tobin's horse away from any possible ground fight.

Both Kaeleb and Smythe moved over to the last remaining fiend; the same one Emerik was heading to. Without looking at one another both Smythe and Kaeleb thought the same things…or they guessed. What is happening here? What are these things that pretend to be men?

Tobin ran to Emerik's side but standing more at the creature's head. He was ready to strike at the thing but was uncertain how effective he would be after seeing Emerik's blade had done nothing. Smoke still poured from the holes the lance had made. It was till alive! The fiend tried to stand, hatred burned in its eyes as it leered with contempt at Emerik. If only it could reach him. It began to paw at the lance sticking through its body as it prevented the creature from standing upright.

Emerik, as if losing any patience he had, stepped forward and stomped on the lance forcing the fiend back to the ground. He pointed his sword the beast's neck as it writhed in obvious excruciating pain. As it twisted on the road the free end of the lance with the handle danced and struck the packed soil. Fearing it would come free from under Emerik's boot; Tobin swiftly moved to its other side and also stood on the lance. It was now pinned to the ground and unable to squirm free.

"Someone, tell me what Hell this thing came from," demanded Emerik but no one immediately answered. Kaeleb, now close behind him, was the first to speak despite everyone's loss for words at that unsettling event.

"We do not know, Lord Montigan." Kaeleb may have not known his given name but the standard he wore made Emerik's family easy to recognize. Everyone in Paragon knew the Montigan and Drathmoore crests and acknowledged their royal positions. Of course, everyone had to, to not do so was harshly punishable. But just then Kaeleb felt Enki remind him of someone in need. Ah, the elven woman! The priest quickly ran over to the fallen young woman who still lay motionless in the dirt of the road.

"Where are you going?" Emerik spat, his eyes never leaving the creature that was pinned helpless at his feet. While still moving toward the woman Kaeleb turned and answered.

"There's someone who needs aid, milord." He turned back to tend to the fallen woman. Upon reaching her he saw her face was in the dirt. Slowly and gently Kaeleb rolled her over to face him and further positioned her on her back. She coughed. He was happy to see that. She was still alive. Badly hurt and bleeding profusely, but alive. The sword had come out of her belly when she fell, opening the wound that much further. She had been bleeding all that time without aid. Everything was crimson and cold as the blood had begun to dry. Suddenly and image of his childhood friend flashed in his mind. Byron. They were just kids then. Byron was injured. This was another message from Enki and Kaeleb knew what his god intended so he began to pray, "Zi dingir kia kanpa. Lu annu utebbibassu resussun nisme tiit. Elu sinnis wardatu ma naparsudu mudu."

Again she coughed. But this time her hand came to her face and her eyes slowly opened, squinting from the sunlight above. She slowly drew in a deep breath and blinked against the tears forming in her eyes. She could not see. She remembered feeling a great pain in her stomach...the sword! Her hands quickly moved to grasp the blade in her gut. But it was not there! She looked down at her stomach and saw she was covered in blood but saw no sword. In fear she grasped at her shirt and pulled it up, terrified to see the gaping hole she had lost all that blood through. But there was no hole! How? What? She looked up at the man who was speaking to her.

"Good," Kaeleb spoke softly. "You're going to be well. Relax. Lie back." He knew she may not hear him through her panic but he was patient and she would hear him soon. "You are well. Relax."

She lay her head back down on the hard packed dirt of the road. What was the last thing in her memory? Pain? Fear? She struggled to remember but could not recall her last thought. She remembered being the forest, or what was left of it, scavenging for food. Her village was getting hungry, along with her, and would begin to starve soon. Then everything became difficult to discern. *Was I grabbed? Hit? I do not remember.* Suddenly, her wits came to her with a much focused look.

"Who are you?" she pointedly asked the human at her side.

"Kaeleb," he spoke with a smile. "My name's Kaeleb and I am a priest. You were being taken by some...men and we came to your aid." He had hoped that his pause had not alarmed her nor raised her curiosity. There was no way to explain the existence of the things they fought. Besides, traumatizing her again by informing her that something quite inhuman had dealt her a fatal blow and by all accounts she should be dead now did not seem the least bit appropriate to the compassionate priest. He was quite happy she was still alive and that, by the grace of Enki, she would be all right.

Just outside Silverwood on the same road

Same Afternoon, a short while later

At last she came to her senses. Exactly how long she had been running she did not know. The sounds of her panting for breath began to subside. Ruelina checked herself to see if she had been wounded but, surprisingly, she found herself quite unscathed and kneeling in the soft dirt. Where am I? Looking around she could not tell at first but then her surroundings became familiar. The kind of lush green hues of the trees and the types of scattered underbrush let her know that she has fled south of where she was on the road. If she had continued for a few more miles she would have arrived at the road leading to Boregar.

Looking around to see if she was, in fact, alone she stood and brushed herself off. This time the idea of its futility did not enter her mind as she walked back to the north, continuing to brush the dirt off her skin and cloths. Nearly satisfied with the amount of cleanliness she could reach while still out in the forest, she began to remember the horrific fiends she encountered. Men that changed before her eyes! Those eyes held so much hatred and lust for blood that they still shook her spirit and gave her chills. Ah! She had run away!

Ruelina quickly read the trees and decided upon a clear path which she hastily began running along. She must get back to Clarissa! Ruelina did not care much for the other two. If they were there to help, then they could prove their worth for a change. She had to prove to everyone over and over she was not crazy even after walking for three months to get from there to Paragon City. Before that, she had been tested against ghouls and had fought for the survival of her home. So, she felt, let them suffer a bit. She did not care.

Clarissa. She could not let Clarissa down. They had known each other for many years and were friends. She even attended Clarissa's wedding! There was no way Ruelina could not find a way to help her. Not another person from Silverwood. Already, she felt she had failed her home by not bringing back adequate aid. She would not fail her people again. Thoughts of her own shame raced through her mind. Images of Clarissa lying in the road, dead and worse, began to haunt her. So she ran faster, sprinting as if some specter were lashing at her and daring her to fail again with a mocking cackle.

She soon emerged on the road, catching herself as if in surprise. Looking around she was indeed stunned that she had ran that far that fast. Where was Clarissa? She hastily searched and finally saw her lying in the road…lying in blood.

"Clarissa?" she called out as she ran toward her fallen friend. "Clarissa?" she called again when she heard no reply and saw no movement. Ruelina ran as fast as she could. She sprinted past the prince and knight without as much as a glance. She cared about Clarissa and if the elf were even alive. Everything and everyone else would have to wait.

Kaeleb heard Ruelina calling out and quickly running in his direction. Clarissa, so that is her name. Good, he thought, a friend beside her will help. She would feel better with someone close to her giving her emotional support. That is the way of healing, he understood.

When Ruelina arrived she saw that Clarissa's eyes were opened. She was alive! She quickly knelt down in the dirt and embraced Clarissa, happy that he she was okay. Or was she okay? There was too much blood for her to be alright. Kaeleb shifted backward slightly to give the two more room. Using the available space, Ruelina began checking Clarissa to see her wounds. Moving Clarissa's clothing around, she found none. Looking at her in utter bewilderment, Ruelina was unable to speak a word.

"She's fine," Kaeleb spoke softly behind her. "She is quite unscathed," he spoke with a slight smile. Kaeleb was happy to be such a useful instrument of Enki. Especially since the god of thunder and war did not always require killing or bloodshed. Ruelina turned to him, remembering how she herself saw Clarissa pierced in the stomach by the blade.

"How's this possible?" There was a distinct measure of suspicion in her voice.

"By the glorious power of Enki." Kaeleb still spoke softly yet directly, all while keeping his friendly smile.

Smythe carefully approached the prince. Carefully, because he did not know if in the passion of fighting the prince would swing on him and cut him down in the road as well as to purchase himself time to generate an acceptable explanation for what he just saw. The prince and his company would not be very receptive or lenient to any explanation that involved the concept of magic let alone the very use of the word.

"My Lord Montigan," Smythe began, beginning where Kaeleb left off. "We are not certain what these are ourselves." He listened to himself and cringed. *That was the best I could say? Truth may be best, but it might also get everyone here killed. How could I sound so stupid?* "We came upon this woman being abducted and came to her aid. When we first saw…them…they were men."

Emerik, keeping his foot firmly pressing on his side of the lance that pinned the fiend to the road, turned to the voice and spoke abruptly.

"Who are you that dare address me by name and what is this thing?" Fire shot from his eyes. The speaker had better not be attempting to play him for a fool. Emerik would sooner cut him where he stood than risk being deceived, especially with something horribly unnatural under his foot.

"Forgive me, my Lord," Smythe asked while bowing. "I am Smythe Gibvoy, an investigator from Paragon City, sent here officially to determine the facts concerning the events here in Silverwood and report my findings to my superiors." Motioning over to the priest he said, "That is Brother Kaeleb, priest of Enki and also from Paragon City. Like me, he is here for the same reason and under official order. He was sent by the church."

"What official orders?" Emerik demanded. "Are you here for this?" His eyes returned to the inhuman shape trapped at his feet. Still, he struggled to accept the very existence of such a thing, whatever it was. How is it he found himself with the same internal struggle again? This time, he sought to come here. He invited this. But this was different than before. How would he solve this?

Smythe took a brief moment to choose his words carefully before offering his explanation.

"We were sent to Silverwood to investigate the nature of the troubles there. Since we have just arrived we have no time to deduce if these things are, in fact, part of those troubles. The elf-woman Ruelina is a native of these woods and is our guide."

"Not part of the troubles?" Emerik bellowed, having seemingly skipped over all the information past that point. Suddenly he felt he was speaking to an idiot. Being too rattled from fighting something inhuman and again struggling to accept the existence of something that could not exist, Emerik could not think into what he was being told. "Have you really looked at this thing, man?" *Are you mad?*

Not good, Smythe thought to himself. If he was not delicate he would lose control of the conversation and that could cost him his assignment or even his life.

"Sire," Smythe spoke evenly as to not give the impression he was soothing the soldier prince. "I have no evidence yet but I feel that this is not the only issue here. That thing may be part of another and unrelated problem but I cannot tell without further investigation."

"Then get to it!" Tobin interjected. "Do not just stand there!" Although he was a strong man, an excellent battle commander and a member of the other ruling family of Paragon, he was quite ill-equipped for seeing the fiend at his feet. *These things should not be! What is it? Am I really seeing what I am looking at? I am losing my mind.*

"I need to study it," Smythe spoke cautiously as he

approached. "I need to see what it is."

"Study it?" Emerik asked with a taint of sarcasm. He knew what he wanted to do and would carry it out immediately. Looking to his friend he spoke while nodding to the thing's head. "Tobin?"

He wasted no time. Tobin's metal plated boot came down hard on the creature's head. He wanted to steady it so it would not move. Satisfied with the warped fiend's immobility, Emerik twisted and then began to wrench his lance from its rib cage. The crack of bone and the wet sloshing sound of its blood could be heard by all. With a shout that only a warrior could produce, the paladin ripped the remaining length of his lance from its dying body. It still tried to breathe but could not. It wanted to scream a blood curdling shriek to maybe relieve its anguish but it could not. It wanted to writhe and escape the pain but it could not. It looked toward Tobin instead.

The fiend's abyssal eyes bore into Tobin with hatred and vile contempt. If loathing had heat Tobin would be put to cinders in short order. Their eyes locked. Tobin's hair on his arms began to stand as a dark chill crept into his veins. He began to see the depths of hell in its gaze as it stared at him. His own eyes began to widen as his pupils closed. Blood emptied from his face as he turned ashen grey.

The creature was not about to depart this plane alone. It intended to take Tobin with it. Slowly its clawed hand rose as it bent its arm at the elbow. The razors were poising to strike him between the gaps in his armor on the inside of his leg. The fiend almost smiled as it could imagine feeling Tobin's flesh rip and hearing the howl of suffering. Stupid man.

"Tobin!" Emerik's shout shook him from his transfixed state. He stepped back as the lance pierced the creature again.

"Wha…" was all Tobin could utter.

Emerik had been calling to his friend as he watched the fiend prepare to strike. Not allowing that to happen, Emerik raised the lance and dropped it into its breast will all his weight. He impaled it into the road and the last of its blood thickly spurted out from the other gaping holes in its body. It gave no sigh or growl as its now lifeless corpse lay in the road. Its eyes glazed over as any remaining signs of life left its broken body.

Emerik quickly stood and looked at the thing with his lance jutting from its chest for the second time. He eyed it, noting its probable death, as he walked to his friend.

"Tobin!" he shouted again. He grabbed hold of him by his lax shoulders and shook. "What is wrong with you, man?"

He finally snapped out of his daze. Quickly casting a single glance around he ascertained what had been happening while he was incoherent. He saw that Emerik was in front of him, Kaeleb was closing his distance on the fiend looking like he was about to strike it, Smythe was standing off eyeing the fiend and the elf woman had her bow pointed at the creature. He looked to Emerik with his eyes blinking. Had he gone completely stupid?

"I'm fine," announced Tobin, not wishing to be thought of as a mad fool or some amateur that froze in the face of fear. But was it fear? What was that? What just happened? All Tobin knew is that it was something he could not explain right now. Today, for the first time, he looked into a creature's eyes and saw what he would only describe as the black of hell itself.

Seeing his companion still shaken Emerik continued to look at him, not being dismissed so easily, especially when it came to his childhood friend. He had an idea of what Tobin was going through at that moment having been through that himself. He wanted to make certain Tobin was well. It suddenly dawned on him exactly how precarious this little quest could be. Should anything ill befall him, Emerik would hold himself accountable for all of his own days. Tobin finally saw that everyone was either staring at him or the corpse of the fiend, then eventually him. So he straightened himself up and placed the most determined look into his eyes and spoke.

"Yes, I'm alright," saying that more for everyone else than Emerik. It did not go unnoticed and Emerik nodded to him and gave Tobin what Tobin needed, a sound yet reassuring slap on the shoulder. He held his gauntlet against Tobin's pauldron to convey his message. Tobin understood. Knowing someone over twenty years can afford the ability to speak without words. Since Tobin needed to save face and not be embarrassed at the moment the two did just that. Tobin knew they would talk later and also had the impression that Emerik may know more than he has spoken of up to then.

Emerik nodded to him and turned to the fiend and Smythe who was just standing there staring at it. The investigator had wanted to study it further, mainly to see it breathe and move. He wanted to understand this new enemy that chilled his soul. But now that was not possible. The brash Emerik had killed it, ruining that plan right in front of him and there was nothing he could do about it. Smythe was much more shocked than frustrated. He looked to Emerik who stared back at him like a giant bear would eye a coyote around its territory, daring it to do something wrong to justify pouncing on it. Now what was he going to do? Emerik inadvertently proposed a solution for him.

With a strong stare the prince commanded, "Bring this to Silverwood and figure out what it is." Emerik then turned and strode to Kaeleb and Clarissa. His glance to Kaeleb told the priest they would talk later but would get to that at the right time. Right then, Emerik was still trying to get an idea of what he just rode into and the situation he suddenly found himself in. "Who is she?" Emerik pointedly asked about Clarissa.

"Oh," Kaeleb answered in surprise, not thinking Prince Emerik would ask about and elven country girl he did not know. "I had heard her name is Clarissa, I believe."

"From who?"

"From Ruelina, our guide," he motioned over to the rather strong and rough looking elf woman who potentially had no sense of humor she was aware of.

"Ruelina," Emerik repeated. "Is that so?" He walked slowly up to her giving himself time to estimate who he was about to speak with. She looked hard, rough, strong, defiant and somehow…fragile. Ruelina could take on the world, or at least try with little reservation, however a small wound in the right place would do more damage to her than any battle-axe could do landing directly into her skull. Emerik quickly guessed that sensitive area was her home or the forest. But he knew that before this day. He himself had listened to her speak and it was her passion that moved him to go there in the first place. It was also not the first time he had heard a sincere plea of desperation mixed with unnatural fear.

Ruelina watched the heavily armored man approach. Already she was guessing how to fight him if needed. Trying to notice weak places in his protective metal plates she was also confused by how someone would consider draping themselves in so much metal. Could that ever possibly be a favorable thing? To her it was a sadly obscene amount of misused metal. She then wondered what the man was really trying to cover. The ranger did not take a single step backward as he neared. Metal or not, prince or not, fancy and expensive equipment or not, she simply wanted her home saved and this human still had yet to prove he was worth his weight in sunflower seeds let alone be the shining savior of Silverwood.

He stopped in front of her but remained out of striking range. His metal gauntlet squeaked as he tightened his grip on his sword. For a moment he did not speak and nor did she; the two stared at each other. They saw something in each other at that time. Both saw the strength of unwavering determination and neither cared if they ever opposed each other or not. Emerik was dedicated to his god by way of the sword and she was dedicated to her home of Silverwood by way of nature. Neither was going to be swayed.

Finally, he spoke, "I am Prince Emerik Montigan, son of Duke Drakken Montigan from Paragon City. This is Sir Tobin Drathmoore, son of Duke Kyle Drathmoore from Lomar." His eye never left her while he spoke, not even to blink during his introduction of Tobin behind him. "You are Ruelina of Silverwood…and we need to talk." His eyes probed hers and saw her defiance was part of her nature. No matter, she was a peasant in his country and she would do what she was told. "Right now," he added. It was not a subject for debate.

"Fine," she snapped. "As long as it helps my village." Her posture did not change in the least. Someone was going to help and it might as well be the fancy looking demanding prince.

"I need to know what is happening here. Who…or what are these things?"

"I do not know." She feared the conversation would go nowhere and that she would have to walk him through it by hand like a child. "I just came back so I don't know what's happened or what's been happening since I've been away." She saw in his eyes that Emerik did not believe what she had to say. Ruelina felt she now had to force him into doing something other than stand here talking. Stupid Humans. "All I care about is helping my village so…can we go there or not?" She was pushing the boundary of disrespect with Emerik and he began to grow impatient.

"Are these what you were talking about back in Paragon? Are these ghouls?"

"No, these aren't ghouls. I don't know what these are." Yes, she thought, he's stupid and I'm not standing here all day entertaining him.

"So, you never saw these before?"

"No, I never saw these things before." She was really beginning to lose her patience now. This prince seemed to be getting more idiotic by the minute. How was that possible? Was he always this daft? "Now can we go?" She was counting. One more stupid question and she would leave him to play with these things while she took Clarissa back home. If he wanted to frolic in the forest making himself feel important then he could do it without her.

Emerik looked around. He was searching for a decent place to examine these fiends. Finding none he approached Tobin who was in obvious restraint from hacking at Ruelina for her disrespect towards Emerik. Loutish backward peasant.

"We need to examine these things and here is no place to do it." Emerik made no attempt to lower his voice.

"Examine them for what?" Tobin asked with marked confusion. "They are dead, whatever they are- were." The plan was obvious to him: if they were to encounter more...kill those as well. What was the fuss about?

"There are at least two problems at work here," Emerik observed. "First, these are not ghouls and we came here to solve a ghoul problem. That means these are a second problem. We need to find out more about our new enemy and see what is happening in Silverwood."

"That's better!" Ruelina added. Finally, some decision making from the grand leader, even though that was a suggestion Smythe already made.

"What is your problem, peasant?" Emerik turned sharply and began to walk back toward Ruelina. No commoner was going to address him like that.

"Look, I know you're a prince and everything but you have not really done anything to help." Damn this was a waste of time!

"Done nothing?" Emerik was shocked and angered. "Saving your life was doing nothing? Should we have watched safely from our horses while you were slain?" He wanted to smack some sense into her. Was she always that stupid and selven?

"Oh...yeah." Ruelina had not thought of that. He did do that. Now she felt rather sheepish. "You are right-"

"I know," Emerik interrupted. "Now, is there a place to examine these things in Silverwood?" She had better offer some assistance and do something other than complain. He did not come all that way to be bantered by her.

"Yes," Ruelina answered as she thought. "There are people in Silverwood who could help."

"Fine," he said sharply. "Get these...things and we are off to Silverwood." His command was to everyone and not just to Ruelina. "How far away are we?"

"Almost an hour's walk, not far at all," she replied.

"Good," Emerik spoke sternly. "Then we are off."

Kaeleb had been listening to the conversation in silence and noted that Ruelina cared for her village and fellow townsmen. He knew that Clarissa needed help to make the walk to Silverwood because she needed rest and could not do it on her own. Carefully, he approached Ruelina while holding Clarissa at his side.

"Ruelina," said Kaeleb softly. "She cannot walk on her own. Could you help me with her?"

She was lost in her thinking for a moment. Ruelina felt something was not right with those things, those fiends. Certainly, they were unnatural but there was something else at work there; something that she felt in her gut but could not discern. Kaeleb's words help snap her mind back into focus.

"Yeah, I will." That was all she could manage to say. That nagging feeling still pulled at her. What was it?

"Sire," Smythe addressed. "How do we get these corpses to Silverwood?" They were at least man-sized and he really did not wish to be burdened by carrying one of those things for an hour. If there was more trouble, Smythe wanted to be free to move.

"Drag them," answered Tobin. "I do not care." He did not care because he was not going to do that. Carry a bloodied corpse of some unearthly devil through the back woods? To hell with that notion! Someone else could do that drudgery.

"Well, my lord," Smythe spoke carefully. "We could take them by horse." He noticed that there were four very fine horses right here with them. Besides, if they took his suggestion then he would not have to carry one.

"Huh," Emerik snorted looking to Smythe. He was surrounded by impertinent fools, all but Tobin, anyway. "Not on my horse."

"Do not even think to look at mine, either," Tobin said. If Emerik was not going to allow that then he was not either. Soil his finely groomed horse with blood from the trash he just killed? Never.

"Then…" Smythe's voice trailed off.

"Drag them by the squires' horses. They have rope as well. Or you may drag them there yourself. I really do not care. But those… things are not going on my horse," Emerik decided.

"Nor mine," Tobin added.

Smythe and Emerik looked at each other for a short time while Smythe expected Emerik to change his mind and Emerik expected this commoner to do something other than stand there wasting time. The prince counted to seven in his head.

"Dyrrany!" Emerik did not have to speak twice. Dyrrany knew what needed to be done. Both he and Perry began to retrieve their rope from their horses. Drag those to Silverwood? No problem. They would drag them back to Paragon if they were commanded to do so.

While everyone else seemed to be doing something, Ruelina lapsed back into her own thoughts as she helped Kaeleb slowly walk with Clarissa. What else was so wrong? She tried to push it from her mind and think of something else but it did not work, the feeling was too intense. Those things were dead, correct? They no longer posed any threat but she could not help being concerned with them. Frustrated, she attempted another tactic to push it from her mind and that was to talk about something else.

"Clarissa, are you well? How are you feeling?" Ruelina's concern for her was genuine. She would have asked earlier but the thoughts of the fiends were too distracting. She hoped that Clarissa did not think of her as uncaring.

"I am good," she managed. "I am just very tired." She wanted to get home. Rannon, her husband, did not know what had happened and he was the only person she wanted to be with at that moment. If he knew she had been taken then he would be all that more worried and would have come looking for her. Clarissa did not want the same, or worse, for him so she was grateful Rannon did not know anything yet. At least Ruelina was back from Paragon and she brought help. But was there supposed to be more? Only six men?

She could not focus enough to count yet. Maybe there were more on the way, she guessed but hoped for an army.

"Good." That helped Ruelina feel a bit better. But she could not help from asking the obvious question. "What were you doing out here this far?"

"Oh…" She realized Ruelina actually had been away for a long time and did not know how bad things had become. "I was looking to gather food."

"Food?" Ruelina asked with great concern. There was plenty of food when she departed. There was farm land and animals to hunt for in the north and south.

"Yes," Clarissa began to explain. "The blight from the east has grown steadily worse. It is horrible. There are no animals to be found for hours around here. It gets worse," she added, sensing Ruelina's astonishment. She really had been away for some time and did not realize what had happened. "We are running out of water as well. Many of us began to get ill from using the water from the well in the village. So now we must bring water by wagon and barrel from the stream that is even farther away. That means that we have little water for our crops. Those are dying out also." She lapsed into silence. That was enough for Ruelina at the moment. Clarissa could not bring herself to tell her of the others that have vanished or died since she left. For Clarissa, her grief and fear was far too close. But now she was gaining hope because Ruelina was back and she brought help.

"Does anyone know what is happening?" Ruelina asked. The conversation, however disconcerting, was failing to keep her mind off of the fiends. Walking past one, she looked down, seeing its black lifeless eyes glaring up at the sky. The fiend's shady scaled face was contorted in agony and loathing. Dark blood had stopped oozing from the gaping slash in its torso and she could dimly see inside its body into its chest. The thing was disgusting. Nothing like it should ever exit in the entire cosmos. But, there it was, lying dead in the road not but an hour from her home. She glimpsed its heart and lung within, still wet and still looking fresh. Unknowingly, her head cocked to one side as she still stared at it. Kaeleb felt her pace become slower than the already sluggish progress they were making and turned his head to see what she was doing.

"Is something wrong?" asked Kaeleb.

"Hold her," Ruelina replied without taking her gaze away from inside the fiend.

Kaeleb steadied himself to support Clarissa's weight as Ruelina released her hold to kneel down and peer closer. He was more than a bit confused by her actions but thought it best to watch rather than to interrupt by questioning her. After all, she did not have to answer to him.

She took her dagger from its sheath and slowly, carefully placed the blade between its ribs. Prying the bones apart a bit more she was more able to see inside. There was definitely something very wrong. The more she probed the more intense the ill feeling became. Her mind struggled to grasp something that she was seeking but could not identify. She cursed herself for not being clever enough to answer her own nagging issue. What is so wrong?

Meanwhile, the squires were tying nooses into their ropes for dragging the corpses to town. They thought the best way to drag them would be to loop their legs at one end and tie the other to the horn of their saddles. Merely grasping the rope from horseback would not suffice with their individual strengths. Smythe helped with knots that would be attached to their saddles. He was content with rope tying over and above not having to carry a carcass. As he tended to that menial task he pondered the implications of the tensions between Ruelina and the prince. He needed to gather as much information and support from both as he could however, showing that he may favor one over the other could cause unneeded animosity. His mission would then be even harder to accomplish. How could he make the situation work to his advantage? Smythe continued to ponder carefully yet quickly since he did not have much time.

Emerik and Tobin talked about the concerns of gathering needed information about the enemy and what could possibly be done to defeat them. They both agreed that neither had enough understanding for making any sort of sensible plan. Too many questions were still left to be answered and both were boggled by some of the events during the melee. The seemingly most pertinent question, aside from "what were these things?", was the matter of the ineffectiveness of their swords while their lances did abnormally painful damage and produce smoke as if the fiends had been stuck with acid? Magic. No wonder it had been banned so many hundreds of years ago.

Ruelina leaned in and dropped her head in order to get a better look at the organs inside the fiend. From what she knew of man and animals, these seemed to be normal heart and lungs…or were they? The lungs were not quite shaped right. Wet. Its insides were still wet and not drying. It was dead; this thing should be drying in the mid-afternoon. Her body jolted in surprise. She blinked. Did she just see movement?

Its heart beat again! Ruelina yelled in shock and fell back, scrambling rearward on her hands and feet away from it. Everyone heard her scream and instantly stopped whatever they were doing to look. Instinctually, Emerik's hand grasped the hilt of his sword.

"It's alive!" Ruelina shouted while trying to compose herself. "It is not dead!"

Impossible!

"How can this be?" Emerik hastily approached the fiend Ruelina had just recoiled from while drawing his sword. Behind him, Tobin also drew out his blade and make quick stride to join Emerik. These could not be alive. Ridiculous!

Smythe swiftly made his way to the other carcass. The gaping holes in either side of its chest still lay open and it seemed to still be lifeless. He briefly glanced over to the other fiend and, seeing that it was not moving, decided to kneel down aside it. Placing a hand near its head for balance he leaned forward to get a much closer look.

"It is not dead!" Ruelina repeated to Emerik. Standing and readying her sword she continued. "It's healing itself. Its heart's beating again."

"This is not possible…" Emerik walked to the same side of the thing that Ruelina was on to see what she was ranting about. Ignorant peasants had a way of not understanding many things and this could be another one of those instances. He knelt down to see for himself.

Smythe peered into its black and lifeless eyes. It was not moving. Could it be an overreaction from an uneducated backwoods dim-wit? Ruelina never gave him the impression that she was mentally slow, but then, they did not encounter shape shifting fiends before now, either. Perhaps she had her wits scarred out of her during the fight? He felt disturbed as he gazed into the dark orbs, feeling the unearthly characteristic emitted from the demonic fiend. Looking ever closer into its eyes, Smythe could almost see his own reflection. Then he noticed it, the subtle yet indisputable motion of its eye refocusing…on him.

Smythe's head quickly jerked back away as he sat bolt upright with a gasp. Using the air he now had filled his lungs with he loudly made the announcement.

"Ah…she's correct." He composed himself enough to speak coherently. "This one is alive!" Now what? These terrors were supposed to be very dead!

Emerik and Tobin look to one another as if seeking unspoken advice. The decision that must be made is clear. Surprisingly, both speak the same words at the same time.

"Kill them!"

Emerik and Tobin raised their swords at the same time. Emerik paused to stare at the apparently lifeless fiend. For a moment his heart beat in fear. He was concerned, deep down, that he may not be…enough. Perhaps, when a crucial time came, he would discover that he was not as strong or as well trained or as equipped as the believed himself to be and that those who depended on him would be severely let down by that failure- his failure, the failure of just not being enough. His grip on his sword weakened. Was he enough? Was he really doing what was right coming here?

Tightening his grip, Tobin also began to feel fear. Unknown to Emerik, Tobin eyes had widened in obvious fright. He hated himself for it. A warrior should not feel this kind of fear, he thought to himself. What do I do? This was not the same reaction he had back outside of Southmar. This was different. He suddenly felt cold as he began to sweat and his heart pounded in his ears. Realizing from the skirmish with these unearthly monsters just a few minutes ago that their swords were of no use…what was he to do? A few measly peasants to fight that were masquerading as ghouls? Bollix! He was not ready for this! But he should be ready for this; he was a Drathmoore, by Heaven! No one ever saw a Drathmoore shake from fear or wet themselves! He was definitely not going to be the first in recorded history to do so, either. His chest tightened as the self-loathing fought for dominance over his welling sense of fright.

Suddenly, from between the two of them, a single yet swift sword stroke fell into the creature's head. From closely behind the two, Ruelina shouted in as much anger as unsettled shame. She fled in terror from these things and it almost cost the lives of people who needed her to be strong. As a hiss of smoke began to rise from the open cleave in its skull, her sense of humiliation went with it. Never again would she bolt in fear from an enemy such as these. Her village needed her, her friends needed her and these stupid humans, like it or not, also needed her.

Smythe, however, had quite a different perspective than the others. While all eyes were on the prince and screaming elf woman, he decided to do the illegal act of using magic- right in front of a prince of Paragon. With a short gesture and quick chanted words he drew power from the air itself. All that only took but a brief moment but time seemed to slow a bit as Smythe felt the energy rush up his spine then down his arm. He touched the creature and it convulsed, only for the briefest second, then it was done. If anyone else were to be standing close by they would have heard a confusing crackle of energy. But Smythe had his answer and was pleased with it. These monsters were not resistant to magic and spells that evoke or invoke power would do quite well if they were to encounter those again. He watched it for a time before he was assured that he killed it, then stood and brushed himself off. When he looked up toward everyone else, he was face to face with a most unhappy looking Tobin.

"What were you doing?" he asked through gritted teeth.

"Wha...I was...umm...I..." Smythe managed to utter little since his heart now leapt into his throat and threatened to choke the life from him.

"Prince Emerik and I ordered these things be killed." Tobin was not amused at the notion he had a traitor in his midst. This sweet tongued boot licker better have a satisfactory explanation for not trying his hardest to beat that thing to death and he had better be acceptable or Smythe would look far worse than these things.

"Yes...ah, yes you did!" He thought quickly.

"So, why were you not killing it?" Tobin's grip tightened on his sword. Maybe his bade was unqualified to hurt these things but he was quite certain it would do very well against Smythe.

"I...I was wrong...my lord."

"Wrong?" Tobin's forehead wrinkled as his eyebrows narrowed. "Wrong about what?"

"I..." Smythe looked away and pointed to the thing. He was still trying to think of something to say that was not damning to himself.

"SPEAK!"

Smythe's body jolted and head jerked back toward Tobin with eyes widened.

"It was dead."

Tobin starred at him with disbelief while Smythe continued quickly, almost in a pleading voice, in an attempt to spare his own life. "I was wrong, it was dead. It was not alive."

"You said it still lived," Tobin recounted.

"I was wrong," Smythe lied. "I was just finished checking it as was coming to tell you." Please, he thought, believe that rubbish and let's be on to Silverwood.

"You were wrong," Tobin repeated coldly.

"Yes," Smythe said with an almost apologetic voice. He even managed to lower his gaze to the ground at just the right time.

Tobin leaned in and whispered through tightly drawn lips, "Don't ever be wrong like that again."

Smythe looked up and their eyes locked. He saw that Tobin was quite serious and do him great harm if he thought it necessary.

"I will not, my lord." He knew at that moment Tobin was not going to kill him and he felt pleased with his skills.

"See to it," he said definitively before turning to walk back to Emerik.

Good, Smythe said to himself, the two of you are more pliable than I first guessed. This may be easier than I thought.

As Tobin walked to Emerik he saw it would be a short stroll because Emerik was already coming to him. With an unhappy look and an impatient stride, Emerik furtively glanced at everyone as he passed them. Suddenly he felt that Tobin, his best friend, was his only friend and the only one he could really trust all the way out here. Out here. Here, was so far from Paragon. But, yet again, he found himself in a remote location, with little to no resources to draw on, battling something unnatural and having only one person he felt was trustable. How did he get into this mire twice in his life? The questioning thought was fleeting. Emerik pushed it from his head and focused on the tasks and matters at hand. From experience, the battle veteran knew he would have plenty of time for reflection later. Sensing Emerik's need for some measure of secrecy, Tobin spoke with a low voice while looking to see if anyone could possibly overhear their conversation.

"What's wrong?"

"I've had enough of lingering on this road," Emerik answered. "And... I..." His voice trailed off, getting lost for a moment reflecting on what had happened to him almost three years ago.

"What?"

Snapping back into the moment, Emerik said what he hoped he did not have to.

"I do not trust them...and all this milling about is beginning to irritate me." He looked briefly into Tobin's eyes then cast them back around the road again. He needed his friend but was not yet ready to disclose those horrifying events from the past. "I want off this road and into Silverwood."

"Well," Tobin said with a stern nod. "Consider it done." His friend needed help and he was not about to let him down. With a yell to everyone in ear shot, and perhaps farther, he announced, "Alright! We go to Silverwood…now!"

The Thorp of Silverwood

Later that same afternoon

No one spoke on for the final hour of the journey because the overbearing silence of the forest seemed to transfer to them as well. Even though the sun shined brightly and cast its rays through the dense canopy of leaves, the party felt something...wrong. The closer they neared Silverwood the more silent, and paradoxically, the more restless they became. From somewhere deep inside themselves all of them felt they were going in the wrong direction, that Silverwood was not a place they wanted to be. Even without knowing, all of them began to walk slower and the horses, striding with more listlessness, seemed to be drained of their energy. Silverwood felt like a place of death although it did not look like it. The road to there was green and with blossomed flowers. It was just too...silent and something did not feel right.

Ruelina felt it also but perhaps more than the others. It did not feel the same as when she had left just a few months ago. Had it been so long? The journey back seemed longer than the trek to Paragon. But what happened to this place? Everything looked the same as she had expected but the feeling was wrong. This all felt wrong; the fiends, Clarissa being out this far from the village and something else. Something, somehow much darker but she could not place what it was. It was something stronger and far worse than she felt with the shape changing creatures they had just fought. Even her reaction was different. Before, she felt frustrated with herself for not being able to name what it was she felt. This time, she felt too tired and agitated. Again, though, she was unable to discern why. Why feel distressed? She was finally coming home was she not?

The only other who seemed, again, to feel it was Kaeleb. However, he too said nothing. There was something unnatural at work here, something aberrant and vile. To Kaeleb, it looked like the wondrously beautiful forest they had been traveling through for the last few days, but as he to neared Silverwood something inside him was trying to tell him that danger and doom were near. Even as he and everyone else saw the Silverwood trees for the first time in their lives their reaction was not as uplifting as it should have been.

Silver. Somehow, and from somewhere, silver had actually become part of the trees here. Veins of silver, like glistening frozen veins of blood, could be seen in the trees. Running like a network of circulation from the trunks all the way to the leaves themselves, silver shines brightly in the afternoon sun. How could this be? Silver did not grow into trees. Silver was mined from deep in the earth from inside rock. Since there was no rock within one hundred leagues of here, how did this possibly happen? The new comers' reaction should have held more awe and wonderment however, that was vastly overshadowed by the dark feeling they experienced. Still, none the less, they were stunned.

"Incredible," Smythe managed.

"It looks beautiful," Kaeleb added.

Ruelina remained silent. Yeah, just wait…we'll see how beautiful you all think it is in a few minutes.

Emerik was about to utter his own exclamation of awe but as they passed from the forest into the town itself, all of them halted and his words were immediately lost. They were in shock, paralyzed with astonishment as they could only stand and stare at the dismal sight they witnessed. Past the magnificent architecture of Elvin culture, past the beautiful trees that still glistened in the sunlight, on the other side of this poor tiny village they saw a sight that could only be described as horrific.

To the east, as far as their rapt eyes could see, the forest was a misshapen cemetery of decay and death. Every tree, every plant, was dead. Nothing lived. The silver that was part of the majestic trees remained standing like saddened twisted skeletons in a vast field of demise. This was far worse than any, especially Ruelina, could have ever imagined.

She stood motionless, gripped by the feelings that reeled though her. Quietly, and unnoticed by the others except Clarissa whom she still helped to walk, Ruelina trembled with dismay. She could not utter a single word since none could even be formed in her mind. It was not like this when she left. Sorrow and grief gripped her chest and she found that she could not breathe. She could not take a step. She could not take her eyes form the devastation she now saw. There was only one thing she could do, cry in silence. Tears began to stream down her face as she saw everything she knew, from as far back as she remembered from childhood, standing before her dead. The forest was her home and her life. Every plant, bird and bee were things that she grew up with and felt connected to. Now, all of that was dead. Ruelina came home only to find herself standing on the edge of a cemetery that was the sum of all her memories in her life. All she could do was stand, stare and cry.

Clarissa felt her despondent reaction and, although very weakened, griped Ruelina tighter to offer as much reassurance and condolence as she could. Ruelina had been gone for some time and did not know what all had happened. More so than herself, Clarissa knew Ruelina had an attachment to the land. Like her father, Ruelina was one for the forest and for the life that thrived there. Clarissa resided here in this village but was not like Ruelina. She was not a ranger. Ruelina was connected to the land and was taught by her father along with Barbas, the village druid, to become one with the forest. Sill, Clarissa was not without her own distinct sense of sorrow and loss. Each morning she reluctantly awoke to see death as it threateningly crept toward their homes. Waking in the morning soon became waking at night and she would stare out her window at the ever expanding death of the forest with fear and dread. Sometimes, rather than awakening at night, she would just not sleep at all.

After the long pause it was only Kaeleb who found within himself any focus with which to speak. His voice still cracked with bewilderment and came out softly as if there was something terribly fragile in the air he did not wish to break.

"What...happened here?"

That was all he could manage.

Smythe, who was standing just behind him, absently remarked, "I do not know..."

"What could do this?" Emerik asked and immediately followed with another question as if the first was rhetorical. "Is this...was...did ghouls do this?"

"I don't know." Ruelina tried to remark while still trembling, "This is what I was trying to tell you."

"Ghouls do not exist," Tobin added. He was seeking some sort of rational and sound handle on the surrealistic nightmare he found himself staring at.

"Yes they do," Ruelina quipped. "You still do not believe me?" She felt Tobin's remark was as ignorant as it was dismissive. Did everything have to be proven to them first? What would it take, for a ghoul to actually chew on them before they believed? Stupid humans.

"We'll find out soon enough," Tobin challenged. This was obviously some sort of trick and he would not entertain the tart commentary of an ill-bred back wooded peasant. How dare her! Who did she think she was?

"Yes," Emerik interrupted with a stern yet even tone. "We all will. But right now we must press on. Staying here to argue about it will not help." Even he felt it, the agitation in the air. Something here was causing anger to quickly heat within them. Before it boiled over and lead to a direct confrontation he had better maintain the lead and keep everyone occupied. Where was that coming from? Was it in the air? It was then he noticed while looking around that the shadows seemed thicker here and all colors seemed to be subdued as if they were standing in the shade when they were not. He felt that if they stood here long enough he would see one of the shadows itself move. Deciding to think on that later, and before she could respond with another insubordinate comment, he asked Ruelina directly, "Where can we take these corpses to be examined?"

Snapping out of her confrontational mode of thought, Ruelina mustered a quick and helpful suggestion. "We can take them to the stables. Vasala, our village animal caretaker, could help us."

"Ah..." Smythe began, "Would these not disturb the other animals there?" Thinking of the dead fiends that still seemed to come back to life, he imagined some rampaging horse, terrified and dangerous, causing too much trouble for them at the moment.

"No," she answered, "not at all." She still faced the decay of the forest she once knew and wiped her face of the streams of tears. It was only then that she even noticed she had cried.

"Why is that?" Smythe's face twisted in obvious confusion.

"Because," she turned to him just after drying her cheeks. "Our animals ran away a long time ago." Or were eaten first, but she did not add that. Their disbelief in ghouls would also have them not accepting that they ate Silverwood's livestock.

"They ran-" Smythe began but was interrupted by Emerik.

"Good." Pointing at Smythe, Tobin and his squire Emerik ordered, "Take these to the stables and wait for us there." With a nod of his head to Ruelina, his voice softened as he spoke further. "Where is her family?"

"Just past the inn to the north east," she answered in surprise. But not in so much surprise that she may have forgotten that he had not shown he is here to help or not. "Rannon is her husband's name," she added, in case his memory had lost any fragment of compassion. Emerik, however, continued to surprise her. He stepped forward slowly toward Clarissa who was still being supported by both Ruelina and Kaeleb.

"We are taking you home. You are going to be alright." Turning to Dyrrany he said, "Take my horse with you. We will meet you at the stables soon."

Clarissa nodded with a wordless thank you.

Emerik came over to where Ruelina was standing and stared at her as if he expected her to do something. Not knowing what that could be she felt compelled to ask.

"What?"

"I don't know the way. You do," he pointed out. "Let me help carry her."

"She is from my town I will carry her," she said defiantly.

"Fine, lead the way. But as we go, tell me in detail exactly what happened and where I can talk to your mayor....what's his name?"

"Matchok," Ruelina added in a firm voice, "His name is Matchok and we pass his home and the town square on the way to her place."

"Good...Let's move before we have no more daylight left." He said that knowing it was still early in the day.

Carefully, they moved Clarissa back to her home in the north east of the tiny village. Since they entered from the south west they had the entire place to wind through before they reached their destination. Ruelina pointed out some of more notable structures in the village: the stables just south of the garrison, the temple of the Earth God called Enlil which was to the west of the garrison the inn and lastly the library that was just south of the inn.

The mentioning of the library made Smythe's ears perk up.

"A library? You have a library here?"

"Yes," Ruelina answered. Did she not just say they had one? Doesn't everyone have a library in their town? Stupid humans.

Passing through the remaining buildings scattered between bright and dark green trees that contained no silver. Emerik asked some general question so he had an idea of what was around here. Ruelina, thinking they were useful questions, was more than happy to answer as they walked. The village only ever had about forty people living here and they were dispersed into just over twenty structures. Some of the buildings had been abandoned years ago by families who died off and did not leave the dwelling to anyone. The village kept them in decent repair in the event they may be needed in the future. Most of the work here was farming or hunting. No one trapped because the elves considered that cruel to the animals. There had always been a small militia of fighting men here that numbered about ten for as long as Ruelina could remember and they had resided in the garrison. Interestingly, the garrison had three levels and could easily quarter and train over thirty. However, the small band of ten had died off or disappeared since the emergence of the ghoul attacks so the structure was now vacant.

There was one temple that was dedicated to Enlil, the god of the earth, and it had two priests, an older one named Ben and a younger man named Nellron. Ben had been there in Silverwood for almost thirty years and Nellron was just recently assigned as a replacement for his aging superior. As mention before by Ruelina there was a stable there that could house almost ten horses.

The aforementioned library had two floors. The ground level held all of the books while the second served as living quarters for the only librarian who was an aging elf named Jotham. The library itself had over one thousand books inside and was described by Ruelina as "having something about everything".

The town now had no smith since he was also part of the garrison and was one of those killed months ago. The forge however, still remained intact in the basement of the garrison. Also, there was an inn although Ruelina could never recall anyone coming to Silverwood to visit so it served as a place to eat and gather.

The only real knowledgeable people to speak to were the village elders, of which, only three remained: Matchok the mayor, Jotham the caretaker of the library and Ben the aged priest. She did not mention Absalom since she and most everyone else felt he was struck in the head too many times and it had knocking something rather important loose in his skull. Sadly, even she had first left, both Jotham and Ben had fallen ill. Seems old age claims everyone unless one dies young.

"Matchok is this way," Ruelina directed.

"No," Emerik objected. "We will do that later. Right now it is far more important to see her home and back to her husband."

"Rannon," Ruelina added. However she was stunned that he cared that much for someone he did not know.

"Yes, Rannon." He corrected himself and they continued to her home while he asked a few more questions about the area and its history.

After the educating walk they had reached the home of Clarissa and her husband Rannon. The two settled here over twenty years ago and opened a general store where people could purchase items that may be needed in or around the home such as plates, eating utensils, linens and the like. Anyone in town could place an order with them for nearly whatever they wanted and the two, bases on the need and amount of other orders to be filled, would make the trip to the nearby trade city of Boregar. Being that it was only a full day's ride away most people would have their requested items in less than a few weeks.

When Rannon saw that his wife was being supported by Ruelina in obviously poor condition he took not time to race from their home to come to the side of his wife. He was naturally quite excited and spoke rather quickly.

"Are you well? What happened? Where did you go? Here come inside…" He nearly pushed Kaeleb out of the way and accepted help from Ruelina his fellow townsman. Kaeleb was not offended in the least but followed closely behind them as they passed the doorway. He stopped at the threshold as called inside.

"My I come in?" He did peer inside, though, having never seen elven architecture and decoration before. This journey would have been worth just that if it were not for the forest dying, people being killed or disappearing and the whole ghoul issue and apparently, the new fiend problem they encountered on the way here.

"Yes," he heard Rannon reply. "We are in the back."

Kaeleb carefully made his way to the sounds he heard toward the rear of the home. He did have to admit, elven wares were quite skillfully made. But then, it made sense since the elves lived longer and could spend much more time developing their skills for crafts and arts.

He reached the door and saw that Clarissa had been taken to

their bedroom and that Rannon and Ruelina were making her comfortable. Kaeleb entered the room and approached her husband.

"She is going to be well. She just needs to rest," he assured him.

"I see blood covering her but I see no wound…how is that?"

"It is possible because of the blessings of Enki." Kaeleb admitted.

"I don't understand…What potion did you use?" Rannon was not in the mood for games.

"No potion. It was done by the blessed grace of Enki."

Rannon stopped to really look at Kaeleb for the first time. He studied him for a few moments before speaking again.

"You are a priest?"

"Yes, from Paragon City. I am Brother Kaeleb Azhwan Miryd and this is Prince Emerik Montigan."

"Oh, I am Rannon…And you were able to heal her because of Enki?" There was lingering doubt in his voice and the word "prince" seemed to escape his ears.

"Yes, most certainly," Kaeleb insisted.

"You know that no one has been able to do something like that for about four hundred years?" There was a hint that Kaeleb was potentially lying, crazed or being truthful all in the same question.

"No, I did not know that," Kaeleb admitted. "I only know that she is well because of the blessings of Enki."

Rannon stared at him for a moment and believed that Kaeleb believed in what he said.

"Well, I thank you for helping her and bringing her here."

"No," Kaeleb said with a smile. "Do not thank me. Thank Our Master Enki for healing her and for putting me here to help her."

Rannon did not follow the path that Enki led, although he did recognize the deity and gave his due respects.

"I will, but thanks none the less."

Kaeleb merely smiled.

"What happened?" Rannon asked while returning to his wife's side.

"We came across her on the south road," Ruelina explained. "She was being taken by some men. We confronted them and…they…changed…they were no longer human."

"What?" Rannon was confused. "No longer human? What were they then?"

Ruelina paused at the risk of sounding completely mad.

"We honestly do not know," Emerik said cautiously yet had enough of being out of a conversation in his presence. "We brought the bodies back here for someone to look at…they…look more like lizards that move like dogs…or…something."

"What?" the elf was shocked.

"Have you, or anyone else, ever seen anything like that around here before?" Emerik asked.

Rannon paused to think and push the amorphous image from his mind. He had difficulty picturing even roughly what they had described.

"Ah…no…never."

Kaeleb frowned.

"That's not good…because now that means there are two problems. The ghouls and…whatever those things are," Emerik deduced.

"Three," Ruelina corrected.

"Sorry?" Kaeleb asked. Did she just correct a member of the royal family without even the slightest bit of respect?

"Three problems." She counted on her fingers. "Those things from earlier, the ghouls that no one wants to believe exist and, if you did not happen to notice, the large dying forest outside."

"I saw that," Kaeleb defended while almost sounding sheepish.

"Right," Ruelina said. She turned to Rannon. "Maybe you can take her to the temple priests or ask that they came here…or something."

"Ben is still ill and has only gotten worse after you left," Rannon explained with his brow showing concern.

"Everything is going hell here," she said under her breath. "Very well, then see if…Nellron can help." She canted her head to tell Kaeleb it was time to leave and then began to make for the door.

"Where are you going?" Rannon asked.

She answered with a sigh, "Insane."

As they exited the Rannon home, Emerik took little time to address Ruelina.

"Take me to see…Matchok. Is that his name?"

"Matchok," she corrected. "With a "t" in it."

"Alright, Matchok then...Take me to see him."

Ruelina paused before answering, mostly because she did not like to be told what to do. "I do not have to."

Emerik looked to her with a raised brow.

"What?" He stopped walking. If this was to be a problem he would certainly solve it right there and then.

"I don't have to take you to see him...he is walking this way," She answered with a hint of smugness.

Emerik glanced ahead and noticed an elderly looking elf ambling rather gracefully in their direction. He was the height that Emerik had thought he would be for an elf and possessed the very same pale features with long brown hair streaked with grey and silver from age. But that is where the elfin resemblance ended. Matchok, so unlike typical elves, was noticeably plump and it was Emerik's turn to be stunned. He had never seen a portly elf and never thought they even existed.

Matchok walked straight to Emerik and bowed. He had a stone like appearance to his face and his eyes seemed polished.

"Welcome to or home Prince Montigan." Matchok spoke while staring at the packed dirt of the ground, "We are most honored to have you here."

"Thank you," the prince responded properly however, he felt that propriety was something that seemed somehow trivial standing in this surreal village. The wall of death, as he ad recent come to call it, had not passed that far into the village yet so they were still surrounded by lush green foliage and flowers in full bloom. However, even while standing in the midday sun he noticed what he did earlier, that the colors were not as bright and that only the hue of black was sharply noticeable. "How do you know who I am?" He needed to talk about something other than death, decay, darkness or shadow.

"Oh," Matchok said without looking up. "Your family crest on your tabard is easy to recognize. I know you are a Montigan but I do not know your given name."

Emerik caught himself since he was not normally this formal.

"Please, rise," he said to Matchok. "My name is Prince Emerik Montigan son of Duke Drakken Montigan of Paragon City...and this is..."

"Oh," he said as if picking up the cue. "I am Brother Kaeleb Azhwan Miryd from the Temple of Enki in Paragon."

"...and you are?" Emerik give him no time to perform the pleasantries. He favored short introductions and little chatting.

"Matchok," he answered quickly. "I am Daucian Matchok, the appointed mayor of Silverwood."

"It is good to meet you," he politely replied. Emerik stopped for a moment as if he just now listened to what he was told. "Appointed mayor?"

"Yes, I am not elected but am appointed by the village elders."

"Oh, very well," he accepted that but also had to ask. "Who are the elders?"

"Ah, well...there are only three remaining here now."

"Three remaining? How many were there before?"

"Ah," Matchok was a bit uncomfortable and that did not go unnoticed. "There were Six."

"Six? What happened to everyone else?" asked Emerik.

"Yes well...Barbas walked out into the forest some time ago to investigate the cause of the blight but never came back. Jotham is here but has fallen ill and the same is with Ben. Absalom wanders around fairly well still but he is never in a predictable location and, of course, me." He said that and looked away as if to hope it was time to go. Sadly for him, it was not.

"Five," Emerik stated.

"I'm sorry, milord. Beg pardon?" Great, he had to get the smart member of the royal family here.

"You listed five but said there were six. Who is the sixth member?" Emerik asked.

"Ah," he stalled. Damn, I wish I knew how to lie better. "The other member is Naia." There he said it. "But we have not seen her for a long time," he quickly added. It was a little too quick for Emerik's liking.

"Really? Well, when did you last see her?"

"Oh...um...about...oh...eight maybe ten years ago."

The prince's frowned.

"Eight maybe ten years?" Those were strange numbers to put together. If the aged elf would have simply said "ten" or "eight" it would have been believable but not "eight maybe ten" so Emerik knew he was being lied to but did not want to make a problem about it right then. He decided to play stupid and act as if to have accepted it, for that moment. "Ah, that's too bad. It would have been nice to speak to...him or her?"

"Her," he said quickly from not having expected that question.

"Hmm..." Emerik pretended to think for a moment. "We came across some...creatures that first appeared to be human. We were on the road to here...know anything about those?"

"Creatures? Appearing human?" Matchok was bewildered.

"Yes, they...changed into something far less than human. Something dog like with the skin of a lizard," Emerik tried to describe.

"Um, no. Never heard of anything like that." His ignorance was genuine.

"Um, very well. We brought the bodies back here and need to study them. Where can we do that and who can help?" He asked already having an idea of the answer.

"Ah..." The elf pondered. "Maybe Vasala can help, he is in the stables."

"Right," Emerik responded swiftly. "Those are the stables with no animals...What does he do here?"

"Who?" The elf noticed Emerik thought too fast for him to keep up.

"Vasala, at the stables. What does he do here in Silverwood?"

"He cares for the animals," Matchok said.

Emerik just stared at him. Everyone around there had gone crazy.

"Fine," the prince said. "There is an empty garrison across from the stables, correct?"

"Oh yes, sire." He almost sounded happy about that. "It is still in fine shape as-"

"Good," he spoke authoritatively. "We will be staying there tonight. Where can we get food?"

"Oh, we all gather at the inn just behind me." Matchok motioned to the two floor building very near to them. "We eat breakfast, lunch and dinner there...but it seems like you already missed lunch."

"No matter," Emerik said dismissively. "We have traveling provisions but would like to have dinner there."

"Oh," he saw slightly stunned. "Why yes, of course! We would be happy to introduce you to everyone."

Great, Emerik thought. It will be the social event of the year.

"Excellent." That sounded more flat than enthusiastic. "Then we will see you there." He turned to walk away. "We will be at the stables or garrison until then, should you need us."

Emerik walked off leaving Kaeleb to stand there. He looked to Emerik then to Ruelina and Matchok then back to Emerik before nodding "goodbye" to catch up with the prince. Kaeleb knew that the study of those fiends would begin shortly after Emerik arrived and he did not want to miss any of it.

Matchok and Ruelina found themselves abruptly standing by themselves. A faint breeze blew a thin cloud of dust along the ground at their feet.

"Um, Ruelina..." Matchok asked.

"Yes?" Here it comes.

"That," meaning Emerik and Kaeleb, "Was the help from Paragon?"

"Well, no," she sighed. "The prince and his friend, a Drathmoore, met us on the road. Paragon only sent two."

"Two?" He was shocked, insulted and worried all at the same time.

"Yes, two...investigators."

"That's all?"

"Yes," Ruelina said with a frown. She stared at the ground feeling useless and helpless. Maybe she could have tried harder while she was in Paragon City?

"I wonder," Matchok interrupted her self-rebuking.

"What?"

"Did things just get better...or worse?"

Ruelina looked at him squarely.

"I honestly don't know," and then followed after them.

Kaeleb caught up to Emerik easily and was met with a short glance but no pause as the prince kept walking. Neither of them liked the silence nor the strange feeling in the air. Both wanted to speak but Emerik did first.

"I have heard about you," he stated.

"You have?" Kaeleb did not think of himself as important enough to have reached the ears of a prince. "Oh...was it good?"

Emerik shrugged.

"Seemed to be. The rumor is you are one of Enzi's chosen, something which has not been seen for a few centuries."

"Yeah, I heard the same thing," Kaeleb admitted unenthusiastically. He did not want to be special or treated any different from anyone else but somehow that was just not going to happen.

"So it is true?"

"Is what true?" Kaeleb disliked conversations like those. Never did they end well. There he was, having another one of those conversations as he walked, with a prince, in a small creepy village, to a stable with no animals.

"Are you or are you not one of the chosen?"

"I suppose so...but I do not know. Such things are not up to me."

"Oh? Who is it up to then?" Emerik asked already knowing that question.

"Enki, of course," he answered with a most confused tone. "But then I can probably say the same about you, Prince Emerik."

"How so?"

"No one from the royal family has been a paladin since the Great War." Emerik was not the only one who could hear rumors. "Now there are two."

Emerik thought for a moment while they still walked through the soundless village of green trees and elven buildings.

"That's true," was the best that Emerik could conjure at the moment.

"Looks like the world is changing," Kaeleb observed.

"Agreed," Emerik noted and then stopped just outside of the stables.

The two could hear the other talking inside as their voices echoed off of the wooden walls.

"But," the paladin began, "What do you make of this place?"

"You mean here? Silverwood?" He looked around at the darkened shadows and felt a chill in the summer air.

"Yes."

The priest turned to face the paladin.

"I think this place has become evil. We are surrounded by it. It is an angry and hungry evil."

"Well..." Emerik began. "Here I thought I was the only one who felt that."

He turned to enter the stables.

Inside the building were what anyone would have normally thought would be inside stables. There were stalls for horses, pens for pigs and a large area for feed and hay. There were, of course, no animals and therefore there was also no need for animal food. The place was empty and rather dismal. There, around the middle of the room, tables had been set and the corpses lay twisted atop them. Everyone else had gathered around to gawk. Standing there were Smythe, Dyrrany, Perry, Tobin and a new person, an elf. He must have been Vasala.

"Prince Emerik," Tobin half announced and half greeted. His bellowing tone was more for everyone else than for the prince. "How goes everything?" He must have noticed the expression on the paladin's face.

"Things are reasonably well. Clarissa is back with her husband Rannon and he is much happier with that. Also, we will be staying our nights in the garrison." He paused to survey the room and everyone's demeanor. "How are things here?"

"We are waiting for you," Tobin replied. "We also just informed Vasala here about the events of the morning. It seems he can be of some help."

"Good," Emerik stated then looked to Vasala. "How can you help?"

"Ah, well, I can take a good look at these things and tell you about them," the middle aged elf replied. He, like most elves, was of a slight build and had the typical sharp features. His pale skin seemed to match well with his white hair although he was not elderly. The elf's hands showed wear and darkening from years of manual labor with animals and he was not devoid of some old scars from the occasional bite or injury he received. Like Matchok, he also was dressed comfortably yet not in the fashion of a stableman since he was not wearing boots or sturdy clothing.

"What makes you qualified?" Emerik asked bluntly. That was

a question no one else had thought to ask up to that point.

"Well, sire. I was taught by the best."

"And who would that be?" Emerik pressed.

"Well…Naia, of course." He looked to the door at Ruelina who was just then entering. "She can tell you."

Everyone looked to Ruelina then fell silent. Were they actually supposed to know who that Naia person was? Emerik noted that he was the second person in a short time to mention that name and say it with great respect but that so far Ruelina had yet to say anything about this woman. There was really something not right about this place.

"Very well," Emerik said. "You may begin."

"Please, wait a moment," Kaeleb requested while he took his pack from his shoulders. "I wanted to take notes." He produced many sheets of paper bundled together and rummaged until he found his charcoal. He made his way to an unused chair and placed the papers on the seat. He knelt down to write.

Damn, Smythe thought, *what didn't I think of that? He's going to make me look bad if he keeps that up.*

When he was ready, Kaeleb apologized for delaying everyone and got ready to write.

Vasala then cocked his head and began to talk to Kaeleb while he inspected the outside of the creatures. They were predominately dark brown to black in color and had scales for skin like that of a lizard but they reflected light differently depending on the angle in much the same way as some poisonous snakes. This would sometimes give the scales an illusion of depth with a brassy hue. The fiend's hands and feet ended in claws that were not like the talons seen on most other lizards. Those were solid bodied suggesting they might have grown straight from their bones.

The muscle structure, Vasala told them, was quite well balanced in the front and back so that they were adept runners and climbers. With their limbs having mostly all ball joints and not hinge joints, the elf guessed that they could turn most of their body to face or do things in different directions. Unlike a human or elf that could only move their elbows or knees in certain directions and could not, say, rotate everything to face and effectively grasp something directly behind them, especially above their own waist. The fiends were much suppler and that gave them no weak direction or vulnerable angle to attack.

The elf became particularly horrified yet fascinated when he looked at their heads. Inside their mouths were two rows of sharp curved teeth that could extend or fold like those of a shark. Their nostrils were slotted and implied they did not breathe through their noses. When Vasala searched for how they breathed he suddenly stepped back in utter astonishment.

"What?" Tobin asked.

"Gills," the elf answered with a twisted expression of horror. "They have gills. They breathe under water."

"Yes that is strange indeed." Although Emerik agreed he did not fully understand.

"Why is that disturbing to you?" Smythe questioned. He may not know everything, but when he did not know facts or information he knew people and that usually got him the facts or information.

"Well," Vasala gathered himself. "There is no large body of water near here. There is only a swift river near Boregar."

It took some time for that to sink in. No air meant no life. For these things, no water meant no air. Since there was no water around Silverwood...

"There is no water around here?" Kaeleb asked as stopped writing. The papers were roughly tossed in a pile beside the chair.

"No...ah...we do have a well but we fill that with buckets. It is not large enough for these to live." The elf searched his mind for a good explanation but could not find one as if his own thinking kept slamming into a wall inside his mind.

"So...where is a large body of water that could support these things?" Smythe asked.

"Well, there is Lake Grydell but that is over two months travel by horse."

"Where else?" asked Emerik.

"There is the ocean," Vasala answered but in a tone that suggested that it was not possible.

"How far is that from here?" Tobin inquired.

"Over," he paused to look at the ceiling while he thought, "Over three months, closer to four. Yaddith is the nearest place. It is a port city in Ib far to the north east."

"Great," Emerik said with a touch of sarcasm. "So...that means..."

There was a pause where almost everyone looked at each other and almost spoke at once.

"Where did they come from?" It echoed in the empty barn. Shortly after, everything was again embraced by the discordant stillness.

After a while Vasala had gathered enough courage to approach the table and begin where he had left off. He glanced at its face but tried desperately not to look really at it. Eyes. Next he was going to look at its eyes. He brought his face closer to the creature's so that he could get a really good look at its eyes. Black. Iris and pupils seemed to be no different. There was no white or lines of blood vessels. Again, it resembled a shark.

Looking closer he saw another clear cover, something like a sheath that could cover the eyes and still allow it to see. A cat and sheep had those. What the hell was this thing? Was this some sort of newly pieced together race or had these things been around for a while? He swallowed hard and stood. There was only one way to know for certain if these were creations or if they grew.

"Um...someone please get me an axe."

"A what?" Smythe asked.

"What do you need an axe for?" Ruelina had to enquire. Although completely destroying these things seemed like a very sensible idea to her.

Vasala sighed, "Well...I need to see if these things grow or not." He lowered his face back down closer to the fiend's. Suddenly, he became acutely aware of the double row of sharp teeth that loomed list below his own vulnerable neck. Then he saw it. Quickly he pushed back from the table with a loud shout of terror and pointed at it, unable to speak.

"What?" Ruelina asked with marked fear in her voice.

Emerik and Tobin began to move closer to the tables while Smythe began to move farther back. The elf continued to point and stammer.

"The...tha...the...th...a...tha...i..."

"Speak man!" Emerik shouted.

Vasala looked to Emerik with widened eyes and trembling with fear.

"It moved its eyes! It looked at me! It's not dead!"

"Damn it!" shouted Tobin while drawing his sword.

"How?" Emerik asked the elf. "How do we kill it?"

Vasala stood shaking and he could still feel the malevolence from the fiend's gaze.

"Vasala!" Emerik shouted.

The frightened elf turned his quivering head with a gasp and looked at the paladin whose eyes burned with fire.

"How…do…we…kill…it?"

"F…Fi…Fire." Finally he mustered his courage. "Fire! They must be burned! White hot!"

"Where can we make a fire that hot?" Tobin demanded.

"In the basement of the garrison. A forge!"

There was a pause. Everyone seemed to stop moving at once except Emerik and Kaeleb who looked at each other a little confused.

"Let's move people!" the paladin shouted.

That seemed to snap everyone out of their bizarre trance. Kaeleb and Emerik again looked to one another. We'll talk later, they said wordlessly.

Dyrrany and Perry moved to one fiend and grasped it by its shoulders and legs.

"No!" Emerik shouted. "Take them on the tables!"

"Those are not your tables!" Ruelina bawled.

"What do you expect to start a fire with?!" Emerik bellowed.

Ruelina's mouth opened then closed again. She then scurried away to the table that Dyrrany and Perry were at.

"We can tie them down," Kaeleb suggested as he and Smythe moved to the second table.

"Yes," Tobin agreed.

"Use the rope we drug them here with!" Emerik commanded as he raced Tobin to the third table. They did not wait for the rope, however and lifted the table. Making their way out of the large doors Emerik and Tobin headed for the garrison. From inside the stables Ruelina shouted to them.

"I thought you wanted them tied down!"

Without pausing, slowing or looking back, Emerik shouted over his shoulder.

"You can wait if you want! I am going to burn this thing as quickly as I can!"

"Hurry!" Tobin shouted. "Unless you want them to wake up on the tables!"

Damn this! Ruelina spat to herself. She struggled to loop the rope around the table while the fiend lay motionlessly on it all the while with an impending sense of urgency that at any moment it would sit up and being tearing all of them apart like bed sheets. Her hands trembled and she was vaguely aware the other table was heading out of the door without any rope to secure the unconscious monster.

Finally she secured the knot and immediately after, Kaeleb and Smythe lifted the table and awkwardly scrambled out of the large doors. Ruelina stood and began to run to reach Dyrrany and Perry who were carrying the second table.

While running sideways to the garrison, Smythe and Kaeleb looked to one another with apprehension as a fiend lay between them, loosely tied to the flimsy table. Both felt a shiver dance over their bodies.

After passing through the opened gates of the wall that surrounded the stone structure, Emerik and Tobin reached the large reinforced metal doors to the garrison itself and kicked. With a loud echoing groan they gracelessly swung open. Sunlight dimly poured into the stone hall. They paused to look around. Neither knew how to get to the forge in the basement.

"Now where?" Tobin hollered.

Ruelina was franticly trying to tie a knot in the rope looped around the jogging table. She shouted in frustration in her inability to secure it.

"In the back, right side!" she yelled back.

Emerik glanced over his shoulder and began to move as quickly as he could. The sounds of his and Tobin's metal armor clanked loudly like broken gongs. They reached the door and found it was already ajar. Going through it they saw two sets of stone stairs, one leading down the other leading upwards. Downward was the obvious choice and they scrambled as quickly as they could while trying not to trip on the stone steps.

There in the basement they found themselves lost. There was a large corridor leading straight away from the stairs with arched doorways on either side. They looked to each other knowing that time was short.

"Where?" asked Tobin while trying to catch his breath. Running in sixty pounds of metal armor while lugging a table with a two hundred pound fiend was quite tiring.

"Don't know," Emerik said between gasps.

"Where would you build it?" Tobin asked.

"First floor...less running."

Tobin looked around as they stated to make their way down the wide stone corridor.

"Back...it would be in the back," Emerik said as if he remembered.

Picking up their pace, Tobin asked him, "How...do you know?"

"I read it...in the history books...they used to...always build...the forge...on the north side." He could not seem to get his breath while carrying this table.

When they reached the end of the corridor and entered the left door, both discovered that the history books had been correct. There it was on the north wall, the largest forge the two had ever seen. It was pristine while marble and covered as if it were an oven. The entire place was immaculately clean. Did they ever use this place?

The two continued to make their way directly to the forge after realizing that they both had stopped to stare at this room in surprise. Placing the table down in front of the furnace they looked at each other. How were they going to burn the table with this thing still on it? It would take far too long to get hot enough if the table were still in one large piece. They looked around for something to start the fire with. Luckily, there to the right of the kiln and lined along the wall, were enough logs and kindling for them to start, as well as flint and steel to get a spark.

As Tobin ignited the kindling Emerik stood over the fiend and stared at it. He needed to know more about this enemy before he faced them again. However, fate seemed to not grant him this luxury. Both could not hear the others clamoring down the stone stairs while shouting to one another.

The squires, Dyrrany and Perry, anxiously reached the bottom of the stairs. They did not like being that close to the monster between them. After the last step they hurriedly scanned the corridors not knowing where their knights went. Then they heard a voice from back up the stairs.

"Wait for us!" said Smythe excitedly. He did not want to be any more lost than he already was.

"Eala you, run faster!" replied Perry.

The two squires began scrambling down the larger corridor while shouting.

"Prince Emerik?"

"Sir Tobin?"

They shouted into the seemingly empty place. That was it! Dyrrany thought to himself, Silverwood has been made empty, as if something should be here but is not. He would have to speak to his teacher-paladin later.

"Bastards!" cursed Smythe. They were not stopping.

Kaeleb was satisfied with the nation of trying to sprint with this table rather than give in to being frustrated or angry…which is what this places wants.

"We'll be fine," he tried to console Smythe. "Just don't stop."

Smythe's anger flashed like a barrel of lamp oil exploding. Ruelina was just behind Kaeleb when it happened.

"I know not to stop! Do you think I am stupid?" Smythe's voice came fast and sharp. "You don't have to be some holy priest from some distant monastery to know these things are dangerous!"

What was he talking about? Kaeleb thought. His mouth opened to ask Smythe a question when Ruelina spoke first.

"Calm down!" she ordered.

"Eala you! Calm?" Smythe's face was turning colors and his veins stood out from his skin. "Did you happen to forget about these?" He motioned to the fiend on the table he and Kaeleb were carrying. However, since both of his hands were occupied the table tipped. Smythe lost his balance.

"Damn!" He cursed before falling down the stairs and taking the table with him as he tumbled.

Kaeleb's mouth hung open for a different reason now and the blood drained from Ruelina's face as they watched the table toppled down the stairs and slammed heavily into the solid stone wall. The sound of splintering wood echoed loudly against the stone as the table shattered.

When Smythe stopped rolling he groaned in discomfort from having bounced off the stonework. Vaguely he remembered getting quite angered. What had happened? The table!

Ruelina was the first to the bottom of the steps and, passing by Smythe, she approached the fiend and drew her sword with noticeable fear. The priest came and helped Smythe to stand and looked him in the eyes as he did. It was as Kaeleb expected. The angered investigator had a different look in his eyes and his face was no longer twisted in rage. Something was influencing people here in this village, something strong and malevolent. Kaeleb said nothing but patted him once on the shoulder as Smythe's eyes averted in shame from having lost control then both looked to the fiend on the floor. It was freed from its bonds. With the table splintered the ropes now hung loosely around its body and it felt as if it would jump to life at any moment.

The fire was not burning large enough in the time they needed it to. Tobin glanced around the room for something to help. As Dyrrany and Perry entered the room carrying their table, his eyes landed on the bowl lamps that flanked the archway.

"Bring those lamps here!" Tobin shouted. "And don't spill the oil!" Demons, fiends, monsters, ghouls, silver trees, he had had enough already. No wonder his ancestors had outlawed magic. Look at the trouble it causes!

The squires promptly placed the table onto the floor and looked around for what lamps Tobin was referring to. Dyrrany, seeing the ancient styled oil lamps, pointed and rushed over.

"There!" directed Dyrrany.

As the squires moved to retrieve the oil everyone heard the tumbling and splintering of wood. Everything fell silent as if they were afraid to move for fear of rousing one of these creatures.

Emerik, however, took the risk thinking that if they were going to fight these again then they were going to fight these again and there was little to gain by prolonging it.

"What happened?" shouted Emerik.

The paladin's voice carried easily down the corridor to the ears of the three who were staring at the fiend.

"Just dropped a table," Kaeleb shouted back.

"Quit playing around and get that thing in here!" demanded the paladin.

"How?" Smythe wondered while not wanting to even touch it.

"Grab the ropes," said Ruelina as she stepped forward. "We'll drag it."

Without sheathing her sword she grasped one of the loops with her left hand. The two men followed suit and they began to tow the monster down the corridor.

The squires gingerly rushed over to the kiln holding the glass bowls of oil. Not wanting to wait Tobin grasped the lamps, one in each hand, and tossed the lamps into the furnace. The glass shattered against the bricks and oil splashed everywhere inside. There was a whoosh as it ignited and flames quickly rose inside.

"More wood!" commanded Tobin.

The squires raced along with Tobin to gather more wood from against the wall. Emerik turned the table onto its side and began to break the legs off and toss them into the furnace.

"This is actually faster," Smythe observed as they were now almost able to run. He was trying to be funny to break the tension.

No one replied and Smythe quickly decided to shut up. They rounded the corner into the forge room, following the sounds of clamor from within, and moved straight to the kiln with the fiend in tow.

Ruelina stopped at the opening, took a deep breath and then bent down to lift the thing by the ropes. Kaeleb quickly moved across from her and helped.

"What are you doing?" questioned Smythe. He suddenly felt…odd, like a hundred cold and tiny insects were crawling on his back. Did the shadows just get longer and deepen? Did the room appear smaller?

Without stopping Ruelina quipped.

"Burning these things. Remember?"

Ruelina and Kaeleb looked to each other, nodded and swung the load toward the flames. Its shoulders struck the sides of the opening and did not enter. The fiend was too large or the kiln was too small. Perhaps the forge was not designed to burn man-sized creatures. Kaeleb looked to Ruelina with panic on his face.

"Now what?" the priest asked.

Ruelina shrugged and stared at it.

Smythe canted his head. His expression had changed to one of an unnerving calm.

"Make it fit," he said distantly.

"How?" Ruelina questioned as she looked up at Smythe.

"Tear it apart," Tobin spoke unemotionally with the same tone as Smythe. "It would do no less to us."

Emerik's gaze shifted from Smythe to his lifelong friend then at everyone else. Those were not the words of Tobin. He did not know Smythe but he knew his friend and Tobin did not talk ever talk in those tones. However neither sounded like they did earlier before they reached this forsaken village.

"How?"

"With these," uttered Smythe while drawing his own sword. He stepped forward to the creature that Ruelina and Kaeleb still held suspended. Again, his head canted. Kaeleb noticed the expression on his face and mannerisms were quite different then what Smythe displayed in the past few months of travel getting to Silverwood.

With a strange and somewhat unnatural motion, Smythe grasped the motionless fiend by the throat and shoved his blade into its armpit. He began to dig and pry at it shoulder. The priest and the Ranger, Ruelina, dropped their hold on the ropes and stepped back in horror. Dark viscous blood oozed from the wound as the metal ground against bone.

"What in the hells are you doing?" She was shocked and repulsed.

Smythe stopped and slowly lifted his head. She was looking at the face of a different man as he slowly spoke with a methodical tone.

"I am removing its limbs," he turned back to the monster and began again. "It must fit inside to burn…it must…"

The priest, who stood behind Smythe and watched in horror, became more disturbed at what he witnesses when he noticed that he had nearly taken its arm from its body in that short time. Smythe, along with his other mysteries, seemed to know much about humanoid anatomy with threatening detail.

Smythe stood and placed a foot on the creature's chest and pulled while twisting. Dark crimson thickly squirted on him but he gave no reaction as if he were more focused on his gruesome task. With a sickening snap of ligaments, the arm came out of its socket. He then unceremoniously sawed through the rest of the tissues freeing the arm from its body. He glanced back at Kaeleb with a calm almost trancelike gaze then turned back and tossed the limb into the kiln.

Lifelessly, it slammed into the back of the furnace and lay motionless in the flames. Everyone stopped to watch. Everything was silent save for the roaring breath of the fire and the occasional pop of burning wood. No one could see if it was actually burning or not.

Smythe, the man who just a few minutes before did not want to even graze these things, bent down to begin on the other arm.

"We need more oil," Tobin suggested as he walked near to Smythe.

Perry instantly began to look around for more lamps or any container that held oil.

"Sire?" Dyrrany asked.

"Help him," commanded Emerik who knew what he was asking about.

The two squires began to hastily search.

"What if this doesn't work?" Kaeleb inquired.

"Then we kill them again," Tobin coldly began. "I will go looking for Vasala." He did not add, and maybe toss him in there. Damned magic. Why can't people just stay with using swords? Was that so difficult to understand?

Inside the kiln, the dark scales began to change colors, bubble and smolder. Yes, these fiends do burn. Tobin bent as he drew his own sword and began to cut into its hip.

The two holy men were horrified like all the others but felt something different. There was an unnatural force at work here. They watched, witnessing the horrifying influence and realized then just how dangerous this place was. Anyone at almost time could become psychotic and dispassionately commit ghastly doings with seemingly no remorse. The problem in Silverwood was far worse than these fiends. Again, the priest and the paladin spoke to each other wordlessly. Silverwood had become corrupted and they would have to be careful if everyone was to leave this place alive or sane.

The squires returned from a distant room bearing a small cask of oil. They two became paralyzed with disgust when they saw Tobin and Smythe impassively dismembering the second creature. It was not just that they were doing it but what made it worse was the way they were. Neither expressed any feeling, not of anger or even disgust, as they mutilated it.

"S...Sire, the oil," stammered Dyrrany to his teacher.

The prince quickly came to them and took hold of the small cask.

"Fine work," he spoke quickly and stood between them and the horror to block their view. "Ah...go and see if...if..." He struggled to think of something for them to do but would not take very long since he did not want anyone to be alone in this village. That was far too dangerous. "Bring our horses inside the garrison walls and close the gate."

"Sire?" Perry asked with a mark of concern and confusion.

"And if the gate can lock, indeed do so," he commanded.

The two moved away as the paladin watched them disappear around the corner. Emerik had become acutely concerned for everyone's safety. His glance fell to the ground as he remembered when he convinced his friend to join him in coming to this place. He also remembered asking himself, am I doing the right thing? Standing in the cold stone corridor as his friend and a stranger mutilated an unnatural creature in a most horrifying fashion, Emerik resented himself for even suggesting the notion. Maybe I am not that good of a friend. Maybe I am just not that good at all. He scolded himself. Maybe I am not really worthy of serving Enki. He strongly shook his head as if his scalp was suddenly covered with tiny spiders. He returned to the kiln.

The ranger and priest were staring at Smythe and Tobin in total distress. Neither had ever seen such a horrid display before. Both men were covered in thick dark goo that dripped like slime from their clothing.

"What?" Smythe asked them after the last leg of the fiend was cast into the forge. What are you staring at?

Neither could speak.

Emerik came over and looked at his friend drenched in gunk. He frowned and shuddered with the notion his friend was going mad.

"You...ah...you're a little..." He could not conjure something constructive to say. "Are you well?" He finally decided on.

Tobin blinked.

"Yeah, I am good," he sincerely replied. "I was just...doing what needed to be done." Tobin shrugged.

"Maybe you should get cleaned up." Emerik was at a loss for words and felt he was no longer speaking to Tobin.

"Yeah," he looked down at himself. "Maybe your right. No point going to dinner like this."

"Dinner?" Ruelina asked in shock. *How can you think of eating after that? I may not eat for a week.*

"Of course," Smythe added. "I'm hungry too."

They're crazy, she thought to herself. *The stupid humans also went mad.*

"Where can they get cleaned up?" Emerik asked her.

"Um…" She did not really know the garrison. "Upstairs, I think to the back left of the building."

"Good," Emerik quickly came to her and grasped her arm. Leading her out of the room he said, "Show me."

As they strode quickly down the corridor she kept looking at his gloved had that still held her arm and wondered what had gotten into him as well. When they reached the top of the stairs he released her but did not stop walking. He was obviously upset.

"Tell me," he started. "What is this place?"

"What do you mean?"

"I mean what is this village? Who lives here? Why is this even here? What is this place for?" asked Emerik with great agitation.

"I am sorry but I do not understand what you are asking."

He sharply turned and leaned in nose to nose and pointed back the way they had come.

"I just watched my friend, who I have known all my life, act like someone I do not know." He took a breath and glanced to see if they had been followed. Even though he did not notice anyone he lowered his voice just to be safe. "He did not talk like my friend, he did not sound like my friend and he even started to not look like my friend." He paused to let that sink in. "So I want to know right now what in the hells is going on here."

"I don-"

"Don't tell me you don't know," he interrupted. "I have lost my patience with not getting any answers. Tell me what is happening in this place. Start from the beginning and you had better not leave anything out."

Ruelina swallowed. *Finally he takes an interest.*

"From what I know, it actually started around two suns ago in the spring…"

After an hour of Ruelina speaking quite quickly Emerik's lips pursed. He thought for a time before he said anything. The situation seemed worse than he thought, especially if she was correct and accurate with her tale. Somehow that stone hallway had become quieter, darker and colder. Finally, the paladin spoke.

"Tell me about Naia."

"Naia?" she questioned.

"Yes, Naia. Vasala said you can tell us so I am asking you. What can you tell me?"

Ruelina took a deep breath. It figures he would as about the village enigma.

"Well, I know a lot but also very little."

"That makes no sense," he humorlessly stated.

"Well…if you want to know what she looks like I cannot tell you." Ruelina was serious.

"What?"

"No one can."

"How can you live with someone in a small village like this and not know what they look like?" He did not like someone playing with his mind or trying to trick him.

"Veil."

"What?" he blinked and leaned in as if he may have heard her wrong.

"She always wore a veil," she explained. "She said there was a problem with the way she looked and did not want anyone to have a problem so…she always covered herself."

Emerik just stared at her.

"She did, really," Ruelina affirmed, knowing that he did not believe her.

"Fine, what else? What did she do here?"

"Do?" she was a bit confused. "As in her work?"

"Yes," the paladin replied.

"She worked at the library…and was a teacher."

"Yeah, the library…" his voice trailed off for a moment. "What did she do there?"

"She was a scribe and book maker."

He nodded.

"That would explain why she knew many things," he thought aloud. "What did she teach?"

"What did she teach?" she repeated with slight chuckle. He was not going to like the answer.

"Yes, what did she teach?"

She went quiet for a moment so he could receive the full implication of what she was about to say. She leaned in and looked him dead in the eyes.

"Everything."

The two stared at each other saying nothing for a while.

"Is that all? There are no other surprises? Nothing else to tell me about?" Emerik asked with raised eyebrows.

"No," she reassured him. "That is all I know."

He exhaled with a frown and then turned away from her to walk back down to the basement. He stopped and looked back to her. For the first time he saw Ruelina, a woman born and raised in a tiny forest village whose only goal was to save her home. She looked strong like one of stout silver trees outside yet vulnerable as paper in a coming rain.

"You can stay here with us tonight if you want. It would probably be safer."

She thought for a moment before declining. "No, but thank you. I will sleep in my own home tonight. I have not been there in over six moons." Being home was a warming thought for her.

"Very well," he said with gentleness in his voice. "We will see you at the inn in the morning."

She turned to leave.

"Sleep well," he added.

"You also," and with that she left, closing the large door behind her. The echo danced everywhere in the hall and the air became thick. The prince suddenly felt alone. I hope we all can sleep tonight, he thought. Sleeping well would be a blessing.

They had cleaned in a stone tiled bath in the rear of the garrison, just as Ruelina said there was. It was strange for a bath to be located inside of a military building, especially one as old as this. Also, Emerik thought it was quite odd that the bath itself was so…ornate. The colored tiles were quite small, being only a bit more than an inch square, and there was well over a thousand placed on the inside and outside of the bathtub itself.

While everyone bathed, Emerik gave himself a tour of their temporary home and base of operations. The entire structure was stone and was quite old. Interestingly, the place was situated in an elven village however, was not of elven architecture or design. The more Emerik studied of the garrison the more convinced he was that it was not of Paragon style design either.

In the basement, there was the forge they had discovered earlier, a kitchen and a small jail or prison area that had long since been converted to storage. Why would they need a jail here in the middle of the forest? Also, predominately throughout the entire garrison, the stones were pale grey and almost white. While the iron was the typical deep black with swirls of what looked like silver. He knew enough about metals to know that iron when mixed with silver produced a weaker alloy. So why use it in a garrison?

The main floor consisted of a barracks to the right and two large training rooms to the left. The quarters had beds with matching chests neatly positioned in the room and numbered thirty. Thirty arms men? Why thirty for such a small place? Within the training rooms were weapons placed in racks that had not been used in decades. The prince noted another oddity. The weapons were not elven but were of an ancient design he had read about in history books. The weapons were, in fact, new creations but were fashioned in a design that had not been widely used in over six hundred years. He would ponder that more at a later time. Additionally, on this floor was a room that seemed to be a war room located in the central rear of the entry hall. Inside this chamber was a stone table engraved and painted with a map of this surrounding area, very strange indeed.

On the second level were more rooms. On the west side were two large rooms that were one the garrison commander and his second. To the right, or east side, were a study that was now devoid of books, a game room that still had its chessboards and another storage room. Emerik took an interest in the chess board after looking at the empty shelves of the study. It was strange to vacate a garrison and take the time to remove the reading material. What did these soldiers read, anyway? Looking at the chessboards he became amazed. There were three and all three were different.

The first two were normal boards of sixty-four squares of black and white with sixteen playing pieces per side. The figures themselves seemed to have been intricately carved from ivory and oiled ebony wood. Both materials were far from indigenous here. The pieces themselves were positioned for a game already.

Emerik tilted his head at the next chessboard. Actually, it seemed more like boards. There were two boards connected by pedestals so that one was atop the other and were both round. The board colors were still black and white however the lines were like a spider's web with a central circle in the middle. The pieces were not so very humanoid here and seemed to resemble fanciful and mythical creatures. They were four colors to the pieces, tan, white, black and yellow, and they were positioned as if someone were playing a game. Emerik could not discern what piece or color belonged to what side. It seemed as though some of the pieces could also move from one level to another since some of the same colors, namely tan and yellow, were on both boards.

Last, he discovered the stairs that lead to the roof of the garrison but did not venture upward. He was hungry and wanted to eat more than he wanted to see the village from a higher vantage point at that time. He would wait until later.

As he made his way back down he surprisingly ran into Smythe who seemed to be looking around as well.

"What are you doing here?" asked the prince.

"Ah, I was actually looking for you, sire." He was clean and had a different look in his eyes. It was the same look that Emerik remembered the man had when they first met.

"Why? What do you need?" demanded Emerik.

"Vasala had just left," Smythe offered.

"He came here?" This not being told things needed to end.

"Yes, he wanted to see if the fiends burned."

"They did," Emerik stated the obvious.

"Yes, that is what we told him." Smythe's mind wandered for a moment.

"What else?"

"Sire, do you recall that he requested an axe just before he suggested we incinerate them?"

"Yes, vaguely. Why?" Emerik's brow creased.

"Well, sire," Smythe began. "I had asked him about that and he explained that as bones grow they form rings that one could see and count to guess an age. He wanted the axe to cut the large leg bone and see those."

"Well, he does know a great deal." Emerik stated thoughtfully. He shifted his attention immediately back to Smythe. "What else did you need of me?"

Smythe stared at the floor before taking a deep breath and looking back to the prince.

"I wanted to come and...offer my apologies," Smythe answered humbly.

"Apologize for what?"

"For my...ah...lack of control earlier." Amazing how he could not find an articulate phrase.

"You mean for you going insane and hacking that thing apart like you enjoyed it?"

"Yes, for that." Amazing how straight to the point the prince could be.

You were not the only one, the paladin thought of Tobin.

"Why do think that happened?" Emerik wanted to see how aware or unaware this stranger was and possibly how much he knew.

"There is something in this place. I do not think that it was always here, but something is influencing this village." That was about as near as he could figure. Also, he decided, he was going to punch Scarecrow in the face for sending him here. Never, in all his years of investigating magic, had he ever experienced an area such as that as in Silverwood.

"Do you think it is coming from the forest?"

No...from somewhere else...

"Actually, milord," he glanced around to ensure no one unwanted would hear him speak. "I think it is from somewhere else, as in from somewhere...below." Before burying himself Smythe quickly added, "However, that is just a quick theory. I still need to conduct my investigation to be certain."

"I can understand," said Emerik. "But, who do you investigate for, exactly?"

"Wha...well I...ah..." That was a surprise. "I am an investigator for the Golden Council, milord. My report will be read straight away by the Council members themselves."

The prince nodded in acceptance. The Gold Council answered directly to the king and advised him on all matters concerning the kingdom laws, history, foreign relations, military, finance, everything.

"Good," the prince began. "Then you can utilize your skills for me while you are doing so for the Council. I believe it is relevant to the issues at hand here but is rather buried under layers of lies and deceit." His tone and look became quite serious. "I want you to unearth it and come directly to me when you have. Understood?"

"Ah, well, yes I do understand but what is it?" Smythe was intrigued that the prince may have noticed something he had not.

"I believe there is a shroud of intended concealment pertaining to the village elders. There are certain inconsistencies surrounding them and I want to know what you uncover."

"Certainly, sire." Great, now he was being sent on another wild chase that may only result in his wasted time. "May I ask what inconsistencies?"

"I would not want to bias your investigation. Just let me know what you discover." The tone suggested that Smythe had is new yet small assignment so he should quit asking stupid questions and get too it.

"May I at least have some names so I can more direct my energies?" Smythe needed at least something to go on. It was difficult to see though fog.

"Yes, of course. Ah…" Emerik thought best about how to put it to him. "There seems to be a leading circle of elders here, just as in most small villages, like a council. From what I can tell, Matchok is appointed by this elder council to manage Silverwood. Which, that is strange in itself since most elder councils do not give away power but rule through a group. Anyway, most have gone missing or fallen ill."

"Fallen ill? Vanished?" Smythe reiterated.

"Yes. It seems Ben, the local priest of Enlil, and Jotham, the librarian, are both ailing."

"At the same time?" inquired Smythe. Sounds like poison or something else.

"Ah, yeah," he did his best to hide his suspicions to not sway Smythe's thinking but failed miserably at it. "Also, Barbas, perhaps a woodsman, vanished some time ago when we walked into the forest and never returned. Then, there is Naia."

"The woman that Vasala mentioned?"

"That would be the one, yes. She is…well…there is something very strange about her."

"How is that, milord?" Smythe was intrigued. Nothing charged him more than uncovering things people did not want found out. For him that was the ultimate game of chase.

"Well, her name was mentioned twice by two different people as someone that holds a great amount of authority and, it would seem, is very knowledgeable and wise."

"Knowledgeable and wise?"

"Yes, did you see how quickly Vasala had detailed information about a creature he had never seen before just by glancing at it?"

"Yes," remembered Smythe. "He also mentioned that Naia was his teacher."

"Correct."

"So where is Naia now?" Smythe wondered.

"She is on the list of those who had vanished. Seems she did that some time ago as well."

"May I ask how long ago?"

"Well…" Emerik breathed. "About eight to ten years ago."

"Eight to ten?" Smythe's brow creased.

The prince nodded.

"That is a peculiar range. Someone so important and they do not know when they left?"

"Yes, it would seem that way…" Emerik's voice also suggested it was a lie and they both knew it.

"Is there anything else you can tell me?" Smythe's mind had already begun chewing on it like a wolf gnawing at a very large bone. He would not stop until it was completely finished.

"No, that would be all," he said dismissively. She is ugly and wears a veil but I do not believe that for a moment.

"Yes, milord. May I begin in the morning?" He at least wanted to eat and rest before attempting anything very mentally taxing.

"Certainly, tomorrow is fine." He moved to leave then paused. "I will be speaking to everyone tonight during dinner. I trust you will be present?"

"Oh, yes." He said that a little too eagerly but hunger can do that when someone mentions food.

With a nod and no words Emerik turned away and made his way downstairs. That is when he, and everyone else here, heard the loud pounding on the reinforced doors. As the prince crossed the floor toward the entrance, he was beaten there by Perry who reached the doors and shouted.

"Yes? Who is it?"

"It is Matchok, we have brought food." The voice was muffled through the thick metal.

Perry looked around and noticed the prince still nearing the door. Dyrrany, Tobin and Kaeleb appeared from the barracks room to see what was happening. Emerik merely nodded to Perry and stepped back at a safe enough distance in the event it was an ambush. He may be a royal but he was not that stupid.

The squire pulled the heavy bolts on the doors and struggled to open one. With a loud groan as before, the door opened. Emerik took note of how much noise it made for future reference. Why, he did not know but he felt that it may become important to remember sounds in this structure.

In the open doorway, the face of Matchok appeared. He glanced in before stepping through the threshold and was followed by three others, an older elf, though not as aged as he was, and two young elven women.

"We brought some food for you here. We did not know if you would be coming to the inn or not." stated Matchok with a gentle and understanding tone.

"Ah, right," the prince answered. "We had planned on not, until the morning. But we thank you for bringing us this."

"Ah, no thanks needed. It is our honor, especially you being a prince from the capital and having come all this way for people you don't know." The smile on the old elf's face was genuine. "It is the very least we can do."

"Well, we offer our thanks anyway," stated Emerik.

"Where can we put these?" Matchok inquired. Certainly those metal serving trays full of food could not weightless.

"Ah..." he quickly glanced around. "The war room would be fine." He managed to just get that out before anyone behind him could speak.

"Excellent! You're getting an idea of the lands here?" Matchok's enthusiasm sprang out a bit. Anyone that seemed ready and willing to help the village was quite uplifting.

Emerik and everyone followed the wafts of real cooked food

into the back room.

"Well, trying to anyway," he stated. "I would like to speak to you further in the morning after we have had some rest if that would be fine?"

"Oh yes, certainly! I also imagine you will want a better tour of the village and the area after breakfast then?"

"Excellent idea," the prince commended.

"Then I will see you in the morning at breakfast. Usually we eat within one hour of sunup."

Emerik nodded.

"Then we shall see you there."

Matchok bowed and like a gust of wind everyone left. The place became silent again.

Everyone just stood and stared at the food without touching it. Mostly it was comprised of vegetables, bread, some fruits and one bowl of mushroom soup. There was no meat. But there were two jugs of water and two bottles of wine.

Everyone began looking at each other then back to the food.

"Well," Dyrrany began. "If indeed they are stupid enough to poison it they will kill their only hope for survival. But they do not look like the sort ready to commit suicide."

"Agreed," the paladin said. He stepped forward and grasped a whole loaf of bread. "Good point." He broke open the loaf and took a bite. He chewed and watched the ceiling as everyone else watched him. After he swallowed, and since he was not dead, he passed the loaf to Tobin and the other half to Kaeleb. After that, the food was eaten in short order by the hungry men.

When it looked as though most all of the food had been scoffed up, Emerik addressed the group somberly.

"Gentlemen," he began with a sigh. "I have never been one to speak at length since I prefer to be brief. We came here for the same reasons but with different motivations. Right now, I suggest that we all have the same plans and agendas. First and foremost, we must keep ourselves and everyone here safe. That also means keeping a watch on each other and ourselves. There is something about this place that…affects the mind and changes a man. So be careful. Second, we have a few issues that must be investigated. The creatures we burned and the blight in the forest." He could see some trying to remind him wordlessly about one that he apparently forgot.

"And, no, I have not forgotten about the ghouls. But I have not seen one yet either. We do not know what the changing creatures were nor do we know what is killing the land. Also," he said gravely, "There is something important about this place. Not only does silver obviously grow in the trees here but there is another less apparent reason why these people have not abandoned it in the face of doom."

He looked around at everyone while pouring another metal cup of wine. He continued, "When we discover what is so important about Silverwood then I think we will uncover what is happening here, why it is happening and who is doing it."

No one said a word but held a look of exhaustion on their faces. The road was long and now everyone's belly was full they all, Emerik included, became too sleepy to think.

"So with that I suggest we get some rest and begin in the morning." He finished the cup and placed it back on the table. "Tobin, there is a room upstairs that may to your liking if you would like to inspect it."

"Excellent, I could use a comfortable bed," he said standing.

"Dyrrany," Emerik addressed.

"Yes, sire?"

"If you could be as so good as to close and bar the gates to the garrison it would be most helpful."

"Of course sire," Dyrrany said before abruptly leaving.

Perry glanced at his teacher before he received the nod of approval to go and help Dyrrany.

"I will retire upstairs...men, sleep well tonight. Starting tomorrow, I do not think the coming days will be very restful."

With that, everyone went in their ways. Emerik and Tobin retired to the second floor while Smythe and Kaeleb returned to the barracks room and to the beds they had already picked out. Before completely retiring for the night each and seemed to have his own ritual before sleeping. Kaeleb had his prayers, Smythe had is meditation and reading and so on.

Most people wanted to sleep when it was quiet but there was very different. In the gloom of the night, Silverwood became forebodingly silent in a most surreal and eerie manner. No one slept soundly.

Ruelina had stopped to stare at her house. Technically, it was her parents' house but they had both died and did not actually "give" it to her. They never had the chance. She felt good being home but then also realized how much she missed her father and mother, becoming painfully aware of the cold empty feeling in her chest.

Feeling herself wanting to see her mother as she opened the door or hearing her father humming a tune as he strode through the forest brought a well of tears to her eyes. With a quivering chin Ruelina pushed open the door and pushed back her sob. There was no need to have locked the door. Under the circumstances, it had seemed like a useless notion.

The house was exactly as she had left it, a little dustier, but everything was here none the less. Walking inside, she dropped her backpack onto the floor and closed the door behind her with a heavy sigh of relief. Family or not, it was good to be home.

She made a fire to heat water for her bath. While that was warming she rummaged around for a bottle of wine. Although it was an apple-strawberry wine, it would do well. When her water was ready, she removed her dusty clothing and slipped her athletic frame into the steaming wooden tub. Taking long sips of her wine with her eyes closed, Ruelina tried to relax. She knew it would be a long time before she had that chance again.

Inside the Silverwood Garrison

Early the Next Morning

The night was not very restful. Visions of battles, sinister lurking shadows and distant unidentifiable wails, haunted their dreams. Also, for those who were not accustomed to such quiet, the utter silence was quite bothersome. Even when people needed "quiet time" to relax and get away from stresses, whether they walked in the forest or sat beside a calm lake, there were still sounds. One could still listen to the ambience of birds, insects or even the barely perceptible sounds of nature around them. In Silverwood, however, none of that existed any longer. Everything was dead quiet and the sound of deathly silence was unsettling to everyone.

There was also the unearthly permeation that caused discord within people. It seemed to agitate and rile even the most calm. Tempers rose quickly, patience was lost sooner and some people even acted as something other than their normal selves. Emerik and Kaeleb first recognized that in the form of a feeling, a preternatural discomfort in reaction to that environment. After the previous day, the others came to acknowledge it as well.

The first one to awaken that morning was Kaeleb. Dim sunlight crept into the large barracks room where he, Smythe and the squires slept. Rising as quietly as he could he eased off of the bed, knelt facing the rising sun and began to pray. That was his morning ritual. Before he did anything, prayers and thanks to Enki would be offered. Following that, he would meditate. That morning, he would focus on Silverwood itself and what was happening there.

While one holy man was in meditation the other was waking. The paladin opened his eyes and starred at the strange stone ceiling. He was not used to being here yet and he did not wish to become accustomed to sleeping there. Emerik wanted his stay in that bizarre hamlet to be as short as possible. He stood from his temporary bed, although it was quite comfortable, he did not find it was restful. With a sigh, he stretched and looked for the direction of the rising sun before kneeling down to pray. His heart was heavy yet full of purpose. The previous day he witnessed his lifelong friend behave as a complete stranger. It was something he never wanted to witness again. That morning, while talking to Enki, he asked if anyone were to be corrupted again that it be him. The prince felt guilty for bringing his friend here and wanted nothing more than to help this place and be off. Little did the paladin know that Enki had been listening and would soon answer his prayer.

A short while later, the others had awoke and begun going about their morning routines. The warriors of Paragon, namely everyone except Smythe, were soon practicing just as they did every day. Yes, even Kaeleb the priest was among those who wielded a blade. Although not as skilled as the knights and their squires beside him, the priest was still schooled at the capital and was considered competent. Smythe, on the other hand, bore a sword but his proficiency could not be compared to that of the others. To them he was an amateur at best and would be put in the same regard as a common foot soldier. But such was Paragon. To live and die by the sharpness of the sword was simply their way. However, Smythe viewed the world through a slightly different set of eyes and thought it best to live and die by his own wits and as quietly as possible.

Dyrrany and Perry sparred one another with sword and shield and spoke in low tones as they did. Both agreed that they needed to speak to their respective teachers about the events, specifically concerning the fiends. They found themselves quite distressed with the ineffectiveness of their weapons and morbidly fascinated as to why the lances produced smoldering wounds. Perry was the first to approach is mentor but was closely followed by Dyrrany as they walked.

"My lord," addressed Perry with a sharp bow.

"Rise," Tobin said calmly. "What do you need?"

"Sire," he said as he stood. "I am needing some guidance concerning my use with the shield and sword."

"Very well." Tobin noticed Dyrrany standing quietly by waiting for his chance to speak to Emerik. "Come then and tell me of your question…Emerik, seems like you have a question waiting for you as well." With that, Tobin and Perry walked to a striking target and spoke softly.

Emerik turned his attention to his squire and another jolt of guilt shot through him. He also brought poor Dyrrany into this mess as well.

"Yes, Dyrrany, how can I help you?"

"My lord," he awkwardly began. "I was wondering about strategy and tactics…" His expression told that he was greatly concerned about something greater he had yet to mention.

Emerik's heart sunk. He felt he knew what Dyrrany was distressed about.

"What tactics and strategy?" Emerik asked anyway.

"Well, milord…It is about yesterday…How can we fight an enemy that is not harmed by our weapons?"

Emerik looked at him in silence for a few moments. He was this squire's mentor and he was supposed to have a good answer to offer. But the paladin-prince had none. He took a deep breath and fully faced Dyrrany.

"I do not know yet," he said truthfully. "Unfortunately, I do not yet have many answers at this time. However, as you noticed, we defeated them. Every creature great and small has a weakness. For this new enemy we will treat it no different than any other. We will study them, learn what will work best to best them and smite every last one for Enki and Paragon."

Dyrrany merely nodded. Doubt still filled his face. Maybe as the prince or a paladin he could do it but not the squire. Emerik felt the weight on the young man's shoulders and sighed, patting him on the shoulder.

"Don't fret," said Emerik with strong conviction. "We will be fine. It will not be easy, I will say, but we will be fine nonetheless." He gave the man a tight smile. When Dyrrany returned it Emerik smiled broader and slapped him on the shoulder.

"Now," Emerik spoke with a deeper tone. "Let's get cleaned up before we stink everyone out of their breakfast."

"Yes, sire," he replied with a smile and trotted off. As soon as he left the room his grin instantly fell from his face. With a deep exhale he fell back against the wall and bit his lower lip. *Eala, we're in trouble.*

The paladin looked to see Perry sauntering by. He gave the prince a tight lipped nod and continued on his way. He looked as frightened as Dyrrany. Emerik frowned.

"He is very afraid," Tobin voice said behind him.

"Yes, Dyrrany the same." He turned to face his friend who also had a concerned look in his eyes.

"Me as well," he spoke honestly. "I do not know how to fight something I cannot hurt."

"We did hurt them and killed them if I remember."

"True," Tobin began. "But that was not from our swords it was from our lances."

Emerik again frowned.

"So...I am wondering, what is so different about our lances?"

Emerik shook his head. "I don't know...I really don't know."

Tobin glanced at the ground for a moment then tapped his friend on his arm.

"Let's try to get something to eat. Maybe we can think better on a full stomach."

After their practice that morning, they bathed and made their way the short distance to the inn where everyone in town was gathering for breakfast. The sun shone bright that morning and the air was cool. From outside it seemed that everyone was quite happy judging from the cheer in their voices. The group was confused.

"They cannot be that happy just for us," Smythe stated. It would have been nice to get that warm of a breakfast welcome but he felt that would have been too unrealistic judging from their profound under reaction the previous day.

"Agreed," the prince added.

"Well, I don't really care," Tobin said dispassionately. "I am too hungry right now."

The group continued and when they reached the front door they smelled it. Someone had cooked meat! Where did they get that from around here?

"Do I smell..." Emerik never finished.

"I thought Ruelina mentioned that there was none around here even before she left," Smythe recalled.

"So...then where did it come from?" questioned Kaeleb.

"I don't care, I'm hungry!" Tobin grumbled.

The prince opened the door and Matchok eagerly bound across the floor to meet them. Behind the jogging elf the group could see who was left in the town...and it was not many. The room was fantastically decorated with flowing lines of symmetry and blended texture carvings that anyone would expect from elven design. These however, did not embrace the beauty that could be found in contrasting colors but utilized earthier tones and was contrasted by bright hues of the same yellows, reds, oranges, blues and whites that one would see in a meadow of wild flowers. Having the contrasting colors in minimal display as an occasional rendering produced a beautiful motif. It would have been more beautiful if the colors here were not mysteriously subdued.

As they glanced around Smythe briefly eyed one of the carvings the framed the inside of the door. At first it seemed quite intricately carved. As he neared it however he realized he did not understand how elaborate it truly was. It was thoughtfully carved in layers upon layers so that the longer one looked upon it the more detail one would see. It was quite amazing. Knowing he did not have much time to study this he cast his gaze around the room and noticed that everything was made this way, the walls, the frames around the windows and doors, the tables, chairs, at a quick glance it seemed almost superficially decorated…until you looked closer. Smythe was awed.

Everyone else, Smythe not being discounted from this, was awestruck by the smell of fresh cooked meat. It was something that was missing from dinner the previous evening and, as they were told, was also something not to be found around here now. There, however, despite what had met their ears, were two decent sized deer that had been cooked and were being enjoyed by the remaining villagers. Everyone was smiling except the group of newcomers who either had their mouths agape or dumbstruck looks.

"Welcome, my lords! Welcome!" Matchok sounded jovial.

"Thank you," was all Emerik managed to say before the plump elf continued.

"Please, come this way! We have a table already waiting for you!" He motioned toward their seats with a warm smile and an outstretched arm. Ruelina was already seated there.

"Come! They're here," he said to one of the young elf girls the group remembered from the previous night. She was the one carrying the mushroom soup. "Get them some food."

He then turned back to the group who were shuffling to seat themselves. My lords in heaven help me, Matchok thought. What will become of us now? He then approached the table where he was seated and was eating and sat down. It just so happed, quite purposefully, that all of them were seated together. Matchok and Ruelina included.

The prince was about to speak to Matchok when he overheard the irritated voice of a man from the line of people waiting to get food. When he looked over, he saw a tall and darkly dressed figure at the front of the line slapping food onto his plate and a younger elf looking at him.

"Hey, there's a line you know?" the boy spoke it with the message get to the back of the line.

"Yeah, I know," the figure replied without looking at him.

"Well, this is not the end of it, its back there." The boy pointed behind the last person in line and was slightly more irritated.

"Yeah, I know," the figure repeated slower and turned back and ignored the boy.

He finished putting food onto his plate and walked over to an empty table against the wall but did not sit. He tried to eat while standing. When he took a bite his head jerked back and his stomach churned. I will never get used to the food here. The two knights watched as the dark figure slowly choked down his food. They thought he would vomit at any time.

Rude ungrateful bastard, Tobin thought. These people took the time to cook a nice meal and you act like they could have done better? Insolent prick.

Just then, their plates of food had arrived all six hungrily leaned in over their meals and began to devour them. The prince, not wanting to be rude, thanked the girl and asked her name. She was shocked after hearing rumors that royals cared little for servants and only spoke to them if there was a problem. She could not think of anything that she had done wrong. Tobin still simmered about the dark figure after tasting the food and thought it had a good taste.

"I...I am...Ielenia," stammered the girl.

"Please," the prince reassured her. "Relax, I am merely trying to get to know everyone here."

Everyone at the table, Ielenia included, all looked to him at once. That was not common princely behavior since most were too pretentious to illicit any conversations with a commoner. Emerik was showing how different he was time and again. The "People's Prince" was at it again. Tobin shifted his glance back to the dark figure that had finally sat down but had quit trying to eat. The man seemed to be deep in thought and the knight had already decided he did not like the man.

Damn it, I am too late. She has already gone and this place is going to hell. The shadowy man thought to himself. It is even beginning to smell like it. The odor that was imperceptible to everyone else was making him nauseated and grumpy. He did not like hell and no plans of ever going back. His internal monologue was interrupted when he heard one of the armored men talking about him.

"Who is that?" Tobin pointed to the solitary brooding figure.

"Oh, that is Thelial," Ruelina answered calmly.

"So, he has been here before?" asked Smythe.

"Yes," Ruelina said while trying to remember. "He comes and visits from time to time."

"You know him, then?" inquired Emerik.

"No," she answered thoughtfully. "I didn't really ever speak to him."

"Oh?" Tobin piped up. "Who was it he came to see then?"

"Um…I think he spent more of his time at the library and the temple." Ruelina was trying to figure out what all this had to do with saving her home but was coming up short on any justification. Thelial, after all, looked nothing like a ghoul. "When I saw him here, that is," she quickly added. Hopefully they would concern themselves with more important things…like what was killing her home.

Unfortunately, that small comment only served to raise their suspicions. The figure was a dark brooding stranger who snuck into town for some furtive or clandestine dealings, only to vanish again like the wind. He was a perfect suspect. For what, the two knights did not know, but they made him a suspect anyway. Smythe, on the other hand, being accustomed to such modes of operation, did not pay him much attention as far as considering him part of the troubles. The man was rather strange but then when he thought about it, all of them in this little hamlet were odd in one way or another.

Apparently having enough of his nauseated contemplation time, Thelial stood and made his way for the door. The bad part of that was he had to [ass quite close to the table where the knights sat and studied him.

"You there," Tobin bellowed. "What is your business here?" Matchok was mortified.

"None of yours," answered Thelial quite dispassionately.

"Excuse me," Emerik began with a different tactic yet one which still did not invite any forms of noncompliance. "I am Prince Emerik Montigan and this is Sir Tobin Drathmoore. We are from Paragon City and these others with us are official investigators from the Council."

"Well," Thelial glanced at everyone. "I am happy for you..." He started to turn to leave when Tobin's rather unsatisfied voice stopped him.

"We want an answer..." Tobin commanded.

"We are here officially," added Emerik.

"You are doing what then," Thelial remarked. "Investigating?"

"Yes," Emerik stated firmly.

"Well then I wish you luck with that," again he turned to go.

"What are you doing here in this town?" Tobin was about to boil over.

Thelial looked to him like a piece of stone. No one was going to intimidate him into answering anything he did not want.

"It would help us if we knew," Smythe joined in. "We are just trying to be thorough." Add some sugar when you want something.

Thelial merely studied their faces for a moment before considering all of them amateurs. Suddenly they seemed more pathetic and infantile than capable.

"I am here to deliver a message," Thelial told them

"A message for whom, may I ask?" Smythe continued.

"A message for Naia."

"What is the message?" Tobin was as subtle and graceful as a mallet. Smythe closed his eyes knowing he just ended the conversation and he may never know.

"Tell me," Thelial began. "Are you the woman called Naia?"

"No, of course not!" Tobin sounded insulted. Me, a woman? Ha!

"Then my message is not for you..." Thelial glared at everyone. "...any of you." He abruptly turned and left he inn, leaving the people at the table to sit and stare at one another for a time. Ruelina smirked and sipped her tea. She did not ever really speak to him much but she already wished she had. He was likeable.

"Forgive him, my lords," Matchok spoke respectfully. "He has not eaten in three days."

"Bah!" Tobin stood. "If I had my way it would be much longer before he would eat again, disrespectful cur!" He spat and walked over to inspect the table of food to see if there was anything else he wanted. Besides, that Thelial character made him restless and edgy. Who did that filthy peasant think he was, anyway? Talking to a noble like that was just plain…deserving of a whip.

Matchok watched as Tobin walked away and leaned in to Emerik.

"Don't be too hard on him, sire," he still spoke of Thelial. "He brought the two deer here for us."

Emerik looked puzzled.

"But," he glanced to Ruelina. "I was told there was no game here for over a day's travel."

"That, my lord, is true."

"Then…where is his horse or wagon?" questioned Emerik.

"He does not have any," Ruelina stated. "Never did."

The prince looked to her then back to Matchok.

"Then how did he get them here?" In his mind, Emerik dared them to say "magic".

"Well, milord," Matchok thought of how to put this as simply as he could. "He carried them."

"What?" The prince's mouth dropped.

"Yes," Matchok nodded. "He carried the two for a day."

Emerik sat in silence.

Outside, Thelial calmly strode toward the north and walked into part of the forest that was still green, following a wagon path that had been used for many years. It was silent here, just as everything else was. He continued inward until he felt no one could casually spot him before bending down to retrieve a dried leaf from the ground. He peered at it, studying its brown textured surface before bringing it to his nose to smell it. There were so many things normal people missed in their everyday lives, including the smalls of dried leaves.

He put the leaf next to ear and crumpled it while listening to its crinkle. Placing the roll carefully back down onto the ground he looked around as if searching for some hidden detail that was directly before him, somewhere tacked to a tree. He listened. He looked. He smelled. He touched.

This place was damned and he knew it. It was in the air and in the ground, something vile and malevolent. It was ancient, angry, cold and hungry. Worse than that, Thelial noticed it had the feel of being…familiar. He frowned darkly.

Standing, he made his way farther north along the wagon trail and thought about the knights from Paragon. Poor bastards, they were sent here under equipped and uninformed about their enemy. How were they supposed to "investigate" things they were not taught about? Someone must not like them, he realized. This was as close as sending someone to their death as you could get without hiring the ambush yourself. Sending people with no real magic power to fight a supernatural enemy as dark as this? *Stupid humans.*

Then, he reached it, the end of the trail. Here, just short of a creek bed that cradled a small stream that ran eastward and into the decaying lands, was the reserve well that Silverwood was using for water. Looking at the packed dirt he could see this trail was more used in the recent days. Again, he glanced around the silent forest before walking straight toward the well itself. He peered down into the darkness of the short square stone wall. Shocked, he tried to look closer by leaning over the edge.

Abruptly he righted himself and glanced around hurriedly. *Bastards! Where is it?* He began to search in a wider circle and patted his breast pocket in his jacket. Good that the vial was still there. His head shifted from side to side, looking, searching. *Where is it?*

Finally, just a few yards away, he saw the crumbling stone ruins of some ancient building. The remnant of the wall, barely rising to his shoulders, was shadowed and moss covered from the ages of being out in the weather. What ever happened to the building that was once here, had long been forgotten. But that did not matter to him. Thelial rounded the corner of the wall and began searching the ground.

He began to thump the soil with his closed fist. *Thud. Thud.* Again, he began to search in a broadening circle. *Thud. Thud. Thud.*

Thunk. He stopped. That sounded like wood. *Thunk*. He struck it again. Yes, wood with empty space under it.

Thelial's dark face slowly produced a sinister grin. *Stupid Humans.*

Inside the inn, the group learned about the town and its history a bit more. Asking of the whereabouts concerning some of the villagers, the investigators began to form a plan of how and where they would begin. They learned that Barbas and Ineas, both were Ruelina's teachers and both and vanished just a few weeks before. Barbas, who they found out was a rather odd druid who decided to reside inside of the town, went out into the dead land to discover the cause and report back when he had found something. That was over one moon ago. When he did not return, Ineas went looking for him and was not heard from again. Ineas, Silverwood's last ranger, departed a few weeks before.

There was only one general store in town and its proprietors were Rannon and his wife Clarissa, both of whom they had met the day before. Once or twice a month, the two would depart for Boregar for supplies and then quickly return filled with complaints of the noisy city and how crowded it was. The existence of this shop rather perplexed Smythe. With no form of organized labor or established economy in Silverwood, he wondered where the gold had come from to purchase anything. Rather than ask directly he raised an oblique question concerning harvesting the silver from the trees for economic gain. This idea was stomped on quicker than if he suggested to burn down the temple and use the remains for a small arena.

"No!" almost everyone nearly shouted at once. "The silver is never to be taken from this land!"

"Why is that?" He did not understand.

"Because! These trees are sacred and this place serves to protect it!"

While that gave a reason for the existence of Silverwood out here it still posed a few other questions that Smythe decided to hold for another time. One obvious question was: So, as guardians of this forest, what are you all doing while it is dying? But he thought such a question would only serve to insult and not aid anything at the moment. What he did manage to ask seemed to stun everyone.

"So…what is so sacred about Silverwood?"

"Did you notice the trees have silver in them?" The tone suggested his capacity for extreme stupidity.

"Of course. It is quite beautiful as well." Smythe calmly said without taking their bait to look like a fool. He was used to playing these games and they were not.

"Yes, and that was made by a goddess herself. She walked here and thought this land was beautiful. So now you have the silver forest and Silverwood."

That simplistic explanation seemed flawed to the arcane investigator. But rather than directly confront the issue he came at them sideways and with a smile.

"So, who were the first to settle here?"

"Oh, that would be the town founders," Matchok stated with rock solid confidence.

"The town elders?"

"Goodness no," the mayor replied. "We elves live for a long time but not that long. Silverwood was made just after the Great War. None of us are over four hundred years old. No elf lives that long."

"Ah, yes." Smythe nodded his head and placed that remark into his mental list of things to look into later.

They also learned about the inn and it was managed by another aging elf named Miklosh with the help of his four daughters, Ielenia, Anituna, Miaree and Xelozia. Ielenia had introduced herself earlier and the others they had seen wandering around completing their various chores. The innkeeper's wife, Silaqui, a sweet grandmotherly type elven woman had sadly passed away quietly in her sleep some years ago.

Another oddity was the library. This small hamlet actually had a functioning library of some decent note. The keeper was one of the village elders by the name of Jotham. His responsibilities were gradually taken over during the preceding years by his daughter Maura because of his failing health. Old age claims everyone unless someone dies young. Maura Ilphunodel, or "Moon Blossom" as it would be called in Common. Everyone thought it was a joke or an exaggerated mistranslation. No one could possibly be called "moon blossom".

After collecting their news, the group went about digging, so to speak, around the hamlet to uncover what they could. The two knights, followed closely by their squires and Kaeleb were escorted by Ruelina who also served as their guide and one to fill in missing pieces of information. Smythe wandered in a different direction.

The main group headed straight to Barbas' home at the edge of the woods. All began to slow their pace as they neared the vast twisted skeletons that writhed in frozen mockery of nature. The closer they drew to the dead forest the more eerie the sight became. As far as they could see tarnished frames from the dead trees towered before them. It seemed to be an endless landscape, crowded with dark misshapen scarecrows, that was keeping all life and sanity at bay. What worsened the scene was the darkened cemetery of Silverwood that dominated the foreground just inside what was a tree line. Death and more death.

"By the gods!" Dyrrany exclaimed. This looks like hell should look.

"What the hells is this devilry?" spat Tobin.

The priest and paladin could only stand and gawk as they were rendered wordless. Emerik blinked in hopes that this nightmarish countryside would vanish. Sadly, it did not. He tore his eyes from the grotesque to see, there, where the woods were quite dead, another peculiar detail that none of them could yet understand.

"How can this be?" Emerik asked agape.

"I don't know," admitted Ruelina.

"It looks like there is…a…a wall. An invisible wall of death that is moving through the town." While some part of the priest was disturbed at the notion, something else inside him had to say it to get the words out. Perhaps in hopes of lessening the tension from the mental strain of trying to understand what he looked at as it struggled with his innate sense of impending doom telling him to run as fast as possible back to the safety of Paragon City. Kaeleb thought if he lost control that he would crumble into a quivering mass of mental and spiritual anguish.

There was a distinct line that was slowly passing through the forest and moving westward. Everything to the east of the invisible line was dead, not dying but already decaying dead. To the east of the barrier everything was still green. Even at the points where the "line" was still passing through a tree, half of it was dead while the other half remained seemingly alive. Although alive, it would not be for much longer.

Emerik had moved closer to the absent druid's humble shack of a home to look at its wooden frame and siding. None of the lumber used contained any amount of silver. However, what struck him the most was the wood itself.

"Come here and see this," he said more to Tobin but everyone responded and gathered to see what it was. The paladin was pointing to the wood and looking at where the "wall" was that Kaeleb had noticed.

Tobin looked over his friend's shoulder.

"Woah, how can that happen?" he asked with unsettled bewilderment.

"I do not know," the paladin admitted. "But it seems like the wood in the house is rotting with everything else."

"Yes," Kaeleb added as he stepped back to look at the whole structure at once. "Part of the house is crumbling and the other part is not. It is in the same progression as the rest of the forest." He spoke while moving and he unwittingly crossed over the "line" he noticed and into the dead land. Suddenly the priest felt alone, isolated and cold. He slowly looked around not understanding what had just happened. The hair on his arms and neck began to rise as he felt he was being leered at with extreme hatred by some unseen eyes. Quickly he moved toward everyone else while whirling around to confront his invisible adversary. He saw none.

The rest of the group became wide eyed and the knights began glancing for an opponent to cut down but could see none. They could only hear the panting breath of their comrade.

"What is it, man?" The paladin demanded.

"Wha...the...there is something here," stammered Kaeleb. He could swear that if he lingered where he stood a moment ago that something would have hissed at him.

"Where?" Tobin asked while still looking at the air. "I see nothing!"

"It was a feeling...something...knows, it thinks..."

"Quit talking nonsense and spit it out!" spat Tobin.

Emerik felt he understood and cautiously walked over to the border between living and dead earth. He stood at the edge and then knelt down as everyone else loomed behind him. Slowly, the paladin took off his glove and placed his open hand onto the ground. After a moment, he quickly retracted it as if he had placed in hot water and immediately stood, putting his glove back over his shaking hand.

"He's right," Emerik announced. "There is something evil here and it has a conscious."

"What?" Tobin asked. Why did everyone stop taking in plain language?

"It thinks," the paladin said to his friend. "It is evil, it thinks and it reacts."

"Told you," Ruelina quipped. "But nooo, no one wants to believe me."

Tobin flatly ignored her.

"What are you saying? What do you mean "it thinks and reacts"? I don't understand." Tobin's words came out like a waterfall.

"I felt it," Emerik breathed. "I felt it and it felt me." He paused for a moment to say this as plainly as he cold without causing any of them to flee in panic. "It knows we are here and it knows what I am. It can…feel that I am a paladin and that he is a priest." He stopped with that. Emerik did not wish to add, it knows and does not care. It is not afraid of us.

The group stood in silence for a moment as the darker parts of the implications began to sink into their skulls with a chilling shiver.

"Let's continue and see what we came to see." The paladin did not want to be standing out here while something lurked in the twisted skeletal field that lay just a chillingly few yards away.

When Ruelina knocked on the solid wooden door there was no answer. Everyone stood and stared at her like she had just lost her mind and forgot that no one was at home since Barbas had not been seen for over a month. Feeling they were looking at her she looked back at them.

"What?" she asked. "You never know." He could have come back that morning and no one would have known. She did not want to be rude.

Pushing the door open it groaned and the hinges squeaked making an odd reverberating chord that echoed in the lifeless abode. As the dim light came into the room Ruelina stood stunned. The home was ransacked. Various articles from cabinets, drawers and chests littered the floor while dust illuminated by the sunlight hung lazily in the air.

"What the hell?" She slowly stepped in as if timidly avoiding disturbing something.

The knights were next, followed by Smythe, Kaeleb and the squires. None of them were expecting that.

"Does this always happen when someone leaves their home?" scorned Tobin.

Ruelina merely shat him a glare and did not answer.

"I wonder what they were looking for." Kaeleb posed.

"Hard to say," Emerik noted. "It would be almost impossible to tell."

Smythe's experienced eyes told him a slightly different story of the events. He looked at the layers of tossed articles and a pattern of movement began to form in his mind. He could imagine someone as they moved around the home. Where they went first then next and then next all became clear. Whoever they were Smythe had quickly determined they were sloppy and rushed while having no idea where to look.

"They left a mess," Tobin stated the obvious. "They covered their tracks well."

"Beg pardon, sire," Smythe began. "But no, they did not."

"What?" the knight asked.

"They did not cover their tracks well," began Smythe. "In fact, they did not even try to cover them. This was the work of a sloppy amateur at best."

"You said 'a'. Do you mean just one?" Kaeleb questioned.

"Yes, just one. He was in a hurry, probably nervous, and did not know where or how to look for whatever it was that he wanted." He walked over to the fireplace at the rear of the room.

"How do you know this?" Tobin demanded to know.

"That, sire, is my job." He spoke without turning his head to him. Smythe meant to disrespect, he was fixed in concentration and deeply focused. His mind had something active to do now. Probing in the fireplace he smelled the faint odor of fresh ash. With no surprise he discovered the charred remains of a book. The other papers and articles were destroyed by the fire.

"Ah ha," uttered Smythe.

"What is it?" asked Emerik as the crossed the room to see what Smythe had.

"This..." He began. "This is what the person was here for. They were not looking to thieve or to burgle. They were here to conceal."

"Conceal what?" The prince became most curious now.

"Conceal a crime of some kind." Gingerly he opened the burnt volume.

"What crime?" To the paladin this had the potential to become quite a quagmire of mystification.

A thin smile crept across his face as he identified the nature of the book. Leafing through it more quickly he noted from the partial spine that it was a diary of some kind and that certain specific pages had been torn before it was set ablaze. Smythe ventured to guess that the ashes in the fireplace were the pages in question.

"I do not know exactly what yet, but...here are the remains of Barbas' journal."

Smythe handed the book to Emerik who took it and opened it to a random page.

"We will need to go through this and see if there is any useful information..." the prince strongly suggested. It sounded like a logical course of action however, Smythe had a differing opinion.

"No, milord, I do not think that will be of any value."

"Why not?"

"Because, milord, if you look carefully you will notice that some pages are missing." Emerik looked at the book and noticed what Smythe had just told him. "And, if you look in the fireplace behind me, you will se the ashes of those pages. Someone came here to hide what they were doing or to conceal something Barbas discovered. That means someone who is part of this is human or elf and that they feel fear."

"Fear?" Perry asked.

"Yes, indeed," Smythe turned to him and spoke. "They are afraid of being discovered. Which also implies they fear punishment or some still feel that what they are doing is wrong...And that is a good sign."

"Why?" Perry was suddenly full of questions.

"Because," he explained. "If they are discovered and face punishment it may be quite severe and knowing that what they are doing is hurting others it could be bothering them. Because of that, we can be a little confident that they will make more mistakes that will lead to their capture."

"I don't understand," Perry continued. "Why is that?"

"When someone does something they feel is not right, however little that may be, they can do things which will lead to them being discovered…" Smythe could tell that what he just said was not understood by most everyone in the room. "Take for example someone who is having an affair in their marriage but knows it is wrong- feels it is wrong. They will do or say things that will subtly let their spouse know they are unfaithful even if they are not aware they are doing it. It's the same with this person here. They could have stayed to ensure all of the book was burnt but did not. At some point they could have guessed that, in a small place like this, someone would come into the missing person's home to investigate. I would venture to guess that this villain may have had something to do with Barbas' disappearance as well as some of the others as well."

"Wait, you are going too fast," Ruelina said shaking her head and raising a hand for him to stop. "He had something to do with Barbas vanishing? And the others? Is this person responsible for the forest?"

Smythe chuckled.

"Now it is you who is going too fast. There was something that Barbas had written about which this person did not want to be discovered. It would be convenient for anyone who finds out the same thing to "vanish" as well as destroying anything that would lead to the discovery. Concerning the forest, I do not know about that yet. We would have to find the source, a central or starting point for the blight in order to learn more."

Everyone fell silent for a few moments as is digesting what Smythe had just told them.

"So who do you think this person is?" Emerik asked.

Smythe thought for a moment before answering. Careful wording was always prudent. "Who they are, I cannot yet say. I do, however, have a good idea of where they are."

"Where is that?" asked Tobin. He needed a direction to point his sword.

"They are here in Silverwood."

"What?" Ruelina spoke as if she had just been slapped in the face.

"How can you be certain?" Emerik asked. If Smythe proved correct then he would believe this man to be the very best sleuth on the planet.

"Well," Smythe's lips thinned and pursed for a moment. "Ineas went into the forest a few weeks after Barbas, correct?"

"Yes," answered Ruelina. "He went to look for him."

"Good," Smythe spoke with a confident nod. "Then if I am correct, Ineas' home will be in the same condition. And, if we discover any diary or journal, it also will have pages missing and be in the fireplace…Most criminals work in patterns. When you know their pattern they are easier to predict."

"Then let us be off to Ineas' place," Emerik commanded. "No sense in searching a place already searched."

At that, they all exited the modest home and made their way to the dwelling of Ineas. The walk was not long since the home was quite close but it was closer to rest of town than where they had just come. The wall of blight had not yet reached there.

At Ineas' home, it was just as silent as the rest of Silverwood and the home felt empty. Upon reaching the door, Ruelina did not knock this time. She just pushed open the door and peered inside. Here, the trees formed more of a canopy that could not afford the same illumination as Barbas' home had. However, despite the gloom of the shadows, the place inside could be seen. Smythe proved correct. The home was in shambles in the exact same manner as the other home.

Smythe pushed past everyone and made straight for the fireplace.

"Is it the same?" Emerik asked as he still glanced around at the disorder.

The investigator stood while brushing his hands free from ashes.

"There was nothing left of it," he said with a frown. "It also seems there were other things in there as well. Something made of wood maybe but there is too little of it left to identify." He looked around this place in the same manner as he did at the other home. He discerned layers of clutter and another pattern of movement. It was much the same as before.

"What do you see?" Perry asked.

"Hum?" Smythe looked up at Perry. "Oh, well, it seems they were in less of a hurry here but not quite as careless. I am beginning to think they believed no one would be coming here to look. Perhaps they thought there would be no one here to do so. But..."

"But what?" asked Kaeleb.

"Well, the other place is in much more disarray then here."

"Why do you think that is?" Kaeleb responded with another question.

"Well...maybe because he started here first then found he was running out of time or was almost discovered while in the Barbas' home." Smythe was still thinking as he spoke. He was not yet convinced of that theory.

"He?"

"What?" Smythe looked around. He did not know who just spoke to him or what they said.

"He," Emerik repeated. "You said "he was running out of time". How do you know it is a 'he' and not a 'she'?"

"Just a feeling," Smythe was guessing. "Maybe because I feel a woman searching a place would be a bit more careful however...that is more a bias opinion than an educated one. I merely said 'he' without consideration and not as an identifying word."

Emerik nodded.

"I noticed gravestones nearby...if there is nothing more to do here I would like to go and inspect them," Smythe commented.

"Why do you want to go poking around in a cemetery?" Tobin was a bit concerned at such an odd request considering their surroundings.

"She said there were ghouls here," Smythe motioned to Ruelina.

"That's right," she added. Finally maybe someone was listening.

"Well, I would like to go there. I hear ghouls eat dead things so it seems like a good place to start looking for them." He turned to go but the threatening tone in Emerik's voice stopped him.

"What else do you know about ghouls?"

Smythe paused and looked back to Emerik.

"I know they are not supposed to exit."

As they neared the cemetery with Smythe in the lead they felt a pull from deep within themselves that told them al to leave. Normally, people ran in at the premonition of danger, but they seemed to walk straight into it with complete disregard for their intuitive warning.

The cemetery was oddly circular and at its center stood a monolithic tree. This one also was quite dead but it was the largest tree in the forest. Even from that distance, the group guessed it would take four men to encircle it. Also, most cemeteries were aligned in rows. The one in Silverwood was not and this one mostly seemed to use slabs rather than head stones. The carvings were ancient and weather worn. The lettering and other identifying marks were quite difficult to discern. It was as if the blight also took life from the stones as well, causing them to decompose.

With a deep breath Emerik stepped over the invisible line and into the dead lands while Kaeleb stood at the edge and watched him. The paladin shuddered but pressed onward, grinding his teeth and making his hands into fists. Whatever was happening to him he did not say nor was he daunted. With that encouragement, the priest closed his eyes in a mental prayer to Enki and stepped in. Instantly, images flashed in his mind. Blood, screams, moans of the dead and writhing shadows. He became nauseated. Swallowing hard, he trotted to walk closer to Emerik.

Slowly they passed between the crumbling stones. Usually graves were quiet but this one was different. There seemed to be something about the land, something drawing everything downward. The sun passed behind a group of clouds lazily making their way across the sky. When the light dimmed the shadows became so very pronounced that the group suspected they would spring to life and attack them. Most everyone gasped and a shiver moved though everyone at once. For a moment no one dared even move.

"Let's be done with this," Emerik spoke through clenched teeth.

"Right," agreed Kaeleb.

They carefully walked to the gigantic tree in the center of the cemetery. This tree, different from the others, gave them a profound feeling of injustice or wrongness that it was dead. It was as if something unique and significant had been callously murdered and they stood gawking at its carcass. Somehow, everyone felt angered by this site but could not explain why. Even the insensitive knight Tobin felt iniquitousness of it.

"Something's going to pay for this," was all that the knight managed to utter.

Ruelina had not stepped onto this soil since she had left so many months ago. Just then, she began to grasp the seriousness of what was happening. It was something much greater than the land and trees dying. Kneeling down, she touched the earth. It felt cold like a corpse. It had no life. She fought back the tears of anger and sorrow that formed behind her eyes. As she glanced toward the horizon she felt the cold heart of death. East…it is in the east.

"What is this?" Smythe's voice shot out and startled everyone. They looked to him expecting to see something unearthly or grotesque. Instead, he stood before a statue and stared at it. Slowly everyone else began to gather around him and it.

"It is statue," informed Tobin.

Smythe just looked at him.

"That sounds like something I would say," admitted Smythe. *Huh, well he's a smart ass also.*

"It's a grave statue," Ruelina spoke from behind them as she stood and walked over.

"For who?" The prince asked.

"Lady Gajana."

Everyone stopped and stared at her.

"What?" Smythe did not believe what he just heard. Somehow his ears deceived him and he thought she said Lady Gajana.

"This is the grave of Lady Gajana," repeated Ruelina. *Are they deaf as well as thick skulled? Stupid humans.*

"The Lady Gajana?" Emerik asked in disbelief. Inside, the unnerving feeling that he was being stared at by unseen eyes made him quite uncomfortable.

"I don't know of any other, do you?" Yes, they were thick. *Stupid H…*

"I thought she was buried somewhere else," Tobin fought to recall where that place was but could not.

"Ilranik," Smythe volunteered. "The capital city of Rokal."

"Well," Ruelina pushed through them to stand beside the sculpture. "As you can see, She is here."

Their eyes all at once shifted to the effigy. It was a life sized stone carving of a standing woman with partially folded wings, closely resembling an angel, holding a sword pointed to the ground with her head dropped in sorrow. The figure's carved hair, at a quick glance, looked like a hood that blended with her robes. The details were incredible. Even with the decomposing stone, they could tell the craftsmanship was astounding.

Smythe saw the base of the statue and quickly knelt down to get a closer look. There, around the bottom, were two lines of inscriptions. Both were in different, yet quite ancient, scripts. Smythe instantly recognized them. The top line was in a form of ancient elven called Quyndrian and mostly it was only used for religious or arcane writings. There, however, at the base of the statue, the alphabet seemed to have been used a letter replacement for Common and read:

Here IS Gajana chosen EN THE Eyes Of Anu

Smythe at first thought he read it incorrectly however, even with its misplaced capitals and misspellings, it was there.

The second script put a bead of sweat on his forehead. This language, Awatium, was only used by his order and no one outside the society was supposed to know of it. But there it was. Again, it seemed a letter for letter replacement for common was used. This line of text read:

May Heaven'S Light Rise OVER you as
Thou have dONe For us

His blood drained from his face. How can someone know this? Better yet, how can someone know the alphabet and still get it wrong?

"Something wrong?" Kaeleb asked him, feeling uncomfortable himself in this unholy place.

"What?" He looked up trying to think quickly. "Ah, no." He looked back down to the carvings to stall for time. "I was just looking at...at this old elven writing here."

"Do you know what it says?" Emerik asked him.

"Ah, yes I do. It reads 'Here Lies Gajana, chosen in the eyes of Anu' right here." He pointed and hoped no one else noticed the other language and the bead of sweat that now dripped from his brow. Was there someone else from the Brotherhood here in Silverwood?

"See?" Ruelina quipped. "Like I said, this is Gajana's grave."

"Well, it is an amazing looking statue," Tobin stated.

"Yes, too bad it is now inside of a dying forest," said Emerik.

"But we can do something about that part, right?" Ruelina felt that she had to keep reminding them or they would forget. "Remember? Dying Forest? Ghouls?"

"Yes, but we must look around more to get a good idea of what is happening here," explained Smythe. He would support any distraction away from this statue and would return to it at a later time. He looked up at the sky pretending to search for the sun.

"What time is it?" Emerik asked.

"Looks to be about…just after noon time now," Ruelina answered.

"Very well," the prince began. "Let us leave here and get something to eat. Besides, after that I want to look in on Clarissa to see how she is faring." He turned to walk away. That nagging feeling of something that did not like his presence there did not ever quiet.

Ruelina was again shocked that he even cared and followed everyone out of the forest cemetery. She had hoped they would help them soon but she began to guess that there were too many things which they did not know. Those were things she grew up learning and it would be unrealistic of her to expect them to know all of that in one day. A shiver crept up her spine as she walked. She felt something staring at her, something unseen. It whispered.

Save me…

Quickly she whirled around with a start and a shout escaped her throat. Ruelina rapidly scanned her area but saw nothing. The voice sounded wet and like it was right beside her ear. Everyone else had stopped and turned as well, reacting to Ruelina's yell.

"What is it?" Kaeleb asked. He was the closest one to her and already was grasping the hilt of his sword.

"I…I don't…nothing. It is nothing. I thought I heard something." Turning back, she walked quickly away from the dying forest and did not want to tell them she heard a voice since disbelief seemed so popular among them. "This place is just too creepy and I am going."

Without another word the group turned and lumbered to the inn for food. Not that any of them were particularly hungry but an empty inn was far better than the chilling shadows of an unnaturally dying forest. Behind them, and quite unnoticed, a single shadow against a dead tree moved.

When they reached the inn, most of the food for lunch was already eaten. Matchok and some others had saved some of the food for them, knowing they would be hungry at some point. They were not wrong. The group found that as they departed the dead forest they were indeed ravenous.

While eating, Emerik had asked about the water supply and food. He was informed that the well inside of town was poisoned and they had not discovered it until some of the animals and townsfolk had perished. That was a few weeks ago. Tobin immediately inquired if anyone had seen Thelial at the village around that time but Matchok admitted that no one had mentioned him being there. Tobin frowned.

When asked about where their water was coming from, the plump elf told them they had to make regular trips to another well beside a stream to the north. Tobin inquired as to its more specific location and was told all anyone had to do was follow the wagon trail to the north and that it would lead directly to the well. Being that it was the only place the trail lead to it should be quite easy to find.

The group thanked their hosts after finishing their meal and stood to leave. Everyone decided to go visit Clarissa and further tour the town, except for Smythe. He mentioned he wanted to take a closer look at some of the other buildings in the village and left on his own.

Quite craftily, utilizing the focus on the main group, Smythe skillfully slipped away between buildings and stood nonchalantly amongst some trees there. He watched as the knights, their squires and Kaeleb, all escorted by Ruelina, made their way northward to visit Clarissa. Satisfied that they had departed he decided to eye Matchok for a moment. He watched the plump elf turn and walk around the inn. Smythe remembered that his home lay in the general direction and did not take further interest. He slowly took a step backward and bumped into a tree. Fearing he would be punctured by silver he quickly turned. Smythe only found a thin specimen, older than a sapling yet younger than the other trees here. His head cocked to one side and he reached up a plucked a leaf from its branch. The leaf was green and soft. There was no silver in it. What the hells?

He looked around the village at the other trees between the buildings and noticed something quite peculiar. None of the trees within the village perimeter seemed to have any silver. How bizarre. So that meant there was a circle of silver trees that grew around Silverwood but not in Silverwood. What did that mean? He added that to his list of things to look into at a later time. Right then, he wanted to see inside Naia's home.

He easily reached the door of the modest house. It was a single story dwelling that used stone for its foundation. How strange. They were many miles away from any mountains but here was stone, enough stone to build a temple, a garrison and part of her home. This place was very strange indeed.

Pushing on the door, he found it to be locked. Hum...Barbas and Ineas did not lock their doors but Naia did. Was there a thief about that no one else knew about? Did she not her place ransacked? No matter, he was getting in anyway.

With an examination of the lock he observed it was a simple lock. Nothing intricate or even imaginative, it was just an uncomplicated warded lock. Retrieving his picks from his hidden pocket, Smythe went to work on the catch and in short time he heard the click of it opening. He briefly worried that this was far too easy, but dismissed that notion and slipped inside. The door was closed quietly behind him.

He paused and blinked for a moment before making his way farther into the home. It was quite neat and tidy. Did she have a maid that was keeping this place in order while she was away? There was very little dust and everything was neatly arranged in a proper place. That was a stark contrast to the two other places he had been to that morning. Even the dust was thick in the air but not here.

Taking a closer look at the furniture and decor in the home he wanted to know as much about her as he could glean from the articles she left behind. There was a cabinet of obvious elven design however it did not resemble the wood elf craftsmanship he noted earlier. He had seen this type before from the high elves of Ib.

Looking down, he found himself standing on an ornate rug from Pnath. She gets around as much as I do.

Stepping into the living room he was stunned. In a completely different motif, the room was filled with Sydathrian furniture, a rug, rosewood carvings and even two masterful pieces of calligraphy that were framed in silk brocade and hung on the wall. She travels and is very wealthy. How did she find the time to collect all those things? It would take anyone almost a year to get to Sydathria from here and get back again. But to transport all this furniture without any damage would be a feat of itself. Granted, he had just returned from Sydathria as well, however part of that journey was made by boat and he was not lugging delicate items and expensive furniture. Naia had just became top on his list of people to meet and get to know…if she was still even alive. That would be a horrible shame if she were not, a tragic waste. No wonder she was one of the village elders.

Passing into her bedroom he was again stunned. There was a Sydathrian hand carved bed, the type given to people who were newlywed. His mouth dropped open. Running his hand along the polished wood he identified it as mahogany. It was simply incredible. There was also carved wood paneling on the walls and masterwork ink paintings there. He was amazed. How much money did this woman have?

Eyeing one of the ink paintings he walked closer. In exquisite detail was painted a bird on a cherry blossom tree in the winter. He could almost feel the snow falling. He shook his head in awe and walked over to another picture. There was a painting of a mountain scene with a waterfall. He felt it was absolutely beautiful.

With his curiosity getting the best of him he wanted to look closer at the wooden frame to see how it was made. He tried to move the painting from the wall but found it was somehow quite securely fastened. He pulled on both sides. That did not work. He tried to lift it from the bottom. That did not work. He tried to reach the top and pull it down. That did not work either. Stepping back in bewilderment he stared at the painting. Why do that? Somehow he felt the painting was laughing at him.

Smythe made his way to a third painting and did not really look the work itself, he just wanted to see if it was also stuck to the wall. Pulling on both sides did not work. Lifting it did not work and pulling down did not work either. What the hell? In frustration he pressed on the corner and felt it shift. He froze as if he expected it to fall with a loud crash. But it did not. Cautiously reaching to the painting he pushed on it again and the same thing happened. Smythe stepped back and smiled. It could not be that simple. He reached for the corner and felt slightly behind the frame. There it was. It was a small latch. He moved it and pulled. The painting swung away from the wall on a concealed hinge on its left side.

That was clever. He looked behind the painting only to find a small stack of gold coins on the bottom shelf numbering about twelve. Twelve gold? Who would go through all this trouble just to hide a measly twelve gold coins? He moved the coins to a higher shelf and began knocking on the wood. In a short time he found it and smiled. Part of the bottom shelf was false and was a removable panel. Lifting it out, Smythe peered inside. He saw a sturdy looking wooden handle.

Smythe just stared at it. If I pull on it and it is trapped, I just lost my hand or worse. If it is not trapped then it will open or move something. Let's see if it's trapped. He closed his eyes and spoke a short chant while drawing in the air.

"Usmi aksu masku arnum." He opened his eyes and saw everything differently. He had cast a spell he learned from the Brotherhood to detect traps. It allowed him to know if they existed in his field of vision and, with further concentration, he could tell how it was constructed. Normally he would not resort to magic but with his hand at risk and with the devices so far being quite a bit more sophisticated than the door lock he did not wish to take that risk.

Happily, he found none. Smythe dismissed the divination spell and reached into the wall to grasp the handle. If I'm wrong…this is going to be very difficult to explain. He pulled.

A short series of clanks and grinds sounded before a bottom panel of the wall slid open. He had already released his grip and counted his fingers just to be sure. Smythe walked to the new opening in the wall and knelt down to peer inside. He saw a chest.

Carefully, he searched for traps before grasping the box itself. Finding none he tried to lift it and discovered it was quite heavy. Instead, he chose to drag it out from its place. It slid heavily across the floor with a grunt from Smythe.

It was a wooden box with metal reinforcements. On the front were two latches and a single lock while on the back he could not see any hinges. Clever, he thought. They are on the inside of the box so no one could get to them and open the box that way. He popped both latches and lifted the lid. Amazingly, the lock was not secured. Lifting the lid so he could peer inside and then he quickly closed it again. It slammed harder than he wanted. There was no way he saw what he did.

Opening it again, slower this time, his gaze revealed the same that he saw before. The box was filled with gold bars. He reached in a picked one up. It was four inches by two inches and about half an inch thick of solid gold. Looking at the others inside counted the number widthwise and lengthwise. Guessing at the number down into the box he quickly estimated there were approximately three hundred there. She could buy Silverwood!

What puzzled him the most was why she left all this gold here? Was Naia coming back? He closed the box and shoved it back into its hiding place. After it was returned to its same position Smythe pushed the handle in the wall back down and watched the panel close. He replaced the false panel and carefully replaced the twelve coins back to their original places and closed the painting.

Shaking his head he walked directly out of the bedroom and entered another place off from the living area. There was no way he was going to take any of the gold. First, there was no place he could take it to. Second, he could not just carry that heavy box down the street without being noticed. Third, if someone had that much gold just lying around they probably had a lot more and people like that could also afford to send many mean people to chase you to the ends of the earth. Fourth, he was just not that kind of person. Lying to someone for personal gain was acceptable but stealing was not. Also, if he were to get caught he had two knights from the royal family to contend with and when the Brotherhood found out he would be expelled. Being expelled from a secret society usually meant no one ever saw you again. With all of those factors, Smythe decided to put off his early retirement for another time.

This new room appeared to be study at one time. It was not a study any longer since the shelves that would once hold books were now empty. Smythe scratched his head. *Why leave all that gold but take your books? Who the hell was this woman? Was she a maniac? Well, let me try her second home, the library.*

He walked to the door, carefully opened it to see if he would be spotted. Feeling confident that his surreptitiousness would not be noticed, he quietly closed and relocked the door behind him and then strolled casually to the library. Smythe looked up at the sun in the sky and hoped it would cast more brightness on this dismal hamlet.

When he reached the library he paused before opening the door. He had hoped it was a "public" library and that anyone could just walk in and look at the volumes. The building was a two floor structure that looked more like a house than a library. The only way he could tell was that he could read the elven word for "library" artfully carved into the small sign hanging from above the door. He thought it was strange for a hamlet of only about twenty structures to put up a sign. One would think the elves did not have such short memories. Also, considering the few number of visitors they had here, anyone could point someone in the correct direction. The posting of signs, then, was rather peculiar. He turned the latch on the door and stepped inside.

Books, there were books here. Naturally one would expect there to be books in a library however Smythe did not expect that many. At a quick glance he estimated there were over three hundred volumes in the room. That was a large number considering how small this place was as well as the cost and time of actually producing a book of almost any size. None of these were small and were all very well bound.

"Hello," he cheerfully called out.

There was no reply and he strolled further in.

"Hello? Is there anyone here?"

Along the far wall there were two other doors, one to the left and one to the right. He decided on the left door and found it was locked. With a frown he walked between the bookshelves to the other door and knocked.

"Hello?"

From a distance he heard a crash as if something fell and tumbled on the floor. Shortly following he picked up a faint young female voice but could not make out what she said. Then he heard footsteps hurriedly thumping toward the door. Noticing it opened outward he stepped back so as to not get hit when it swung. It proved to be a productive idea. The door swiftly opened and a panting young elven looking girl stood there catching her breath. Smythe merely smiled at her and imagined the wood door smacking into his nose had he not moved.

He eyes widened a bit when he looked at her. She had brownish hair and big light brown eyes. They were a perfect complement to the smooth tanned skin of her short attractive figure. Her face actually seemed to illuminate when her small mouth stretched into a broad grin when she looked at him. Perhaps for the first time in his life he actually felt what it was when someone looked at him and not just in his direction. It was penetrating and warming, yet a little awkward since it was a first.

"Greetings," she said with distinct bubbly cheer. The young elf had a distinct accent that was different from the others he heard speaking in the hamlet. She quickly rolled her "r", pronounced the "i" like an "e" and over pronounced the "s" like a "z" at the end. Smythe was used to listening to things like this and was likewise taught to notice small details about people. He could not, however, seem to place where she might have gotten that accent.

"Greetings to you too," he said with a slight bow.

"Whaaa," was all she said and in that accent she spoke with the same intonation of a euphoric thirteen year old. He had guessed her age to be about eighteen in human years so her manner of speech was a bit odd.

"What is that?" He asked her in a very polite tone.

"Hum?" She batted her big eyes at him.

"You sounded a little surprised."

"Oh, yes, that…" Was she always this cheerful? "We don't get many strangers here."

Smythe nodded.

"Do I look that strange?" He quipped while looking down at his clothing. Humor, he found, was sometimes the best way to relax someone and make friends.

"Ha! You sure do!" she giggled.

Did the girl not understand the joke? No matter, he would continue to be charming. Extending his hand he introduced himself.

"I am Smythe Gibvoy-"

"From Paragon!" she interrupted as if happily involved in a guessing game while shaking his hand in large swings.

Smythe paused for a moment. He began to think he was addressing a child in a young adult's body. She did not stop shaking his hand yet.

"How did you know—"

"Oh, everyone knows that," she interrupted again.

The looked to each other again. Her big brown eyes gleefully drilling into him with a toothy grin. He noticed she did not introduce herself.

"I'm sorry—"

"For what?" Again she interrupted him and had still not stopped her handshake.

Yep, he was talking to a child.

"I did not get your name," he said with a smile.

She burst into a short laugh and covered her mouth with her empty hand.

"My name's Maura!" She renewed her vigorous handshake with far too much enthusiasm for Smythe and he eventually peeled his hand from her grip. Again he smiled.

"So...Maura—"

"That's me!" Interruptions were habitual.

"Yes, um...what do you do here?"

She looked around quickly.

"You mean here at the library?"

Smythe slowly nodded with a tight smile.

"Oh!" She paused, looked back at him and burst into a loud cackle that quickly ended. "I write books!"

That stunned him.

"You write books?" He pointed around the room. "These books?"

He was answered by another cackle that was a bit too loud and bit too long this time she bent at the waist.

"Oh, no! I did not write these."

"Ah, so which books did you write then?"

Her face crinkled in confusion.

"I wrote these," and pointed to the very same books he had just been told she did not write.

He was baffled. She was bewildered.

"Stop," she put up her hands as if he was walking somewhere but he was not. "You are confusing me."

I am confusing you?

"What are you asking me?" She questioned.

He blinked.

"I was asking if you wrote these books," he spoke slowly.

That did not seem to help her.

"What do you mean write?"

She had not just asked him that.

"Um..." he struggled for a way to put this that would not take all day. "Did you take a pen and ink and some paper and write the words into the books?"

"Oh!" exclaimed Maura. "I am so stupid," she smacked herself in the head. "Oops, I'm not supposed to talk like that." She suddenly looked sheepish then it quickly changed back to being jovial. "I only wrote some...they were getting old."

Smythe blinked again.

"They were getting old?"

"Yep!" She turned at her back and forth at her hips while curling her lips in.

"The books were getting old and you wrote them?" He was not sure what the hells she was speaking about.

"Yep, they were hard to read so I wrote them...like a...a...scrub"

Now he understood.

"Oh...you copied them. You were a scribe."

"Yes!" her face lit up and she pointed at him with both hands. "That's it, a scribe." Then she paused as if she forgot something important. "What did I say? Oh! I said like a scrub!" Again she bent over and burst into a loud cackle. "I'm so stupid."

You have no idea.

"You said they were hard to read?"

"Yep!"

They looked around the room at the books.

"How many did you read?"

Her head snapped back.

"Why...all of them," she talked as if he was the stupid one.

"You read all of them?" His mouth fell open.

"Of course."

"But...but...there are..." slowly he pointed.

"One thousand four hundred and seventy eight," she said beaming.

Smythe had to pause.

"You read one thousand four hundred and seventy eight books?"

She did not say an answer but moved her head in an exaggerated nod. They both stopped moving and looked at one another for a moment before she burst into another giggle. Somehow, he felt like laughing with her.

"That's a lot of books to read."

"Yep," she shrugged.

"Who first wrote these books?"

"Oh! That was Naia," she spoke as if he should have already have known that.

"Ah…" He nodded. She was a very busy woman. "Is that who taught you to read and write?"

"Yep."

"Um," he spoke thoughtfully. "What else did she teach you?"

"Lots of things…she taught me everything I know." She played with the fabric of her shirt as she spoke.

"Is it just you here? By yourself?"

"Ha! No, of course not," she smiled.

He waited for the rest of the information but it never came.

"So…who else lives here?"

"My father. He's upstairs in bed. He's been sick lately and I am taking care of him."

"He's sick?" Sounds like more trouble. "What's wrong with him?" This had better not be some mysterious illness.

"He's old! He is almost three hundred and thirty now!"

Smythe declined the reply, yeah, for being that old he should have died a few decades ago.

"Um…would you mind if I took a look around?"

"No, not at all! Feel free!" Her hands rose on outstretched arms that offered him run of the whole place.

"What kind of books do you have here?"

"Oh, we have books on everything," she clasped her hands in front of her.

"Everything?" He vaguely remembered Ruelina mentioning

that earlier.

"Yep!" she said with a big nod and began counting on her fingers. "Anthropology, zoology, botany, architecture, history, languages, meteorology…"

"Wait-wait-wait." Smythe stopped her. "You have books on all this? Naia wrote books on all this?"

"Yes," her rhythm slowed like she was talking to a child but never lost its joviality. "One thousand four hundred and seventy eight of them!"

He paused and just stared at her for a moment.

"Speaking of Naia…do you know where she went?" He used the softest tone he could generate.

"No," she frowned. "She did not say."

"Did she say when she would return?"

"No, just that she would be back as soon as she could."

Smythe could tell that Maura was most unhappy with that lack of information.

"Did she say what she was going to be doing?" Come on Maura, any little piece of information would be helpful here.

"Not really, she just said that there were many people that needed her help and she was going to help them…and off she went." Maura shrugged and looked like she was about to cry.

Smythe, thinking quickly, changed subjects again.

"What is in that room there?" He pointed to the locked door.

"Oh, that's a special reading room." Volunteering information was not in her capacity.

"May I see it?" he asked with a warm smile.

Her lips pursed.

"I don't know…it's only for special guests."

"Well…I'm a guest here in Silverwood…and I am special since I am the only one here like me, right?"

That caused her to laugh.

"Well…" she said with a smile and looking at the ceiling. Smythe already knew her answer.

"Oh, come on…" he said with a broad smile and melodramatically joking tone.

She blushed and turned back and forth shortly before finally acting.

"Very well," she felt like she was helping him and she liked to help people.

"Thank you," he said gratefully.

"Just don't tell anyone," she suggested.

"I won't," he promised. "My lips are sealed. Naia will never know."

Maura stopped cold and turned to him with a stern look.

"Of course Naia will know, she knows everything…I was talking about my father."

Smythe was surprised by her forwardness and considered asking her how Naia would know if no one told her but rejected that notion based on his conversational experience with the young girl up to that point. He would just be satisfied with getting into the room.

After opening the door she told him, "Now then, I will be upstairs if you need anything."

"Good, you will be the first one I will come and find," Smythe spoke with warm grin. When he tried to walk into the room she stopped him and had a confused look on her face.

"What?" he asked.

"You're going into a reading room," she pointed out.

"Yes," replied Smythe.

"You have nothing to read."

Oops, missed that part.

"Well, you have so many books here…I don't…I don't know which one to read." He sounded sincere even though he was lying through his teeth.

Maura laughed at him again.

"You're silly," she said as she turned away. "So what would you like to know about?"

"Um…anything?"

"Anything," she said with a confident tone while playfully jutting her jaw.

"Magic."

That stopped her. Smythe watched her confidence drain from her body.

"We don't have any books on that…that is not legal here." Suddenly she looked concerned.

"No…no…no, I was joking," he reassured her. "It was just a joke." Not really, but that is what I'm telling you.

"It wasn't funny," she pouted.

She walked over and grasped a volume from another shelf and returned. Maura thrust the tome into his gut. He grunted.

"Here you are," she offered with a smug look.

"What's this?" He asked while looking down at it.

"It's a book on Sydathrian philosophy. Their way of thinking is good for a quiet mind."

Quiet mind? What planet is she from?

"Do I look like a need a quiet mind?" He tried to say it with a joking tone.

"Absolutely." She pushed him back into the reading room. He was stunned at her doing that and especially how strong she was at doing it. Once he was through the threshold she reminded him, "Remember, I'm upstairs if you need something."

"Upstairs if I need anything, I will not forget." He spoke with a deliberate nod.

"Good."

The door closed in his face.

It was a little dark in here and he could hear her footsteps as she left, locking the other door behind her before climbing the stairs. His only light was one meager candle on a polished wooden table. Who leaves a burning candle in a locked room of a library? Did she not imagine books can burn? Looking at the soft glow he realized that it was the center one of five candles on a candelabrum. He removed it and lit the other four before putting it back in place. He slid the book onto the shiny surface. The impact was muffled slightly by the carpet beneath the heavy table. Quiet mind, he scoffed. Very pretty girl but daft as a shoe.

He was taken back when he saw another bookshelf in this small room. There were no windows and only that one small door for an exit point. Taking only two steps he reached the shelf and peered carefully at the books. They were old and worn from much use. When he eyed the titles his mouth fell open. These were books that many would pay thousands of gold for! There were books outlining the technology of ancient magic, the psychological impacts of faith and philosophy, harmonic construction of buildings, detailed astronomy and planetary movements, the framework of consecrated ground and even an atlas. An atlas of the world! No one has this! Most all records of towns and cities were destroyed during the Great

War. Very few survived and detailed ones were almost nonexistent. This discovery was an incredible find. He quickly removed five of the twenty odd books and put them on the table.

He slid out a chair and sat down like hungry child to his mother's cooking. He grasped a random book and then flipped through it. He was astounded. The level of knowledge, vocabulary and skilled command of the language let him know he was reading the works of an accomplished sage. If Naia indeed wrote this then she would be one of the smartest people on the planet. Even the skill of her calligraphy was beyond masterful. He picked up another and found the same thing. It was written in the same style and tone, only the subject had changed. One after the other it was the same. Naia was an authentic genius. But that just told him what she was, not who she was. He wanted to know much more. This person was quite intriguing and he had a strong feeling that somehow the things that made Silverwood unique were somehow intertwined with her.

He closed the last book and stood with a stomp of his heel. Smythe froze. The floor under the rug sounded different here. He pounded his foot again and heard the same sound. Finishing his movement to stand he took a few steps and stomped. There was a different sound that was less hollow. He smiled. Clever.

He moved the candelabrum onto a chair so he could sill see. He placed the small stack of books beside the door. Picking up the table end that was farthest from the door, he slid it across the rug and up against the wall. He then circled around and threw back the carpet. There it was, a square trap door neatly placed in the floor. He bent down to grasp the handle and open it but stopped. There was no handle. No handles? How do you open this thing then?

He knelt down at one corner and ran his fingers around the edge. There was no way to get fingertips into that small space and still expect a firm enough grip to lift it. He sat back on his heels and frowned. He thought for a moment then it struck him, I can pry it open.

Retrieving two hidden daggers he carefully wedged the tips between the door and floorboards. He was careful not to leave obvious marks that someone was tampering with the concealed door.

He was about to apply pressure then he stopped. Something inside told him that it was a bad idea. Smythe reviewed everything for a moment and then dismissed the notion. There was no space for a trap and even if there was a poison gas or other device, he was confident he could reach the door. Just to make certain, however, he produced a handkerchief and wrapped it around his nose and mouth, securing it at the back of his head. Now he was ready. He grasped the handles of his daggers and levered...

He could hear the distant sound of a rumble but could not tell what it was. There was a bright yellowish orange flash before he felt weightless. The only reason he knew he stopped flying was that his vision was jolted. He could only hear bells ringing. Shaking his head and blinking the reality was brought to his attention. The room was on fire!

Eala! A fire trap in a library? The roar of the flames and feeling of searing heat pressed against him. He turned quickly as the tiny room began to fill with black smoke. He pulled the door open and fell out into the main area of the library. With a fresh supply of air, the fire roared louder and poured like liquid along the ceiling and into the room.

Damn! Damn! Damn! Damn! He quickly reached in and grasped the five books and made his way to the closest window. Finding it open he tossed the prized books out then turned to run back to the other door.

"Maura!" he called out. "Maura!" He pounded on the locked door but stopped when he tasted smoke on his tongue. Smythe stepped back and then kicked with all his might at the door. It cracked but it was not nearly enough. He kicked it again and again before it split. By that time he could hear Maura yelling as she scrambled down the stairs.

"What happened?" She was wide eyed and full of fear. The roaring fire was getting louder.

"Fire!" Smythe yelled. "Get out of here!"

"My father-"

"I'll get him!" he interrupted as they shouted over the roar of the blaze. "You go now!"

He grasped her and pulled her from the doorway and then pushed her in the direction of the exit. Not looking to see if she was actually leaving, Smythe turned and bolted up the stairway that was filling with smoke. When he reached the next floor he yelled.

"Hello? Hello?" He could feel the floor warming and the heat was rising to this level quite quickly. He scrambled around from one area to another before finding a bedroom with a wizened elf lying in it. Thick smoke was close behind him.

"Hello, we have to get you out of here," he said as he rushed to the bed. The aged man had an ashen look to his skin and his eyes were nearly lifeless. He looked like he was going to die at any moment.

"No...don't..." he said softly. It was the only volume he could manage.

"But we have to save..." Smythe was frantic.

The elf slowly shook his head.

"It's my time, boy," he told Smythe. "Where's Maura?"

"She's safe outside. But..."

"Take care of her...she means...everything...understand?"

Smythe nodded but the elf knew he did not grasp what he was trying to tell him. Sadly, they had no time. With his last bit of strength he firmly grasped Smythe by his arm and clenched as hard as he possibly could. A cracking beam was heard behind him as the blaze roared in the house.

"She means everything...protect her...she must be kept safe...she's not ready to be on her own...she's not ready..." The old man struggled to get the words out with blazing eyes.

Smythe felt a surge of nobility and worthiness. He looked the old elf dead in his eyes and spoke to him but before he realized what he was saying, it was already out.

"I swear by my honor to protect her as long as I live," his voice was strong and earnest but inside, after he listened to himself, Smythe cringed. *What in the name of all creation did I just say?*

"See that you do, boy." The man released him and fell back onto the bed. Looking up at the ceiling through the smoke he knew Smythe had little time to get out if he wanted to live. But there was just too much to say in too little time. "Listen close..."

Smythe leaned in to hear over the rising volume of flames that reached up into this floor.

"There is a puzzle...twenty eight pieces...put it together...you will know...when its time...they...try to hide...but the lines were...already drawn in the first war...the enemy is known..." He never finished. His body became limp as the smoke stung Smythe's eyes.

Taking a deep breath from as low as he could, he stood and

rushed back down the stairs. As he came down he felt dizzy from the heat and he could not see through the smoke with his stinging eyes. He fell down the rest of the way and slammed against the bookshelf just outside the door.

He did not remember how he got out. He only remembered there was water being poured on him as he lay outside on the dirt. The sun was close to setting and there was a clamor of commotion around him. Everything was moving in slow motion. He rolled back onto the dirt and grunted. Darkness embraced him as he lost consciousness. In the distance he could hear a fading sound of ghostly laughter.

When she reached the air outside Maura began screaming at the top of her lungs for help. The town's people naturally came out to look and when they saw the building was quickly being swallowed by flames they all rushed to aid.

The inn was the closest place for any water and so they decided to sacrifice their last amount of drinking water in the hopes of claming the blaze and save her ailing father, Jotham. They formed a line with buckets as the only measure they had.

The nobles, the priest and Ruelina had just left Clarissa and Rannon's home and had discovered that Nellron, the younger priest of Enlil there in the village, had called on her earlier. She was not well. Her condition seemed to be worsening as her skin looked paler and thinner. Clarissa's once bright eyes had become tired and sunken in. She appeared to be dying.

Kaeleb was aghast since that had never happened before. Whenever he healed someone from wounds or a sickness in the past they stayed healthy and strong, especially the next day after one night's sleep. It was not so with her. The sight disturbed Kaeleb and he somehow felt he had betrayed Rannon and her. The priest felt helpless.

Nellron had suggested that Clarissa be moved to the temple so that he could watch over her closer. At first Rannon rejected the idea in favor of caring for her himself. However, the knights and Ruelina had convinced him that it may be for the best. With a mark of reservation, Rannon nodded and promised to take her there in the morning.

With a displeased eye he watched Kaeleb exit his home. As the priest turned to walk away with the rest of the group he could hear the door being locked. The sound saddened him. Dejected and bewildered, he shuffled in behind them as they went back to the inn. Their quiet pace was disturbed by the shouts and screams of villagers from up ahead. Without deliberation, they took to a run to see what was happening. Racing through the scattered trees and homes they could see the plume of smoke rising above the tall foliage.

When they reached the clearing the elves were throwing buckets of water against the burning building. The knights and their squires dashed to the large barrels of water and, with their superior strength, moved them closer to save time and then immediately began helping with the battle against the flames. Ruelina, meanwhile, rushed to see if anyone was harmed. She found Maura but did not see Jotham. Smythe was lying on the ground covered in black soot.

When asked, Maura did not know what had happened. She tried to explain through tear streamed eyes while watching her home, with her father still inside, and everything she knew quickly burn to the ground. She had the realization that she, her whole life and everything in it, was fragile enough to vanish in a moment like a wisp of smoke. If that happened, who would remember her? Would she be forgotten? Who would ever know she existed? Maura's head slowly fell into Ruelina's shoulder and she cried. The hardened ranger put her arms around her and said nothing. Bit by bit her home, their home of Silverwood, was being destroyed. Her faith in the strangers, the new humans in town, was quickly diminishing.

After a while of feebly casting their water against the burning structure, all of them stopped when they heard the beams cracking. They watched as the roof collapsed in, knowing there was no way to stop the blaze. They would only make certain the nearby trees would not burn as well and cause further damage to the surrounding homes. Everyone's heart sunk as Maura fell to the ground sobbing. Her father was burned alive.

Emerik crossed the remaining open ground and strode directly to a sooty Smythe who was just now sitting up and trying to drink some water. The prince remained standing as he spoke.

"I see you were…close to the fire." There was a hint of edginess.

"Oh, yes sire. I got Maura out but sadly I could not save her father," Smythe replied as he wiped black from his brow.

Everyone nearby was listening intently, including Ruclina and Maura.

"And...what exactly happened?"

Smythe swallowed hard and explained, "Well, I was inside the library reading some very interesting material when I heard this loud noise and everything around me was engulfed in flames. I barely made it out alive and went looking for Maura. I got her out and then went upstairs to get her father but I could not save him. He was very worried about her...so, I promised him I would take care of her."

That stunned everyone.

"What?" Ruelina asked as if she was just spat in the face.

"You promised him to take care of her?" The paladin wanted to be clear on that point. Knights, and especially paladins, did not take promises lightly.

"Well...it was more like a vow, really," Smythe admitted.

"A vow?" Emerik wanted to be very clear. Vows were heavier than promises but not that much dissimilar, only in formality.

"Yes, I swore on my honor." Smythe swallowed hard again. *Did I really say that? Did I go that insane?*

Tobin scoffed loudly and turned away. "Honor," he echoed.

The prince thought for a moment then spoke clearly and carefully to Smythe. He wanted no misunderstanding as he spoke, "You realize we are still in Paragon."

Smythe nodded, "yes."

"You know this vow to protect her is now something you must hold to."

Smythe nodded again, "yes."

"You also realize that we," he motioned to himself, Tobin and their squires. "We all know of this vow of yours by your own admission."

Smythe nodded.

"If you break this vow...the penalty is prison for eighteen years."

Smythe again nodded, "I will not break this oath, my prince. I swore to a dying man." *Someone, stab me in the head.*

"See that you don't," Tobin warned. Looking at the little girl with the mixed blank yet worried look on her face Tobin walked over to her. He felt an unidentified bolt of animosity toward the little elf. Without a tight grip of control the words flowed venomously as he faced the girl down. He looked at her yet spoke to Smythe as if she was not there or was incapable of answering for herself. "So...who is this?" he asked with superciliousness.

"This is Maura." A small lump formed in Smythe's throat.

"And...who is this Maura, exactly?" Tobin found himself regarding her much the same as he would rotten paper.

"She is the woman I vowed to protect, sire."

"Really?" Finally speaking to the shrinking girl he said, "So, tell me, cute little lass...what can you do?"

She looked at him and blinked with a blank expression. "I don't understand," she said. The question was confusing to her.

"What...can...you...do?" Tobin spoke slower and louder as if he were addressing someone deaf and dumb. *Why are most of the pretty ones so slow?*

"I heard you," she said backing away. His unfriendly face and volume caused her to draw back. "I just don't understand the question." There was something acute about him Maura did not like, something was suddenly making her skin crawl.

Tobin's face hardened. *I can see why he wanted to "protect" her, cute and stupid.* However, he had more pressing concerns than the habits of a brainless tramp.

"What are you good at doing?" The answer better not had been "entertainment" or he would have to slug Smythe in the head.

"You mean, what do I do for work?"

He sighed and glared at her. No one could be that dim-witted. "That's a start," his head slowly nodded.

"I was a...scribe in the library." Happily, she did not say "scrub" like she did with Smythe.

"That's the place that just burnt down?" He callously motioned to the still smoldering building.

"Yes, there."

"Not working there anymore," he blurted offhandedly. "What else can you do?"

"I don't know," she answered with a growing dislike for the large metal clad tormenter.

"You don't know?" He leaned in and she leaned back.

"No."

"Did you learn to use a sword like every other elf?" He straightened and looked down at her.

"No." Maura was shrinking.

"A spear? Anything that could be used in a real battle?"

"Battle? No."

"Great..." His sarcasm was thick. *I'm not helping to defend this whelp until I know she's worth saving.* "Know anything about forests?"

"A little..." *Why all these questions? Why are you acting so angry?*

"Dying ones?"

"No."

"So...you're useless," he concluded.

"I don't understand." *How can anyone be useless? What is wrong with you?*

"Of course not," he mocked with a fake chuckle. "You...can...not...do...anything...useful. You can't fight, you can't tell us what is happening here and...you're stupid."

Maura just blinked at him.

"Yes, you're stupid." He repeated it in case she did not understand it the first time.

"That's mean," she could not comprehend anyone talking the way he was.

"I don't care. I don't have to be nice, especially since you're stupid." He turned to walk away while shaking his head. *I cannot believe this. Where do these people come from? They stay in a dying forest with someone poisoning them to death and they still worry about coddling their hamlet idiot.*

Maura's lower lip quivered looking like she was about to explode into a bawling mess. Ruelina quickly came to her and put a reassuring arm around her shoulder. Her head sank into the ranger's chest like a puppy.

"Don't be nasty," she spoke to the back of the knight's head. "She doesn't deserve this." Tobin did not answer. She petted the back of Maura's head. "It'll be fine, Maura. Don't worry about the big mean man. He makes everybody cry...he's like a monster."

While everyone began to shuffle off in different directions Kaeleb made his way over to Emerik. Looking around so that no one else could hear, he spoke to the prince. Emerik noted the priest's need for discretion.

"I need to talk to you," Kaeleb said in a hushed voice.

"About what?"

"Clarissa...That's never happened before."

"What do you mean?" the paladin asked as he kept walking away from everyone else.

"When our Master Enki has healed someone though me they have...stayed healed. Never have they gotten worse. It's very strange."

The paladin pondered for a moment before replying, "What do you think is happening?"

"I don't honestly know," Kaeleb admitted. "I'd pray over her but Rannon doesn't trust me."

"I noticed...but here in this place, none of us are." He shook his head. Hour by hour it seemed the Emerik had less and less answers but was drowning in questions.

"True, but its different when they think we- I am intentionally doing harm."

"Agreed," not that he wanted to admit that but it was the truth. Something seemed to be plotting to destroy these elves' hope. "So...do what?"

"I suggest we all be careful. If things like this continue, they may not treat us very kindly anymore." Kaeleb, although he said that, was far more concerned about the people in the village coming to further harm. He did not care if they were run out of town because of misunderstandings so much as he worried about the elves here being slowly killed off by this unseen darkness. He shivered at the thought.

"As in the library?"

"Both Clarissa and the library," the priest noted. "They used a lot of their water in fighting that fire as well. But ever since we arrived, we have been watched and something does not want us here."

"Yes," the paladin said reflecting. "I noticed that as well...Today has been a busy day. Get some rest and we'll discuss this further in the morning. Maybe tomorrow we can help them gather water as well."

"Yes, milord," the priest bowed and turned to walk away.

"Sleep well," Emerik bade, borrowing the phrase from Ruelina the other night.

Just after dinner, as Smythe ambled toward the garrison with Ruelina and Maura in tow, he thought of the how comfortable that uncomfortable soldier's bed he was sleeping in really was. Running around in a burning building proved quite exhausting and he needed to sleep. Making their way between the long dark shadows of the night Ruelina and Maura spoke behind Smythe. They had already decided not to speak of her deceased father. The young elf was really not prepared for those words yet. Ruelina changed the topic, slightly.

"We'll need to get you some new clothes and a new place to live," the elf suggested. "But you should be okay in the garrison for a while."

"I don't care about that," Maura said truthfully. "Are you staying with me as well?"

"Well, I had not thought of that yet." The protective ranger thought of a lecherous Smythe drooling over Maura while she slept. "Yes, I can. I will. I will stay tonight and then move some of my things there in the morning."

"Good," Maura felt relieved. Someone familiar would be with her and she did not know any of these new people. "Father is gone now. Maybe that's better? It was not good for him to suffer like that." Trying to prevent herself from crying, Maura changed subjects like an ocean wind. "I am going to miss my flute. It was a nice flute. Naia gave it to me as a gift. She made it, did you know?"

"We can get you another one," Ruelina tried to console her but knew those words would have little consolation even before she said them.

"Not like that one." She remembered playing it the way Naia taught her to. She always liked when the animals gathered to listen, especially the rabbits.

Smythe's eyes were half closed as he was on the brink of stumbling or finding a way to sleep while he walked when he suddenly felt a sharp blow on his head. He cried out in pain and shock as his hand came up to cover his skull. They all stopped.

"Ow! What the hell?" Smythe blurted. He was awake.

Behind him the women stopped.

"What is it?" Ruelina's hand went to her sword but Maura did not react with any concern.

"I don't know," he said rubbing above his ear. "Wait there with Maura." He slowly approached the shadows. Looking at his hand in the dim moonlight he could not see any blood and the lump did not feel wet. He thought that was a good thing and cautiously approached the darkness beside the stables. It was quite black there.

Twenty men with large axes could be standing there and he would never have seen them. Slowly and quietly he drew out his sword and swallowed hard. If anyone was watching him approach they would have certainly seen him take out his blade. He reached the corner and peered into the black.

"You don't need that," said a whispering voice.

Smythe stepped back when a dark figure emerged from the shadows as if it had stepped out of them. It glided with unnatural fluidity as it slowly came toward him. Smythe shakily placed the point of the sword between himself and the figure while his heart pounded in his ears. The shadow continued to advance without care. Smythe trembled even more.

"M- Maura!" He managed to shout as he felt himself getting smaller and the soundless form getting larger and darker.

Maura's cheerful voice shouted back, "Hello, Thelial!"

Smythe heard the name and was instantly bewildered. *Thelial?* He glanced over to Maura who was in the street happily waving her arm and then he felt like he was not holding anything in his hand. He looked into his empty palm and noticed his sword was gone! The image of his own sword cutting through his body flashed though his mind like lightning.

"I said you will not need this," the voice was a bit more impatient this time. He expected the robed man to listen the first time. People were frightened so easily. Smythe looked up at him with wide trembling eyes as Thelial was giving him back his sword, handle first.

"How did you..." the investigator's voice trailed off.

"Small rock. So...the library burnt down, huh?" The darkness spoke quietly while calmly waving an arm to Maura. He ignored the half question, *how did you get my sword from my hand so easily?*

"Wha...y...yes. Yes it did." Smythe slowly came back to reality and stood in a more natural posture. His heart still drummed in his hears, though.

"I heard your explanation earlier...Nice of you to get Maura out." Thelial continually nodded while he spoke.

"I did what I could."

"That's a stunning feat of dexterity to tie a cloth over your nose and mouth before going to look for her, especially while being in the middle of a raging fire." He stopped nodding and looked the investigator in the eye. Smythe just stared while he began to sweat and his ears turned red. Those eyes were more than just a little piercing. "So, will you still lie if I asked you again about the library?" Thelial's expressionless face looked quite lethal.

"...Yes, I probably will." Smythe swallowed hard.

"Fine, let's get her inside the garrison then." He turned and glided over to Ruelina and Maura like a wraith. Smythe looked at the dirt as he passed. Thelial made no noise and left no tracks. *Was he even human? Who was he? What was he?*

Thelial despised the fact that the library was gone. He would miss Jotham and those long talks more than the books. The old elf was a good man. After hearing their conversation from the comfort of the darkness, Thelial also realized he would really miss the special sounds of that flute. He liked the rabbits, too.

That night, everyone was quite exhausted and slept like stones. Everyone save the priest Kaeleb who tossed around in his own sweat. He dreamt of fire and sulfur. There was a river of blood with twisted monsters drinking at its banks. The sky was red and black and spun with lighting and rumbling thunder that sometimes sounded like a growl. A sobbing feminine voice and wailing baby echoed in the distance. Then the priest heard a girl's unearthly voice in a harsh whisper.

Save me, Kaeleb...

Inside the Silverwood Garrison

Early Next Morning

She had been watching him all morning and into the early afternoon. It can be amazing how many times someone can see another but never really look at them. That's how it was with her just then. For years she barely gave him a passing glance and never tried to speak to him. He always came, usually once a year or so, and only spoke to Naia. He never stayed at the inn and never ate with them. He was just known as that enigmatic fellow who came to visit every so often and consistently brought a gift for the townsfolk. That time it was food. Everyone knew him as Thelial and somehow everyone knew better than to ask about him. More mysteries would have been the answer anyway. But, he was a good enough chap and they had accepted this, especially being that he was Naia's friend.

Ruelina, though, thought different that day. She had witnessed him stand up to the high and mighty from Paragon without care and they backed down. To her, he was strong, intelligent, skilled, independent and, actually, quite humorous. But that was not what she really was thinking about. It was a look he gave her early that morning. She had been talking to Maura about what clothing the girl may want when she could feel him looking in their direction. It was without thought that she had glanced over Maura's shoulder just in time to see Thelial's deep piercing stare above his amused smile. For a brief moment, one that vanished in the beat of a hummingbird's wings, she saw his eyes soften as their glances met. He abruptly turned and went about his day, which was outside of the garrison.

Since Silverwood was a small place, it was difficult not to find him again. Even if it was just to catch a glimpse of him from a distance, Ruelina found herself peering between trees and homes just for the remote chance of seeing him.

After lunch, when mostly she just sat and watched him eat, the group scattered in different directions as they poked and prodded around the hamlet trying to ascertain what exactly was happening. Curiously, Thelial did not seem to be asking questions nor did he seem to be investigating anything. He just seemed to be wandering from one place to another looking at inconsequential things. When she found him inside the garrison doing something with many bottles and jars, mixing this and smelling that, she drew up her courage to actually talk to him. She rehearsed it before getting there but it did not come out the way she planned it to.

"Hello." That was a bad start. She felt like a fool but recovered well. "I never got a chance to meet you. I've seen you here before but never talked to you." *Damn it!* It was supposed to be something more intelligent and stronger than that.

"Most people don't," he said quietly and without emotion. He continued to mix, stir and watch his bottles.

"Well, I'm Ruelina," she said extending her hand.

"Yes, I know," he said putting down his small jar and shaking her hand. "Nice to meet you." His touch felt strong and electric. He never smiled and went back to his collection of small vials.

"And?" She thought he would have volunteered the information.

"What?"

"What's your name?" *Great, he thinks I'm dumb and wants nothing to do with me.* Even though she knew his name Ruelina wanted to hear him say it. Thelial regarded her in silence, as if he watched her internal monologue scroll down her face.

"I'm Thelial," he told her with a dispassionate tone. She thought of asking for his family name but decided that it would be worse than trying to get Tobin to relax.

"Good. Any friend of Naia's…"

"Yeah…" he went back to stirring.

"I heard you were looking for her."

"That's right." He held the small vial up as it changed colors and then frowned.

"Will you help us?"

"That depends," he said looking to her as he carefully placed down the bottle.

"On what?" *Oh, you're as much help as the other useless people here.*

"If it fits into the plan," said Thelial uncaringly.

Ruelina blinked.

"Plan? What plan? Your plan?" She was ready to belt him.

"I don't make plans." His tone said *I do what I'm told because I have less responsibility.* "What do you want, anyway?"

"Well," she began with a huff. "I really wanted to know what part elven you were."

"What part?" Her reply was confusing to him.

"Yeah, you're not full human and you're not full elf either. So…which kind elf are you? Grey? High? You're not wood, wild or snow."

"A kind not from around here," he answered dispassionately.

What the hell kind of answer was that?

"Fine…your human part then?" Her lower jaw began to jut out and her foot tapped.

"That's not exactly human either…But nobody's perfect," he added with a smile.

That was it, he was jesting. She laughed with him and thought he did not like his half human side. Little did she know that he was being truthful.

"No, but seriously, where are you from?" Her chuckle died.

"Very, very far away from here…sort of," Thelial said calmly.

Again, she paused and blinked before asking, "Are you always this cryptic?"

"No…If you get to know me I'm just very evasive."

Both looked at one another and laughed. His eyes were dead and sad. Her eyes were alive and sad. They did not share that sadness but for a moment they touched without moving a finger.

"What are you doing anyway?" She asked while getting her breath. She probably would not have resisted if he grasped her, pressed her against the wall and roughly kissed her.

"I'm identifying the poison that is in the well."

"What do you plan to do then?" That was something quite useful he was doing. Unlike the others who seemed to be bumbling fools, and one of them called Maura stupid?

"You mean after I know what was used?"

She nodded.

"Well, I'll do what I can." He did not say what he really thought. *I'll hunt and kill everyone who remotely seems to be involved.* He thought that admission would be a bit too much for her to hear, no matter how true it was.

After dinner at the inn, the group sauntered back to the garrison. Smythe had rested all day after being prayed over by Kaeleb the previous night. The priest stayed close to him all day in close observation since he was concerned that Smythe would relapse in the same manner as Clarissa had. Happily, the investigator did not. He seemed to be doing quite well and was fully rested. Having enough energy, Smythe wanted to show Kaeleb the inside of Naia's home, in hopes the priest would notice what he could not.

On the way, Smythe pondered the writing on the statue that supposedly marked the grave site of the famed Lady Gajana. That was too impossible. Gajana was buried in Silverwood? It had to be some manner of jest, some sickened form of a hoax. Still, there was the matter of the writing with misspelled words and, apparently, misplaced capital letters. How bizarre. What could that mean? "Here IS Gajana chosen EN THE Eyes Of Anu" and "May Heaven'S Light Rise OVER you as Thou have dONe For us." Mentally, he removed the lower case letters and was left with "HISGENTHEEOA" and "MHSLROVERTONF." *What in the name of Heaven did that mean?* Smythe continued to brood over that in silence as they walked.

No one had noticed Maura began walking a bit slower. She felt the shadows around her grow and become cold. She felt icy fingers tickling her neck and back. Worst of all, she felt she was being watched with tangible, malicious and hungry eyes. She began to hear a raspy breathing in the shadows of something that did not need to breathe. It had some semblance of a mind, it was conscious and sentient and it was more than one...

She stopped walking and began to tremble.

"Nooo...I don't want to go."

Smythe turned to her, "It's alright you're safe." *Damn,* he thought, *I was getting somewhere with that code as well.*

"No...it's not right," she insisted with a shaking head and looking very upset.

"Naia will understand," Ruelina tried to soothe. "It will be fine."

"Remember," Smythe added. "I'm here to protect you."

Ruelina shot him an angry glare that he did not see.

Kaeleb, approaching Ruelina from her back, whispered to her, "Does she always do this?"

"I don't know...I really don't know her." Ruelina did not know whether to be more compassionate or more upset. Maura felt the cold come closer and heard the raspy sound of air moving in and out of dry decaying lungs.

"Nooo!"

"What's wrong?" Smythe felt he was at a loss.

"Bad...Very bad things!" she blurted.

"Maura, you don't have to go into Naia's house," Kaeleb offered.

Maura energetically shook her head while trying not to cry. The cold, the breathing, the thoughts of inhuman predatory things observing her as food were quickly becoming a cacophony.

"Yes," Ruelina agreed as she picked up on Kaeleb's idea. "You and I can just wait here."

"I can't protect her if she is not near," Smythe insisted. The vow was sincere but no one believed that. Even him, but he made it and he was stuck with it. Ruelina gave him a cold stare that he did see that time.

Smythe was about to discuss the point with Ruelina when Maura blurted, "I want to go! We have to go!" She sounded like she was about to shatter.

"Why? What's so bad?" Kaeleb asked softly. He never got an answer.

Maura screamed with an ear piercing shrill.

Out from the shadows, lumbering like broken beggars, hobbled a small band of pale humanoid monsters. Their taunt grey skin was stretched tight across their bones and was even rotting in some places. Their eyes were completely black, but glowed in the center like burning embers, and dripped with malevolent ravenous hunger. Menacingly clawed hands reached out for the four victims as the creatures fiercely attacked all at once.

Smythe was caught by surprise as one lunged at him like a crazed animal. The full flying weight of the thing knocked him to the ground. The creature landed atop him and Smythe could smell its rotting flesh as it hissed. Sheer panic gripped his heart.

The priest instinctively spun, making a potentially decent blow become a glancing one, while grasping his sword as he turned. He trembled in fear, drawing his breath in short gasps. Without hesitation, another one of the things was on him and he fought to get enough distance to use his blade.

"Ghouls!" Ruelina shouted and fell back while shoving Maura in the direction of the garrison. Her eyes narrowed. While drawing her sword she tried to yell to Maura to get back into the garrison but her voice was interrupted by a creature that lunged into the air at her while another dashed directly for her. She could see their razor like claws reflecting the moonlight.

Kaeleb reached out by reflex and grasped the thing by its throat and pushed hard. That gave him the space he needed and, with a shout, shoved the point of his sword deep into its body. He felt the steel slide through and out its back. But it did not care! It seemed to feel no pain and continued to fight and snarl without pause. The priest became terrified.

On the ground, wresting with one of these things atop him, Smythe could not draw a weapon or use any magic, but he could scream wildly. He was stuck. Franticly he writhed and twisted and shouted, trying to get out from under this thing while also trying to avoid the sharp teeth that were snapping perilously close to his face. Then it happened. Yet another that was still looming in the rear of the pack dove forward, closed its grip tightly on his leg and sank its teeth deep into his thigh. The pain shot through his body like a white bolt of lightning and a scream of agony escaped his throat. The ghoul atop him used his distraction at his pain to drop its teeth into his shoulder. A sour burning radiated down into his chest and arm. His scream became one long agonizing howl. Then something else began to happen. He felt as if his veins pumped acid instead of blood. It was excruciating and he began to curl into a ball as all his muscles contracted at once. Smythe was in agony feeling his muscles melt with an acerbic burning, unable to move and quite helpless. *No! No! No! No!* What was worse was that he was still somewhat aware of what was happening. The two above him peered down as he folded into a fetal position in the dirt. He thought for a moment they had smiled.

Ruelina swung hard, and again, and again, and again. Anger boiled in her veins. Her hatred for the foul things allowed her no fear. Instead she trembled with rage. She did not stop for a moment sometimes striking at one then the other as she tried to keep both at bay. Sometimes her blade struck and sometimes it hit air. Even when it did land solidly the creatures did not react as if they had been cut. But she knew how to fight them. With these things they had to be rendered incapable of moving. A slash to its gut would never do. If you wanted on to stop running you had to take both of its legs.

Nothing less would work. After shoving one to the ground she sliced the other across its jaw. Its head snapped to the side and she brought the sword down across its skull. The steel passed from it temple to its opposite cheek. The dome of its skull fell from its head. Ruelina gripped her sword with both hands and sank her whole body into the cut with a roar. Even with half a head it still remained standing. It did not, however, after her sword sank deep through its shoulder and down into its gut. Ruelina kicked the unmoving creature off of her sword in time to stab the other in its hip. She cursed it through clenched teeth.

Kaeleb had been cutting and slashing his one ghoul but it did not stop attacking. *What do I do? What do I do?* With a quick glance around to the enemy and his allies, he realized that this was not a fight they could win. They needed help and they needed it fast.

"Help!" he cried out while still fighting with his snarling opponent, eyes wide and heart thumping. "Emerik! Anyone! Help!"

Inside the garrison, Emerik was getting ready for bed. He was tired and not feeling very cheerful. The events of the past few days wore heavy on him and he wanted nothing more than some direction or solution. *Someone, somewhere, Enki, please give me a direction I am to look in.* His squire had already retired for the evening and left him in dejected silence. The prince was in over his head and did not know what to do. Sluggishly and with a deep frown, he shuffled over to his borrowed bed. His armor was off and he was about to change into night clothes when he faintly heard someone yelling.

His canted his head not certain if he heard it or not. Making his way to the door of his room he heard it again, it was the sound of a woman screaming. Without pause, grasped his sword and shield, opened the door and stepped into the hall. He looked around then quickly went to the end of the hall at the front of the building. He heard a door opening behind him.

"What was that?" Tobin asked him. Evidentially he also heard it and emerged in just a shirt and trousers. He was already strapping his sword to his side.

"I don't know yet," he made his way to the window and peered down.

Then he heard it. The priest Kaeleb was shouting, "Help!

Emerik!"

The paladin saw them surrounded and in a chaotic melee with some grayish colored humanoid creatures. Something in his chest suddenly felt an icy chill.

"They're in trouble!" he said as he turned to run.

Tobin was closer to the stairs than he was and ran down them like a shot. He was already out of the main doors when the paladin reached the bottom of the stairs. Tobin did not know what he was running into as he sped. The sounds of yelling and fighting weakly echoed in the stone garrison.

Maura, looking rather weak and helpless, shrank in the presence of the snarling ghouls. Her face was twisted in panic as their black orbs pierced through her body. She tried to turn and run but her muscles would not obey her commands. She was too horrified and moved in slow motion, too slow. The two were upon her in a flash.

The ranger, still with her sword in the flailing creature's hip, twisted violently and thrust. She felt its hip joint separate with a crack. It felt it as well and fell to the dirt with a thud, hissing and gnawing. Unable to stand and not fully realizing why, the ghoul still attempted to run which caused to spin around in circles on the ground. It swiped it claws and thrashed its limbs as furiously as it could. The sight made it appear more terrifying. Ruelina paused to time her next blow and brought the strike down heavily into its other thigh. As the bone split from the steel passing through it, its leg barely clung to its body by rotting sinew and flesh. It did not stop its assault for even a moment.

Even after Kaeleb had removed its left arm during his last good strike, the thing kept clawing. The severed appendage lay motionless on the ground. Why won't it stop? By the gods what is this? His next thrust entered beneath its chin and snapped its head back. Kaeleb shouted and pushed forward into a run. The point passed inside of its face and stopped at the top inside of its skull as the priest drove it backward. When it slammed against the outside wall of the stables, the sword pierced it skull and stuck into the wood. It hung, pinned through its head, against the wooden planks and never stopped attacking. It could not see anything but the night sky since its head was tilted back however it still scrambled wildly with unknown rage. He stepped forward, shoved his boot heel onto the ghoul's chest and ripped his sword from the plank and out of its skull. Its head hung loosely and with a large split in it. It staggered, giving Kaeleb the time to aim his swing for its neck. With a dull thud its head hit the dirt before its body. Both parts remained still.

The unarmored knight rounded the wall of the garrison with his sword drawn and ended up standing a bit too close to two corpse-like creatures that were dragging a helpless Maura. She was curled tight into a ball like she was having a seizure and her face was wracked with pain. He looked down then back up. His mind could not get past the fright he felt as he stood in their presence. The two dropped Maura to the ground and pounced on Tobin.

Ruelina's ghoul, finally realizing it could not walk or even stand, decided to crawl to kill her. It scrambled like a twitching crab as it swiftly came at her. Avoiding its claws she thrust her sword into its back and pinned it to the ground. With its two useless legs flopping behind it and its good arms swiping at the air, it writhed franticly trying to free itself and attack the elf woman at the same time. It howled in what was more like a hiss with enraged frustration.

Kaeleb saw that the elf had pinned one but that it was also not defeated. Quickly he ran to her and it. Hearing the swift approach, Ruelina turned to fight another opponent. His fist cocked back with grim determination.

"No!" Kaeleb shouted to her and immediately stopped advancing. "It's me, Kaeleb!"

Ruelina blinked in recognition then shot her glance down to the thrashing ghoul at their feet.

Emerik rounded the corner just in time to catch one of the grayish creatures about to bite into Tobin's head. His friend was curled up and frozen in a silent scream. He paused for a moment being taken back the sight of these things then rushed forward with a swing of his sword.

"Get off him!" he shouted.

The thing hissed and tried to stand but the prince's blade split through the top side of its head and exited its armpit. While turning to face the other, it had already struck under his shield and raked its claws across the paladin's thigh. The slashes were deep and blood spurted in pulses. Emerik yelled in pain and swung feebly at it. The acidic pain and contractions were already setting in and he fell to the ground. His heart beat wildly in his chest. When he heard the distant clank of his sword hitting the dirt his heart sank.

Tobin watched helplessly as Maura was drug off into the night.

The priest raised his sword to get ready to cut at the prone creature as the ranger circled around behind it. She placed her boot firmly at the base of its spine and rocked her sword, which was still lodged in its spine, back and forth with a vigorous motion. Its head rose in anger bring unable to strike effectively at her. This gave Kaeleb the chance to drive one solid stroke into the nape of its neck. He pulled the sword from the dirt below it as the head rolled a short distance away from its body. Finally, it had quit moving.

The priest looked to Ruelina and then toward the garrison. He saw Emerik and Tobin lying vulnerably on the ground outside the wall.

"Emerik!" he hollered and burst into a run with Ruelina very close behind him.

Emerging from the quiet shadows they lumbered up out of the ground. The first sniffed the air then looked around the empty cemetery. It crawled a few feet away and then another emerged. It was followed by another and another. Lastly, one surfaced that seemed to move different and look different than the others. It was more controlled, more intelligent and more…cunning. It looked to the others and they moved into Silverwood in mass.

A shadow lying across the ground away from a nearby tree silently rose and followed behind them. The shape became more menacing the farther it moved from the graves. As it glided with the second ghoul party it drew out a dark sword with so much of a hiss. It stalked. It was hunting. In the distance, it could hear the sounds of fighting and could see the shapes of the humans as they battled the first group of ghouls. If it had a face, it would have smirked.

The white haired ghoul stopped suddenly. The others stood still as well, along with the shadowy figure that glided to a halt. The ghoul leader looked around as if it felt not right. It knew there was an unidentifiable something that was amiss. The others began looking around as well but did not know what they were looking for. The black wraith drifted to the center of the pack. The leader looked over its shoulder to the moving shadow, but it was too late.

With a blur, the shadowy figure cut through the leader first then swiftly and accurately dispatched one after the other. The only sound that could be heard was their motionless bodies landing on the soft dirt and the occasional swish of the dark sword as it cut through the night.

With the ghouls lying on the ground the figure crouched and carefully looked at each one to ensure they were slain. It reached up and pulled back its hood. Thelial stared darkly at the corpses that lay around him. He frowned and reached out for the one that was their leader. Grasping it by its long white hair he yanked its head so he could look at its face. It was frozen in a stare of hatred and a silent scream of malice. "Huh," he scoffed at it. "At least you're easier to kill than the ones back home." He released the head and it flopped to the dirt.

A movement from the corner of his eye caught his attention. He looked over his shoulder in time to see a third pack moving to the garrison. Damn, he did not expect that. *How many of those things were there?* He pulled his hood back over his head and melted back into the shadows.

On the way to the prince, Ruelina noticed Smythe lying between two ghouls and was about to be eaten alive. Smacking Kaeleb firmly on the shoulder she abruptly changed directions and made her way toward Smythe. The priest quickly followed.

When she reached the first one, its back was to her. As it turned her sword struck downward through its face, knocking it back. The other stood and Kaeleb thrust forward piercing it in its chest and twisted the blade back out. It swiped at his head but missed. Being careful not to step on Smythe, the priest moved around to draw the thing away from him.

The ghoul Ruelina cut stood but could not see well with its face split. It eyes hung differently in the sockets and its head waved back and forth as it tried to focus on a target to hit or bite. With its aim not well, Ruelina parried with the sharp edge of her sword until she had a clear opening to strike. He was hoping to take at least on hand by doing so.

The other ghoul lunged at Kaeleb with a snarling hiss, its claws outstretched and ready to sink into the priest's flesh. He ducked down, nearly flattening himself to the ground. The ghoul sailed over him and that is when he stood and swung upwards. The sword slashed from its ribs to its hip, straight down its body. It was knocked off balance and landed with a thud. Quickly scrambling around, it leapt at him again. The priest stepped to the side, almost too far, and swung downward. He felt the claws catch his tabard and rip through it with little effort. Thankfully the razors did not catch and rip his armor. He could imagine that being his flesh. The blade cut through its back but did not penetrate through its ribs and it was knocked heavily to the ground.

The pain was subsiding and he could begin to move his fingers. He let out a loud gasping yell as he rolled onto his back. Smythe was happy his muscles no longer painfully spasmed and that his blood slowly began to replace the acid. Taking a deep breath, he groaned. Rolling prone he forced himself to stand and look around. He gasped with a start as he saw a ghoul not more than four paces away. It quickly stood and lunged back at Kaeleb. To his other side Ruelina was slowly hacking away at another ghoul. His breath caught tight in his chest when he caught the sight of movement in the distance. Another pack of ghouls came lumbering through the darkness. Did that one have white hair?

Painfully he stood and watched them draw nearer. Smythe was becoming ambulatory but it was not happening quickly enough for his liking. The other ghouls would be there soon and he needed to have his full movement if he were to be of any use. He scrambled, mostly limping, toward them and ducked into the stables. Crouching painfully behind one of the large doors, he quietly flexed his limbs against the resounding discomfort in the hopes of speeding his recovery. Happily, those paralytic effects seemed to be temporary but the oozing bite marks were not. As they closed and their attention became focused onto the fighting he suddenly considered that there may have been something else lurking inside this stable with he snuck in here. Peering into the darkness he hoped that notion was very wrong.

Emerik and Tobin lay there in the dirt and stared helplessly at one another. The pain was incredible and they could not move. Emerik could barely move his eyes and when he did he looked right into Tobin's stare. He was lower than he ever had been in his life, feeling powerless, useless, ignorant and foolish. The "People's Prince" was close to getting everyone here killed. If he had ordered the evacuation of the town then no one would be there. If he had believed Ruelina from the beginning, then they would have been better prepared. He would not be watching his friend suffer like this just a few feet away. If only he could stop second guessing himself. If only…

The process of recovery was going quicker now that he had stood and moved around. From his concealed position behind the barn door, Smythe quickly rolled and flexed his fingers. Wishing he had something to bandage his injuries with and Breathing deep to calm himself, he fought to steady his mind as he readied for the battle. He knew it was against the law. He knew that if he were caught he would need a good explanation. He decided to concern himself with that later. Right then, he felt that if he did not act and do something, it was quite probable that they all would die.

He peered around the corner and spied the ghouls lumbering toward Kaeleb and Ruelina. He readied himself, took one last deep breath and then quickly moved from behind the door. Instantly he drew a glyph in the air with both hands as he rapidly spoke a few words in an arcane tongue. Three bolts of magical energy shot forth from his fingers and struck three different creatures. All of them were caught unaware. The three, obviously wounded, tried to lumber as best they could to attack him. Again, Smythe completed the same movement and the same words. Energy poured in from all around him then shot from his fingers. The same three were struck again. Smythe, now confident, taunted them.

"Come then!" he challenged. "I can do this all night!"

As he began the same motion again the ghoul with white hair cocked its head and crouched lower.

"*Tear off his flesh*," it slowly hissed.

Tobin let out a growing yell as Emerik moaned beside him. Both could feel their muscles relaxing and the burning slowly subsiding. The knight grunted with each panting breath.

"Hells…What…ahh…what…was…that?" He forced the words between painful breaths.

The prince rolled onto his back and slowly moaned. Blinking, he tried to focus on the night sky through watery eyes. He agonizingly and clumsily patted the ground for his sword.

The priest turned sharply toward the hissed words. He saw another pack of ghouls and was gripped again with renewed fear. *How many of these are there?* He saw what he could only describe as bolts of energy shoot out from Smythe's hand, arc independently through the air in different paths and then strike some of the ghouls as they closed on him. *What the hell? I saw that just a few days ago. That was him!* He remembered the fight against the men who became fiends on the road to the hamlet. This was the same magic only now he realized it was Smythe who was doing it.

The elf wasted no time watching the dazzling display. She dashed to the closest one and swung as hard as she could. Her sword bit into its neck and sliced out through its ribs on the other side of its body. The ghoul leader looked to Ruelina and then back to Smythe. It stood up, as much as its twisted and decaying form would allow, and began to hiss in an arcane language.

Smythe's head snapped toward the ghoul with white hair in time to see it was also casting an evocation! *What? How can it do that?* He watched with marked fear as a small flame, the size of a single candle, formed in the air in front of it. With a roar, the small flame quickly spun into a large one and formed a sphere that stood almost as tall as a man. The burning globe then began to roll directly toward Smythe as quickly as a person could run!

"Damn!" he cursed before limping off away from the stables as quickly as he could. Looking back over his shoulder he wanted to see, out of morbid curiosity, what damaging effect the magic would have on the wood of the building. He did not want to see the sphere turn as it rolled to follow him.

"It turns! Eala, it turns!" He pushed himself harder in sheer panic wondering where he could go to hide from a five-foot-tall flaming globe. He could feel warmth running down his leg and down his body as he awkwardly hobbled and knew it was his own blood. But right then, he felt it was better to bleed than to be burned alive.

The paladin stood just in time to see a large rolling sphere of fire chasing after Smythe. In the distance, a gray creature with long stringy white hair held his hands outstretched and always in the direction of the sphere. His eyes blinked for a moment before he recovered his sword and shield and then slapped Tobin stiffly on the shoulder. The knight turned to Emerik with an angered yet worried look on his face.

"Damn, magic," said Tobin.

"Let's kill it," Emerik suggested as he ran, more jogged, toward the fray. His legs were not quite following his commands just yet but he was not about to wait in safety while people in his country were being killed. He pushed himself a little faster while he heard his friend grunting behind him. Both pressed to ignore their painful wounds and Tobin was about to pass him as they moved.

Ruelina struck another, one that was wounded by Smythe's magic, but it did not fall. Keeping in the fight, it continued to slash wildly at her while gnashing its teeth. Kaeleb flanked it and slashed its leg. As it turned, it dropped to one knee and swiped at him, hitting him in the side of his chest. The ringing of his armor told him the claws did not penetrate but the force of the blow knocked the wind from his lungs. The ranger swung straight down and split into its head and neck. The momentum finally stopped and the blade was wedged all the way down between its shoulders. She cursed as another ravenously scurried toward her.

Tobin pushed past the ranger like a charging bull. Without stopping his run the knight cut into the creature. It spun as Tobin charged past it. When it turned to face him and give chase Emerik slammed into it with his shield. It sailed ungracefully through the air and Emerik chased it. As it came down it was struck again. Emerik stabbed it through its skull as it thudded onto the dirt and kept running.

Kaeleb fought to get the air back into his lungs while trying to run with them. He watched as another ghoul dashed at Tobin. The knight merely stepped to the side and cut without stopping. Emerik, close behind, cut it again as he ran past. Both seemed to be charging through to the ghoul leader on the other side of the stables. He decided to help and Ruelina was close on his heels.

One creature leaped at Tobin head on. He could not step to the side quickly enough and instead he held is longsword out in front of him. The creature howled wildly but was unable to control itself. Attempting to twist in the air it only succeeded in allowing the point of Tobin's blade to pierce its ribs and exit its other shoulder. Tobin swung downward, slamming the thing onto the ground and wrenching his blade free. He stepped forcefully onto its head before cutting deep through its badly damaged chest.

Hearing a snarl behind him he pivoted to receive its charge. Emerik suddenly stopped between the two and the creature bounced off his shield as if it tried to run through a stone wall. The paladin raced forward and cut it in its leg when it landed on its back. Bringing the sword around his head Emerik struck again and slashed across its arm and shoulder. He spun to his left and dropped his body. Briefly the creature saw his back and took the opportunity to sink its teeth in. Emerik, though, never stopped his spin. The shield came around first, slamming into its head and side. While off balance the paladin swung his sword into its jaw. The top of its head dropped from its body as its lower jaw hung loosely by its neck. Emerik was standing again and rushing to the leader as it fell.

The priest slowed to a stop and surveyed the battle. There were still a few ghouls remain aside from the leader. Emerik and Tobin needed help in getting to that leader in safety. He held his sword outstretched and pointing to the sky. "Zi denger kuan kanpa talamu iskaku!" Unseen power fell from the heavens and a faint sword, translucent and free moving, projected out from Kaeleb's blade and sped toward a ghoul he focused on.

Smythe never stopped running. He raced around the building and approached the leader from the rear. As he rounded the corner he could see it was occupied with another matter. There were to knights cutting their way through the ghouls as they raced toward it. Slowing to a stop he fought to catch his breath. Smythe would help them without their knowing.

The knight sprinted the last remaining distance. He could see the darkened hatred burning in its eyes like glowing coals from a furnace. From the corner of his eye he could see a ghoul, snarling and hissing, suddenly be cut by swinging blade of insubstantial force. It was quite distracting. He watched it cut again and again without someone grasping it! Emerik sped past him focused on those glowing eyes and wanting to cut a sword between them.

The creature hissed in its arcane tongue before Smythe's transmutation was completed. Quickly the area around it became dark. There was no moonlight to penetrate and no starlight as Smythe's work took effect. Emerik disappeared into the area of darkness as the creature became stunned. Not knowing about this new magic but detesting it with every fiber, the paladin guessed where the creature was and struck. The thing could see in the darkness but did not fully understand what had just happened. It watched, rather perplexed, as the paladin's sword came down across its body. It fell back from the force of the blow and landed on the ground. Not knowing where it was, Emerik swung again and again trying to hit something in this inky blackness. His blade passed harmlessly above its head. Slowly, as it regained its wits, it crouched like a coiling spring to pounce on him.

The other ghouls were having a difficult time with Ruelina, Tobin and that enchanted weapon. Kaeleb felt Enki's power surging through him to the blade his god granted him. When he noticed the area suddenly darken from the air itself he changed tactics. Running toward where Emerik once was, he guessed, the priest called out for Enki to aid the paladin.

The creature was poised to strike and watched intently as Emerik swung in different directions trying to hit it. When it felt his rhythm it readied to pounce. But the black vanished! The area that was dark became light. The sudden illumination hurt its eyes and it shielded itself for a moment. The paladin felt the light shining down on him and now looked for the creature. He saw it. He struck. He watched it fall.

Looking around for another opponent, Tobin found none. Ruelina did the same, as did Kaeleb. Emerik panted and shouted in a triumphant challenge to any other creatures that could hear. None of them answered but Tobin and Kaeleb did. They both shouted in one loud bark. All of the warriors of Paragon did. Those that did not were fallen in battle. With stern faces the warriors regarded one another and sheathed their swords. The fight, for now, was done.

"Emerik?" Tobin called.

"Here!" he answered while his friend jogging to him. The paladin's eyes never moved from the creature with the long matted hair. Smythe limped from the shadows. He ran with open wounds and opened them more and was covered in blood.

Tobin reached his friend Emerik and panted, "What...the hells...were those?" He managed to speak between gasps.

"I don't know, sire," Smythe answered firmly, thinking the knight was speaking to him. His eyes were closed as he lumbered and did not know that Tobin was not addressing him.

"Those..." Ruelina said as she walked to them, "...were ghouls."

"Ghouls?" questioned Emerik.

"Yes..." she sighed.

"All those...monsters are ghouls?" the priest asked.

"Yes!" the ranger shouted. She pointed. "*Those* are ghouls! And *those* are ghouls! Believe me now? They are not people trying to scare us poor stupid peasants from our homes. They are ghouls!"

She wanted to slap one of them. Ruelina did not care who, anyone would do just fine.

Emerik looked to her for a few moments then spoke softly. "I am sorry we did not believe you," he apologized.

She wanted to say, *well then maybe next time you'll believe me and not think I'm stupid or had no learning, pompous prick! Or better yet, next time I'll just let them chew on you and ask if you believe before I help you!* Instead she uttered something like, "Just save our home."

Kaeleb had wandered away from the group not wanting to be seen. He was dripping sweat and felt his hands tingling. He sank to his knees and felt the world spin. His adrenaline had faded. The non-existent ghouls had been defeated. It was time for him to vomit.

"What do we do with them?" Smythe asked while looking down at the ghoul leader. He remembered he needed to bring back proof of their existence but thought it would be quite odd in front of the prince and knight if he cut off a hand or head and stuffed it into a small sack. The explanation would be more unpleasant than the questioning.

"We have been burning them," the ranger offered.

"Then let's do it!" Tobin agreed.

Smythe turned away as he imagined a task from his mission literally going up in smoke.

"Um..." Smythe looked around franticly. "Where is Maura?"

Ruelina's face drained.

"Maura!" Kaeleb called out.

"She was taken," Tobin admitted.

"What?" Both Smythe and Ruelina managed to pronounce it at the same time.

"She was drug off...a few minutes ago," he was careful not to mention, *while I was lying helpless in the dirt.*

"Where?" Smythe asked.

"What direction?" Ruelina was ready to sprint.

"Um...that way," the knight pointed vaguely. It happened to be back toward the cemetery. Without a word, thanks or curse, Ruelina shot off in the direction of the graves. Smythe was close on her but did not run as fast as the athletic elf, especially since he was still limping in pain. Ruelina left him behind and called out for Maura as she ran.

The snarling ghouls kept dragging her. She wanted the pain to stop so she could cry. Her teeth were grinding together so tight she thought they would break. With a faint movement from her eyes she could glance down and see blood flowing from the slashes in her stomach. She wished Naia were there.

Abruptly she felt herself being dropped to the ground. She rolled onto her other side and watched dimly as the ghouls ran off. She could hear the sounds of fighting but could not see what was happening. Then it stopped. She could hear something limping toward her and then stop. It grasped her knee like a vice and began dragging her again. One of the ghouls was gone but the other still dragged her through the hamlet. In a quick blur, something dark and swift like the wind passed overhead and smacked the ghoul. The shadow glided off noiselessly into the night as the ghoul picked itself up off the ground. It looked into the distance but evidently did not see anything. It turned to grasp Maura when the soundless shadow slammed into it again. It was knocked behind Maura and she could feel the ground vibrate with the force of its impact.

Something above her head was quickly limping toward her. The scraping of claws in the dirt told her it was the other ghoul. He heart pounded rapidly as she saw it pass in front of her. Its lower leg was broken and dragged its dangling foot by rotting flesh without care. It stopped and looked around. The shadow seemed to suddenly appear before the ghoul and struck it. With a sharp thud the ghoul left the ground as it was knocked from her field of view. She heard the other creature scamper toward the shadow before she remembered it too was a ghoul. The shadow spun and struck, knocking the ghoul fell to the dirt where it stood. Swiftly it stood and thrust out its claw. The shadow grunted and pulled its long razors from his abdomen. His foot came up in a blur and the ghoul's head snapped back. He then made a small circle and turn with his body. The ghoul flew into the air and inverted before landing on its skull with a dull crack. It spun around on its head, its limbs flailing in violent rage.

In the distance, Maura heard the comforting sound of Ruelina calling her name. The shadow looked in the direction of the shout and paused. Scrambling to its feet the broken ghoul regained its balance and crouched to lunge at the dark figure. With little regard, the shadow kicked it solidly in its knee and put it back down in the dirt. Before the ghoul could stand the whirling darkness was gone. The ghoul was not without foes, though. But in its broken state, it was no match for an enraged Ruelina and a grimly determined Smythe.

The shadow watched from the rooftop. It saw how the ranger and the Craftuser fought the injured ghouls. He smirked. His bleeding had already stopped and he was not concerned about the unnatural toxin from the ghouls here. He found he was immune long ago, but he also knew he would have to more careful next time. He was careless and that's why it got him. *Lesson learned*, he told himself.

While the corpses were being stacked the members of the hamlet peered out from the safety of their windows. They watched the entire struggle, from Kaeleb's first shout and all the way to the pile of bodies. When the pile was ignited and the soft low crackled in the night they finally left their windows with some measure of satisfaction. The strangers were there to help. They helped each other and they helped poor Maura as well. Maybe they could be trusted. Most all of them just wished Naia was there. Things like this never happen when she was around. They never saw a ghoul, never had a dying forest and never had any real troubles.

The villagers would have helped but they knew they could not. That tactic had already been tried. In a posse they grasped their torches and lanterns with good solid weapons from the garrison and marched into the cemetery to defend themselves. Within the hour, the ghouls had more food. Days later, the townsfolk found shambling ghouls that were the townspeople that fought before. Their own people had become corrupted. The false sense of security was enough for the villagers to remain indoors at night. Ghouls never came in the daytime…well, mostly never.

Inside the Silverwood Garrison

Early Morning

Maura tossed and turned in the early morning, hours before sunrise. With a gasp she sat bolt upright in the darkness. As her chest still heaved she looked around the room. Everyone was still sleeping. Catching her breath, she slipped quietly from her bed and padded softly across the floor to the window. She looked up at the night sky, being streaked with clouds, very little moonlight passed to the gloomy hamlet. Her home was that gloomy hamlet. Trying to see past the clouds, hoping to get a glimpse of a star or two, her thoughts went to Naia. She missed her mentor and friend very much.

It had become a quiet ten years since she had left. The place became cold. Cold? Like icy fingers sharply dancing into her spine. Maura trembled and part of her mind was now under a shadow of malice. She felt something digging into her mind, splitting her skull. No, not again.

She ran to Ruelina's bed where the ranger was sleeping, crawled on it and began to shake her with tear streamed eyes.

"Wake up," she sobbed. "Please wake up." Maura glanced to the window and Ruelina stirred beneath her.

"Um…what is it, Maura?" Ruelina was half asleep.

"Something's coming…they're coming back…please get up…"

That woke her up. Ruelina sat up and saw Maura's tears shining in the dim light.

"What's coming?"

"Them…they are coming back…please…"

"What is it?" the priest roused and sat up in his bed.

"Maura," Ruelina answered while standing. "She's acting the same as she did the other night before we were attacked. Get everyone ready."

"Please hurry!"

"We are, we need to wake everyone first," Ruelina told her.

Maura took a deep breath and then screamed at the top of her lungs.

"Wake up! Wake up!"

On the second floor Maura's shrill stabbed their ears like a hundred pointy daggers. Emerik shouted and fell from his bed. He scrambled to get up and grasp his sword. Tobin was already in the hall with a drawn sword and shield but no armor.

"What is it?" asked Emerik while panting.

"I don't know, I just heard screaming," Tobin remarked.

Thelial emerged from the room next to Tobin's at the end of the hall. He was fully dressed and looked rested.

"Its Maura, she did this before."

"Maura?" The knight was not in the mood for that witless twit and a bad dream.

Thelial nodded.

"Just last night before the ghouls attacked. She felt them coming."

"Felt? She can feel the ghouls before they come?" asked Emerik with earnest curiosity.

"Apparently so." Thelial walked to the window and peered out.

"See anything?" the prince asked.

"No, not yet," answered the assassin.

"You're not taking this seriously, are you?" Tobin pleaded with Emerik. The man had gone crazy.

"What do you need?" Emerik asked Thelial.

What does he need? By Hell's wrath, this turning out to be a bad night.

"Ruelina, she's good with a bow." Thelial's posture suddenly straightened. "And tell her to hurry."

Outside in the gloom of the cold drizzling rain, Thelial saw dim shapes of lumbering forms making their way through the hamlet. They were searching.

"How many?" the prince asked.

"About...eight so far."

The prince looked at his friend.

"Yes, I am taking this seriously." He turned and headed for the stairs. He stopped after a few steps and looked back. "Tobin, come with me, we'll stop them if they come through the front door. Thelial, stay here and shoot whatever you can. Ruelina will be here shortly along with the others."

"What?" Tobin asked.

"If the ghouls get by us then they can hold here on the second floor for a while. Or we can have a fall back point if there are too many."

"Too many?"

"We can fight in shifts on the stairs if need be."

"Wait, wait…how many are we expecting?" Tobin asked while grasping his arm.

"Eight…a hundred…does not matter. We're killing every ghoul they send tonight." With a stern nod they headed down the stairs.

At the bottom they met Ruelina and their squires in the great hall heading toward them.

"It's Maura, she started-"

"I know," Emerik interrupted her. "Get upstairs with Thelial and take your bow. Shoot as many as you can. You two are coming with us." He strode into the barracks and looked around, taking everything in at once. "Smythe, take Maura upstairs. Stay by Ruelina and Thelial but keep away from the windows."

"Yes, milord," Smythe quickly answered. "Come on, Maura. We'll go upstairs."

The three of them quickly ran to the second floor.

"You," he said to the squires. "Barricade the door. There are two solid beams to buttress them with already there. Go!"

"You've changed," Tobin regarded.

Emerik merely shot him a glance and turned to Kaeleb.

"These things are unholy so we'll need you down here with us."

The priest nodded.

"Men," Emerik addressed them all. "Our goal is simple. We keep them outside. If they come in they do not leave and none get past us. Hoowaa?"

"Hoowaa!" They all shouted and turned to the door. If the gates were to suddenly burst open or shatter into tiny splinters, none of them would have been surprised. *The prince's stare could have burned a hole through the thick beams. Come on then! Paladin or no I'll slay all of you.*

Upstairs Ruelina ran directly beside Thelial while Smythe took Maura to the sitting area to the right of the hall. Nervously, she sat down and was still upset. Maura glanced around as if expecting something to jump out at her and trembled.

"What's happening?" the ranger asked Thelial.

"We have eight ghouls heading this way. They don't seem to know exactly where we are yet." His voice was even and controlled and he spoke with the same regard as he would speak about the neighborhood cat.

"How can you be so calm?"

"These don't frighten me."

"They don't? What does?"

He never answered and never intended to. It was an answer that she really did not need to hear...ever.

"Can we hurt them with these arrows?" Ruelina was concerned that their weapons were useless against the walking dead.

"Well..." He reached down and handed he a heavy quiver. "We can with these." His face formed a wicked smile.

Ruelina had never seen arrows that size before. They were almost half an inch in diameter and a few inches longer than she was used to. The tips were not bladed but were sharpened metal points instead.

"What are these?"

"Be careful," he said while turning his attention back to the outside. "They explode when the shafts break."

"Explode?"

"Fire," the grin returned. "Lots of fire."

"Why fire?"

"There're only a few things that can harm most walking dead: anything holy or blessed, usually something silver and...fire. Tonight, we are using fire." He honed in one lone ghoul and smirked. "These are much heavier so you have to aim high. Now...watch..."

Thelial drew back his composite bow and aimed carefully. It was carefully constructed to allow someone with greater strength more damage from the arrows. Ruelina watched the muscles flex in his forearms and hands before looking out the window. She felt her mouth become dry even while on the brink of a fight.

"There, by the stables," he told her where to look.

Squinting, even as an elf, she could barely see the creature shuffle along the wall.

"I see it," she admitted. Before she could ask how he could see that far, he spoke.

"Shiny."

There was a dull twang of the bow string and arrow sped into the night. Soundlessly it sailed through the air toward the unsuspecting ghoul. It looked side to side peering with its burning orbs to find the humans and elves that still lingered here. It was hungry. All of them were hungry. Their numbers were too many and food was too scarce. They needed to feed. But it never saw the arrow coming at it in the night nor did it see where it came from. It briefly felt the point pierce the side of its chest before the shaft broke. With a flash of orange light and a bellowing clap the ghoul burst into pieces. Dry bits of it scattered with the rising cloud of dust.

Thelial grinned smugly and reached for another special arrow. On the first floor the fighters heard the rumble outside and looked to each other with welling concern.

"Magic?" asked Perry.

Emerik commanded Dyrrany, "Go and see if everything is good upstairs."

Immediately he bolted for the stairs and bound up them as quickly as he could, skipping two or three steps as went. When he reached the top he heard laughter.

"Is everything well?" The squire yelled.

"Oh, yes, we're fine," Ruelina shouted back with a wide grin.

"What was that?"

"Arrows," she giggled.

"Arrows? I never heard an arrow do that before." Dyrrany challenged.

"They're special arrows, filled with chemical fire."

"Oh," he wished he had some. "Well, just be careful." He bounded back down the stairs.

"Report?" Emerik asked him.

"That was them upstairs. Chemical fire in the arrows, they said."

"Chemical fire? Why didn't I think of that?" Tobin mumbled.

One detonation after another erupted outside. The ranger and assassin shot one ghoul after another as they found out which building to attack. Scanning between the buildings and trees, Thelial saw something curious and disturbing. Two ghouls with long while hair spoke to one another before one darted off into the night. The remaining one looked up at the window and slid off behind the stables. Thelial became worried. Before he could say anything behind him Maura began to whimper.

"No...no...no...too fast...too dark...too fast...no..." She got up and ran to cower in a corner.

Thelial and Ruelina looked at one another after watching what Maura did.

"That's not good," Ruelina observed.

"You may want to get downstairs and warn them," suggested Thelial as he looked outside.

Too late.

Maura screamed.

The assassin saw the swift movement of a shadow race through the hamlet and into the garrison gate. It took the thing less than a second to pass through half of the village.

"Damn it!" Thelial cursed as he dropped his bow and pulled his sword. He ran toward the stairs. "Stay here!"

In the great room, behind the buttress, the warriors stood poised. They only heard Maura scream once before the shadow slid through the narrow space between the doors. It moved like a swift wind. The shadow became partly solid and slashed Tobin and Emerik as it sped soundlessly by them. There was no hiss, no growl not even the sound of moving air. There was just this shadow that had passed into the middle of the room.

The priest got the best look at it since it seemed to abruptly pause and look at him. It was taller than a man and had wings that never flapped. Dark matter poured from it like wisps of smoke from a candle. He had to do something and fast. Kaeleb moved to get some distance between him and it. Did it smile mockingly at him?

As quickly as it came it glided to Kaeleb. Everything became black. It flew up to the second floor in silent laughter. The murky black around the priest began to burn his skin like acid. He yelled from inside and tried to run in some direction that would lead out. But the darkness followed where ever he went! Kaeleb howled in pain and panic.

Upstairs the hallway became darker and Thelial crouched

while pointing his sword. Ruelina gasped as the shadow sped in the narrow hall. Thelial grunted and then the shadow howled moving past her and out of the window.

"Coward!" Thelial yelled from the hall.

No sooner did Ruelina turn to look at him did he suddenly appear beside her. He scanned the outside for the shadow with a snarl on his lips. Seeing nothing, not even a ghoul, he hit the metal frame of the window in disgust. Ruelina jumped from his outburst and watched him walk down the hallway.

Kaeleb was frantic as the pain continued to hurt more and more. If he could see he would swear his skin was being burned from his body all at once. In the midst of the chaos he remembered the thing reaching out to touch him. Again he howled and ripped off his shirt and threw it from him. The darkness stayed and he dropped to one knee. He knew he would die soon if he did not do something quickly. With another grunting hiss through clenched teeth he took off his belt and threw it.

He panted. His watery eyes opened and he saw blurry light. He yelled in thanks to Enki for guiding his thoughts while listening to his skin hiss. Emerik saw the thin smoke rising from the priest's body like he had just been taken from a boiling kettle. There in the corner was an area of swirling cloudy darkness. Thelial emerged from the stairs and strode into the great hall. He looked at the inky blackness in the corner as he passed it. Huh, he thought. That works here too.

"Where is it?" Tobin asked while standing. He held his chest as it dripped blood from the large gaping claw marks.

"It gone...as in gone out the window." Thelial looked at everyone surveying their damage. They were all lucky, this time.

"What was that thing?" asked the prince. He never needed Enki more than he did then.

Thelial paused and looked at Tobin. His silence brought the knight's eyes to his.

"That," he paused. "Was a scout."

"A scout?" Emerik asked.

Thelial nodded.

"Yes," he frowned. "Now they know how many of us there are, how we are armed, how well trained we are against them and...where we are weak. As soon as it gets back to who or what sent it and tells them what it saw here. They will make an attack plan and then rip this little place apart. They'll hit fast and hard."

"What do we do?" Tobin needed a counter attack plan. He would not just sit and wait to become food.

"What can we do?" Thelial asked coldly.

They paused in silence as the weight of impending doom pressed down on them.

"Abandon this place," Emerik said assertively.

Everyone stared at him.

"We have to get everyone out as soon as we can." The prince was not normally for running but he knew that he had to go and seek the temple or he would be no good to anyone.

Thelial moved toward to Kaeleb who had stopped smoldering. Kneeling down he spoke to him.

"You alright?"

"No...that hurt." The priest winced.

"Yeah, it looked like it would. But, you don't seem to be hurt on the outside."

"It felt like my skin was burning off." He struggled to stand and Thelial helped him. When hands met his body it did not hurt him anymore than he already was. Looking down he saw no damage to his skin. "What did it do?"

"I don't know," Thelial lied. He did not feel bad at all lying to a priest and would probably do it again when he had the chance. "Let's get you lying down."

"No...what if they come back?"

"Not tonight they won't," he reassured the agonizing priest.

"How can you be so sure?" Emerik asked.

"Because, they got what they came for. We probably have a day maybe two at the most."

"That soon?" questioned the prince.

"Would you give you that long?"

He slowly walked with Kaeleb into the barracks and gently helped him into his bed.

Late that morning the ranger was the first to rise. Considering everything that happened the night before, she was still up just after dawn and felt rather rested. She was not feeling very energetic but awake, still, none the less. Ruelina glanced over to

Maura to see if she was well. They young elf girl already had her eyes open and was watching the ranger.

"You're awake?"

"Yes," said Maura as she sat up. "Not very long though. It's still raining outside."

"Ouch..." the priest grunted from his bed.

"You're awake too?" Ruelina looked in surprise.

"Yes, but everything does not have to hurt so much," he grunted. When he moved he realized that the discomfort was from overworked muscles and not from the thing earlier that morning. He sat up and rolled his neck.

The squires stirred as well as did Smythe. Everyone sat up and just stared at one another. None of them were very tired but no one offered any explanation as to why they all woke up at the same time. Smythe was about to open his mouth when Thelial stepped into the room. His face became grim when he saw everyone was awake.

"How are you this morning?" Smythe asked him.

He looked as if to say "don't ask that" but did not answer.

"Dyrrany, Perry, you're going to be needed upstairs soon," the assassin said to them.

"Why, is there a problem?" Perry asked him.

"No, not yet..." Oops, that came out too early. "Your masters are awake and will need help with their armor." He crossed the floor and went to the barred window. Looking at the ground and sky he frowned darker. The sky had a tint of dark red. He did not like that.

The two squires rose, dressed and went upstairs. Ruelina stood and looked at everyone looking at her. Smythe never really noticed how athletic she was for an elf. She may not have had a very pretty face, as elves were concerned, but she had an appealing frame. At that moment, Thelial was staring at Maura, as was Kaeleb, but for an entirely different reason. Maura had felt the ghouls before they came, twice in a row, and with stunning accuracy. She also noticed the shadow before it arrived as well. That meant her extraordinary perception was not merely limited to walking dead like ghouls. She was aware of incorporeal fiends also. Maura suddenly became not so dumb and useless; the elf girl had become a thinking feeling individual with a greater perception than either of them possessed.

Without a word, the two wondered what other secret or unknown things Maura was capable of.

With a loud crescendo of clanking the prince and knight emerged into the great hall. Emerik, of course, wore the gleaming armor. Interestingly enough, it seemed to befit him well, as if it was his all along. The knight looked into the room at everyone and slapped his gauntleted hands together.

"Let's eat!" It sounded more like a command to children than an invitation. Without awaiting a response, the two strode off and went outside.

Everyone slowly stood and sauntered out. Thelial was the last to leave being that he stayed by the window trying to discern the uneasiness he felt. Kaeleb, although he did not mention it in the least, also was inwardly struggling with the same thing. Something had changed. Something was worryingly different.

Smythe nonchalantly walked slower than the others so that he could get nearer to Thelial. He knew the man knew far too much about what was happening here to be just a normal smart guy. When the darkly dressed Thelial came near he decided to ask the question.

"Um, Thelial, you've been here before, in Silverwood, right?"

"Yes, why do you ask?"

"I was wondering...if you could tell me, where can I find a good cloak?"

Thelial looked at him for a moment as if he were about to unemotionally and swiftly cut Smythe's head from his body. He knew the response, they both did. But where was Smythe in all this? Was he part of the problem, part of the help or part of the unknowing? From what he had seen up to that point, Smythe seemed to Thelial that he was part of the unknowing. That could be good or bad.

"Why do you ask?" Thelial gave an incorrect response.

"Ah, well, you know..." Smythe stammered. That was not the response he was expecting and that made Thelial all the more threatening. Someone out in the world will all that bizarre and unearthly insanity in full bloom around Silverwood, who also knew as much as he did, could not be good if he were not part of the brotherhood. Smythe continued. "Since its raining I thought I may need one."

"Yeah..." Thelial saw a flash of fear in Smythe's eyes. He

was part of the unknowing and was actually one of the good guys. "Well, around here there are none to be found." He subtly emphasized the words incase Smythe was a bit daft. "So it looks like you're going to get wet, just like the rest of us." Without another word Thelial walked a bit faster to the inn.

Smythe trailed behind thinking to himself. *Thelial is one of us. That's a relief. But...he's not an investigator and I was told I would be here on my own. Since I was sent and here is here by his own accord, looking for Naia, then he must really know something the rest of us don't. Naia...Naia...She's a teacher and sage. She knows a great deal about magic and many other things it seems. Was he coming here to ask her something or to tell her? He mentioned a message so he wants to tell her...what? Also important, what does he do for the Brotherhood?* There are only three types of Brothers: Mists who investigate, Guardians who keep knowledge and...Smythe stopped. *Agents...he's an agent. He's an assassin!* Smythe swallowed hard. Agents were special and especially deadly.

At breakfast everyone ate slowly and very little talking. Most heads were pointed to the plates of rice, vegetables and fruits that were getting a little too old to eat. Silverwood was running out of food, it had no decent supply of water and it was losing hope. Still, the elves stayed. Sacred land? What was so damn important about this place? The prince would have to know and Smythe was a bit slow on his investigation. He was gone most all of yesterday and the prince had yet to receive a report as to why and where he was or what he was doing.

"Mayor Matchok," Emerik addressed. "Please come here for a moment."

The fat elf wobbled over.

"Yes, sire. Is everything alright?"

"No, it's not," he answered somberly. "In light of a new enemy that appeared last night I am insisting that Silverwood be abandoned...today...immediately."

Everyone in the room stopped moving. No one could have breathed without everyone hearing it.

"Um...leave Silverwood..."

"Yes, it is neither a suggestion nor a request. Make any and all preparations to evacuate this village as swiftly as possible. Before nightfall, I want everyone on the road out of here."

Matchok opened his mouth to speak but the prince cut him

off.

"Everyone."

"Yes, sire." Matchok bowed and wobbled off with a distressed look. Even under threat of doom and certain death no one wanted to leave from this place.

"Smythe," Emerik called even though he was sitting at the same table.

"Yes?"

"What happened to you yesterday?"

Smythe paused trying to think of what to say and what not to.

"Speak quickly, we have much to do."

"Well...I believe I found the origin of the dying forest," the investigator blurted.

After a pause Emerik simply urged him, "Go on."

"Um...There is a hill about a few hours' hike from here. The hill has stones on it, eleven of them, and has an altar in the center. And...I think I know what happened to some of the missing villagers."

"What is that?"

"They're dead, milord. Not just killed normally, sire. They...they were...twisted like rags."

Smythe then told them about the stones and about the altar. He spoke of the porous stone that could only come from the depths of the sea. He also showed them the rubbings and they discovered that only Kaeleb seemed to know what they were. They were described as being emblems of the Ancient Ones, the dark gods that fought against the Elders but were defeated. Defeated but not destroyed. The Ancient Ones were the rulers of the Underworld, the darkest of the vilest divinities.

As Thelial listened he could only think to himself, damn it, he found it. He decided to forcefully change the subject.

"So, great prince, what is you master plan? Where will all these people go?" His added sarcasm would definitely bring an end to their other conversation.

"They will all go to Boregar. I am going there ahead of everyone to make arrangements for them. That good enough for you?" Anger flashed in his eyes.

"It's not good enough for them. If you remember they went to Boregar for aid and received none. That is why you saw her in

Paragon City." The extra stresses on the words were meant to ignite a fire. It did. Thelial got what he wanted. He distracted them from the notion of venturing out to the hill. He knew what was out there and knew they could not protect themselves any more than he could protect them. They were ill-equipped for that enemy.

"I don't care! They are not staying here to die!"

"Dying in Boregar is better?"

Ruelina looked around not wanting to become part of this senseless fight and then finally offered a solution that some of them had come to before she had even left for Paragon City.

"Ib," she said loudly. "We'll go to Ib."

"What?" Tobin shifted his attention from considering cutting Thelial down where he stood to Ruelina who just mentioned the elven kingdom to the north.

"Some of us decided that if we had to leave Silverwood that we would go north through the Implan Hills and go to Ib." Her voice was exasperated. "Now if the children at the table could just stop fighting it would be much better."

The two men looked at each other and quieted. Emerik and Tobin glared at Thelial who just happy to choke down his food knowing that they were not going to the hill. But none of them knew that. Emerik abruptly stood and took a large swallow of his water.

"Dyrrany, finish up quickly. We're leaving for Boregar as soon as possible." His tankard was loudly placed onto the table. Staring at Thelial he continued. "Tobin, you are in command while I am gone. See to it that everyone gets out of this town before sunset today. After that, secure this place and I will return from Boregar with force. We will then hunt down this enemy and slay every last one of them."

"Excellent idea!" agreed Tobin.

"Is it?" Thelial asked.

"I'm wondering the same," Kaeleb mentioned. "Our weapons do not seem to harm them."

"It has been decided," Emerik spoke coldly. He walked off and Dyrrany chomped down some of his remaining food and rushed after him.

"What's wrong?" Everyone heard Smythe ask. Looking to see what he was talking about they all noticed Maura sitting bolt upright and trembling. Sweat ran down her forehead and she clutched her seat as if afraid she would suddenly fly off of it. The blood had drained from her face.

"Maura, dear, it's okay, it was just a stupid fight between stupid men is all." Ruelina tried to console her. Maura never answered. She just continued to stare ahead with wide eyes and shudder uncontrollably.

Then Thelial felt it. He looked up as a dark chill shot up his spine and into his skull. As he stood the priest felt the hair on his arms and neck stand. He glanced to Thelial who was already bounding through the room toward the back. The assassin felt his heart pounding in his ears as, for the first time in a very long time, fear squeezed his chest. Maura let out a shrill scream as if she were being stabbed to death, sounding far worse than her reactions to the ghouls.

Outside the rain stopped abruptly and the sky darkened. There was a low hum, almost like a vibration, that shook everything in the village. The prince looked up at the sky, just on the other side of the inn, and saw the air bend. He saw it stretch into a point as if it were being drawn into another place. The point became swirling black and the sky all around became dark red. Thunder cracked with the voice of an unearthly groan.

From the churning dark mass in the sky, three very inhuman figures emerged and it felt as if even the dirt on the ground became afraid. The center imposing figure held a sword pointed to the ground. They were too tall and too thin and were clothed in worming shadow. The prince could feel his legs beneath him buckling from weakness. He fell to his knees as he looked into the murky faces. Sound from the very air itself was drawn from all around the hamlet and built to a crescendo before forming a voice that was too loud and too low to be from the natural world.

"*This place…,*" the one in the center spoke. "*…is damned.*" He thrust his large blade into the earth. Somewhere, from in the distance or down below, they heard a scream of pain that was masked by thunder.

The earth began to bleed…

Abruptly the figures receded with claps of wailing thunder and the sky became normal again. Only the reverberating sound of the fading rumbles could be heard and it chilled everyone to the bone. The air itself seemed scarred and silence gripped the world with an icy claw. No one moved. No one spoke. No one breathed. The prince could not take any more.

Emerik let loose a blood curdling scream that mournfully shattered the stillness. He stood and ran. He did not know where he was running but he felt the insane need to flee somewhere, anywhere, as fast as he could. Kaeleb rushed out from the inn in time to see the prince sprinting and shrieking. The priest cocked his head as he watched Emerik literally running around in a large circle and wailing his head off.

Tobin came up from behind Kaeleb and shouted to his friend but got no reply. But then Tobin paused and cocked his head to the side. Confusion disturbingly gripped his hear with icy fingers as he watched his dear friend completely lose his mind. Tobin felt utterly lost.

"What do we do?" he asked the priest.

"We have to stop him…somehow. Before he hurts himself," answered Kaeleb. "Let's go get him."

After timing his movement, the priest lunged at Emerik and seized him. They landed in the soft muddy earth and slid to a stop. Tobin was not far behind after hesitating with the notion of tackling his friend. Emerik flailed for a time while Kaeleb and Tobin clutched him. The prince slowly calmed and sobbed. The knight and priest cast concerned glances at each other as they all lay in the mud.

Inside, Maura looked around while trying not to do anything so daring as to even breathe. She was frozen from the fear that the entities would find her. Maybe if she moved slowly enough they would not see her.

Ruelina timorously made her way to the window as she listened to the prince howling. They seemed to be gone and the rain had come back in their place. She softly crept over to Maura. Like everyone else, she was afraid to move normally from a fear of attracting attention. Even though the entities had gone it was as if their very presence scarred the very air.

When she touched Maura the girl shattered. She bolted like a terrified rabbit. Hitting the wall did not stop her, she ran along it until she found and open place to dash farther. It became very bad when she scurried into a corner and had nowhere to go. Maura sank to the floor clawing at the wood and sobbing in gasps. The ranger slowly came to her to hold her. Pulling her close she noticed that

Maura had wet herself from terror.

Gradually everyone began to stir but no one had returned to normal, especially the prince and Maura. None were more shaken or visibly more disturbed than those two. But they never shared their horror. Neither of them spoke much to anyone.

Eventually, Emerik waved a farewell and he slowly rode out of Silverwood on horseback. Images of the figures flashed in his mind from time to time as if he were having a nightmare while still awake. Quietly behind him, Dyrrany followed and felt utterly helpless. The cold sweat ran down from Emerik's brow as he shuddered in secret on his horse. Never had he felt more powerless and small then he did just then.

Tobin breathed a sigh and strode over to Ruelina, who happened to be standing beside Matchok. His face was grim yet painted with a bit of uncertainty.

"Matchok, get everyone ready as quickly as possible." His tone was not forceful and he did not have to explain why speed was important. The knight was glad he sounded even and in command even though, beneath his clam exterior, Tobin himself was about to lose control.

By the late afternoon, under the invisible weight of gloom, most all of the preparations had been made for the inevitable evacuation. Everyone was almost packed but they would have to leave on foot. There only two horses left and they belonged to Tobin and his squire Perry. Neither of them was giving up their mounts to carry other people's meager possessions. Besides, Tobin fought better from horseback and if the need arose, he could not do it with a burdened horse.

Ruelina looked up in time to see new people walking through the town. It was two women. One was dressed in dull metal armor and the other was clothed in trousers and a loose shirt. Neither of the two looked lost yet neither looked like they knew exactly where they were going either. More strangers? Human strangers at that.

"What's wrong?" Tobin asked from behind her.

"New people." Ruelina nodded to the women who were walking directly toward them.

Tobin's brow creased.

"You there," he called to them. "Who are you?"

They walked closer before answering.

"We are from Ilranik," the woman in armor answered. She waved her black locks away from her face as she spoke. "I am Leannii Blacktower and this is Desia Tourrin. Are we in Silverwood?"

Tobin and Ruelina looked at one another then back to the two strangers. Thelial watched from the shadows as they spoke while Smythe and Kaeleb openly strolled and stood beside Ruelina and Tobin.

"Yes," the knight began. "You are in Silverwood. But why are you in Silverwood?"

Leannii thought for a moment.

"Nice armor," she said quickly, regarding the polished plate Tobin wore. "We…are looking for ghouls." Her smirk came without her consent.

"Ghouls?" Tobin asked.

Ruelina blinked in surprise and disbelief.

"How do you know about ghouls?" Smythe questioned.

"Well," the woman laughed. "That's what we were hired for." Her hands came up from her sides. "To investigate ghouls." She spoke with a humorous smile on her face.

"You're from Ilranik you say?" Tobin asked.

"Yes, we are."

"Where is that?" The knight continued.

"It is the capital of Rokal…about four months from here." Smythe answered for her.

"I see…" Tobin studied her for a moment. The woman's armor looked to be masterfully constructed. It was a formfitting articulating breastplate with chainmail support. Tobin had seen articulating armor before but did not regard it with much appeal. It allowed the wearer to move about freely but offered less protection than his plate. Hers was formfitting so it was made expressly for her body contours, which the knight had to admit, were quite attractive. However, a shapely form and a beautiful face were not enough to pull his attention away from duty.

"I'm sorry. We did not get your names," she said with a smile.

The large knight smiled back, but it was more of a smirk.

"I am Sir Tobin Drathmoore from Paragon City."

Leannii looked to her companion Desia, "Where do I know

the name Drathmoore from?" she whispered.

"Drathmoore is one of the founding families of Paragon," Desia whispered back.

"Oh..." Her smile quickly faded.

"Yes...This is Brother Kaeleb and Smythe. They are both official investigators from Paragon City."

Great, Leannii thought, all my luck. I go to the middle of nowhere in this crazy country and find more officials and royalty than I would in a proper city.

"So, let me ask you again...Why are you here?" Tobin folded his arms.

"Well," she breathed. "As I said before, we are here to investigate ghouls. That's what we're paid for."

"So...You're mercenaries then?" the knight asked with a sneer. Mercenaries, nothing is lower than a mercenary.

"Yes, you could say that," Leannii answered.

"Hum..." Tobin grunted with a condescending nod of his head. "Tell me what you know about ghouls." A tight smile formed on his lips.

"Ghouls?" she asked with a laugh.

Tobin laughed with her, "Yes, funny isn't it?"

"Very," she agreed still laughing.

"So what do you now of them?" Tobin still acted amused.

"Ha! They're not real! Some superstitious story told by backwooded peasants like ghost stories." Her laughter trailed off when she noticed Tobin was not laughing. In fact, no one there was laughing but her and Desia.

The knighted leaned forward and humorlessly said, "Bollocks!"

"What?"

"They are very much real and very much here."

The two women paused and looked at him.

"You're serious?"

"Do you see everyone leaving?" he shouted. "Look there at the dying forest! This place is damned." Tobin suddenly felt like breaking something inanimate.

Leannii and Desia both looked to each other in silence for a moment then burst out laughing. Leannii laughed more than Desia but both did nevertheless. Their mirth died off and they stared at the villagers with blank faces.

"Woah, you're not joking...You are serious." Leannii could not wrap her head around the fact that someone was taking all this superstitious ghoul nonsense gravely. Either that or this place has somehow driven them mad. Maybe it was something in the water?

"Well," Tobin began. "We are staying at the garrison."

"There's a garrison here?" The mercenary was a bit taken back. "Wonder what that looks like."

"It's the big stone building down the lane, you cannot miss it." Tobin gestured.

"Oh, alright...well, thanks." Leannii was a bit more confused at his apparent generosity.

"Pardon? Thanks for what?" the knight said with feigned ignorance. "Oh, I'm sorry. I thought I said we were staying in the nice safe stone garrison. You are not."

"What?" Maybe he's not so apparently generous.

"Since you have trouble believing in the...ghoul problem here, then I elect that you can stay outside."

Leannii blinked at his childishness.

"Whatever, we don't know the secret handshake of your little clubhouse anyway."

"And you won't, either," the knight said haughtily.

Looking over his shoulder she motioned with her chin, "Is that the inn?"

"Yes, but it's being abandoned so you're on your own." Tobin turned away from her and shouted to the villagers. "Move out, now! Be as far away from here as you possibly can in the few hours of daylight you have left!" With that he walked to Matchok and the two spoke as they walked from their home. Most looked back, some eyes watered and everyone walked slowly.

Ruelina frowned at the back of Tobin's head as he walked away. She walked to Leannii before the mercenary had time to turn away. Smythe and Kaeleb were not far behind her but each for their own reasons.

"Greetings, I'm Ruelina from here in Silverwood."

"Hello," she looked up and down the ranger. "I'm Leannii and this is Desia...in case you hadn't overheard."

"Oh, don't be too upset about the ogre in armor, he's like that with everyone."

Leannii's eyes passed over each of Ruelina's shoulders at the two men who came to stand at her flanks.

"Greetings, my name is Kaeleb Azhwan Miryd and I am a priest from the Temple of Enki in Paragon City."

"A priest? Of Enki?" She asked with some apprehension.

"Yes...is there a problem?" he sounded concerned.

"No, no, not at all...just wasn't expecting to see one of you out here."

"I'm Smythe Gibvoy, also from Paragon City."

"Yes, I head the...knight mention your names. You two are investigators?"

Both nodded.

"What do you investigate? If you don't mind me asking."

"We are here to investigate the matter of the ghouls terrorizing this hamlet, among other things," explained Smythe.

"Oh, I see. Well, good luck with that," she replied with a forced cheer. They were mercenaries who worked as far away from the eyes of the law as possible but found themselves in the company of those who enforced laws in a very strict society. Leannii again silently cursed her luck behind her fake smile.

"We would like to talk to you about why you are here. You know, who sent you, exactly what your task is, you understand." Smythe did a very good job sounding official.

"Um...certainly. But, could we talk tomorrow? We have had a long trip from Ilranik and we need some rest." She smiled to be polite but she really wanted to tell them it was none of their damned business why they were there. However, that would have probably gotten them tossed in a cold cell somewhere uncomfortable.

Smythe was about to object when Ruelina stepped on his toe with her heel.

"I'm sure our investigators understand. Not long ago they also had a long journey that lasted a few months and needed to rest as well. I would think they could be patient and compassionate enough to wait until tomorrow."

Smythe grunted through his teeth instead of yelling out loud.

"Yes...that would be fine."

She abruptly removed her heel from his foot and smiled. Pointing behind her Ruelina said, "The inn is behind us and you are welcome to whatever food has been left."

"Thank you," Leannii said to her.

As she turned to go, the three looked at one another. None of them were happy with the knight's decision and thought he had placed them in a deadly position. The strangers would be alone and unprepared for the ghouls. It was just a question of when the next attack would be.

Leannii sharply whistled and after a few moments two others appeared from around the buildings. One was carrying a bow, had sandy blonde hair and weathered Caucasian skin. The other was curiously dressed in clothing from a different culture, had slanted eyes similar to a wood elf but had a different tint to his skin. He was obviously Sydathrian and was a very long way from home. They came up to her and stopped.

"We're staying in the inn behind me for now. Keep your eyes open and be careful. We are not alone here. Kerrison, Chang, this is Smythe and Kaeleb, officials from Paragon City."

Both hesitated then greeted them.

"Ah," Kerrison was a bit edgy around officials from anywhere. "What kind of officials are you?"

"The investigating illegal things kind," Smythe said with a tight smile.

"Oh, well, if I can help at all...you know."

Leannii shot him a look that shut him up.

"We'd better get moving," she said to everyone in a way that it was not a hint.

As they sauntered to the inn Leannii felt Kaeleb grasp her by the arm. She turned to see what he wanted but calmed once she saw the look in his eyes. He was sincerely concerned.

"Listen," the priest spoke in a low tone. "I don't know why all of you are here and I can guess that you don't believe in ghouls yet. Be careful tonight. If you need help, just call."

"We should be fine, thank you," she said dismissively.

"No, I'm serious...yell for help, if you can."

He released her and everyone parted. Leannii regarded the priest with a curious expression. Was he crazy or was he speaking the truth?

That night, after the sun went down, the screaming started. At first it was echoing in the distance and then it became louder and louder. The mercenaries were running to the garrison and the ghouls were snarling and howling behind them. Inside the garrison, they could not tell which was more disturbing, the growling of the ghouls or the helpless cries of the people. Maura looked worried. "Can't we help them?" Maura pleaded. "They're dying…" "If we help them Tobin will lock us out." Ruelina said with a frown. "We'll see," Thelial said coldly. "I'm not sitting here and listening to that." He stood to walk out of the barracks room.

"Where are you going?" Ruelina asked him.

He stopped and looked to everyone grimly.

"To do what's right." He walked straight to the front door.

Perry moved to stand in his way.

"I cannot let you back inside once you go out." The squire did not sound pleased but an order was an order.

"Listen," the assassin said threateningly. His icy glare gave the squire a shiver. "I am going out that door. Lock it behind me if you wish."

"What?" The ranger was not happy with that either. "I'm coming too!"

They could now here Leannii kicking at the front gates and shouting for them to be opened. More chilling inhuman and human shouts and screams rose outside.

"If you stay inside, that is on you. I'm going." Thelial decided and no one was going to stop him.

"I'm also coming," Kaeleb said while standing and grasping his sword.

They lifted the two beams that buttressed the doors and pulled. With a bellowing groan the massive barriers yielded and swung open. They could now see the solid gates outside but could not hear anything beyond. They looked to each other and raced down the stone stairs and began to open remove the metal bar. Behind them the group could hear Tobin stomping down the stairs.

The gates swung open and they saw Leannii, panting for breath, feet spread apart ready to fight again and with a darkly furious look in her eyes. Around her on the ground lay the slashed bodies of ghouls and her three companions. They were curled up into balls shivering. Everyone knew what had happened to them. Thelial could see that there were ghoul bodies strewn almost all the way back to the inn. The group was stunned speechless.

Tobin emerged from the garrison and stopped in the gateway.

He was chewing one of the remaining pears and spoke between bites.

"So...you believe in ghouls now?" He took another bite and chewed loudly.

"You bastard," Leannii spat. "You left us out here to die!"

"No...I left you out here...to learn a lesson or two."

"The only thing I learned is that you are a pompous prick!"

"I see...that you still have not learned one of them." He tossed the core aside and brushed his hands.

"Sod off," she glared at him and turned away to check on her friend Desia.

"What did you just say?" Tobin was looking for a fight.

"What?" Leannii whirled around. "Is your helmet on too tight? You're an arrogant, selven, spoiled little rich boy who couldn't live without his precious title. Ealaing bastard."

His eyes widened as if he had just been slapped in the face. No woman was going to speak to him like that, especially not some brash lowlife mercenary from another land. Ruelina smirked and Thelial shook his head. Only Smythe really noticed that, even with all of the ghouls lying slain around her, she was completely unharmed.

"Is that so?" He took a solid step forward.

So did she.

"Maybe I should show you what holds this title," he drew his sword.

"Yeah," her voice darkened. "Come show me..."

He advanced with a powerful swing. Leannii casually ducked beneath it and swung, hitting his shield. Immediately he pressed forward and swung downwards. Spinning away and blocking with her shield she slashed his leg. Losing his balance he moved backward, swinging his blade to cover his steps. She raced to catch him. When he saw her quickly closing on him he swung again but left himself open. Parrying with her shield Leannii kicked him squarely in his chest and spun, cutting upwards with her heavy blade. Tobin did not see that coming. The steel cut across his chest and sent him sprawling backward. With a loud clang and a dull thud, he landed on his back...and did not move.

Panting, she looked at him lying there on the ground. Softly he groaned. He was not dead. Everyone was surprised at her next motion. Leannii stepped back and put her sword away. That was quite unlike a mercenary to do.

The priest ran straight to the fallen knight as did Perry. Checking his wounds, Kaeleb prayed to Enki for the knight not to die. Behind him, Leannii was catching her breath and watching him chant. Her jaw dropped when she heard Tobin cough and they sat him up. No one could do that! No priest could actually heal another. That was...was...old legend, fairytales!

The semi-conscious knight was lifted and carefully carried back into the garrison by his squire and priest. The ranger casually leaned against the gate and watched them slowly pass.

"Yeah, that showed her," needled Ruelina.

Tobin said nothing as he weakly tried to glare at her while passing by.

Smythe now looked at the mercenary woman with very different eyes as she tended to her friends. Gingerly he approached her being careful not to provoke her and end up worse off than Tobin just did.

"Um, Leannii?" he addressed.

"What?" she said sharply.

"Don't worry about him. Please, stay inside the garrison with us," Smythe calmly suggested.

Quickly she stood and gave him an icy glare.

"Why, so he can whack us in our sleep?"

"No, no. He's...someone you have to get used to. Being from a noble family, well, nobles are like that."

"Are they?" she spat. "Or just the ones from here?" She carefully helped Desia stand on shaky legs. "He doesn't act like any noble I have ever met."

"Have you ever really met one face to face before?" he pushed and was met with a fiery glare. That was apparently the wrong thing to say. "I apologize...the question I should have asked was, have you ever been to Paragon before?" Smythe tried to tactfully back out of the mess he just made while feeling his heart thump in hears for a moment.

"No...I have not."

He nodded and hoped she understood.

She paused to think for a moment.

"Fine, we will, as long as it doesn't cause an issue with that dog. I don't want him to start pissing to mark his territory next."

Ruelina's laugh burst out but was quickly grasped in her

control again as she helped Leannii's friends into the garrison. Thelial also smiled and disappeared inside.

Later that night, Chang shuddered in his bed with a cold sweat. His skin had become dry and pale and his lips were blue. He would not talk but kept drinking cup after cup of water. Beneath a pile of blankets, the Sydathrian still shivered from a chill in the warm night.

"I've never seen this before," admitted Leannii as she helped him drink more water.

"Nor have I," said Kaeleb. He was trying to discern what illness the mercenary had contracted but could not. The man's pulse was threading and slowing. His body was actually becoming colder not hot like a normal fever.

"I have." Ruelina voice sounded distant. She sat between the shivering man and Maura with a wary eye.

"What is this?" Leannii questioned. "What's happening to him?"

"Well," the ranger sighed. "We called it ghoul fever…To be honest he'll die tonight or tomorrow night. After another night he'll rise as one of them."

"What?"

"It's true," she said sadly. "We never found a cure or a way to stop it."

The room fell silent except for Chang who continued to shiver in his bed.

"What can we do?" Leannii asked.

"I don't know. What can you do?" Ruelina remarked dejectedly. She was hoping to never have seen that ever again.

"Desia, was this ever mentioned?" the mercenary leader asked her.

"Um…not in detail like this," the young woman answered. "Just that people can get sick, die and come back as ghouls. It's how they…reproduce or increase their numbers, she said."

"What? She said? Who is she and what did she say?" The questions flowed from Smythe's lips but no answers flowed from anyone. Especially, none from Desia who really did not want to remember her meeting with Mishka…ever.

Jonathan Graef

Covenant Manor, Just outside Ilranik City in Rokal

Early Morning, Five Years Ago

The sun seemed to rise a bit later and a bit colder that day as she watched it begin to peek over the distant trees on the horizon. The sun left the previous evening and was followed by a moon that came and went as well. Still, she sat staring out of her window. All night she searched for an answer but even as the sun greeted her, she was still without the solace she sought. She had not really moved all night and nothing around her gave her any comfort. Ordering her servants from her bedchambers and never retiring to sleep, the lady aimlessly wandered in the room until she came to sit sometime in the early morning and had not risen since. Now that the dawn came, her situation worsened.

Most people would have envied the thought of how she lived her life being surrounded by the finest goods that her parents' money could purchase: the softest silks from Sydathria, the best hand carved furniture of mahogany or teak and the finest tailored clothing that could be found, nothing was beyond the wealth of her family. She attended the best schools in the capital city and would attend the best university in the land as well. She drank from goblets of silver and gold and ate from plates of the same. The mansion employed over forty servants ranging from cooks, maids, farmers, herders, stable hands, grounds keepers and tailors. This number did not include the family lawyers, accountants, scribes, tutors or guards.

After the Great War, the Covenant family helped restructure the lands here in Rokal. Reconstruction was their greatest effort and they were quite successful at it here around the capital city of Ilranik. Agricultural and herd lands were reestablished along with innovative companies for construction, real estate and trade. Included in the list of duties the Covenant family undertook was the defense of the emerging city and protection for the followers of Lady Gajana after her passing. Along with her followers, the first University of Thaumaturgy was established with businesses from the Covenant family directly involved with the management, construction and planning.

Recently, a family friend who had become the Covenant's

financial advisor was looming about the mansion even more this past month then he ever had before. Xergo Wallance, as he was called, had been an employee of their family for more than a decade now. Xergo knew much about business and banking and had done well with the family financial planning. There was no record of the Wallance family name in the local magistrate's office however; Xergo was able to produce excellent references. His increased presence in the manner did not especially alarm anyone nor did it seem strange that he poured over maps and papers from the Covenant archives. Only Leannii seemed to not be comfortable around him and the only other who felt that way was Haverest Covenant, her grandfather. However, he passed away some years ago but not before announcing to the family that he felt Xergo was up to no good. Haverest bellowed and complained endlessly about Xergo each time he laid eyes on him. That had begun when Xergo was employed and continued for two years until the grandfather's death.

One day, however, Xergo stood outside a door while he listened to Leannii and her mother loudly shout at each other…again. Screaming matches between the two had been increasing with the older Leannii had become. It seemed the stronger she was the more she resisted her mother's ways and demanded to be her own person. Lady Fabiana would not have that in the least. With another loud slam of a door, Leannii came stomping from the room and into the corridor where Xergo pretended to be idly strolling through. Their eyes met and Xergo spoke before Leannii tread heavily too far out of normal talking range.

"Hum," he sounded. "Another fight?"

"Obviously," she spat but did not pause or slow her pace.

"She should look at you more," he said empathically. His plan was working.

Leannii stopped and turned on her heels and her long silken blue dress ballooned outward then fell gracefully against her frame.

"What?"

"She should look at you more," he repeated feigning surprise that she did not understand his meaning. "You have grown up and are no longer a little girl." The bait was laid out.

She saw shocked that anyone had noticed and was too upset to perceive the game that was being played.

"Yes, well…that is my life as a woman in the Duke

Covenant's home."

"But you have become a fine woman and have grown to be so strong…" he looked around as if not wanting to be overheard and stepped closer to her. "…Much stronger than your older brother." More bait.

Again, she was shocked that anyone had ever noticed. All she ever heard was how great her brother was and how wrong she was. It seemed that it would never end.

"I did not think anyone here saw that."

"Ha!" he scoffed with an almost melodramatic tone. "How could anyone not? Besides, do not worry about that. Your day will come."

"What do you mean?" she asked him, quite puzzled with that cryptic reference.

"One day your brother will need you," he whispered and stepped almost against her. His eyes burrowing into hers and she had not noticed the swell of her breasts in her dress rubbed against his chest, exactly the way he wanted. "When that day comes, my dear Leannii…" His hand gently brushed her chin upwards and for a moment he thought of crushing his lips down onto hers and forcing his tongue into her mouth. However, he held is desire and set his trap. "You will become the family savior and they will have no choice but to see your strength." His breath was hot on her chin and her lips parted slightly. Abruptly he stepped away and smiled. "You will see," he spoke while turning to leave her standing there alone. You will see…

She felt alone and a bit cold after the warmth of his body departed. Someone actually sees me in this house. Just as soon as the smile crept up to her face it was wiped away with her mother bursting open the doors to the corridor. Xergo chuckled to himself as he casually walked down the spacious corridor, listening to the echoes of their continued battle.

Just a few weeks later and after this long and sleepless night, she realized when she stood after hours of sitting, that she should have spent more of this night in prayer and meditation in lieu of sulking and moping. She knew better than that because she trained different. So why did she anyway? She thought of that herself and generated only one possible answer. The lady chose to feel sorry for herself instead of doing what she needed to. Inside her, the warrior wanted to go and do something but the intuition in her felt that she would never see her brother again. That is what this was all about. Her long black locks hung around her face like a cowl a helped her look as if she were already in mourning and her sadness darkened her already deep green eyes. Later, during her morning prayers and meditations, she would beg Enki for forgiveness and to help her be more resolute and disciplined in the future.

For now, though, she feared her brother would not return. She felt that deep in her chilling bones and was paralyzed by it. Standing with a frown, she peered from her balcony at the front of the house to where the party began to gather. Horsemen and wagons were packed and ready for their journey with glints of sunlight dancing off of their polished armor. Soon, her brother would join them. Not wanting to miss sending him off she turned with a sigh and made her way down through the mansion. Her pale silk dress flowed with her in the early dawn. She resembled a ghost as she glided beside the banister and silently down the great stairs.

The two doormen snapped to attention and opened the large entry for the lady as she approached. With a deep echoing groan the massive portal was pulled open with the grunts from the men. This mansion had stood since the War and these massive doors held for over five hundred years. Their intricate carvings told a story that has long since been forgotten. The writing in the some strange tongue now went unread and not understood but was preserved as some testament from an ancient tradition that was also forgotten. The lady's grandfather remembered and was strictly adamant about the preservation of many old family traditions and history. Unfortunately, before his passing, he had passed on none of his wisdom. Even when asked while he still lived the aged man would sternly yet enigmatically command, "These things should never be forgotten!"

When she emerged from the house her breath caught in her throat with an audible gasp. Her brother was already here and tending to his horse! He, just like every other man in the courtyard, was dressed in armor and ready for travel. His horse's saddle was packed with everything he could think of to take with him, including a spare sword and bow. Leannii instantly felt more distressed because she was almost late and did not want to be late, not for this.

She quickly strode toward him, extending her gate in such a

way that suggested that she was more comfortable in other attire rather than that fine silk dress. He heard her coming and knew who it was without even having to look. He knew the sound of her strides enough to also guess with great accuracy as to what mood she was in before is sister ever uttered a word. This morning, her steps sounded desperate and unhappy with an overbearing sense of aggression that was not outside of her normal nature.

"Thalorn," She called with a stressed voice. As she came around the rear of his horse he interrupted her before she could continue.

"You are not going to talk me out of this, so don't even bother yourself." He did not even look up from the knot he was trying to secure his saddle.

"Why not?" she pressed.

"Because, we already spoke of this every day for the past few days. And every day you try to talk me into not going and every day I insist that I am going." He looked up and into her eyes. "So this morning is no different unless you have something different to say."

"As a matter of fact I do."

"In truth?" He was not surprised in the least but in his manner he obviously did not believe her.

"Don't go," she said firmly.

"Well now," he sarcastically spoke with a shaking head. "That does not sound any different than before."

"I should go, not you."

That however, was quite different.

"What?" That was all he could manage.

"I should go and you should stay here," she said definitively.

"You have gone mad." He thought this was another ploy to talk him into staying and that there was no possible way she could be serious in thinking she should go and fight rather than him.

"No I have not!" Defiance, her other common tone, was thickening.

"Very well, little sister." He leaned into her face as he spoke as if challenging her and little sister came with a bit more condescension than she was willing to tolerate. "Give me one good reason." He smirk did not help. She wanted to smack him in the head but, as usual, she did not want to embarrass him in front of everyone and stayed her clenched fist at her side.

"Because..." She struggled for restraint. "I am much better at fighting than you."

His head threw back with a mocking roar. Her jaw clenched as she ground her teeth feeling heat pour into her face.

"Oh my," he said while still chuckling. "You have gone mad. What makes you think that?" Some of the nearby men heard her answer and chuckled as well.

"Because, I could always best you when we practiced."

"Ha! You lie! I always beat you!"

She took a step toward him with a burning rage.

"I always let you win! By Enki, how embarrassing it would be for you to always get pummeled by your little sister!"

He said nothing but shook his head in disbelief.

"Fine!" she shouted. "Have it your way then!" Quite swiftly she reached for his saddle and drew his reserve sword from its scabbard. Her grip tightened and she almost was snarling at him. Taking a step back to give him ample room she screamed, "Come then!"

His brow rose in complete surprise. This was not what he had expected. His sister never acted like this and he could not remember ever seeing her so enraged in her whole life. She truly has gone mad. He did not want to fight her and right now all he wanted was to be far away from here but before he could leave he had to calm her down.

"Come now," he said with a forced softening to his voice that almost sounded like patronization. "You don't really want to fight...here...now."

"Yes I do, you arrogant horse's ass!" He was wearing plate armor reinforced with chain mail, but she wore none. She held a reserve sword that was not made of the finest craftsmanship while he wore one made of much finer material. However, even though he was better armed and much better protected she did not care.

"Why?" he demanded. This had gotten ridiculous. "Why do you want to fight me so bad? Do you hate me that much?"

"No I don't hate you!" she shouted in reply.

"Then why do you want to try to best me here and now...in front of all these men? Why let me win before only to fight now? Why?"

Why could he not understand? "Argh!" She screamed to the

sky in fury before turning her attention back to him. "Dung eating fool! I would rather smack that cocky smirk off your face myself than to have you die!" She began to sob.

He could only stare in shock with a black look on his face.

"Don't you understand?!" She continued as tears streamed down her face. "You're a moron! I love you but you're a moron!" She dropped the sword as she stood and sobbed with bending knees as she felt her legs weaken and chest tighten. It was hard for her to breathe but she kept talking to her brother who just stood unmoving and stared at her. "D...don...don't go. Please...don't go...I will never see you again."

Then he moved. He came a caught her before she fell. Slowly, he helped her to her knees while holding her tightly to his chest. She gripped his armored sleeve and began to gasp a bit less. Shifting her weight to lean against him, she jolted with sudden discomfort from the hilt of his sword jabbing her in the ribs. He felt this and released his embrace. Both looked down to the sword at the same time and she began to chuckle.

"Ouch," she said with no conviction.

They both laughed. She reached down to move the handle away when she saw it and stopped moving. Oblivious to his sister's action he absently said, "Sorry about that" while he still laughed. When he did not hear her joining him he looked at her and noticed she was staring at the sword he wore. He also knew why.

"Yeah," he said absently. "I know."

"Enki in Heaven, that's..."

"...Grandfather's sword," he finished for her.

She looked into his eyes with sincere concern and puzzlement. It was not her turn to think their sibling was insane.

"I am only borrowing it," he said to excuse himself. "I will return it when I get back."

"That sword is over five hundred years old!" She barely spat in a whisper so no one else could hear. "You should not have it! Are you out of your mind?"

"Why? Grandfather is not going to miss it."

"Our Master Enki called him home years ago but that's not the point!" She was losing her patience again but did not want anyone else to hear their words. Still, she was being the over protective little sister. "It is an heirloom of our family. You know how closely grandfather guarded that! If you do something…"

"Do what?" he challenged. She had better not suggest that I would damage this sword.

"Something stupid," she answered. "You are really not thinking this through and, as Enki is my witness, I think you will do something stupid."

"Why? Why would I do something stupid?" His voice rose and was matched, or more it was exceeded by his sister.

"Because you usually do!" That was a bit louder than she wanted. She looked around to see who was listening and, much to her dislike at the moment, everyone in the courtyard was watching in attentive silence. "Listen to me, that sword is special. I do not know how or why but it is and nothing had better happen to it."

"How do you know it is not just some old sword that was very well made?"

"Ah!" She could not believe he just said that. "You really don't think, do you?" Yes, she would have to explain this as if he were a child. Even being four years her senior, he was still like a little boy. "Grandfather's books speak of this but do not say why it was made, nor by whom. Also, because I do not think you even noticed, grandfather never had to sharpen it or polish it."

He did not understand that last point.

"Most swords will rust and become dull." Pointing sharply at it yet trying to use a small motion so as to not draw unwanted attention to the sword, "That one does neither."

The blade was unquestionably different in its construction. Being made so long ago it was a mystery where the technology came from as only recently had swords of that make been thought of as useful. This type of blade was longer than a one handed broad sword yet shorter than a two handed great sword and was named a "hand and a half" sword for lack of something better. Its earned nickname was "bastard sword" since it seemed to make many children fatherless on the battlefield. However, that was then and not five hundred years prior. This kind sophistication did not seem to have existed until those recent times.

Despite this particular blade's difference in length it had much more weight than its modern types. Also, there was an issue of the shifting that one could feel when the blade was swung. Some manner of weight inside the sword would transfer toward its point, away from the handle, thus giving more power to the strike but seemingly harder to control. This was, obviously, quite a perplexing function. There was additionally another matter of its metallurgy. Some quite different materials were mixed together causing a strange silvery grey hue in the blade. Strange engravings and glyphs were expertly placed on the sword in some purpose that had long been forgotten and therefore added to its obscurity. Last, there existed the truth of what she had mentioned: this blade never rusted nor dulled. This is a magic sword, he thought. Impossible, things like this only exist in fairytales and old legends.

"Well then," he said standing. "I had better take good care of it then."

He was so stubbornly stupid. The fool was still going after all of that.

"You had better or I am coming after you." There was something in her voice that made him feel it did not warrant a sarcastic remark. Instead he merely smiled and helped her stand.

"I will be back, you'll see."

"Where will you camp?" She was already planning to follow him and search for him. As unwanted as the notion was, she could not help that deep feeling which chilled her bones telling her he would not return alive.

"It is a two day ride with wagons to the Blacktower just north of here. There are reports of only ten to fifteen bandits. So, two days to get there, two days to find them and serve justice and two days to return. You will see me and all fifteen of my men before Sunday."

She did not feel this would happen. There was far too much an overshadowed feeling of dread.

"You have six days. If I do not see you here in six days I will bring hell with me to find you."

"I know." He embraced her again to say farewell for now. "Thank you for coming out this morning."

"Did you think I was not?"

"Well, with father gone to Thran and mother...doing what she does, I knew you would be the only one here. Still, I know you had no sleep last night so I thought..."

"You thought wrong," she said a bit accusingly. But she did not want her parting words to bare any illness and quickly changed her tone. "Even if mother were here I would be the only one standing out here with you right now." She tried to change but did not change much.

"Yes, well. She loves us none the less," he said reassuringly.

She was surprised in how he said it, it even sounded like he believed it himself. He really was stupid and did not see. She loves you not me. She was not a son and in this family, just like many others, daughters were treated much like dogs. If her brother were in the same room, she felt she may as well not even be at home. Notwithstanding the fact that regardless of how correct her words may be, her brother would always be right. This frustrated her more knowing he was not all that bright. The best answer she could give him was silence.

Still thinking about what she said concerning her letting him emerge in victory each time they sparred, he could not help feeling that it was not an embellishment. His ego and curiosity finally got the best of him at this most inappropriate time.

"You always let me win?"

She was caught by surprise. He was such a little boy.

"Yes."

"Always?"

"Always."

"How?" He had to ask. "How were you always able to beat me?"

If this continued her new word for him would be infantile. "Do you really want to know?"

"Yes, I do." He shoulders were straight toward her with his arms at his sides. The same posture was taken by him when he was about to be corrected by one of his teachers.

"You always make the same mistakes." He asked for it. "Each time you swing with force you try too hard. You swing from your shoulder instead of from your back leg. Very wrong." If he were going to leave she was hoping this very pointed lesson would sink into his thick skull before he had to fight. Maybe then he would have a chance. "When you do that your opponent will always know you are about to strike and…when you do it your shield arm drops, leaving you exposed."

"Truly?"

"Yes!" she scolded. "So by Enki, stop doing it!"

"You always were the smart one." He admitted that much but would not say the rest.

"I know," she said flatly. "And the fast one, the strong one, the pretty one, the funny one…" She was smiling but not gloating.

"Alright, I get it." He tried to force a laugh but it did not work well because he knew that she was correct. She was better than him at everything. Maybe not this time, perhaps this time he could be her equal when he returned. With that thought he placed his boot into the stirrup and got on the saddle. He really was leaving. Stupid little boy.

"Six days…You have six days then I am coming after you."

He looked down at his sister from atop the horse. He frowned. Even from this view with her wearing a dress she still looked stronger and more capable than him.

"You know if you did that mother would be furious with you."

"Not my problem. She can argue with Heaven about it. Nothing stands between a paladin and divine providence," she said without a pause. "Six days," she said again in a reinforcement of her convictions. Her words were repeated more for him than for herself.

He smiled down at her and bent his head to her. She quickly reached her hand to his hair and kissed him solidly on the cheek.
"I'll see you soon. I will be back before you know it."

With that he turned his horse and led the men out of the courtyard. He left her standing there watching him leave. One final cold chill sent shivers down her spine as he passed out of sight. *Why is he trying to compete with me?* She knew him better than he knew himself because, after all, she was the smarter one. Turning briskly she strode back into the house. There was much that needed done and she had very little time to do it.
"Walter!" she called out. "Walter!"

From another part of the mansion she could hear footsteps running down a corridor as he raced to answer her call. He had served the family for many years and was not about to let anyone down at any time. Bursting through the doors he looked quickly for where she was.

"Yes, my lady?" he addressed while panting for breath.

"We have a lot to do. First, I want my armor and sword sent to the smithy. I do not care if it is polished. I want it strong and usable and the sword sharpened as best as he can do. Also, I need some supplies for traveling. I am going very light and must travel quickly so only gather what is absolutely necessary." She spoke as she walked through the house to the stables outside in the rear of the property.

"Are you going on a trip, my lady?"

"Yes, Walter. I am going to Blacktower forest."

He gasped.

"My lady, that area is full of bandits and is much too dangerous. Perhaps you should wait for your brother to return."

"No, I am leaving in six days to go find him."

"You do not think he will return?" He did not want anything to happen to her. All these years he watched her grow from an infant struggling to take her first steps into a strong young woman. As strong as she may be, he did not want her to step in harm's way.

"No." She stopped. Her thoughts arrested her mind for a time as she imagined her life with her brother over these years and how she was usually always there to help him. In the company of their parents she took a step back and let him be the son they wanted all the while knowing that she was more like their ideal image than he was. But she was not a son she was a daughter and no daughter would ever hold an equal place as a son, even if she were older. But there was no time for reflections such as this. She would hold her word and give him six days. Fearfully and deep down inside her, she knew that was far too long to wait. "I will travel only with one other rider and will take no court clothing with me."

"As you wish, my lady." He had been hoping she was not going to do this but since she was set it was his duty and pleasure to help in any way he could.

"Oh…" She turned to face him. "One more thing."

"Yes, my lady?"

"Quit calling me "my lady" or "duchess" and please use my name when it is just the two of us."

He smiled because he forgot and kept forgetting. Bowing his head he spoke.

"Yes, Leannii."

He ran for his life. Trees raced past his ears as he barely darted between them trying to see through the blood in his eyes and listening in panic to the sounds of his pursuers. Whooping and taunting calls echoed through the forest as they gave chase. He did not know where he was going he only knew he was being hunted and had to run as fast as he could or he would die. He retained his shield and loosely gripped his sword as he sprinted.

He thought this was a stupid idea and wished he had never left. He came here for the wrong reasons with wrong information. He was ill equipped, outnumbered and now he was alone. Ten he was told, ten to fifteen bandits. Who could not easily and swiftly deal with ten to fifteen untrained men? But that was not the truth. Ten was more accurately forty and untrained was also just as fallacious. Everyone else was dead within one day of their arrival. From just three days after leaving home, he was the only one who survived and he was now being chased through the trees for sport. They could have shot him with many arrows many times but for them it was much more fun chasing the duke's only son to his death.

As he ran he felt his legs begin to burn like his veins pumped acid. He kept running. They did shoot some arrows at him earlier just to terrorize him. It worked. He could hear their bellowing laughter as he tried to dodge arrows that were really in no danger of striking him. He imagined he looked like a fool…and he was not wrong. These men fought and terrorized people for their livelihood. He had never been in a real fight but came here anyway, secretly hoping his small body of guards would handle whatever needed done and he could take credit for leading them through battle.

He was a fool. Mainly he wanted his sister to look up to him or at least think of him as equal to herself. What an idiot! She was his sister and loved him but there he was, going on an expedition to prove something he did not need to prove.

Something caught his attention from the corner of his eye. He saw an arrow that was shot into a tree. His heart skipped a beat and his breathing became more ragged. He continued to run as fast as he could but he felt like he was constantly tripping and would fall if he stopped. He looked over his shoulder to see where his pursuers were. Much to his dismay, he saw they were jogging after him and not running. He felt his heart suddenly become heavy with the weight of realization that they were merely playing with him and took great amusement in his plight.

He slowed to a stop and fell against a tree unable to breathe. For a moment, the whole world spun and he thought he would fall unconscious right there and then. Blinking through the blood that smeared his face and blurred his vision he saw them swiftly surround him. He knew he was going to die. For him there was only once choice left: he would fight them and die quickly hopefully taking some of their numbers with him. He tightened his grip on this grandfather's sword and pulled his shield closer to his body. Still gasping for air and now surrounded by insane killers he turned and faced the closest one.

The one he picked was a taller but lanky man in mismatched leather armor. His blonde hair was wild and unkempt and his eyes were fierce like a razor. He smiled with a grin that should have dripped venom.

"Look here, boys. The rabbit wants to play." His voice was deeper and rougher than Thalorn had imagined. The bandit was answered by many angered shouts and mocking laughter from between the trees. "Is that what you want, pretty boy? Rabbit want to play?"

Thalorn gritted his teeth and, with the best yell he could muster, swung the heavy sword at the man's skull. The bandit effortlessly stepped to the side evading the haphazard attack. As Thalorn went stumbling by he kicked the boy solidly on his ass and drew a roaring laugh from his fellows who watched the poor man slide through the soft dirt on his chest.

"Is that your best, little boy?" He walked over and retrieved a sword from the circle and casually walked back to Thalorn who was still trying to get his feet under him. His lungs hurt and his whole body ached. Maybe if he had been practicing his skills as much as his sister was things could have been different, the thought. Turning back to his opponent he readied for another attempt at the man's head.

Again he cut the air. But this time the blonde brought the flat of his blade swiftly against the side of Thalorn's skull. He was still being played with. Thalorn saw a flash of white light and his teeth rattled in his head. He did not know when he fell again but he felt the soft earth beneath him again as he began to feel a metallic taste in his mouth. He was struck with such force on his head that Thalorn tasted steel. Feeling a warm fluid flow onto his shoulder from the side of his head where he was just hit, he struggled again to stand.

Tired, sore, bloodied and ashen in color he still found some determination to stand. Last chance he said to himself. He hoped this old relic of a sword might actually do him some good. Thalorn reached deep in himself to draw on every last ounce of strength he could and channel it into a strike. He no longer felt the pain nor did he feel out of breath. Was he drawing power from this sword? He steadied his shield, raised his sword and with a determined yell, Thalorn swung. Everything became silent and everything slowed down. He lost all peripheral vision and he could only see what was directly in front of him. He watched the event unfold in horror.

He was a spectator to his own body; all he could do was watch and could do nothing to change it. He watched, just before his swing, his right shoulder dipped. He did swing from his shoulder. This dip caused his shoulders to cant and his shield arm lowered, tilting his shield away from his body. All of the constant repetition of incorrect movement took command and he moved incorrectly as he fought. His sister was correct. Horror came as he observed the bandit's as it sliced slowly through the air and met an even plane with his own neck. He did not listen to his sister.

All Thalorn felt was a slight pressure at his throat before his eyes became dark and he felt, at last, cold. The last sound he heard was the bandits' riotous laughter.

He had his six days. She waited long enough. That evening, even before the sun fully set, she would leave. The horses were ready, she and her guide were packed and in that afternoon just after her prayer and meditation, she and her mother predictably fought.

Brother Quinn, one of her teachers, had come calling that morning because he had seen a change in her over the previous few weeks. Leannii had become more withdrawn and distracted. She seemed constantly tired and her moods began to unpredictably shift but most of the time she had become increasingly more irritable and showed very little patience, even for herself. They only spoke briefly that morning but Brother Quinn did the best he could under the circumstances.

"I am concerned about you," he plainly stated.

"Oh?" She sounded like she was only half listening and did not really care. "Why is that?" It sounded like a rhetorical question.

"You have not been yourself these past two weeks."

"Really?" She was thinking of something else. "Who have I been then?"

Quinn slammed his palm down onto the table. The loudness echoed abruptly throughout the chamber and jolted her in surprise.

"Do not mistake me for a fool, young lady. I will not have it," he spoke with the sternness of a sword, not unlike the one he wore just then. It was unusual, if not outright forbidden, for priests to bear arms. The only exception was concerning the priests who worshiped Enki, the god of war. Brother Quinn was such a priest and also was a top instructor at the University of Thaumaturgy. In addition to that, he served on the Council of Temples for the city of Ilranik and was the highest level instructor for those of the paladinhood under Enki. All of those made him her teacher in more than one facet.

As a teacher he was rather strict and "severe" as some would say. He was as hard as a tree trunk and could speak with the same precision and sharpness as the sword he carried. Sometimes he would joke and call himself a "tired old man" however, not even the more youthful city guards would challenge him. There was much to be said for wisdom through experience and he had plenty of both.

Leannii looked up to him in shock. Sometimes the old man seemed frail and somewhat fragile. But his eyes, voice, and the occasional slam on a table, quickly reminded everyone that he was not so fragile and could hold is own quite well.

"Sorry, Master," she spoke while lowering her head. "Please forgive my insolence."

"Only if you tell me what is happening in that head of yours."

She knew there was no escaping this so with a sigh she told him about the bandits and how her brother undertook the responsibility to bring them to justice. She also spoke of his inability to fight and why he went on this quest in the first place, which was to compete with her. She omitted no details.

"So, today is the sixth day, then," he mentioned.

"Yes, Master."

"You intend to arrive there at night under cover of darkness?"

"Yes, Master. It would be better that way." No one would see her coming. Actually, she hoped it would be raining hard when she arrived. No one would hear her coming either.

"You had better get moving then. You do not want to be late."

She looked to him in surprise with her eyes blinking as if someone else would suddenly be sitting there in his place.

"You are not going to talk me out of going?"

"Ha!" He scoffed. "Why would I do that?"

She shrugged in an honest gesture of ignorance.

"Are you a paladin?" he asked as he leaned in toward her, eyes blazing.

"Yes," she answered.

"Is a paladin charged with defending those who cannot defend themselves?" He did not even blink.

"Yes." Leannii said again.

"Is it a paladin duty to be the sword of justice in the eyes of Enki against those who would inflict evil on the innocent?"

"Yes," she replied.

"Is it also in our code that we maintain peace and will answer the call to battle when it is needed?"

"Yes." Leannii nodded.

"So…why would I talk you into staying here? Would not acting when it is obvious to do so break your code of honor?"

She nodded. Yes, it most certainly would, she thought. He stood to leave after seeing he talked some sense into her.

"With that I will be off and expect to see you again when you have returned." Adding a final thought he turned back to her. "Do not forget to find me after you get back."

She smiled and nodded again.

"I will not forget." She walked him to the door but stopped him before he left. "Oh, before you go, this will be my first battle…do you have any advice for me?"

"Yes, I do." He sternly looked at her. "Do not forget what I taught you or you will come home in a box." He was about to turn to leave when he added, "Oh, and use your head for more than just a shield or a place to wear a helm. You do not have to be a genius of war to come home alive. Be simple. When you have decided to end someone's life then go do it and let nothing stand in your way. When you have decided on a course of action then follow it through to its end. You cannot attack when defending. Always bring more weapons than you think you will need. You remember any of this?"

"Yes, Master. I remember well," she spoke with a smile.

"Good! So when fear grips you, make sure you do not forget then either." He did not smile.

With that he abruptly left. Never once, even after all those years, did Brother Qinn ever tell her how rare paladins were. He did not know why they were rare. People had just ceased receiving The Calling. When she received her Calling it was something special. Her grandfather predicted it although no one would listen to him. He saw what no one seemed to, that Leannii was special. But no one, aside from him, ever told her so.

As she watched Qinn walk away without the slightest hint of him looking back to her she tried to imagine what his last comment could mean. When the fear grips you…do not forget. She could not understand what fear he was speaking of. Inside, she shrugged it off and went about her tasks before leaving. There was still much to be done and she had to be ready by nightfall to leave. Both she and her guide would travel by night as swiftly as they could yet still be rested for a battle upon arrival at Blacktower.

What a strange place for bandits to gather. There were a few of those ancient black stone monoliths scattered around the continent. Their exact purpose could only be speculated since all of the key questions remained unanswered. Who built them? Why where they built? When were they built? Why build them where they were? No one knew the answers to these questions. The few facts that were acknowledged were that these were constructed of the same kind of obsidian, they had been there for over two thousand years and none of the writing or glyphs inside could be understood. Being fashioned from obsidian, and also remaining complete enigmas, granted them the simple and ominous title of Blacktower.

Each also had another name to identify their locations so that the scholars could understand in a simple statement which one the other was speaking about. This particular tower that Thalorn rode toward, where the bandits had possibly camped was called the Blacktower of Saques, which meant the Blacktower in the forest land. Even though each tower was given a name, each tower was also greatly avoided. Superstition and wild notions ruled and very few made their way to one of these places. The stories themselves varies depending upon who was telling it however, most spoke of shades that moved in the night, hearing strange noises or howling and the occasional foreboding tale of someone who ventured to a tower and never returned. All of these were unsubstantiated campfire stories that were not believed by the more educated academic communities. Over the past four hundred years most every tale concerning the towers, and many others as well, were thoroughly investigated for any hint of validity so that civilization might begin to relearn the world around them. Finding no moving shadows, strange noises or any actual reports of people who had vanished, all of these stories were balked at by the investigators. Still, the rumor mill continued to faithfully produce more and more each season and the towers remained a place to avoid by the general populace.

So it was rather bizarre that a gang of bandits would make a base of operations by a tower. Either they wanted everyone to fear them more and not come seeking justice or there was something else a bit stranger at work. Either way, she would discover what they were doing, serve them their due justice, find her brother and return home…but not before another argument with her mother.

As soon as her mother, Duchess Fabiana, learned that her daughter was about to embark on something unladylike again, she had a conniption. It was bad enough she felt her daughter acted more like a boy than a young lady even as Leannii was growing up but now her daughter was about to go gallivanting across the countryside. For what? As if her older brother, the son of a duke, needed help from his younger sister. Fabiana scoffed while being mortified. She felt Leannii needed to stop all this paladin warrior mannish nonsense and relearn how to be a proper lady and good woman or no man would ever want to marry her. Who wants to marry a woman who is so inappropriate so as to tromp through mud as if it were fun? Leannii was a noble woman who was supposed to act like a lady! What was that girl's problem? Already Leannii was seventeen and no man was interested in being her suitor. How embarrassing. Now, she was trying to prove she was something she was not? Lady Fabiana would not stand for it.

Amazingly, Leannii held her passions in tight control. Her mother also tried to stand in front of her and stop her from leaving all while screaming red-faced at the top of her lungs. All of Ilranik might have heard Lady Fabiana that afternoon but Leannii kept calmly moving around her mother, not fighting with her and trying to leave as peacefully and as quickly as possible. Even when she was threatened with being disowned, Leannii did not falter.

"Don't come back here again!" Leannii heard her mother scream as she mounted her horse to leave. "From now on, I have no daughter!"

The rider with Leannii looked to her with great uncertainty and concern but his glance went unrecognized. Leannii kept staring straight ahead as they passed through the gate and headed northward. As soon as the path narrowed, she motioned for him to go ahead of her. When he did, Leannii quietly lowered her head and began to cry.

For the next two days Leannii and her guide, Oleg Samman, did not speak much. Their ride was mostly quiet. After the events of the preceding day, Oleg did not want to press Leannii feeling that she did not wish to speak much. However, speaking was exactly what she needed to do. There was too much pent up energy that needed to be released and Leannii, for many years now, had gone without any sympathetic ear. Oleg's silence and awkwardness did not help her in the least. It had only served to further bury her feelings and become more frustrated and sad. She felt she hated her life, hated all of the demands on her, hated pretending to be who she was not and hated even coming out here after her brother. He was an idiot, she felt. If he was so perfect, then why did she have to come out here? Perhaps, it was Leannii who was the overprotective one.

Finally, while over half finished with their early supper, Leannii spoke. She had been playing with her food more than eating it.

"Oleg," she began. "Did we prepare well enough?"

"Sorry, milady." He was confused. "What do you mean?"

"Did we pack what we needed? Are just you and I going to be enough?"

"There is only one way to know that for certain...that is to get where we are going and see for ourselves." He tried to think quickly for something helpful to say. "I am sure your brother is fine. These are, after all, just bandits- poor untrained hapless men who prey on the weak because they have no strength...You will see." He began to chuckle as if enjoying some comedic thought he generated in his own head. "They will probably wet themselves at the sight of properly trained soldiers."

She tried to laugh with him but could only pretend to smile and share even a little mirth. That dreaded feeling of her brother's demise and the echoes of the argument with her mother still held too great a grip on her heart. She had brought an extra broad sword, three extra bow strings, over eighty arrows, five daggers, a flail and two gallons of oil, just in case. Always bring more weapons than you think you will need, her teacher told her. Slowly her smile faded from her face.

"What do we do if he is dead?"

He just looked to her and did not have any answer since he did not even consider for one moment this whole time that it was remotely possible for Thalorn to have been killed by those ruffians.

"Honest question, Oleg. What do we do?"

He starred at her without forming a word. The thought was too shocking for him to get past.

"I cannot lose my brother." Her words were dark and serious enough to concern Oleg. "He is really all I have." She cast her gaze into the firelight and hoped he was still alive despite her feeling.

When they arrived in the tower area it was just before nightfall. Twilight had set in well and it was already difficult to see. Clouds covered the starry sky hiding even the most ambient moonlight that could have helped. Trying to follow the wagons' path in the dark proved most difficult and next to impossible. Neither having any decent skills in tracking also did not aid them to find their wayward fellows. It became closer to midnight when the two stopped searching. There was no sign of any camp or a noticeable glow from a campfire. Inadvertently, they found themselves at the base of the imposing Blacktower itself.

It disturbingly stood like a malevolent black giant frozen in stone. Its spire shape and dark feeling was quite unnatural in this otherwise quite natural forest. Neither had been here before and both were viewing this for the first time. Oleg stood in amazement as to its height and wondered how something so tall could stand without decay for such a long time as the stories told. Truly this was a structure to marvel at.

Leannii however, was feeling quite different. Something unearthly and quite disquieting spoke wordlessly to her as she gazed upon it for the first time. She wanted to tear this monolith down and run away as fast as she could. Nothing like this should exist on the earth but she could not tell exactly why. Leannii just felt it was not something good, whatever it was. Cutting through the silence, Oleg's voice startled her.

"Maybe we could climb up and see where they camped?"

"What?" she said with a start.

"At the top of the tower," he explained. "We could see for a great distance and maybe get an idea of where their camp is."

She could not imagine herself getting any closer to that tower.

"Ah…you can go ahead. I will wait for you down here."

While Oleg considered that a typical sign of female fear Leannii knew better. It was not fear that kept her from climbing that tower, but some intuitive sense of malice concerning that structure. By the grace of Enki she did not wish to linger here any longer than she had to.

When he stepped inside what little light from the outside was completely gone within those circular walls. Not being able to see, he quickly made his way back outside, past Leannii and to his horse where he retrieved a lantern. After lighting it he walked back to the tower. She watched him without saying a word. Oleg paused at the archway and peered in, raising the lantern in hopes that it would help him see. It did not seem to help so he adjusted the light so that it was brighter. When he lifted it over his head the darkness inside did not change. Oleg cocked his head in confusion. A brighter light should have meant that it was easier to see inside here but it was not. He adjusted the lantern again, this time turning the light as bright as it could possibly go.

The black walls of this tower seemed to swallow the light and still he could not see well. Glancing outside he wondered if the night was playing tricks on his mind. Maybe the black stone of the walls did not allow the light to shine well. Instead of holding the lantern above his head, he slowly progressed while holding it out in front of him. It seemed to help a little as just a few slow steps later he could see stone stairs, made of the same obsidian, which wound in a spiral against the inside wall upward into the darkness. Cautiously, he approached the stairs and began to climb upward.

Assuming the night was still playing tricks on his mind he reached out and placed his hand on the wall to steady his ascent. Quickly he drew it back against his body. The stone was cold! On this warm summer night the stone of the tower was a much lower temperature than it should have been. Oleg though did not stop for long. Perhaps the stone went deep into the ground and was very thick. That would explain why it was so cold. With an exhale and a shrug, he climbed a bit faster.

When he reached the top he paused to look around first. There was a half wall about waist high that encircled the top floor and only enough room for about eight people at the top of the tower. Also, in the direct center of the floor, there was an odd circular pedestal. It was also made of the same material but was about chest high. Before he looked outside, he wanted to look inside first so he approached the cylindrical stone. What he found was quite strange indeed. In the center of this pedestal was a hole, about the size of his fist, but not very deep. There were no markings he could see, there was just a round hole in a round stone stand on top of a round tower. What was this place?

He ran his hand cautiously around the outside of the opening. What he was hoping to feel he did not know, but he was looking for some kind of clue as to what this place was built for. He felt nothing and nothing happened. Dissatisfied with the lack of information, he turned his attention back to his task. He walked to the half wall and peered out into the darkness. He saw nothing. He looked down over the edge but could not see the ground. He suddenly felt that he was floating in an abyss. There was no sky, no forest and no ground. He lost track of directions and could not tell what direction up was. Everything began to sin. He felt dizzy and reached out for the half wall to steady himself...but there was none!

Reaching out his hands, there was nothing to grasp or lean on. He suddenly felt himself become weightless, falling. Panic gripped him as he quickly imagined falling all the way to the hard ground below. Knowing how long he had been climbing the stairs Oleg knew he would be dead when he hit the grass. It was too far to fall and he was not ready to die just yet.

A yell escaped his throat when he felt something sold and cold touch his palm. The lantern was still in the tight grip of his other hand and he noticed he was on his knees. Expecting to be falling hard against the ground his body lurched and he fell backwards against the half wall. When he realized that he was not plummeting to his death but felt like he was, he quickly stood and looked for the stairs to lead him off of this tower roof. It was then that he noticed there were clouds in the sky and a faint outline of a horizon in the distance.

What is this place? Finding the staircase he descended as quickly as he could while using the tower wall for support. The closer he came to the bottom the more frenzied his descent became. He had to get out. He must get out. When he reached the landing he thought there were more steps and he stumbled out into the night after finding the archway and seeing a glimpse of Leannii outside.

With a gasp he staggered out and drew a deep breath. Leannii glanced over her shoulder after seeing him emerge. Strangely he was perspiring and looked very pale in the bright lamplight. He reminded her of what a ghost should look like.

"Back so soon?" she asked with marked curiosity. "You just went in. What did you see?"

Just went in? He thought. *I went all the way to the top.*

"What do you mean?"

Now she was confused.

"You just walked inside and now you are back out again."

"Just walked back out?" He was very lost. While pointing to the dark sky he said, "I just walked all the way to the top and came back down. I even looked around while I was up there."

Leannii looked up in hopes of being able to see the top of the tower. Catching a slight glimpse of the top against the darkness of the clouds her lips pursed and her brow rose.

"Well," she observed. "You are fast."

He looked up at the tower then back at her. He could tell she did not believe him.

"I did!" He pleaded. "There is nothing up there but some sort of round pedestal with a hole in it."

"Did you see anything else?"

"No, I did not see signs of any camp or anything else. It was too dark." *And I almost felt like I was falling to my death up there.*

She thought a bit then looked around. This was not a good place to camp.

"Lets us go and make camp where it is safe." She turned to walk back to their horses. She had no idea where a safe place to camp would be but they would have to quickly find it in the dark. Also, she did not want to be around this place any longer.

"Where would that be?" he asked following.

Leannii did not stop walking but glanced back over her shoulder.

"Somewhere, not here."

Not too far from the summit of the hill where the tower loomed the night, and not very much later, they found a decent sized group of trees that was not very tightly packed together and its undergrowth was not very dense. This provided for an excellent place to camp and lessened their chance to be discovered while they slept. After putting their tents in the middle of the trees and removing their saddles from the horses to give them a rest, they ate without a fire since they did not want any unnecessary light to alert an enemy to their presence.

Before finally lying to rest that night, Leannii did as she would any other night, she prayed to Enki. He was the God of War and Storms and she was a paladin in his service. Much to the dismay of her mother, Leannii took up what was called the Path of the Blood. It was named this because Enki once had a son, Marduk, who was killed when he battled Ereshkegal, the Great Ancient One. Enki was enraged and the blood of his son became the source of his justification to battle any and all of the Ancient Ones where ever and whenever they were. So, that duty was likewise passed on the holy warriors who took up the call to become his paladins. The Blood was Life and the symbol of their strength. She, like all of her brethren, did not actually hear Enki or see his presence. It was publicly correct to say they did and that Enki's glory worked powerfully in the world. However, in reality, none of them really ever saw undeniable evidence of Enki but all of them continued to go through those motions anyway.

Even her teacher, Brother Quinn, gave her the same impression of being one who just acted the part but did not really have any heart-felt conviction. The only one she thought actually felt the will of Enki was her grandfather and it was because of his passion that she walked the Path. Deep down inside herself, Leannii yearned to feel as he did and believe in something as strong as he did. Therefore, day after day and night after night, she prayed and meditated and practiced.

She prayed that night for Enki to guide her to find what happened to her brother and to give her the strength and power she may need if these bandits were still a threat. She also prayed that Oleg would forever be safe and that Enki could take Oleg into his care to watch over him. What Leannii did not know, praying that night in the gloom of that black spire, is that for the first time her life Enki actually did hear and respond…but she would learn much later to be careful what someone should ask of the gods.

Their slumber however, was not very restful. This journey was not going as Leannii had hoped and she did not discuss that matter much with her guide. She elected instead to think of some semblance of a plan in the event her intuitive feeling over the past few weeks proved correct. She had to accept, she thought, that because of the lack of evidence of her brother and his men that they may have fallen to the worse. If that were true then this was not a safe place for her or Oleg and they would have to be as concealed as possible to learn anything. The most disastrous thing that could befall them was if they were to be discovered by the wrong group.

Their breakfast was cold since Leannii did not want to risk starting a fire and so they ate salted pork and drank some of the little water they had left. Neither spoke much as if there was some thick gloomy yet unseen shadow that cast itself over them. They barely even looked at one another and could only bring themselves to say what was absolutely necessary. They repacked and saddled their horses then rode back to the tower.

This time, in the light of the bright morning sun, the tower did not seem so dreadful. Leannii looked upon it with a different eye and felt that this structure, although still unnatural, was just a black stone spire. Its malevolence she felt the previous night had vanished. Leannii paused for a moment in her mind and discarded the memory to her imagination running wild after such a long ride from Ilranik. With that, she dismounted and walked to the entrance.

Oleg, however, felt much different but she had not noticed. He was still clinging to the image of himself falling from the tower and of the vertigo that had preceded it.

Forcing a strong sounding voice he declared to Leannii, "I'll stay here and watch the horses."

She glanced back over her shoulder but paid him no acknowledgement as she continued into the spire.

Inside was dark but her eyes seemed to adjust to the darkness rather quickly and she could see that the floor, walls and spiral stairs were all crafted from the same dull black stone. Looking to the floor she noticed the glyph engraved on the floor encircled by that indiscernible language she had heard so much about. The large symbol was a complex engraving of a five pointed star inside of a circle, almost like a pentagram; however, the lines making the star were all bent. There were many other lines as well but she could not see what it was they were depicting. Curiously, in the center of all of this, was a recessed square. Its length and width were a little less than the size of her boot and it did not seem to parallel or otherwise correspond to any of the lines around it.

Cautiously, she walked over the glyph and knelt down beside the small square. It was uniform in shape and seemed to be made at the same time as the glyph. This is weird, she thought and cautiously reached out her hand. When her fingers made contact with the stone she was surprised as to how cold it felt. She ran her finger tips along the outside edge then into the center but she felt nothing unusual.

"Huh," she uttered before standing and making her way to the stairs. Looking up, Leannii followed the path of the winding stairs up to the top of the tower. It was amazing to her that she could see all of it when there were no windows to allow any light to enter; there was only the archway at the bottom and the opening at the very top. She cocked her head to the side at that thought and then began to climb up the stairs.

She walked for a while before reaching the top and looked down at the steps to the bottom. That was a long way, she realized and then remembered that Oleg said he came up here just the other night. Impossible, this is just too far. Turning her attention to the top of the tower she took her final step and stood at the pinnacle for the first time. In the center, just as Oleg mentioned last night, was a round pedestal of stone and a waist high wall surrounding the crown. There was no roof of any kind and looked to be there never was one.

Leannii slowly walked to the center where this pedestal was and looked on it carefully. It was exactly as he had described: a round pedestal with a hole in it. It was cylindrical, made of the same stone and had a curious cylindrical indentation at the center. She ran her hand along the stonework and felt nothing different than she had before when she touched the same stone at the bottom. Here also it was hard and cold. Regarding the hole she thought, was something supposed to be put inside of here? However, she could not fathom what that object may have been or why.

She walked to the edge of the low wall where she guessed Oleg was at the bottom and looked down. She was almost correct and adjusted her position so that she was directly above him.

"Oleg!" she shouted. "You were right…and this is very strange, indeed."

He looked up at her as she yelled to him but did not respond for her to hear. In a volume she could not hear he muttered, "Of course I was right…but you did not believe me."

Leannii began to scan the horizon for any trace of a campsite. She could see quite far from up here and began to think that this would make an excellent watchtower. An army could be seen at least a day before it arrived. Was that what these were built for? To be some sort of watchtower?

Moving slowly around the top of the spire Leannii searched close and far away for any sign of her brother and his men. Studying the contour of the distant tree lines and rolling hills she tried to see any regular shape that was man made or any plume of smoke from a fire that would give her a direction to begin looking. Finding none she moved to a different area and searched there. Leannii had guesses that she began looking in the south west, which is where Oleg was, and was turning around to the east. Finally, when she scanned the northern direction, she saw the faint rising of smoke.

There in the distance, perhaps but two hour's ride, there rose a faint pillar of smoke against a sheer rocky hillside. Being that there were too many trees in that area, Leannii could not tell what was making the fire or anything else. But that fire gave her hope. Brother! Thank you, Master Enki! Now she had a place to begin searching. She ran to the southwest side of the wall and shouted to Oleg.

"North! There is smoke to the north!" She then ran all the way down the stairs, sometimes skipping two or three in one stride. As dangerous as that may have been, Leannii did not care. She had to find her brother.

Swiftly, she ran from the tower, mounded her horse and galloped of toward the north. Leannii did not have to tell Oleg to follow her, especially when he did not want to be anywhere close to this tower any longer.

As she rode Leannii thought about what she saw from the tower. Facing north she saw the smoke rising from the east side of the rocks. To the south, closer to the tower, were scattered trees and to the north, past the smoke, there seemed to be a clearing before the trees became dense. Why would he put himself up against a rock face? Tactically that was not a wise decision because it was too easy to be cut off...unless he had plenty of provisions and had chosen to fortify a position. But why would he do that? Was he facing an army? To Leannii, none of this made any sense and it did not seem like something her brother would do.

They stopped short of where they guessed the fire to originate from and tethered their horses to a small tree. Being that there was no road or path here the two had hoped that no one would discover them by accident while they both made their way on foot to investigate. Before venturing onward, they took what they thought they would need for scouting. Oleg brought his broad sword, bow and a dozen arrows. He turned to Leannii ready to leave when he stopped and stared with his mouth hanging open.

Leannii had strapped one of her broad swords on her belt to her left side, along with one short sword at her right waist, her bow across her back with two dozen arrows and three daggers. She had one dagger on each thigh, a third strapped to her left ankle and she was concealing a fourth in the small of her back. Oleg was stunned. Leannii sensed that she was being watched and looked up to Oleg who was motionless.

"What?" she asked with earnest puzzlement.

He blinked. "Do you think you have enough?" By the gods, how many weapons did she want to carry?

Maybe he was right, she began to think. But she did not know what else to do.

"You are right," she finally admitted. Holding up her other short sword she asked, "But I do not know where else to carry this one, I have no more room. Any ideas?"

She was sober? She wanted to bring another weapon? Oleg thought she was going crazy.

"Are you serious?" He could not believe what he was hearing.

"Maybe you are right." She put the short sword back on her horse and took out the flail. "I should take this."

Oleg gasped again. Leannii stopped to look at him just standing there and asked.

"Are you coming?"

Traveling northward, the trees here were much less thick and became more scattered with less and less undergrowth. The only sound that echoed through the trees was of the many dried leaves and twigs crunching and snapping under their feet...and Leannii clanking with all the metal she carried.

Soon, they found the clearing by the rock face and slowed as the sound of many men could be heard. Realizing there was not much of a place to hide the two cautiously dropped down into a crawl and made their way to the edge of the tree line where they could get a better vantage point. They were surprised at what they saw.

There was a log wall that had been constructed that stood the height of three men and each of the tree trunks had been sharpened to a point. The wall seemed to encircle the camp and so was made of hundreds of trees. Also, it was gated however, the heavy wooden doors were wide open and they could see clearly inside to at least part of the camp. To the right of the gate on the inside was a guard tower that was also made of wood but was unmanned at the time. But that was not the important sight. When she noticed it, Leannii's heart leapt into her throat.

She saw, at the base of the tower, one of the wagons from her brother's party! Ha, she thought, my brother is here!

"Look!" she said a little too loud while grasping at Oleg's arm to get his attention. "One of my brother's wagons! They are here!" She began to stand up when she caught herself and stopped.

A man walked past the wagon from further inside the wall and stopped in the door opening. He was not dressed like a soldier. Leannii studied him while trying to deny what she was looking at. The man wore tattered brown and grey clothing, his hair was a mess and he had no armor. He was scruffy, dirty and his dress looked just as bad. He was no soldier...he had the look of a bandit.

"Move, you!" The shout came from inside the wall and was directed at the man Leannii and Oleg were watching. As he stepped aside, closer the wagon, another one of the wagons from Thalorn's group came rolling out. The two who drove the wagon looked just as unkempt as the other man and the wagon itself was filled in the back with lumpy cloth that appeared heavy.

This was not good. Two wagons from her brother's party were now owned by bandits. Something terrible had happened and Leannii desperately needed to discover what. Nudging Oleg without taking her eyes from that wagon that was leaving the camp, she began to crawl in a path to intercept it. This may not be hard since the wagon was rolling quite slowly and neither driver seemed to notice their presence. The wagon seemed to follow a road and they followed the wagon, always keeping out of sight. The road led eastward and it seemed that there was only one cart with no escorts.

When it finally reached a different clearing, perhaps a mile or so away from the walled camp, the cart stopped. Leannii and Oleg again crept to the edge of the tree line to spy on what was happening. Beside where the wagon stopped there was a large pit inside this circle of trees. On the far side of the pit two others, also carrying swords, stood and walked over the cart. They all greeted one another as comrades in arms then began to unload the wagon. In the back were two large barrels that appeared to be very heavy as all four men struggled with them, one at a time, and positioned them at the pit's edge. With the barrels gone, Leannii and Oleg could clearly see with wagon's mysterious contents. It was filled with dead bodies!

Some of the corpses were still partially dressed and most were brutally mangled. They lay haphazardly in a pile after being carelessly tossed into their own wagon like garbage. Blood and other fluids still oozed from the gaping holes in the bodies as even the four men starred at the heap. No one wanted to touch any of them however and it was obvious that the corpses were intended for irreverent disposal in this large pit. The worse of it came when Leannii and Oleg recognized the tattered and bloody remnants of the clothing. They were those of Ilranik soldiers.

A flood tears welled up behind Leannii's eyes and her jaw clenched causing her teeth to grind together. Her face became distorted into some twisted mask of despair and hatred. She almost did not look human. She scrambled to stand, clawing at the dirt and leaves to get to the four men. Oleg quickly wrapped his arms around her to stop Leannii from running into danger and used his body weight to encumber her so she could not move. Although that worked, Oleg failed to cover her mouth ad amidst her struggling, Leannii's cry of anguish echoed through the clearing. Four heads quickly turned in their direction to see who just yelled.

"Damn!" cursed Oleg. Now they would have to fight.

From their distance the four men saw two human shaped rolling in the dirt just inside the tree line. Not liking to be spied on or followed, especially in their careers, the four quickly drew their swords and closed on Leannii and Oleg.

"Come on!" Oleg desperately said to her. "We have to go. Now!" He tried to bring her to her feet while restraining her from attacking the closing men.

"No!" She resisted being lost in her pain and anger. "No!"

"Come on!" he demanded while trying to drag her away to safety.

"No!" Leannii began to fight harder. "Thalorn!"

The four men heard the woman yell and broke into a sprint.

Glancing over his shoulder, Oleg realized he could no longer outrun these men. Reluctantly, he released one hand hold on Leannii and drew his sword. That was all she needed. Leannii broke free of Oleg and darted straight to the four men. The four watched, almost comically, as the furious woman ran toward them and they slowed to a stop with utter disbelief. She was crazy. Leannii began to almost growl like a rabid animal as she neared them.

One man in the center calmly stepped forward raising his fist and punched her in the forehead. With a grunt of surprise, Leannii's head snapped back from the force of the blow and she fell back onto her rump. Oleg was slower in reaching the men but when he did, just a few paces behind Leannii, he swung his blade at the first man he could reach.

He was not ready to be cut with a sword yet not completely incapable of moving. As Oleg's sword arced upward at his chest, the man brought his own sword up to block as he back peddled to gain his footing. Now all four men turned their attention to Oleg.

Leannii's hand came up and she rubbed her brow. Then she realized she was prostrate after being punched in the head. She never saw the fist coming. Now, she was angry. Grasping at her waist for some sort of weapon she scrambled to her feet. It was a flail. That would do fine. She ran quickly, approaching the closest man from behind, and swung the flail once around herself then into the arm of one of the four men. As the metal struck bone she felt it splinter like bamboo and he cried out from the excruciating pain. She got the flail moving again by swinging it once around her head. The injured man turned to see who had just shattered his arm only to look into the rather scary face of Leannii.

The flail came around and she swung it down from above her

and into his head. Leannii barely heard the wet yet hollow sound of his skull crushing beneath her blow. He fell lifeless but she did not notice that either. She had lost all side vision and could only see what was directly before her. Even all sound came to her as if it was from a distance.

As Oleg tried frantically to dodge and parry the strikes of three men, Leannii closed on the next man, again from his back. Using the same arcing attack she did before, Leannii swung the flail into the man who was unaware of her. The metal solidly struck him between his shoulders on his spine. There was a dull crunching sound as his body tried to gasp for air. He was never able to breathe and he sank to his knees, paralyzed. Then toppled onto his face just as unmoving and mangled as one of the corpses in the wagon.

Oleg finally managed to slice one of the men and cut deep into his inside forearm. The man yelled and dropped his sword while scrambling backward to avoid Oleg's next attack. He was unsuccessful and Oleg's sword bit deep through the man's shoulder and into his chest. As the man fell, he looked at the sword jutting from his own chest. His eyes lost focus and glazed over when he hit the ground with Oleg's sword still stuck in his body. The last man realized he was alone and quickly decided to run back to the camp for help. He yelled in fear as he began to turn and run. He did not get very far.

Leannii noticed he was running away and instinctively she gave chase the same way as any wolf or tiger would pursue a fleeing prey. The difference was that Leannii was not brandishing claws or sharp teeth; she carried blades, a bow and a flail. When it first appeared to her that he may possibly outpace her, Leannii did the only thing she could think of. Swinging the flail around her head over and over with loudening barbaric yell, she stopped running and threw it at the back of his head.

The heavy weapon clumsily plunged through the air. Quickly losing momentum and having no aerodynamics it fell sharply only to land on his calves as he ran. With a shout of surprise he tripped from the chain loosely entangling his ankle and tumbled to a rather painful looking halt. Leannii was quickly on him.

Picking up the flail that had caused him to fall she swung it over her head and brought it down against his back as he lay prone and helpless. Bones cracked and he screamed in pain.

"No!" He managed to plead between gasps, "Please…don't!"

Thud! The heavy weight came down on him and again, she swung it and brought it down on the man. Thick crimson splattered up the left side of her body with a sickening wet sound that she never heard. As she pulled the flail from his near lifeless body she was fascinated for a brief moment with the depression the heavy metal ball of the flail made in his back. It was only for a moment though as she lifted the weapon above her head and swung again.

Oleg had finally managed to catch his breath and wrestle his sword from the body of the man he had just killed. Seeing the blood and broken bits of bone made him feel woozy and disgusted. He fell back onto his butt and began to absently clean the drying blood from his sword and was completely unaware of his surroundings. Killing a man was very new for him, having never it before, and his mind wanted to distance itself from that horror as quickly as possible. He was no soldier, he was no great battle hardened warrior, he was a guide who knew the geography of the Covenant lands and had only learned to use a sword for basic self-protection. He never learned that skill thinking he would be where he was just then: sitting on the dirt after having just killed someone he never knew and he was not taking it well. From a distance he could hear himself talking to the corpse saying, "I'm sorry…I'm sorry…I'm sorry."

From somewhere behind him he heard the distant sound of a hammer strike methodically slamming into the earth over and over. Hammer? Here? It took a little time for his mind to grasp where he was and what had had just happened. When he remembered it he wanted to vomit however, the more he focused on that repetitive noise the louder and clearer it became. The hammer was some kind of solid metal and it was striking muddy earth with a dull yet soggy thud. Slowly he began to look around the clearing but saw nothing that could be generating that drumming. His brow rose as he realized it was coming from behind him. With the slowness and dexterity of a drunkard Oleg turned to see what was happening.

Not far from where he was he saw someone pounding the soil over and over again. His head cocked because he could not quite understand what it was he was looking at. Slowly his mind had begun to shape and accept what he saw before him. In shocked disbelief and transfixing horror he managed to stand and make his way over to the scene, all without being able to tear his eyes away.

It was Leannii. With another thud his body jolted as he was fully brought back into reality. She was still pounding the corpse with her flail in a trance like stare. Leannii had pounded all the way through the body and was now striking the ground beneath it. Blood had been churned with the soil and produced a dark red mud that she still pounded, oblivious to the fact that he was quite dead. With the next thud, Oleg turned and painfully vomited feeling that his guts were being turned inside out. Again, another thud could be heard from behind him

He turned and looked to see that Leannii was trapped in the trance of killing someone that was already dead. He scrambled to his feet and abruptly tackled Leannii to the ground. Both fell on dry dirt with Leannii still clawing to hit the corpse again with her flail. Blinded by her rage and horror, she did not understand that someone was holding her from behind. She could only see that her target was too far out of hitting distance and she could not get there to strike it again. As she fought against some unknown force she began to realize that she was being grasped around her waist. Focusing on her freedom and abject need to move her mind began to see what was around her and Leannii saw blood.

When she recognized the color she stopped moving and stared at it, slowly raising her hands to see that it was her that was drenched in crimson. Blood everywhere, mixed with soil, was soaking everything around her and including her. As her eyes widened with terror staring at her hands, she screamed.

Her blood curdling wail of anguish invited the entire forest to weep with her and she then began to uncontrollably cry in long howls. Her fingers curled as she slowly rolled to her side, eyes clenched shut, bawling in gasps. Oleg tightly held her and caressed her matted hair, there in the lonely clearing, both bloodied and spent, until sleep claimed Leannii.

Slowly her eyes opened and she fought to see in the darkness. It was now colder than she remembered and she lay amongst some cool green plants on the forest bed with a familiar blanket over her. The soft glow of a fire hissed from her right. Carefully, she sat up and looked around to find herself in a tiny camp with a small fire. A hole was dug and rocks formed a ring around the top edge of the deep yet tiny fire pit. Oleg was cooking. He was smart to lower the fire as much as he could so as to lessen its conspicuousness.

Suddenly, she realized that she was not in her armor and quickly grasped at herself to be certain. Leannii found her feelings were correct and she was now in a clean dress and she had been washed of all blood and soil. How long had I been asleep? Then her thoughts quickly turned to Oleg who was already looking in her direction.

"Good," he said. "You are awake finally." He continued to poke at the meat he was cooking. "You kept moving and moaning from bad dreams. Are you feeling well?" he asked with genuine concern. She paused for a moment to think. Am I well? I honestly do not know.

"I have on different clothing," she observed. The thought of her being seen naked disturbed her and the thought that anyone may have taken advantage of her sparked a flash of anger within her.

"Yes," he spoke truthfully. "You had so much...blood on you I did not want you to become ill so I cleaned you and redressed you. I hope you do not mind that and hope you do not think I did anything improper, milady."

"Well...I...It's..." She did not know what to say and Oleg knew that she was feeling uncomfortable but sincerely hoped that she trusted and knew him enough to know that her safety and well-being was primary. Of course, the thought has crossed his mind when he saw the beautiful athletic figure of such a gorgeous woman but that was a fleeting thought and he did not act upon it at all. They were in a perilous situation and he had felt far too much guilt over killing that man to settled enough to make any sort of confident advances to any woman, especially one with her temper and current frailty. "Thank you," she finally managed.

"My duty," he spoke with a subtle and polite bow. "There is water to your left and this food is almost ready if you are hungry." He returned his gaze to the fire in an attempt to avert his eyes from hers. He did not want her to think he was weak but in truth, he remained on the edge of breaking down for most of this day after the fight this morning. Killing was not like it was in the glory filled stories he was accustomed to hearing. It was far worse than disgusting and wretched and he could not seem to feel anything other than sorrow for it.

"Oleg," she said with a tone to get his attention. When he looked to her she respectfully said, "Thank you."

That caught him by surprise.

"No problem," he replied while trying to guess what she had so sincerely voiced her appreciation for. Finally surrendering to his ignorance he asked, "What for?"

"Say again?"

"What were you thanking me for just now?"

Her eyes dropped, almost in embarrassment, and then she returned her gaze directly into his eyes.

"For taking care of me when I could not do it myself." She retrieved the water he told her about a few minutes before and continued with an almost confessional tone. "I would really not know what to do out here if I were out here all alone…try to get back home as safely as I could, after…" Her voice trailed off and a look of strong unease washed over her face.

He waited for a few moments for her to answer but when she did not he spoke.

"After…after what?"

She took a deep breath before answering to collect her thoughts and steady herself.

"I want to know, without doubt, what happened to my brother," she said plainly. "I do not want to leave here before I know for certain."

"That could be dangerous…"

"I do not care," she interrupted. "I do not want to put you in harm but that is my whole reason for coming here. If I do not leave here knowing what happened or return without my brother, then I will feel all of this was for not."

Oleg heard the weight of her sincerity in her words as she spoke. With a nodding head he said, "Then I shall do my best to help you. We will not leave here without your brother."

Leannii smiled. That promise warmed her heart and helped her feel a bit better.

"Thank you"

They smiled to each other then began to slowly eat. Both needed food but neither was particularly hungry after the events of that day. That morning changed their lives forever. Before then, neither one had killed before and neither one had ever really been in a life or death fight either. Both ate in silence, being unable to speak made their meal tense.

When Oleg put his head down to sleep Leannii stayed awake for a few moments to pray. She asked for comfort and solace. Leannii actually wished that her teacher, Brother Quinn, was there for guidance. She felt she needed his strength and prayed for her own strength so that she would not need to rely on Oleg or Quinn. Praying for the strength to stand on her own again, she did not know to be cautious or what to pray for.

"Woah! Look at this!"

That woke her up from her dead sleep. He felt hands roughly grasp her through the blanket and clothing. Faintly in the darkness, she could see a few faces illuminated by torchlight and smell the odor of unwashed bodies. She tried to flail in defense but there was a sudden pain on her head that never fully reached her mind and all was black and quiet.

Everything was a blur and she could not focus her eyes nor could she move. Leannii could only listen.

"Well...what is she doing here, then?"

"I guess she is looking for them. She has the same ring as the son."

"...Well then...that must mean they are family."

"...what do we do with her?"

"Leave her here. I have an idea..."

She lost consciousness again as blackness embraced her.

Cold water splashed on her face. She shook her head and opened her eyes to see what was happening. Before her eyes could focus on the floor the pain in her skull reached her brain, causing her to wince and moan.

"Oh, you will be fine, princess." She could hear the voce speaking from somewhere in front of her.

"Oh, sorry...duchess." He laughed and she could hear others laughing as well. Against the pain Leannii forced her eyes open to see where she was. It was then she noticed her hands were manacled above her head and she was sitting on a table against a stone wall. She pulled against the shackles but they held fast and she could not get free. This angered her. Looking up to see if there was any way to get free of these irons, she saw that they were chained to the wall where a beam supporting the ceiling was bolted to another cross beam too far above her head for her to reach. Out of response to frustration she tugged again on the chain with an audible grunt. That was met with more laughter from the room.

Sharply, and with a smoldering fire in her eyes, Leannii looked to who was laughing at her predicament. Four somewhat men, washed but rather scruffy, were sitting at another table while enjoying tankards of ale and leisurely feasting off metal plates of cooked meat, breads and fruits. They carried small weapons in sheaths on their belts and wore boots of black or brown leather with pants and shirts of decent cloth.

"Problems, little girl?" One in the front said and drew a small belching cackle from the others.

"Who are you and what do want with me?" Leannii spat.

"Oh…a fiery little girl." He took a large gulp of his ale, sat back in his chair and then crossed his legs before speaking again. "Well, princess, you are here to help us send a message back to your father."

"I will do no such thing!" she hissed.

He glanced over his shoulder at his comrades, obviously feinting surprise to mock her.

"Hear that, boys?" he asked barely containing his own laugh. "The little girl chained to our wall says she is not helping."

They all roared in laughter but Leannii fumed from not getting the joke.

"What is so funny?" Being bound was bad enough and being laughed at was also infuriating however, for Leannii both at once was getting quite unmanageable.

Gaining control of himself the same man spoke again.

"You, little princess," he laughed some again. "You have no idea and still you squirm!"

"I demand to know what is…"

"You demand?" The voice came sharply from their far left. Instantly, the men quieted as if they had just been caught doing something wrong by a strict parent. Slowly and in a disturbingly controlled fashion, boot steps echoed through the room as the man approached. The closer he came the more uneasy the men were. Finally he rounded the corner.

He was a little tall and had a solid athletic build. Dark hair, worn like a cowl, hooded his face. His clothing was dark as well, hued in charcoal and black. He was an intimidating figure to behold.

He stopped at the table and no man sitting had met his eyes.

"You can demand nothing." His voice was educated and deeper than it should have been and the low tones echoed with an eerie chill in the room. As angered as Leannii was, she was made silent with this man's presence. "You are our prisoner, it is that simple, and what few comforts we give you...I suggest you be grateful." At last he looked at her with a black eyed glance like a razor that dripped venom and caused her to gasp. "Things could be much worse off."

Leannii said nothing as she felt the blood drain from her face and a chill slither up her spine. He slowly turned to the men with a disapproving posture. He still spoke with the same disturbing slowness with which he walked into the room.

"Having a bit of fun, were we?"

"We...we were...um...just...um..." They all stammered. Leannii watched quietly wondering what could make this smaller man command so much fear from these ruffians.

"Just what?" he asked quicker and a bit louder. Everyone, including Leannii, was startled.

"We were just...talking..."

"Who gave you permission to talk to her?!" he interrupted, the anger in his voice sparked like molten metal. The men flinched as if he moved to strike them but he did not even raise a hand, just his voice.

"We're sorry..."

"Yes," he interrupted again. "I know you are...sorry." He stared at them for a time before turning to Leannii. His posture has obviously changed and he was instantly calmer just as he had been when he entered. Leannii wondered how someone could change moods so quickly. Was he in that much control of himself or was he that crazy? He slowly walked to Leannii like a predator approaching a helpless prey. There was no need to pounce; she was clearly not going anywhere.

"We found our men...and what was left of one." He dragged a chair closer to the table and continued to speak as he sat. "Did you really do that? Did you...pound through a man into the ground under him like that?"

She did not answer but cast her eyes to the floor.

"I must say...I am...impressed." His tone had a chilling

admiration. "I have been killing for...well, over ten years now, and I have never seen anyone do anything like that before." He tried to conceal a smile but failed in the end. "That was good. I actually became...worried about who may be out here with us when I saw it for myself." He brushed his hands together as if he were cleaning dirt from his palms but there was none. "Impressive. Most impressive...I did not know your family had that in you."

The mention of her family made Leannii's head snap in his direction.

"What do you know of my family?" she snappishly challenged.

"Oh...I know a great deal about the Covenant family, my dear...Leannii."

She looked surprised that he knew her name.

"You do not understand...that's what this is all about."

Obviously, she was puzzled at that remark.

"Let me help you." He spoke with an audible hint of contempt. "I am Jeral Valancia, son of Adenon Valancia. You see, your father saw it fit to raise the tax value of my family land, which is, point of fact, the very land we are sitting in now...he raised them so high that it forced my family to sell almost everything they had and, when they could not pay, he claimed the lands for his own."

For Leannii, this was all new information. She had never heard of this man, or his family, ever before. For all she knew, these lands were always her family's claim. Leannii had no idea of what he was speaking of.

"I have never heard of you," she admitted.

"Never heard...is that so?" He was insulted and could not hide it.

"I know nothing of the matter that you speak of," she said firmly. "If my father had wronged you or your family I know he would..."

"Know what!?" he shouted and stood. "What do you know he would do?!"

Leannii was frightened speechless.

"I will tell what he did do!" he spat. "When my family contested his claim he sent armed militia to our home and had my brother and father killed in our courtyard before my eyes!" His orbs burned with dark hatred. His brow curled and he suddenly looked less human. "I would have been dead as well but I was too young at the time!"

Impossible! Her father may have been spineless sometimes but committing such acts was too far outside of his character. Such accusations were vilely slanderous and she would not have some book-read forest thief insult her name in such a way. Defiant to the end, as was her nature, she looked into the imposingly dark eyes of her captor and hissed.

"You slithering liar! My father is a righteous man and would, no, could never be capable of such despicable acts that you concocted. If you're going to lie at least have the intelligence to make something believable before you spew your filth. And another thing, you little petty thug, putting me in chains is not going to scare me or intimidate my family, spineless little worm."

He stared at her and did not say a word for a moment. He then subtly nodded and cocked his head to the side and asked, "Finished?"

"Yes." She held her composure hoping that he did not decide to cut her head from her neck. "That is about it."

"Very well," he said calmly. "Wait right there." He walked slowly yet purposely away to the far side of the room. The men at the table looked more worried now than ever before and looked to one another asking the silent question of when they should leave. Jeral grasped something off of a table that ran along the far wall and strode back to Leannii. He carried with him a sword. When he reached the table she sat on, he thrust the handle of the sword at her face so that Leannii to get a closer look.

"This look familiar?" he spoke through clenched teeth.

It was her grandfather's sword, the same one carried by here by her brother. Thalorn! No! Acidic tears welled up in her eyes as the pit of her stomach began to burn.

"You bastard!" she spat. "What did you do to him?" Leannii looked up the bolts of the chain and wanted nothing more than to be free at that time. She tugged frantically against her shackles as she began to sob. "Let me loose! Let me loose and I swear I will rip your heart from your chest! Ealaing bastard!"

"Well…such anger." He leaned in closer to her and hissed through clenched teeth, his dark eyes burning with hatred. "You want to know what I did?"

Leannii tugged once more and stopped to listen still panting for air.

"We killed everyone first, sparing him for last..."

"Ealaer!" She lashed with words, frustrated that she could not slap the teeth from his mouth.

"Then we hunted him though the lands his father, your father, had stolen from my family...We chased him down like a dog and cut his head from his body."

Leannii cast her head back and howled. Her scream started in anguish then turned to absolute rage. Catching her breath she lowered her head back to stare Jeral down and yell back in his face.

"My family will never yield to slime like you, never! My father will hunt you down like the rabid dog you are and have you drawn and quartered, you dung eating snake..."

Her head suddenly snapped back against the stone wall behind her from the force of his punch. Leannii was dazed and could not see past the pain in her skull.

"I guess that hurt." He sharply turned his head and bellowed, "Get her down!" They moved like fire was licking at their heels, scrambling to unlock her from the manacles restraining her. When they freed her, Jeral roughly clutched her by the throat with one hand and punched her in the stomach with the other. She grunted in pain and her breath was knocked from her but could not bend because of the tightening grip on her throat.

"Not so brash now, are you?" His fist came sharply across the front side of her head making white spots appear in her vision.

"You!" he spat to the four. "Leave us, now!"

The men scrambled to leave but knew that Leannii had a terrible fate before her. They left without question knowing that if there was even the slightest pause then they may suffer more than her. Closing the door behind them all four shuffled away not wanting to even listen to what was about to happen.

When he heard the door close he turned back to Leannii. Wild hatred burned from every fiber of his being. Jeral spun her around and slammed her over the table. Her head struck the hard wood with a loud thud and her brow was cut, allowing her blood to ooze from about her right eye. He forced a knee between her legs, spreading her feet. When he felt the first hint of resistance, Jeral scraped the hard sole of his boot heel down the back of her calf.

Leannii's head rose from the table as she yelled in pain. He then held both of her arms with a strong hand in the small of her back while he bunched up her dress in the other hand and threw it over her, exposing her legs and rear.

Leannii panicked. All those years of combat training never prepared her for this. The hundreds of times she sparred with wood and steel never included being bent over a table to be violated. She struggled wildly but could do nothing but wiggle. Jeral had lowered his pants while Leannii struggled ineffectively and he quickly became tired of her thrashing. He roughly grasped a handful of her hair from the back of her head and painfully pulled her face off the table.

"Quit..." Her face was slammed into the unfinished table top causing her to grunt. "Fighting..." Again her face was bashed onto the table. "This..." Every pause resulted in her face being painfully struck onto the rough table. "Just... accept... this... is... going... to... happen... you... witless... sow." He pulled up and turned her head to the side, blood dripped from her chin, cheeks and brow. Leannii's jaw was slack and she felt that she was about to pass out. "Understand, moll?!"

It felt like while that her face lay in her own warm blood but it was only a few seconds before she forcefully gasped from the searing pain between her legs. Her head thrashed from side to side as she gritted her teeth against the agony of him pounding into her again and again. Leannii was determined not to scream and grant this demon any further satisfaction. Roughly, the unfinished wood of the table stingingly abraded her cheeks and nose. She fought to put her mind somewhere else not being able to accept that she was rendered helpless buy this common thug. Her eyes happened to cast behind her to the floor and there she saw her grandfather's sword lying on the stone. She only wished it was within reach and remembered wishing she was free from her shackles.

Sometime later Jeral had finished and Leannii fell to the floor. Agony radiated through her hips and legs while she tried to find her own trembling hands to wipe the blood from her eyes. She was past the point of crying, past the point of feeling much more pain. Leannii felt true shame and learned the terrible lesson of what it was to feel dirty.

When she cleared the drying blood from her eyes, she found herself on the cold stone floor. Directly in front of her face, just inches away, her grandfather's sword still lay. Leannii could only gaze at it. She did not move nor did she even think to grasp it and seek vengeance. Staring at it was all she could muster.

"We are not done here, dear," he began. "Not for a very long time. I am going to send you home to precious family worn and broken like the little harlot you are…maybe I will send you out for sport like we did your brother. But instead of taking your head there are about forty men who could use the play."

Leannii did not hear anything past the part about her brother. The image of Thalorn being chased like a rabbit by these degenerates began to boil her blood. She always felt her brother was her responsibility to protect even though she was the younger. The knowledge of his death was just too much for her then. Irritating as he was, he was all she had in her life as a friend. That only friend was now gone, killed by the one who had just used her for his own plaything. Demented people such as he should not live. Slowly, her hand reached out and grasped the handle of the sword.

"I was just thinking," he laughed while he was straightening his pants with his back to her. Every word her spoke was now intended to further demoralize a defeated woman. Jeral wanted her to feel weak, inferior, beaten and broken. What he did not realize is that, for a woman like Leannii, it would only serve to fuel a fire within her. That fire would become a furnace hot enough to melt the most solid steel. "I think you would look good in a collar with a leash." He smiled at the thought.

He turned in time to see Leannii swinging a sword down into his body. His smile was abruptly torn from his face and he tried to dodge the blow but was not fast enough. The weighted blade of the ancient sword bit into his right shoulder as he attempted to duck and spin away. The stinging agony stole the breath from his lungs as he felt his own bones separate. He fell to the floor and gawked at Leannii standing above him now having the same cold razor like stare he had a few minutes ago.

"Not so brash now, are you?"

His mouth fell open and he scrambled across the floor searching for a weapon or a way out. Leannii slowly and pitilessly followed behind him, looking down in sheer condescension.

"We're not done here, dear," she said coldly. "Not for a very long time…" Her voice trailed off as her lips curled and she spoke through clenched teeth. As quickly as she could he swung the sword in an arc, bringing it down on his shin. The bone split and blood shot across the floor. He wailed in excruciating pain. "I guess that hurt." She spoke his own heartless words back at him just as coldly as he had done to her.

Jeral, resuming his crawling for safety, reached a chair and grasped it attempting to use it as a shield. Leannii cocked her head to the side and drew her lips back much the same way as she would if a small child challenged her with a twig. But Jeral was not a child. Every step she took sent burning pain from her loins as a reminder that he was a grown man…but not for much longer.

Lifting the sword she began to remember the same words he had spoken to her. The first swing viciously cleaved the chair into kindling. Without pause, Leannii lifted the blade again and stuck it into his body.

"Quit," she began, speaking while he screamed from the sword blows. "Fighting…" Again the sword came down into his torso causing blood to spray and pour. Leannii struck him with that heavy blade between every word.

"This…just…accept…this…is…going…to…happen…you…witless…sow!"

Leannii stopped herself when she was able to hear and feel the steel strike the stone floor beneath him. She looked down on him lacking all emotion save one: the utter sickening revulsion she had for everyone that could ever remind her of him.

Just then, the door burst open and three of the four men who departed earlier reentered the room. The all stopped cold when they saw Leannii covered in blood and brandishing a large sword. Without much acknowledgement she looked to them and remembered that they fled and allowed her to be raped. Gutless worms. But this sword was getting too heavy. By the heavens, how did anyone ever use such a hefty blade? Knowing that three rested men could more easily over power her while she wielded such a heavy sword, she decided to change the field of battle.

Outstretching her arm to hold the bastard sword level to the floor, she stopped and looked to them. Raising her brow Leannii placed the sword on a nearby table top then stepped away from it. Opening her arms to invite their advance, she taunted.

"Unless you are afraid of an unarmed little girl."

None of the could ever live without beating the life from her and so all three rushed her at once…how predictable.

Leannii kicked the first one in the knee as she stepped outside his reach to duck below the second man's punch. Rising sharply to her feet she punched the second man in the groin with her left then clocked him across the jaw with her right. The first man fell grasping his knee while the third stood in surprise looking down at his friend. But the time he glanced to Leannii she was kicking him solidly in the chest and delivering an elbow to the side of his head as he bent over gasping for air.

Stomping on the first man's face, she spun to kick the second in his groin. Not stopping to even pause, she firmly grasped his shoulders and repeatedly kicked him both knees until she felt someone grasp her shoulder. Leannii quickly dropped to one knee as she spun to the third man who had stumbled into her and was grasping for support. Using her legs to launch her into the strike, Leannii almost jumped upward into her punch which landed in third man's lower chest. While he was bent at the waist, she clutched his head and began to repeatedly bring his face down onto her striking knee.

She yelled at the sudden pain that shot through her leg. The first man had drawn his short sword and weakly sliced her across her left thigh. Cursing his lame attempt Leannii released the third man and abruptly clutched the man's hand holding the sword to twist it. The point of his own sword now pointed at his own stomach. He noticed what was about to happen and then looked to Leannii with pleading eyes.

"No…please," he begged.

"Shhh," Leannii mouthed as she slowly dropped her body weight onto the handle. The point began to drive into his chest just below his ribs while he still pleaded.

"Wait, wait, please just wait…no, no, no."

"Shhh," she told him. "It will be over soon."

The coldness of her words caused him to panic. He forgot his resistance to her weight and the sword quickly sank into him. He tried to gasp but could not with the steel of the blade preventing him from breathing. Without a word she withdrew the sword from his chest and rose to stand over him.

Noticing the second man still moving and trying to stand, she quickly stepped over to him and, grasping him by the hair on the back of his head, pulled his skull back. With his gullet exposed, Leannii swiftly stabbed the point into his neck and, with a sawing motion, brought the blade out the front of his throat. He gurgled and blood thickly sprayed onto the floor in front of him. She apathetically released his hair, letting his rapidly dying body fall into the pool of his own blood with a wet thud.

Hearing the third man crawling backwards in abject fear, she turned to him and began to slowly close in. His eyes winded with panic and the man began to move faster. Noticing that he could not out pace her by crawling, he changed his survival tactic to pleading, forgetting how little it helped the other man.

"Please, no...there was nothing I could do!"

"Nothing?" she asked with little emotion. She calmly stared into his face and began to raise the sword.

"No! Wait!" He shuddered.

"Why?"

"I can tell you..." He was reaching for anything that could keep him alive.

"Tell me what?"

"I can tell you where we keep our treasure!" He offered.

"Why do I care about that?" she asked flatly.

He could not comprehend someone not wanting wealth.

"Well, whatever you want, whatever you want!" He panicked.

"Really?" she asked and paused. "Anything?"

Happy that he may actually talk his way out of his own death he answered energetically.

"Yes, yes, anything...just tell me what you want!"

With a single nod Leannii answered him, "Very well...I only want one thing."

When he did not hear her desire he asked.

"What is it? I'll do it!"

Gazing down at him she took a breath and then replied, "I want all of you to die."

His had could not shield himself quickly enough as the sword came down into his skull causing his world to become cold and black. Leannii released her hold on the handle and stood after dropping her weight into that strike. The blade jutted from the middle of the man's face after passing through the top of his head and through his left eye. She left the sword in him.

Looking around the vicinity in detail for the first time she realized that this was a storage room. It was filled with chests, boxes and crates, some were opened and some just had cloth tarps haphazardly cast over them, but most were stacked atop one another sometimes four high. It would take a long time to search through this place and she did not have that much time. Grasping her grandfather's sword she strode over to the wall where Jeral retrieved this blade and began her search there.

Reaching the wall there, she stopped to ponder the long flat wooden crates that lay before her. There was a thick sack cloth tarp thrown over them and were flanked by large barrels that were opened and obviously contained arrows in some and bows in the others. She reached out, grasped the cloth cover and unceremoniously tossed it aside. Within the crate were shiny new swords numbering about twenty.

A thin sadistic smile crept across her lips.

The sun was soon to rise but she was finished. Leannii was most interested in sleeping now since she had a busy night ahead. Not knowing how they were found the first time, she decided to do the unthinkable to lessen the chances of being discovered. She decided to make her camp directly against their wall where it met the rock face. At that location, on the higher side of the slope where their main entrance was, there was thick underbrush and a few young trees, just older than saplings. Working quietly through the night while they slept, Leannii dug into the soft earth to make a place to sleep and to hide the equipment she took from them.

She had labored all night carrying those weapons out of that cave. The roughhewn corridor was rather short and only had one curve to the right before she found herself outside but still within their encampment. Behind her loomed the rocky cliff while to her right, and not more than twenty paces, was their wall that she and Oleg watched them from just yesterday. To her left, the hill sloped downward and there laid the rest of their camp. No tents were to be seen since this seemed to be intended for a more permanent settlement. Also, toward her left and inside the rock face, was another cave however, due to the work she had to do Leannii was not able to ascertain what it contained.

Moving as quickly and as quietly as she could, Leannii took as many weapons as she could that first trip. Making her way along the scrub of the rocks she came to the log wall surrounding their camp. There where the rock and wood met, she found that the log against the stone was a bit loose. As quietly as she could, she placed the swords on the ground and began to pry at the log. After some time she was able to push it open at the bottom and, after collecting the weapons, she slid through the small opening. From the lack to any traffic pattern here, she could guess that no one came this way.

The scrub on the outside of the wall there was rather thick and a bit tall with trees beginning to grow a few paces from the wall itself. Thinking this to be a perfect spot to hide for a while she searched around until she found what she decided was the most perfect place. Between a few young trees and think, yet soft, ferns she located a fissure in the rocks extending upward about seventeen feet but, more importantly, it was almost three feet wide at the base with a soft earthen floor. Quickly, she began to dig away at the soil and make a small wall around a bed that was just large enough for her body yet large enough for her to hide in. After that, she began to dig other holes in order to conceal weapons and equipment that she would steal from their camp.

For the remainder of the night, she made many trips back and forth stealing as many items from that cave as she could. With no one watching that corner of their camp, Leannii was able to smuggle many swords, arrows, axes, flasks of oil, rope, hooks, hammers and iron nails. With all of the trips back and forth she was concerned about leaving a trail for someone to discover and follow and on her last trip she swept a small branch with leaves along the dry dirt to conceal any tracks she had left. Returning the log in the fence back into its position, she snuck over to her bed in the rocks and finally lay down.

She did not pray to Enki before sleeping as she always had for the past decade. Leannii simply lay in the soft earth without any thought of it whatsoever. As the sun began to rise she heard the distant rumbling of thunder. It was going to rain. Curling up into a tighter ball she clutched the material of her dress and brought it to her face. When her knees came up to her chest she was reminded of the pain in her loins. Suddenly, as if a roaring fire had just been lit, her eyes squinted tightly shut and she stuffed her own dress into her mouth to conceal her cries. Her teeth gnashed against the cloth and she convulsed while sobbing. As the rains began to fall, lightly at first then fell in a torrent, Leannii cried herself past exhaustion and finally fell asleep.

Explosive thunder and the flashes of lightening did little to disturb her slumber that day, however uneasy her rest was. Leannii was sadly caught in her own nightmare and unable to wake, seeing faces of the dead men and feeling herself bathe in warm blood. She dreamt of the rough table rubbing against her face as she was helplessly violated by Jeral as the hammering storm raged on for most of the daylight hours.

At one point, while the thunder saw still roaring over the countryside, she awoke with a jolt and scream. Sitting bolt upright and fighting for her life in her dream, Leannii struck her head against the inside of the rock fissure. She never felt the sharp pain and she was unconscious by the time her head landed in the soft soil. As her blood trickled down her forehead and over her face the rains continued to fall heavily just a few feet from her.

Slowly, her eyes opened. Sunlight still peaked through the forest and dimly lit the inside of the fissure she was sleeping in. When her eyes focused Leannii saw her dirt bed and equally dirt covered dress, both were same shade of brownish grey. She vaguely remembered digging this bed and fought to remember the events of the night. The pain in her head from knocking herself out against the stone finally became real. Her eyes closed as the excruciating feeling radiated through her skull. Her hand came up to comfort the wound and she felt a good sized lump on the left side of her head surrounded by dried blood. Slowly, as she fought the dulling pain and unclear memories, she crawled to the opening and peered out into the forest.

In the approaching twilight Leannii could make out the log wall of the bandit camp looming not far from her. The bandits. Jeral. Thalorn. Oleg. Suddenly all of her memory came flooding back to her. She felt like she had just been clubbed in the stomach and her breath was violently ripped from her lungs. Gasping for air she crawled on all fours until she stopped and clutched at her chest from the physical pain she felt. He heart pounded in her ears and her chest ached. Her ache spread to her guts and they painfully twisted. Moaning and still not able to breathe her head gradually lowered into the mud. She then heaved over and over with sobs and moans between her gasps for air. "No," she painfully cried in long wails amid her vomits. "Why?" she pleaded breathlessly as her face twisted in anguish. Exhausted, gasping and still crying, she collapsed onto her side in the dense ferns, curling up into a ball.

Images began to flash through her mind: blood, screams and feelings of anger, hatred and uncontrolled rage. The last feeling was that of helplessness and, unconsciously, her hand came to her face where the rough table left its abrasions. Noticing the pain her cheek Leannii looked down to see her own hand, dirty and bloody, and wondered how it got to her face without her knowing. She was feeling defeated, demoralized and powerless. Leannii remembered being shackled and looked down to see the cuts on her wrists from when she struggled against the metal. She recalled being laughed at and her plight mocked by the bandits. She remembered killing them as well.

Oleg. Where was he? What happened to him? Then she grasped the important question: What had they done to him? But, she could already guess what they had done. Oleg, Thalorn, and all those other men, killed, no, slaughtered. Oleg took care of her. Thalorn was her brother. Poor Thalorn...she recalled what Jeral said, those words he spat at her to destroy her hope and confidence.

Then we hunted him though the lands his father, your father, had stolen from my family...We chased him down like a dog and cut his head from his body.

She gritted her teeth.
We chased him down like a dog...
Her fists clenched.
...like a dog...
Her lips pursed and she began to quietly snarl.
...and cut his head from his body.
Her fingernails began to dig into the palms of her hands and pierce her own skin.
...cut his head...
Blood began to seep from her clenched fists.
...from his body...his head from his body...his head...
With a grunt, she suddenly became unnervingly calm. Her hands relaxed and her jaw slackened. Her eyes blinked slowly and she swallowed. Her head calmly looked around at her immediate

surroundings, taking in the ferns and damped soil. Rising to kneel, her eyes traced the contour of the leaves and branches all the way up into the night sky. The night's cool breeze kissed her cheeks. She closed her eyes at its caress. Feeling a slight twinge of discomfort in her palms she brought them closer to her face so she could see why. Not really looking at her hands, but looking more through them, her eyes were wide and she seemed to gaze into another world. Leannii then looked down to her long tattered dress as she knelt in the mud. She grasped the cloth from around her thigh and felt the dirty cotton in her hand as if she was noticing it for the very first time. Absently, she released it and crawled over to one of her holes she had dug the previous night. Methodically, she brushed the mud away and retrieved a short sword from one of the boxes she buried. Again, she looked upon it as if it was the first time she had ever seen it.

Slowly she turned the blade around so that it pointed to the ground. She wondered what it would feel like to have such cold hard steel slide into her skin. She imagined it slowly piercing her abdomen and what it would feel like as the sting penetrated her muscles. Gradually the sword rose above her head as she continued to meditate on the blade, little by little, slipping all the way through her body. Abruptly she stopped thinking about it, pausing only to take a slow and deep breath, and then swiftly brought the weapon down.

It pierced the fabric of her dress between her legs, just above her knees. With a sawing motion, she began to cut the length from her dress. She needed it shorter and less cumbersome, at least for a while, until she could find other clothing to replace it. As she was cutting through the material she noticed her muscles complained of being overworked. She ached from the strenuous use she had put her body through the past few days. Leannii, however, dismissed the discomfort and placed it far away with all the other twinges and aches she felt then. She decided she had no time to be in pain, or sick, or injured. There was far too much to be done.

She tossed the material back side the fissure and rose onto one knee, scanning the log wall toward the makeshift gated entrance. Wiping her sweat from her upper lip with her forearm he eyes fixed on two men talking at the entrance. They were laughing loudly when a third man came to bring them some food, and then walked back inside the camp. The two remained outside as they looked for a place to sit and munch. Leannii sniffed and tightened her grip on the sword as she stood to creep her way to the unsuspecting men. Leannii was hungry and wanted something to eat.

Sneaking along the wall, she made her way rather quietly toward the two men. They ate as they sat on a larger rock and faced away from the camp on the left side, Leannii's side, of the gate. She came upon them from their backs. The scent of meat and fresh bread was heavy in the air. Getting closer to her prey, she realized that there were in fact two men and that she needed a way to do this quietly. How was she going to keep one quiet while she killed the other? Simply asking him would not work. She then thought of knocking one unconscious, killing the other and then returning to the first man and killing him. That sounded like a good plan except that she only brought one weapon. Her pace did not slow at all as she continued to slink toward the men while pondering this problem…until she spied the rock.

There in the mud, just to her left against the log wall, was rock a bit larger than the size of her fist. Cocking her head in surprise at her fortune she reached down and retrieved it. It was a good solid rock that was heavy enough to work for her purpose.

The two ate with a degree of mirth, laughing at the notion that some lone girl was looming out there in the darkness and could possibly pose a threat. Foolish! There was no possible way it was just one woman who killed those four men. There had to have been others…or maybe a traitor amongst their own ranks. Either way, being stationed here was far better than the other tasks they could have gotten this night and, if anyone were stupid enough to attack them here, all they had to do was yell loud and help close the gates. That should be easy enough.

The first man never felt the stone strike his skull behind his right ear and as he slumped forward into the soil, his companion could not react soon enough. In trying to ascertain what exactly was happening he looked behind his friend just in time to see the dull glint of firelight flash across the sword edge before it sliced through his face at his jaw. His teeth rattled and some were knocked clear of his mouth. Blood began to pour from the gash as he stood.

Leannii cursed herself for that inaccurate blow and tried to quickly move in and kill him before e alerted the whole camp. The man turned to stumble away, gurgling through his own blood while she tripped over the unconscious man at her feet.

She dropped the stone and hurriedly grasped the second man's shoulder to keep from stepping out where could be seen. Violently pulling him backward she wrapped her had around his blood soaked jaw and pulled him against her. His blood pumped freely from his mouth as he struggled.

Leannii exposed his gullet so her other hand could slice the blade across his neck; but there in the dark, unable to see and wrestling against a struggling man who was already injured, she cut her own arm as well as his throat. A short grunt came from his gorge and he fell to his knees with a froth of blood gurgling from the wide cut in his neck. Grasping feebly at his wound he slumped forward onto his face and then stopped moving.

When her panting breath reached her ears the sound surprised her. Leannii had not expected to be out of breath from such a small action that was not that physically demanding. She then suddenly remembered there was someone else to take care of.

With a single large step, she placed a foot on either side of body and, as she rolled him over with the support of her legs, she straddled his chest. This first man was still unconscious as she peered down at him. Bringing the sword to his chin to cut his throat as well, she stopped. She could not bring herself to do it. This man was helpless and killing him like this to her seemed...wrong. Leannii knew what he was, she knew what group he belonged to and she also knew, if the positions were reversed, she would probably already be dead. However, that did not change her feeling that killing in this was not right.

The blood trickled down from the slash she made on her own arm. It felt warm against the night air and the sting from the wound did not hurt that bad. She looked around for some kind of support that she knew was not there and, with an exhale, returned her gaze to the man below her.

You can do this, she told herself and then placed the point against the hollow of his neck just between his collar bones. Grasping the handle with her right and wrapping her left around the pommel for extra support for a thrust she determined to end him before he came to.

He shoulders slumped and her teeth clenched in frustration. Damn! What is wrong with me? She closed her eyes while regaining her sold grip on the sword. Biting her lip and stifling her moan, she rocked forward. Her teeth ground together as she felt the most disgusting feeling in her life at the sharp steel in her hands unhurriedly slid into his vulnerably exposed throat. She felt the blade stop on his spine.

Slowly standing, she did not look down at his corpse but turned away to glance at the gates to see if anyone was coming. Fortunately, there was no one approaching, which was good, because she felt too sick to fight just then. But looking back to the rock where she ambushed them, she saw the food that she originally wanted…covered in blood. She still needed to eat, but where to get food? Her pondering was interrupted when she caught the sound of someone sloshing through the mud while heading toward the gates!

Frantically she looked around for a place to hide but could not see anywhere to go. Everywhere was too far to run and she would be discovered before she could ever reach a place to hide. At last, she decided to place herself flat against the log wall just outside the gate beside the rock the two men were eating on. Bounding over the large rock she landed and spun with her back to the log wall. It was then that she realized that she was unarmed. The stone she used for a cudgel was on the ground too far from her and the sword was still jutting from the man's throat. Her mind reeled searching for a way out of her predicament. Then, Leannii suddenly calmed and the panic lifted itself from her. Her eyes focused and her breathing steadied.

The man nonchalantly passed through the gates and took a glance around at the forest tree line with so much of a glance toward where the sentries were supposed to be. He carried a good sized covered basket in his left arm and leisurely tossed an apple in his right as he strode.

"I wonder," he began, speaking as with his back to the gates. "How many of them do you think there are?" He talked with his hand, a gesture that could not hide his nervousness.

There was no reply.

"Yeah, really does not matter. We are killing all of them anyway…Hey, what did you think of Jeral? He's dead so he cannot complain about what you say." He laughed at his own joke.

Again, his question was met with silence and he played with the apple in his grasp.

"Ahh, you can tell me. It's not like he had many friends.

Kalbor was just keeping him around until he made good on his promise." He began to walk backwards, not wanting to turn away from the dark of the trees.

"Hey, you two asleep?" He took a large bite of the apple he was carrying and turned to see why no one was answering him.

His eyes locked onto the white shape of someone else's eyes looming back at him, not more than an arm's length away. The figure was muddy and covered in blood from head to foot and only the whites of the eyes shone through the shadow. It moved swiftly toward him, orbs wild, teeth barred her hair trailed behind her as she ran. She? It is a woman!

He tried to yell but the large chunk of apple stopped any decent volume of sound from exiting his mouth. Dropping the basket and the apple he bit from he fumbled for his sword. Leannii reached out her left hand and pressed it against his forearm stopping him from getting out his blade. Without stopping her advance, she continued forward and brought her right elbow solidly against the side of his head. Her bony joint sounded like it just struck a coconut with a hollow thud. He became disoriented by the blow and feebly raised his right hand as a shield while his left came up to hold the lump on his head. Still, the bits of unchewed apple gagged his cries.

Leannii grasped his sword with one hand and drew it from it sheath. Taking a step backward she spun him around with the other hand that was still grasping his forearm. While he turned, he spat out the apple and managed to regain his footing. By the time he finished his whirl the man was ready for a tussle. What his did not know however, was that Leannii also spun while he was and raised the sword as she did.

Just a slight glint was all he saw as his own sword came around through his head. He never felt any pain, he never felt the impact of the steel on his bones and he never saw anything after. His last image was the glaring eyes of Leannii as she focused on her target.

After wiping the blood off of the sword she returned to the fallen basket to inspect its contents. Turning it upright and opening the hinged lid she found exactly what she wanted. Food! It was enough food to feed two grown men for an entire night with two bottles of drink for some extra comfort. She simply smiled. Taking the basket she left the men where they lay and walked in a long circle to her camp, adding another sword to her collection.

The next morning she did not hear what they had to say about their dead comrades. She did not really care to, either. She lay in the mud, just inside of her own camp and watched their reactions. Even if they were looking for her there she would be hard to find. Taking the time to camouflage herself from every possible view, she nearly buried herself and took extra care not to damage the plants and give away her position. While they scampered like little lost and panicked children, she counted their numbers and weapons while noting who was a leader and who was not. She was especially interested in this…Kalbor. Leannii wanted to see who he was and what kind of man he was. It would help to know the enemy before she killed him, it would make the battle that much easier.

They were fools. Not expecting to be spied on, they made obvious pointing references to places in the tree line they would watch. At some times they would even walk to where they were talking about and motion back to the walls and gates. Sadly, Leannii did not catch any glimpse of one she could consider to be Kalbor. She needed to kill him and do that as soon as possible. Considering their observed behavior, without a leader these men would behave like chickens without a head. Decapitation seemed fitting under the circumstances.

…cut his head from his body…

She forced the memory of those words out of her mind and steadied herself to remain single minded. One single mistake could ruin everything and easily lead to her death. If that were to happen, then no one would ever know what had really happened to her or Thalorn or Oleg. That, for her, simply could not do. So, noting where they would place a sentry that night, Leannii gently closed her eyes for some rest. She planned a busy night for herself.

Just after the sun had set, the men walked out of the gates and into the forest. Looking around, they saw no one and felt quite confident in their plan. Five crossed the open area and into the tree line. Finding the tree they had marked earlier that afternoon, the one chosen man plopped himself in front of the tree.

Thinking the soft ground felt a bit lumpy he bounced a few times to pack it dirt under this butt. Seeing this, his leader was not very amused with the childishness of his actions.

"Comfortable?" he asked the man.

Thinking his leader had just asked a sincere question, he answered with an enthusiastic smile.

"Oh yes, I am good."

"I am happy to hear that," his sarcasm went unheeded. "Do you need anything else? Blanket, wine?" He was losing his patience but the stupid man sitting against the tree was far too daft.

"Oh, that would be nice, yes." Again, with a sincere smile.

The leader had quite enough.

"Shut up and listen...you have one hour checks. Someone will come by to see that you are still good once each hour. Do you understand?"

"Yes, I do," he said blankly as if nothing may have stopped the sound from passing through his ears.

"Do *not* talk to them. You are supposed to be hiding so keep quiet."

"I will." The man nodded with an unintelligent gaze.

"Don't' forget," the leader told him.

"What?" he asked.

"Do...not...forget," he commanded the bowman and walked away, taking the others with him.

The lone sniper man watched as they hurried off and looked into the forest for anyone who was not them. He watched as they went and breathed a sigh that this was going to be a long night. Moving his bow and quivers of arrows to a more convenient place, he squirmed again to get comfortable on that lumpy ground. If anyone else was out here, he was going to be the hero that night. He was going to be the silent killer. He was one of the best bowmen in the camp...or so he thought.

Leannii opened her one eye that was still above dirt and looked around without moving her head. She studied the man's face as he carelessly peered around in the moonlit night. No judgment, no subjective evaluation, she simply had determined that this man, whoever he was, was going to die and she did that before she ever saw him.

After those few moments of consideration of how to best surprise him, Leannii decided to act swiftly. Besides, it was getting quite uncomfortable lying there while he sat on her ribs.

Right on time about one hour later, three men came striding across the clearing from the gate. Walking directly to where the other man was, they made no attempt to hide their movements and strode as if they were meaning to speak to someone. When they reached the tree line, two stayed behind and made the amateurish attempt at pretending to be engaged in casual conversation. Clandestine operations were clearly not this group's strong skill.

While the two muttered, functionally uttering no coherent words, they heard what sounded like a short grunt and the rustling of leaves. Curiously they looked to the tree line then to each other. Did they just hear something? Slowly the two approached the tree where they were all to meet but did not enter the forest itself. They remained in the clearing and just peered into the darkness expecting to spot something. Hearing and seeing nothing they called out in a low whisper that only an amateur would have.

"Psst," the one spat. "Sarom!"

They were answered by silence.

They looked to each other again and then back into the forest. Again they tried to call to their comrade.

"Sarom! Sarom!"

Again, they received no reply.

The taller man swallowed hard with his brow creased.

"Wait here," he said to the other and then walked into the tree line.

The man was swallowed by the darkness of the still night and the last man found himself standing alone and suddenly he felt quite vulnerable. He looked around the clearing and up into the night sky, feeling very small. Then he heard it.

"Help," the voice said, spoken in a forced whisper that came from around the area of the tree they were to meet at.

The clearing became quiet again.

He was not certain what he heard but wanted to take no chances. With his first step toward the tree his heart began to pound in his ears and fear gripped his chest. He was alone and afraid. His position in the bandit hierarchy did not afford him any autonomy nor did his less than average intellect grant him any tools for having a clear perspective. With his leaders somewhere in the darkness he advanced into the dark of the forest with the hopes of finding them.

"Ligraff? Sarom?" he whispered. "Anybody?"

Silence.

He neared the tree after taking one shaky step after another.

There, leaning against it in a standing slump, was his comrade.

"Ligraff! I was scared. Good to see you. It is so dark out here..." His voice trailed off as he realized that Ligraff was not replying or moving. Thinking Ligraff was joking or playing a game, the man started to nervously chuckle. "Come on! You that tired already?"

Again, he was unanswered. Ligraff had not even moved.

"Hey, is everything well?" he asked as he slapped Ligraff on the shoulder, still thinking this was a game but feeling something much worse.

Ligraff's lifeless body fell on the ground with a soft thud at the man's feet. His mouth dropped open in shock but before he could yell or run the hair at the back of head was firmly grasped to expose his throat and he felt the unmistakable feel of cold metal against his skin. He froze in fear.

"Everything is just...perfect, thanks for asking." The female voice whispered into his ear and he could feel her warm moist breath against his skin. Suddenly he felt the strong pain in his back and as he tried to gasp he found he could not breathe. Dropping to his knees he then felt his body shutting off like some had just closed a valve on his life. Before his head struck the forest floor the man was already dead.

After two hours had passed the three men who went to check on the bowman by the tree had still not returned. One of the leaders, whom Leannii had identified earlier, ordered two other men to get torches and to accompany him and check on their absent companions. Probably, they were just talking and drinking together and had forgotten to return. Stupid people. With an impatient stride, he walked out into the clearing and crossed it all the way to the tree line. He stopped there and gazed into the dense shadow. Not a sound was heard, just the faint whispering winds high above him and the distant sporadic cries of the indigenous animals he had listened to out here for years. He began to become annoyed. Halting all semblance of secrecy, thinking those buffoons had botched the entire plan by that point, he called out into the night.

"Get your arses out here now!"

No reply.

"I am warning you, get out here now or I will come in after you."

Again, there was nothing.

He looked to his escorts, first on his one side then the other. Still no one emerged and no one replied.

"That it! You're going to be shoveling muck with your bare hands for a week!"

Briskly he strode up closer to the very edge of the line and stopped. Looking over his left shoulder he commanded, "Go get them out."

The man was shocked.

"Me?"

"Yes you!" He was surrounded by idiots. "You're the one with a torch, now go!"

He thought this was a bad idea but followed the command anyway. He drew out his sword and used to push is way thought the undergrowth while he held the torch out in front of him. Step by step he entered and made his way to the tree. It was still too dark to see, even with that lit torch but decided to look around the area before reporting that he saw nothing.

Outside in the clearing, the watchmen and his other escort observed the dancing torchlight bob around the trees, only giving the bearer a faint outline the shadows. Suddenly, with a cry of surprise like he had just fallen, the man yelled and his torch fell to the ground and went dark. The two could only stare into the darkness and wait as they were too shocked to do anything else. The moments crept by and neither heard anything to follow nor did they see the torchlight return. The forest had again returned to the eerie quiet and murky shadow it had just a few moments ago.

"What's happening here?" the watchman asked rhetorically.

Almost imperceptibly, something fast and dark sped by his face. He would have dismissed it to his imagination however, the escort with him gurgled. Turning to see what had happened, he noticed the man sinking to his knees and dropping his torch while grasping weakly at the feathers of the arrow shaft that now protruded from his neck. As the torch hit the soft earth it extinguished, plunging the watchman into blackness.

He turned back to the trees in disbelief and felt the sharp pain of the arrow as it penetrated his right chest and pierced his lung. He could not scream but he could think enough to turn and try to run. No far away the safety of the gates loomed but seemed to be so much farther back than it was coming out here. He was going to try anyway. His legs barely responded to his commands to run and he seemed to be stuck moving like a snail. Everything crept terrifyingly slow, especially himself. He began to count his running steps as the pain in his lung began to spread into his shoulder.

One...

Perhaps he could make it if only his body would move faster.

Two...

It seemed so far to sprint and at his pace he felt it would take him almost ten minutes to run what it had only taken him a minute to walk.

Three...

Another sharp pain penetrated his back on his left side and took all his hopes of breathing from him. He stumbled but stayed afoot. His hand came up to reach the gate but he was impossibly too far to grasp it. It was more out of hope than anything else.

He felt a deep welling sorrow about his life as he understood that he was about to die. At those last moments he wished he would have gone a different way, done different things. A tear formed in his eye as he slowed to a stop.

"I'm sorry," he pleaded as he felt an icy chill grip his body and cause goose bumps to rise across his shoulders and back.

The voice behind him stole his breath from shocking fear.

"Save it for the other side."

Leannii, from just a few feet behind him, released another arrow into him.

The barbed tip thrust savagely into his field of vision after passing through his face from the back of his head. His eyes focused past the arrowhead and fixed on the gates with the soft glow of light within as he fell to the ground on his side. Another tear fell from his eye as the cold black gripped him. From somewhere in the distance, the last sounds he heard were of fire and a wailing infant.

She quickly made her way back into the forest and returned to the tree they had marked. She had very little time and began to dig up the area around the tree. Not far from her was an open crate of short swords and daggers, along with a length of rope and a lot of oil. She was going to be busy for a while.

The next morning came and did not bring much hope for the encampment. Men were already not sleeping and most all were restless. Something was hunting them and they did not know who or what. They had supposed that some men had come to rescue the duchess and had also assumed, with much rationalization, that she had fled two days ago. None of these ruffians had ever fought a formally trained soldier before and the force that hid their numbers so well struck fear in their hearts.

Whoever was out there was not arresting them but slowly killing them off one by one. The leaders knew that meant this was personal and not official. That above all else, caused them great concern. An official, as they found in the past, could be bribed or intimidated. Someone killing another was fall less... amenable and was exceedingly more problematic. The exact number of men that were systematically slaughtering them still remained unknown. In fact, they knew very little.

Since they came upon the first two five days ago, they had lost four men. Since the woman's escape and rescue, they had lost fourteen more: four during her rescue and ten others after that. Five days later and with a total of eighteen dead, the bandits still had no idea who was after them or why it was so personal. They ordered that no one leave the camp that day and that everyone be questioned as a rough attempt of a counter-intelligence investigation. They had hoped to uncover any useful information concerning possible enemies that the dead had ties with. As the sun fell that day, so did their hope of linking the fallen to a common thread. They realized that whoever was doing this seemed determined to kill anyone who exited this camp.

With regard to that understanding, an order was issued that no one was to leave and that the gates are to be closed and guarded at all times. In addition, no one was to do anything alone, to include relieving themselves, and anyone they did not know was to be challenged on sight. Now, they would wait and see what their enigmatic enemy would do next from inside the safety of their walls.

The problem with that plan was that Leannii was already inside their camp through the secret entrance she found in the wall a few days before. Another problem was that they were expecting a force of many men and not just one man, or more accurately, one woman. Again, using the cover of darkness, she spread oil on the wooden structures and onto the ground around them, linking the buildings together with a thick trail so that all would quickly ignite in tandem. She had guessed that these were barracks for the men or dwellings for the leadership. So, it seemed perfectly reasonable to her that these needed to burn down.

There were only three decently built wooden buildings, all of a single story construction utilizing very little stone work in their foundation even though there was more than enough rock available from the hills so close to where these were built. Well, she had thought, that was stupid of them. Lucky for me, stone would have been much harder to burn.

Using all the oil she had, which was a considerable amount that took four trips to carry, Leannii snuck a safe distance away to a small pool of oil that she had prepared. Using common flint and steel, she ignited the oil and watched it swiftly burn to the buildings which, also just as stupidly, were not very far apart. Within a minute, all three were ablaze and she listed to their cries and shouts of surprise as the men fought to contain the fires. Not wanting to stay and watch, Leannii quietly and easily slipped back out the wall and returned to her hiding place for sleep. Again, in the coming day, she was going to be busy.

The fires burned for most of the night. Not having enough water to contain a fire, much less three, the structures blazed uncontrollably until they were reduced to smoldering ruin. Three more of their men burned as well. They were unable to escape quickly enough and were caught inside. The men were shaken and Kalbor, the actual leader, had lost control. The men decided not to be so passive and had decided to band together and hunt these hunters down and kill them all. The bandits' plan was to search every foot of forest and viciously slay anyone who was not one of their own.

With all of them ready, and much against the directives and reasoning of Kalbor, most marched to the gates. They unlocked them and swung them open wide with a taunting shout to challenge any that would dare confront them. Before their roar fell, some of their men did.

From the tree they had planned to shoot her from, Leannii began to fire arrows with chilling accuracy into the crowd of bandits. Being they were so bunched together, none of them had any chance to seek cover. Leannii, shot one after the other, not intending to wound but took some time to aim well enough to kill.

The doors did not even completely open when the first man fell with an arrow in his chest. The second man fell in a similar fashion before they began to realize what was happening. A third and fourth man likewise fell which gave their mentality a violent shove forward. A few did not heed the pleadings of their comrades and sprinted toward the tree where the arrows were flying from. Shouting in anger four bandits broke from their ranks and tore into the forest.

Leannii had left by then, making a large circle away from the camp. It was her intent to be chased but far fewer took her bait than she had hoped. She heard their screams behind her and she stopped running, notched another arrow and waited between two trees for her pursuers. None, however, came.

The four had sprinted blindly between the trees and did not see the ropes that had been tightly strung for them to trip on. Only too late did the four notice the short swords and daggers planted blade up into the ground. When they fell, the bladed painfully pierced their flesh and their screams echoed off the rocks as they bled to death. Writhing on the soft ground only helped end their torment sooner as they rolled onto and over a field of sharpened blades.

From the gates, the men watched in silence as silhouettes writhed and clawed from amidst the undergrowth until their cries became quiet and the forest returned to its chilling silence. This time, no wind blew and no animals were heard in the distance. Their forest home had become their cemetery.

"Damn!" Leannii cursed. No one was running after her. Cowards. So be it, she thought. You do not want to come after me...then I will come after you. Retaining her stealthy movements, she made her way back to her tiny camp to gather her grandfather's sword and other weapons. She had determined to show them what being hunted was like.

At the same time from within the camp, Kalbor's voice was booming and without any hint of patience. He stomped toward his men as he scolded them.

"You idiots!" he began. "All you have done is let them kill more of us! And for what? There was no victory here! Nothing was gained! This was a thoughtless sacrifice that only helped them!" He pointed outside the walls and stopped where he was. "Do you want to help them kill us off?"

The eyes of many of the men fell to the ground in shame.

"Next time, listen to me or you can join the dead…it is that simple." He turned to stride away and return to the cave entrance. His house was burnt to the ground and still smoldered as residual waves of heat still radiated and smoke still rose. Bastards will pay for that.

As he came to the cave opening, he began to think. What was he going to do against an unknown number of men? Each time he loses more and more. This could not continue much longer and he would not have anyone left here. What enraged and frustrated him the most was that he did not know who their enemy was, how many there of them and why they were doing this. Was this in response to that idiotic plan that Jeral had? Capture or kill the duke's children while his employer ruined the Covenant family from inside their own home? It seemed more than a bit fanciful, but the pile of gold spilled at Kalbor's feet was quite real indeed. So with that, and the letter from Jeral's superior, the bandits became an extension of this plot. Kalbor could not help but to think at that moment that it was their undoing. He decided to call everyone to a meeting.

Almost two hours later, Leannii crept through the secret entrance to the bandit camp. Stopping alongside one of the trees close to the rock face, she lay down on the ground and readied her bow. She was thankful that the clanking of all her weapons did not alert anyone. She looked for where the bandits were at the time since, as enraged as she has become, Leannii had not completely lost her senses. Unnervingly, there were a scant few about. She then decided to move deeper into the camp around where the structures she set fire to just the other night were placed.

Crawling along the ground she made her way to where the first cave entrance was, the very same cave she had escaped from. There, in front of the other cave entrance, the entire camp had gathered. Was this a town hall meeting? What were they planning? She decided to crawl to the far side of the opening and wait to see what happening. The bad part was that someone was exiting the cave from behind her.

He saw the dirty and crusty blood covered form lying on the ground at the cave entrance. Cocking his head to the side he wondered where this old corpse had come from, until it moved. For a time they both stared at one another and it seemed like for almost ten minutes. However, in actuality, a few seconds later she moved. Leannii rolled backward and brought her bow up level with the ground, drawing the string back as far as she could. She saw his eyes widen and she released the arrow.

With a dull thud the arrow pierced his stomach and he screamed in pain. Damn! She quickly fumbled for another arrow and came up to kneel before releasing that arrow into his chest. Again, she drew another arrow and notched it.

Down where everyone else had gathered, they all heard a cry of pain and turned to see where it came from. There, at the crest of the hill beside the entrance to the other cave, a single figure crouched with a bow. This person was obviously not one of them and upon recognizing that, the mob screamed and sprinted to approach while drawing their weapons.

Leannii heard the massive shouting from her right and turned to see that everyone in the camp was running at her. Her eyes widened and panic gripped her chest, capturing her breath inside her. She was able to release that one arrow before she began to run for her life. The arrow unfortunately was shot too high and was of no effect as it passed harmlessly over their heads. The bandits scattered to make shooting them that much more difficult however they still gave chase to such an unwanted visitor in their camp.

She hoped to lead them into the forest where some of her other traps may help her survive this. She had not counted on running for her life. She had not thought of what she would do in this situation. Still, she continued to sprint toward the front gates since she did not want to let them know of her secret passage in case she was able to slip away from them. Never again, she decided. Always check your hiding place and always have a second plan.

She neared the entry and saw the empty makeshift guard tower. Feeling better about her predicament, she ran in a wide arc across the open ground to the gate. The drying earth puffed into dust clouds with her foot falls. She glanced back to her pursuers and saw they were far enough away that it gave her a greater hope of escape. From the corner of her left eye as she glanced back, she caught of glimpse of something she did not think she saw. Looking back at it again, she mind fought to accept the horror of what it was she saw.

There, just at the crest of the hill in front of the gate entrance, stood a tall post of wood with another cross beam making a large "T". Her run slowed to a jog and she could not take her eyes from it as she stared at it transfixed in shock. Both tied and nailed to the posts was a body of a man. He had been there, out in the weather, for almost three weeks. Disturbingly, there was something...familiar about this man that she had the most trouble comprehending. A chill ran up her spine and her heart beat a bit slower and harder as she began to place the color of his clothing beneath the stains of blood.

Her jog became a walk then she just stopped. Her eyes blinked a few times as she wanted this horrific display to be some manner of perverse mirage. However, it did not go away. There, at the top if the center post was a shriveled rotting head. Her face twisted in anguish and tears began to stream down her face. Her mouth hung open and her shoulders slumped. Leannii, after days of waiting, finally knew what became of Thalorn. They had maliciously transformed her dear brother into a warped morbid scarecrow.

She continued to gape at him wondering what kind of degenerates could possibly think to commit such a horrific act. These were not men. These were not bandits. These were not even dogs or any other kind of animals. She had decided they were not insane either. She quantified their manner into a single word...fiends. Only something as unearthly and diabolical as a fiend could ever concoct such a sickening and vile perversion as this. Brother Quinn had spoken of fiends to her before but only as legend. No one had seen a fiend since the times of the last war over five hundred years ago. Was this what they actually meant? Had people become so...evil that they had resorted to soul chilling behavior like this? Evil. She felt she stood in the very presence of evil. This was not some tale from a book of myths. She was a first-hand witness to the darkest parts of human psyche that no one should ever have to see.

The shouts of the approaching bandits brought her back to her situation. She doubled over with weakening knees and began to cry. She felt so cold and suffered a searing pain in her chest as razor-like claws tore at her insides. Her mouth slacked and she dribbled with her streaming tears. Suddenly she arched her back and wailed in such distress and rage like she had never done before. Her wail reverberated off the rocks with such a torment driven force that even the nearing bandits were taken aback by her shriek.

As her howl died down she glanced to her left and right. The gates were closed and she had no time to open them and push the door by herself. She could not get to her secret passage without being seen since they were too close now. Suddenly, she remembered her grandfather's sword on her side. She remembered her brother carried it here to combat these…fiends he thought were men. With a darkened glance like a razor she drew the sword and turned to her approaching enemies. Leannii observed them with a disturbingly predatory bearing and then began to walk toward them.

The bandits saw her turn and came to them and felt unbalanced. With hearing her howl and now seeing her advance without fear and filled with determination, they became rattled. However, most managed to push this down or ignore it because none were to be bested by a woman in their lifetimes.

Leannii knew that she was not strong enough to swing and stop this sword only to try to get it swinging again. She only had one chance to see this through to its conclusion and that was to not let this heavy blade stop moving under any circumstances. Once it stopped they would be too close for her to recover and would easily defeat her. Never again, she determined. I will always be strong enough. With that, she swung the hefty sword to her left side while spinning to the left to help the sword around her body. She felt the weight shift inside the blade giving it that much more momentum.

The first man thought he had an opening to strike into. Leannii's head came around first so she could aim her strike better and brought the sword across his face and twisted again to keep the weight moving. Blood shot from his open gash as he spin in the opposite direction and fell heavily to the ground.

The next man thought he would duck under her sword and strike her flank. However, she stepped sharply farther off to her right in the midst of her rotation and changed her distance. The man swung and missed but continued to move forward and into the arcing trajectory of the blade. It bit into the top of his skull and exited his neck. Crimson and grey spouted from his open head but Leannii never stopped.

For a few rotations, there was no one to strike but she kept spinning her way closer to them regardless. She had learned that she in the midst of spinning that she could control her angle and distance by changing her steps. As the next man came to her she abruptly stepped to the right and swung down on his sword arm. Her weighty blade cleaved the bones of his forearm and she spin in place but brought the sword around level to the ground. As his head came off his shoulders red sprayed in a fountain over her and his corpse.

Steeping to the left she focused on an upward strike and felt the bone of the man's thigh separate as the sword glided through his leg. She pivoted around and sank her weight through his body. The steel opened his chest through his back and the ground became soaked. She managed to change the direction of her turns. Leannii kept spinning as she began to make her way down the slope of the hill.

She was getting very dizzy as the sword cleaved the next man. Leannii could not recall how or what happened since everyone had become a blur and features were indistinguishable. All she could do was strike at the advancing blurry shapes and not allow this heavy blade to stop moving.

Over and over she felt the sword slash through someone or something but could no longer tell what it was. She was past the point of being dizzy and quickly became nauseated. Feeling that she was about to throw up, Leannii let out a long groan and pushed herself to spin harder and faster. But that did not help her nausea. She vomited as she continued to spin but did not stop even for a moment.

Not far away, Kalbor stood and watched her cut down man after man all by herself. He was so impressed by that he was stunned. His trance was interrupted by two men off to his rear left that had quickly approached with bows. Kalbor turned to see them drawing back to fire on Leannii while other men were still around her.

"Stop!" he barked. "You'll hit our own men, you morons!"

The two halted and looked to him. Kalbor wondered why their eyes became widened as they looked to him. Wanting to know what it was they were gawking at, he turned back to the whirling woman.

He was just in time to see the glint of the sunlight on the sword before it sliced though his chest. All he felt was a slight pressure and he looked down to see the gaping slash in his torso.

While he peered down at himself another flash of steel sped through his field of vision and he saw himself falling but he never saw himself hit the ground.

She kept spinning even though Leannii was now to the point that he lost her hearing and what used to be blurry was beginning to become dark like she was walking into a narrowing tunnel. Becoming upset at her weakness and fearing that she would fall before she struck everyone she tried with all her might to stay focused and awake.

After a number of rotations that she could no longer count, she suddenly felt herself become weightless. Without knowing it, she had tripped over a stone and fell to the ground. When she felt the earth beneath her she forced herself to stumble to a standing position and tried to get the sword moving again. The whole world turned on its side then inverted. She never felt herself fall into the soft grass as she fell unconscious.

The sun shone brightly in her eyes but it was cooler than what she remembered and a slight breeze kissed her cheeks. Squinting against the painful light she rolled over only to feel the contrast of the thick soft grass beneath her and the utter excruciating pain that radiated throughout her whole body. A moan escaped her lips while she rolled. Panting for breath against the aches she slowly opened her eyes. There was green grass underneath her shadowed by her head. Painfully she lifted her head and realized the sun was in a lower position than when she remembered it last and the grass was damp with dew. It was morning!

Panic gripped her and her heart drummed in her ears. Must get up, must fight before they get me. Her lips curled back, her eyes sealed shut and her teeth gnashed as she pushed herself up with moans and grunts of agony. She felt that her veins pumped acid and not blood. Every muscle in her painfully cried out against even the most minor of usage. Still, she fought to ignore her own body and struggled to at least a kneeling position.

At last, she sat back onto her heels gasping. She felt like just lying down in hopes the pain would just go away. Never had she felt this much agony from any measure of exertion she had ever done in her life. For a while, she just knelt there catching her breath and waiting for the hurt to subside at least a little so she could possibly form a coherent thought without envisioning searing agony. When she felt able to think past the throbbing she slowly opened her eyes.

Green trees against a tan rock face rose beautifully before her. The colors seemed so vivid against the pale blue and white of the morning sky behind it. Birds chirped and sang not far away while crickets chorused from the light shadows of the foliage. The wind whistled from somewhere overhead and she felt it still gently kissing her at her back and neck. A field of white and violet blooms gently swayed in the distant part of the field below her. Directly in front of her, a lizard scampering across a near-by rock seemed to pause to give a friendly greeting before darting off into the grass. Was this beautiful place the same as where she was just yesterday?

She looked down at herself to see if he clothing had changed. She remembered Brother Quinn had once told her that if she were ever in battle and then quickly found herself in a beautiful field with bright sunlight that she should not worry anymore because she was already dead. But in the afterlife she did not remember him saying that she would feel pain but she inspected herself none the less.

Leannii saw that she was covered in dried shades of dark umber and burnt maroon. Without a clean spot to be found on her and having not bathed in anything but blood for the past six days, she had the appearance of a walking corpse. A light waft of her own odor lightly touched her nostrils and she sharply waved her head at the pungent smell. Not only did she look like a corpse she smelled like one as well. She needed to stay up wind of herself. Suddenly, she stopped moving and only cast her eyes to the glimpse of the horrific scene.

Slowly her eyes moved toward the top crest of the hill to her left. There, scattered along the slope were small clouds of flies buzzing over a field of corpses. These were the men she had slain just yesterday and she slept with the dead this past night. Many yards away, a crow that had been pecking at one of the corpses cawed and then took to flight carrying some part of flesh in its beak.

Leannii knelt there mortified at the carnage that she saw. She had done this and she knew that. Flashes of the previous afternoon whipped wildly and almost incoherently through her mind. Blood, there was so much blood and screaming and none of it was hers. What happened to her? Had she become a monster? Standing on agonizingly shaking legs, she rose and took a deep breath to steady herself. Looking down to her feet, she saw her grandfather's sword and laboriously bent down to retrieve it. It felt far heavier now than it ever had before. The sting on her palms told her that her skin was raw from wielding it. Past the point of wearing blisters most of her skin on her hands had been worn down to bleeding. She moaned as she lifted the sword and slid it back into its sheath that was still at her side. After the sword was safely away she looked at her hands, raw, seeping and excruciatingly red.

She sighed and began to awkwardly trudge her way up the slope. Body after body lay at her feet. All of them bore faces twisted in agony, fear or surprise. Looking at one after the other she could yet accept that she, all alone, had done all of this. The buildings still smoldered as she passed by them and she vaguely recalled setting them ablaze with a dispassionately calculating frame of mind. Was all this really her?

As she passed by the cave entrance where they were meeting she stopped to ponder for a moment. Mentally pushing past her aches and pains she remembered being curious as to why they were meeting. What was so important at that time to call everyone together? Looking around, she glimpsed no obvious clue to that answer but recollected someone exiting the other cave and both of them were quite startled. If everyone was here…what was he doing there?

She clumsily made her way to the other cave. Each step shot pangs of agony through her body. There was not a single place on her that did not hurt. Leannii continued to grunt with every arduous step.

She stopped to catch her breath at the other cave entrance, the very same one she escaped from a few nights ago. The very same one she remembered Jeral in. Her lips began to form a snarl and her jaw clenched with that memory. Deciding that she had rested enough, even though it was only a few seconds, she forced herself to walk into the mouth and look for the man she put two arrows into. Faintly seeing his form the shadow of the natural corridor, she gruelingly lowered herself to kneel beside him. His expression was frozen in astonishment and both of her arrows still jutted from his abdomen and torso.

As she briefly inspected his body her eyes were already adjusting to the gloom. Glancing around, Leannii noticed that he clutched a parchment in his hand. His grip seemed to have tightened as he died and he retained a tight grip on it still. With a frown, she began to pry his fingers open. They did not budge. With a sigh of frustration, she sat back absently and was quickly reminded of her extreme discomfort as pain shot from her legs into her chest. Leannii cry echoed loudly in the stone cave. She cursed herself for being so stupid. She cursed her own body for being able to feel that much pain. She cursed the dead for making her kill them and fought back against an impending flood of tears. Leannii thought she had cried quite enough this past week and resolved herself to not be so damn soft and femininely weak again. She did not care that she was a woman but she did not have to be reduced to a sobbing mess every day.

 Noticing the dead man had a dagger she quickly contrived an idea. If she could not pull his stiff fingers apart then she would pry them apart. If she could not do that, she could definitely cut each one off until the paper was freed. Placing the blade between his ring and middle finger she began to pry. The sharpness cut only a little into his flesh and he oozed only a little but she managed to get enough of a space for her own fingers. Knowing that this was the only way, she resolved herself before briskly levering his finger backward. With a dull crack she broke it and it hung limply by the skin it was still attached by. Ignoring the pain she had just caused herself in her own tender hands by that rough movement, Leannii repeated it again and again until she had fractured all five of his digits.

 When she finished she held her hands open and grimaced at the stinging ache that radiated up into her wrists. With a long grunt she hoped to expel the discomfort and be done with it. It lessened but did not go away. Exhaling with a little renewed determination she returned to her task. Carefully then, she removed the document. Not being able to examine it there in the shadow of the cave she struggled to stand and walked out into the sunlight.

 With shock and dismay she read the letter:

Jeral Valancia,

I understand your Valancia family has recently fallen on very hard times and for that I am expressing my sincerest sorrow. None should have to suffer such as that and I imagine Adenon is twisting in his grave while his death remains unavenged. Also, I am aware of the standards that came to your home last moon and can put a name to that symbol if you would but hear me out.

You and I have a common wound that has become a common enemy. In the words of the old ones, "the enemy of my enemy is my ally." It is that which I offer. That we, at least for a time and for a mutual purpose, become allies to exact justice and punishment on the same enemy that has wronged us both so terribly.

Combining our resources we can strike back at them in the same manner that they had done to us. You can hit them from the outside, strike their trade routes in the north and empty their fat pockets. I, at the same time, will hit them from within their own home. The very place where they rest their heads will become a tumultuous hell.

Without the ability to confront both resounding issues at once, they will fall...hard and with great pain.

Within the chest I have sent with this letter is an offering of 2,000 gold. Use it however you like for it is a gift. If you decide to accept my offer, simply break a dagger and send it to me as a symbol.

I look forward to your reply.

Xergo Wallance

When she finished the letter her blood ran cold. She had not thought once about him and really only had one conversation almost a month ago. That lying bastard! Resisting the urge to shred the document, Leannii methodically folded the parchment and placed it safely into the folds of what remained of her tattered dress.

Despondently, she lumbered toward the scarecrow but did not make it all the way there. Her heart began to pound and her jaw clenched so tight her teeth ground together and threatened to crack. Her pace slowed even more until she just stopped trying to walk. Her hands excruciatingly balled into fists and she glared up at the sky and spat.

"Damn you! I gave my life to you," she shouted to Enki and hoped with every fiber of her being that he listened. She motioned around to the dead and to her brother and to herself. "Is this what you wanted? Is this how you reward? You sick twisted eala!" She spat at her god, the god she decided that she would not follow again.

"I hate you. Do you hear me? I hate you!"

A few hours later she dolefully drove the last remaining wagon from her brother's party back to their home. She had carefully removed his head and body from the posts and gently placed them into the back of the wagon. She never found Oleg. To ensure Thalorn would not fall or slide on the long journey home, she packed boxes and crates around his body and covered him with the tarps from the caves.

For the next two days, Leannii did not eat and barely slept. She would only nod off for a short time but she never left her seat. The road was not well traveled lately because of the problem from the bandits that used to lie in the north. There were forty three when she and Oleg arrived. He killed one, but the other forty two were slain by her. She had to pass through part of Ilranik before reaching her home. Thankfully, Leannii did not have to pass into the city itself but could drive along the north and eastern outskirts. By this point she did care at all if she was noticed but the more people that saw her the longer it would take to reach home.

The guards at the entrance to the Covenant estate were about to pummel this misshapen vagabond for trespassing when one saw through all the layers of dirt and blood and recognized that it was Leannii. The gates were abruptly opened and she drove onward without as much as a reply or glance to the guards. Her eyes were fixed onto a point somewhere on the distant horizon and her face held no expression. Statues had more emotion than she did then.

She stopped the wagon in the same place in the courtyard that her brother had departed from a few weeks before. As family servants came rushing out they gasped at the horrible sight of Leannii's appearance. She had lost weight making her cheeks draw inward, she had not bathed now for about ten nights and she was plastered in layers upon layers of dirt, soot and dried blood. Her dress hung on her in tattered shreds and was cut about her mid-thigh. All over her body, from her feet to her face, she was covered in cuts, scrapes, abrasions, bruises and other injuries. Leannii looked as if she had just waded through hell.

She simply gestured to the back of the wagon where her brother and his head lay under the tarps and she gingerly stepped from the wagon and walked into the house. Her grandfather's sword was still on her side. She passed from one room to another after drawing the sword from its scabbard. After passing through the great hall and into the dining room, her mother was on her heels. Mortified and worried about her daughter yet thinking that she had gone completely mad. Leannii did not hear her mother's words when she saw him sitting in the study by the fireplace.

Quickly she stomped toward him, her grip tightening on the sword handle and her face twisting to a snarl. He looked shocked to see her standing in that room, which he was, he expected her to be held or killed. He had to think quickly to salvage this situation and the best tactic he devised under such short and tense circumstances was to act with friendly surprise.

"Leannii!" he stood to greet her while forcing his best genuine smile. "It is good to…" He never finished his lie when the flat of the weighted blade rung against the side of his head. He fell to the side over the desk placing a hand over his face. He began to panic.

"What's wrong with you?" Her mother shouted from behind her, "Stop this at…"

"Shut up, mother," she interrupted without taking her eyes from Xergo.

She brought the blade up then chopped it down against the back of his leg. His cry of pain echoed outside the room and filled this wing of the manor. Leannii pressed the point of the sword against his neck and spoke evenly but they could hear her struggling to contain her wrath.

"Tell her," she commanded.

"Um…I…I…don't…" he stammered.

"Tell her about Jeral, Jeral Valancia."

Damn, she knows.

"I don't…"

"Tell her what you did to them!" The sharp steel began to pierce his neck and the stinging pain spread into his shoulder and ear.

"Yes! Yes! It was me!"

"What was? Who sent those men to kill them?" Her eyes burned with hatred. "Who?!"

"I…I…did," he confessed.

It never helped him. The sword violently slid into his neck and out the other side. He gurgled and grasped at the blade, cutting his own hands. Leannii twisted and sharply wrenched the sword out of him in a different direction. Dark thick crimson erupted to cover most of the room while her mother screamed in horror from behind her.

Leannii quietly and slowly turned away from Xergo. Her face was calm and disturbingly relaxed. Retrieving the letter from the folds of her dress, she placed is heavily in her mother's hand then pushed past her and shambled into the corridor. Servants stood frozen in stunned silence as they watched her stop and gaze around the hall. The sound of her falling to the hallway floor reverberated around the solid wood and stone.

One day passed into the next while Leannii slept. Within the first week, a fever gripped her. She lay in her bed under many blankets and shivered while she muttered incoherent and imperceptible words. Some nights she would wake the manor with her screams but was too delusional to speak and would only return to her fever-induced trance or restless sleep. Finally, after seven days of battling silently for her own life, her fever broke and she began to move on own. She still required a great deal of assistance since she was so weak but this was a great hope for the family.

Each morning she was gently bathed and dressed in clean linen robes. Directly after that she was given medicine with her breakfast and then she returned to sleep since just doing that for the first week was exhausting for her. Lunch and dinner were the same. Rarely did she utter a single word and sometimes she would spend days in silence and never anything to anyone.

Her father, Urig, upon hearing that she had returned and how injured she was, had canceled all business and official travels to sit beside her while she recovered. For hours each day he would just sit and watch over her. He ensured there was always fresh water and fruit in the event she awoke and wanted anything. Sometimes Urig would send the servants away and just watch over her himself. Sometimes that had allowed him to weep in silence at the loss of his son and what had happened to his daughter. The time he spent in his vigilance became longer and longer each day. Urig had come to blame himself for this tragedy. When she did begin to awaken and move her silence cut into his heart deeply. Upon seeing that, he felt then that he had lost both children and feared that Leannii would never recover.

Almost three weeks passed when she uttered her first words

to anyone. She had just been bathed and her wounds redressed by one the elder woman servants of the house. While being tucked back into bed she gripped the aging woman's wrist and held it tight. Leannii looked to her and spoke.

"Where is my sword?"

The servant was shocked. Her weathered face drew back in surprise.

"I...I don't know, milady. But I will fetch it for you now."

Her arm was released and Leannii's eyelids grew heavy and closed. The woman looked to the scared youth with great concern. Finishing her duties in a most hurried manner, she quietly exited the room and began asking everyone where Leannii's sword was. If that is what the lady wanted then she would be certain to do that for her.

It was then that Brother Quinn and Urig were just speaking about Leannii with unease. Both had noticed that Leannii had changed greatly when she returned. Both heard of battle trauma but this was not where their conversation had led. Leannii had transformed on a fundamental level. Although she could move and speak she did not. Brother Quinn had noted that she returned but had not once prayed since and asked Enki for guidance as to what Leannii was thinking.

The knock at the door interrupted their conversation and upon entry, the wizening woman servant told them of Leannii's request for her sword. The woman spoke with a slight tremble and tones of trepidation. Quinn and Urig looked to each other with bewilderment. The two instantly stood and strode to the armory to retrieve her sword for her, the servant was in tow. The two quickly walked to her room bearing her sword with great misgivings. When the servant voiced that Leannii had specifically told her to bring it Urig reassured her that it was okay and just to wait outside in the event she was needed.

Urig was first into the room and Quinn was close behind him. Leannii heard the men enter and rolled in bed to face them. Dispassionately she gazed upon them and when she saw the sword she merely turned to the ceiling and coldly made the announcement.

"That's not my sword."

Urig looked bewildered. Certainly this was, he had been watching her be tutored for years with this very same blade.

"Yes, this is, dear," he began to explain. "You have been

using this for many years. Look, it's your sword."

She never turned her head and never spoke at all.

Brother Quinn gently yet firmly placed a hand on Urig's shoulder. He turned to look to the priest who nodded his head and dropped his eyes.

"I think I know what she wants." He beckoned Urig to follow him outside the room.

When they reached the corridor Quinn looked to him.

"What sword did she have when she returned…the one she used to kill Xergo?"

Urig thought for a moment then answered.

"That was her grandfather's sword. It is back in his old study…Why?"

"Because," Quinn began. "I think that is the one she wants."

"But it is not hers, it belongs to my father."

Quinn placed a steady hand onto his shoulder and looked him square in the eyes.

"Urig, my friend, I have known you for many years. I also knew your father. I buried Dannum, remember? I know you love your father…but after what she has been through, it is her sword now. He even wanted her have it, correct?"

"Yes, but she is not yet twenty."

Quinn's eyes closed and he shook his head to politely dismiss that observation.

"Friend…please, give her the sword."

A few minutes later, Urig returned with the hefty blade in its aged sheath. He was still uncertain that this was the right thing to do but he followed his trusted friend's suggestion. With a nod and an exhale the two reentered her room. Urig slowly approached her bed with the sword looking to her as he did not quite know what to expect. When he came to within arm's reach, Leannii quickly snatched the sword from his grip and rolled over, curling up around the sword as she would a lover or security blanket.

Urig stood stunned. That was definitely something he did not expect and seeing that from his daughter welled up a great pain of anxiety about her. In all his years he had never seen anyone do that. Quinn was even shocked although he regarded what he just witnessed with a different set of eyes. There was a question he had to ask, something he had no know the answer to. Nearing her bed he stopped and spoke over her shoulder.

"Leannii," he said as softly as his gruff voice could manage. "Why did you want this sword?"

Without turning to face him, she opened her eyes and tears silently began to stream down her face and onto her pillow.

"Because…this was the only thing I found comfort in out there."

Urig heard but did not comprehend. Quinn stood slowly while a chill ran up his spine. He knew because he heard her with different ears. Yes, something did happen to her out there, something terrible. Past the point of her body being violated, past the pains in her flesh, beyond the nightmares and fear that she would feel for years to come…Leannii had lost touch with Enki. She had become corrupted and she turned her back on her god. She was no longer a paladin and Brother Quinn understood what that meant more than anyone in this house. Leannii had fallen from divine grace.

Inside the Silverwood Garrison

Early Afternoon

"I was wondering…if he is alright," Leannii asked the priest as he returned downstairs after checking on the injured knight.

"Ah, well…he'll be fine…after a week's rest." Kaeleb jested while remaining a bit distant. Mercenaries were, in Paragon, very distrusted and thought of as never being capable of honorable behavior.

"Very well," she replied and handed him to cup sized flasks of colored liquid. "Here, give him these." She looked around with a bit of nervousness.

"What are they?" The priest did not grasp them but regarded her actions with curiosity. He did not fear her poisoning the knight, because of the look on her face, but still needed to know what those were.

"Yeah," she breathed and spoke at the flasks. "I know magic is not legal here. But, if it can help save his life…they are healing potions. If he doesn't want them I'll take them back, they're quite expensive. I just hope he doesn't decide to put me in jail for it." Finally she looked at him with sincere eyes. For the briefest moment, the priest saw power deep within her. It felt like the kind of power that Heaven would only have reserved for angels or great heroes.

"Oh, well, thank-you." Kaeleb was utterly surprised at what he felt and to handle healing potions for the first time in his life. He had heard of them before but never actually saw or even touched one before. "I'll see if he will use them." He gently took the flasks.

"Thank you," she said.

"What? No, thank you," he said with a smile. "But why…"

Before he could ask why she thanked him, Leannii walked away. She strode unhurriedly back into the barracks with a dark frown. Looking to Chang's bed she slowed to a stop. *Damn it, it was my responsibility to keep him safe.* She looked over at Kerrison who was sitting with his back against the wall and muttering to himself. The man was slowly losing his mind. She had seen it before but under very different circumstances. Leannii lowered her gaze and looked to her friend. When Leannii's eyes met Desia's, her own heart sank. She brought her only friend into doom and against her friend's objections. For what? Money? Leannii sighed wondering if anyone, herself included, could ever forgive her.

"How is he?" Ruelina asked after tending to Maura. Everyone was getting up late that morning. Even though the ranger did not know Leannii's Sydathrian companion, Ruelina still felt pity for him. No one should have to suffer like that.

"What?" Leannii turned to her, lost for a moment in her own misery and concern. "How is who?"

"Your...the Sydathrian who is ill." Ruelina's eyes held a sincere apology. "Sorry, I don't remember his name."

"Chang," she said coldly.

"Yes, Chang. Sorry," Ruelina repeated.

"He died in the early morning," Leannii answered gloomily. "We're burning him before breakfast."

"Oh, I'm sorry," her own tone reflected Leannii's misery.

"Yeah," the mercenary said. "So am I."

Upstairs, the knight was struggling with the bandages across his chest. He scowled each time the pain shot through him. That street rat would pay for cutting him, the miserable wretch. When the knock at his door came he barked for them to enter. Quietly, the priest shuffled in and sat on his bed, placing the flasks on the nightstand.

"You need to not move so much, sire. You'll hurt yourself."

"Bah, I'm fine," balked Tobin.

"You were almost dead last night, you're not fine," the priest insisted.

The knight shuffled around a bit more as he thought of what to say next. A thousand insults and cursed flooded his brain but something different came out.

"Is...she still here?" He spoke with hesitation and a tint of loathing.

"Yes, she's downstairs and had asked me how you were."

"She did?" Tobin was stunned. "Why?"

"Probably, because she feels bad about last night." The priest looked down at the grown knight in the bed as if he were regarding a sick boy.

"She should," snapped Tobin.

"In all honesty, sire, you provoked her."

"Like the Hells I did." He thought for a moment then frowned. "Unless, I did."

"You did," Kaeleb said pointedly. "And locking them outside was…well, it was evil of you." Priests could have a way of telling someone the truth without them being able to rebut it.

"Maybe," the knight grumbled. It was a token word since both knew Kaeleb was right.

"No maybe about it, milord." Lecturing a Drathmoore on the obvious points of good and evil was not in his plans for the day. He changed the subject. "And you are lucky to be alive."

"Yeah, thank you for that," Tobin said with a humble tone.

"Don't thank me," he said while shaking his head. "Thank Enki for saving you."

After a long pause Tobin replied, "You're right."

Kaeleb nodded but said nothing more about that either. Instead he asked the knight a question. "So, Lord Drathmoore, what are our plans for today?"

"We're going to hunt for ghouls," he answered without pause. The knight already had that intended and said it as if he had readied that reply to that question.

"Oh?" the priest asked.

"Yes, old Absalom told me where in that forsaken cemetery to find them. So find them we will." His vice was stern and confident.

"Very well, then …" the priest reached over and handed Tobin the two flasks. The knight grasped them as his brow creased. "You can thank Leannii for these."

"What are these?" he asked with marked suspicion.

"Those are illegal. Those will heal every wound you have in minutes so you may fight the ghouls with full strength." He stood and walked to the door.

"Where are you going?" Tobin asked while lying in bed and still holding the flasks.

"I don't know what will happen to those horribly expensive potions, sire. I don't want to know what you will do with healing potions, milord…especially when you're so injured and we expect a rough battle later today." Tobin looked at the priest as he closed the door behind him. Brother Kaeleb smiled in the hallway and strolled back down to the stairs.

Just outside Boregar City

Same Afternoon

They had ridden from the previous afternoon. The entire trip was silent, not because of the dead forest, which they had left behind in Silverwood. It was good to hear sounds of life again. It was amazing how much the two missed the ambient noises of the forest and saw the rich and vibrant colors again as if they had been deaf and blind for a time.

Instead, they were silent because of Emerik and the unsettling memories that ran ceaselessly though his mind from the previous morning. The unearthly horrifying hovering figures, the bleeding earth, the ghouls from nights before...

This place...is damned...

He shook his head to knock the imagery from his psyche. It did not help. The only thing that seemed to grant him any relief was putting more distance between himself and that dreaded hamlet. He had promised to return and now resented the fact he did. Seeing Silverwood ever again, or what remained, would be too soon. But a promise was a promise and some of those cannot be undone. First he needed to help himself before he could help that place.

When they rounded the top of the last hill Emerik's mouth fell open from what he saw. He had never been to Boregar City before but had heard many things about it. The tales of her glory and splendor were far and wide. The "Shining Star" of east Paragon she was called. There was a hub of culture and education that brought real civilization to the wild woodlands...but not that day.

He blinked as if he beheld an illusion. The once grand city walls were in disrepair and crumbling. The outside homes and inns were a sad sight of shabbiness and depression. People even looked disheartened, moping as they shuffled along. Beggars were scattered along the outside of the walls weakly raising empty bowls as he rode by.

"Sire, did we make a wrong turn somewhere or come down the wrong road?" Dyrrany asked with his heart in his throat.

"No, there was no other way to come…this must be Boregar…" Emerik's voice died off. When finally arriving at the gate, the prince heard a voice and recognized it as his own. "What happened to this place?"

The Hill of Standing Stones outside Silverwood

Late Evening, Ten years ago

"Can you hear me?"
Where have you been? I've been lonely!
"I know…I have been away."
Doing something more important than talking to me?
"Now, don't be that way. You know you are important to us."
Us? There are more of you?
"Yes, but you have already known that."
Get me out! Get me out! I want out!
"Shhh…Calm down. We will get you out when we can."
Save me!
"We will…but you must be patient."
I hate being here! I want out! I want out! Do you hear me? Get me out!
…
Are you there?
…
Are you there?
"Yes, I am here."
Why did you not answer me?
"You became angry again. That's why the others will not talk to you."
Why not?
"Because, they are afraid of you. They know you can hurt them when you get angry…and that you become angry too easily."
You would too! Damned Gajana, she put me in here! Do you know? I hate her! I hate her!
"Calm down…we talked about this. It is not good for anyone to hate. What happened has happened and no one can change that."
But I-
"Shhh…remember what I told you? A dark heart will devour its owner. Hate will destroy you from the inside. Holding anger in your heart is like drinking poison and expecting someone else to die."
…I remember…but I can only remember when you are here.

"It will take time. You must learn to control yourself and quiet your mind."

Is that why the others never come to me?

"Yes, you have great power but no control. Others have tried to free you in the past, others who wanted to let you out but you hurt them all."

I did?

"Yes, everyone who tried to help you has been hurt by you."

Everyone?

"Yes, dear, all of them over all the years."

I'm sorry. I really am. I just want out. I want out so bad. I hate being here. I hate it! I hate it!

"Tschazzar...calm down. You must learn to be calm and control yourself."

Why?

"We have spoken about this before, dear. You have always hurt those who wanted to help you. Also, there are those who do not care about you but still want you to be free from there."

Why?

"They want to use you for their own selfish reasons."

What do they want?

"They want you to hurt people."

Who do they want me to hurt?

"Everyone."

I do not understand.

"Tschazzar...They want you to murder the world."

Why?

"It would make them happy."

Does the world need murdered?

"No, it is full of many innocent people who do not even know you."

Why kill those people? Are they bad?

"No, most are innocent. None of them are perfect but they do not deserve to die like that."

How do they know I would murder the world?

"Because, like us, they know you cannot control yourself. Especially when you are angry, and you become angry very easily."

...Why do you help me?

"Because, as I have told you before, I care about you. We all do."

Why? Why do you care so much about me?

"Because, Tschazzar...believe this or not, we do love you. I love you."

Then get me out. Get me out! Save me! I want out!

"Tschazzar..."

Get me out! I want out! Out! Out! Out!

"Tschazzar..."

...You don't love me.

"That's not true, dear."

If you did, then you would help me.

"I am helping you. I come here as often as I can to talk to you and help teach you to control yourself."

Why do I need to do that?

"You know why, but it is hard for you to understand right now. You could tear a hole in the earth...imagine what good things you could do if you were not angry. You could help so many people and many would love you for that."

They would?

"Yes, dear. People will love someone who can save more than someone who can murder."

Can I tell you something?

"Of course."

I love you...

"I know, Tschazzar. I know, and you know I love you, too...but I must tell you something you will not like."

What?

"I must go away for a while again."

Why?

"There are many people who will die horribly and very soon if I do not go and help them."

What about me?

"You will be alright...Try to remember what I have taught you and you will be fine."

But I don't want you to go.

"I know you don't. Many others don't want me to go either but I must."

Why can't you stay?

"Because I promised those people I would help them. I made that promise long, long ago, many years before you were born."

Don't go.

"Tschazzar...please, you will make yourself upset again."

I don't care! I don't want you to go! Don't go!

"I must...I have to go now, but I will come back as soon as I can."

No!

...

Hello?

...

Where are you?

...

Get me out! Get me out! I want out! I want out! Get me out!
Save me!
Save me!
Naia, save me!
SAVE ME...
LET ME OUT!

ABOUT THE AUTHOR

Jonathan Graef is an US Army veteran, former college professor and previous licensed martial art instructor in Guangdong Province, mainland China. He has always had a fascination with ancient history and esoteric studies. Conception of this story began in 1987, when his college dormitory lost power during a storm. After lighting a candle, watching the lighting dance and listening to the thunder rumble that night, the first shadows of the tale began to grow. Now, the story is available. Currently, Jon lives near Columbia, South Carolina with his wife and children. He continues to write, spinning more dark tales…usually in the dark.

Made in the USA
Charleston, SC
18 April 2016